The Hong Kong
Foreign Correspondents Club

ANTHONY SPAETH

The Hong Kong Foreign Correspondents Club

A NOVEL

SECKER & WARBURG
LONDON

First published in England 1990
by Martin Secker & Warburg Limited
Michelin House, 81 Fulham Road,
London sw3 6rb

Copyright © 1990 by Anthony Spaeth

A CIP catalogue record for this book
is available from the British Library
ISBN 0 436 48054 9

Typeset in 11 point Baskerville
by Hewer Text Composition Services, Edinburgh
Printed in Great Britain
by St Edmundsbury Press, Bury St Edmunds, Suffolk

For Ritchan

Book One

THE PILLOW BOOK OF ALICE GILES, FOREIGN CORRESPONDENT

These times have passed, and there was one who drifted uncertainly through them, scarcely knowing where she was headed. Perhaps it was natural that such should be her fate. She was less handsome than most; she was gifted, but not remarkably so. As the days started racing by in frightening succession, she had occasion to reflect on the books that purported to describe her kind of life, her cities, her vocation. She found them masses of the rankest fabrication. Perhaps, she said to herself, even the story of her own unsatisfactory life, set down in her own 'pillow book,' might be of interest. It might also answer some questions. Can one be paid to tell the truth? If the truth is embraced like a son, what does one do when the false twin starts to cry?

They must all be recounted, events of long ago, events of but yesterday. She is by no means certain that she can bring them to order. There is some rush, for as the Japanese poem appropriately mourns:

Spring renews everything,
And only I grow old.

'By Alice Giles'

'By Alice Giles.' It's an old byline, you may know it. I am, I have been, I might even continue to be a foreign correspondent. I have a story to tell and, as always, there's a myriad of difficulties in the telling. You'd think I'd be used to it by now. The struggle and the thrill to *tell* – what else, after all, justifies the silly life of us foreign correspondents? The ghastly restaurants, the brothels, the spasmodic snoozes in airplanes, the flarings, fibbings, forgetting of family and friends, the dashing and wheel-spinning, the permanent crick in the neck from the telephone, the debut of the new computer, a machine that can do *anything*, acclaimed industry-wide and, even sooner – in a truly frightening flash! – deemed too heavy, too short on memory, old and unsatisfactory. How I know that passage! Pity that poor computer, pity it for me, Alice Giles, and lay its chips to rest with kindness and fond remembrances of its more electric days. For it was wonderful once! Remember that distant era when it did new things, things never done before in journalism? Please remember!

I haven't been in one of those grimy hotels in a while, with their limp curtains pulled against the dawn as the story, nearing deadline, takes shape. I haven't recently paced one of those airport lounges, half-panicked by a trip to a new country and three-quarters thrilled. But I've a story – such a story! – and I'm totally unconcerned by gaps. At my age, one accepts a sense of incompleteness in life, in love, in the songs one is called on to sing. Everything is never known, and stories still are told. Known/Told. Told/Known. Our own yin and yang. Just when you're starting to know, you're called on to tell. And just as you start to tell, you become cognizant of the things you need to know. It's our business: our tawdry, distrusted, manipulative, agonizing and thrilling business. Us with the epaulettes and the fraying notebooks. With the aggressive questions in the choked voices. Us with the distrustful gazes. Us – the foreign corespondents.

This tale involves people, money, sexual attraction, porcelains, the truth, lots of lies – both big and little – and a dusty brown hat I keep in a bottom dresser drawer. It's a story that reveals, in full, the dirty little secret that my colleagues spend their lives trying to deny. The mouldy skeleton in journalism's smelly locker. The lie! It's a story that sprawls over the region I've called home for eighteen and a half years, and it centres, to my pleasure, on my shining and grubby colony, Hong Kong.

It's a tale of hoaxes, beginning with one printed in the glossy pages of the *New York Tribune* Sunday magazine. Who knows how many people yawned through the ponderous piece with the unpronounceable Cambodian dateline? Perhaps some were pulled in by the photographs of human skulls and memories of *The Killing Fields*. Maybe there are readers who enjoy articles that back into their subjects, that continue in eighteen jumps, snaking around advertisements for Irish hats, mail-order beef, fat camps and military schools. Perhaps meandering prose has its own appeal (that might explain the popularity of the grossly over-rated *Tribune*). All that's sure is that many more would have read to the last fat camp ad had they had known the article was a fake – or had they merely seen the original copy, written in fountain pen on a schoolboy's exercise tablet, bearing the dimples that afflict all compositions done at the bottom of a damp, dangerous Malaysian rain forest.

But that's getting ahead of the story.

My guess is that the guys at the State Department or the CIA were the first to smell a rat. The *Tribune*'s big scoop from the border of Cambodia – the first sighting in years of the faltering figure of Pol Pot, exiting one tent and entering another – was recognized as fiction within hours of publication. Who can imagine the global telecommunication orgy that occurred between Sunday evening and Tuesday morning, or the tumult at the *Tribune*: the heads called for, the careers that faltered, the desperate excuses dreamt up and rehearsed in the men's room mirror? To the outside world, the first sign of trouble was a three-paragraph box on Tuesday's front page saying the ombudsman was investigating the piece. An 'ahem' graf stated the article was written not by a staffer but an 'occasional contributor.' It was another twenty-four hours before the paper admitted the truth: the story was a stinky fish. No one had seen Pol Pot. The 'occasional contributor' had never been near the Cambodian border.

On Thursday the *Tribune* reported something truly interesting: foreign editor E. G. Augenstein ('Ted' to old acquaintances like me) was en route to confront the hoax's perpetrator. Ted's destination: a rain forest in northern Malaysia. The home, or lair, of the obscure contributor with the memorable name, Anton Vavasour.

That's where this story starts.

But do real-life stories begin, like stage plays, so abruptly? What were our players doing before this mouldy curtain was hoisted? If I try to rise above it all, to float free of time and space, an all-wise presence zooming beneath the ozone layer – this is, after all, what we foreign correspondents are trained to feign – I can see my three protagonists before the tale begins.

The first is a full-figured man, in rear view, standing on a stepladder in a Manhattan apartment of modest size but sumptuous decor. Heavy drapes have been pulled against the day to create artificial darkness. Beyond those drapes, life, of a sort, proceeds in lower Manhattan.

The man is making minute adjustments in a bank of spotlights in the apartment's ceiling. He concentrates intensely, and his hand moves with autonomy to smooth his already-perfect hair. Every few minutes, the head snaps around to stare accusingly at the drapes. (I see the face – it's Ted Augenstein!) He seems worried that all his adjustments might be wrong when night genuinely falls.

The second man sits beneath a ceiling fan in the airless office of a bureaucrat with chocolate skin. He is dressed in a pair of old-fashioned black trousers and a white broadcloth shirt. Both garments might have been made for an elephant. Giant triangles of perspiration stain the front of the shirt and the back. His head is shiny and grey, with streaks of greasy hair around its perimeter.

The bureaucrat shakes his head as if to say, 'I'm sorry but no,' and proffers to the man a worn, blue passport. The man glares at the bureaucrat murderously. His fleshy lips move. They say (for I can easily read them) 'Kill him, Ramse.'

This, I'm sorry to say, is Anton Vavasour.

And lastly, we are in motion in Tokyo on the Chiyoda line,

with its lovely green-striped trains. My third man, the youngest and certainly the trimmest of the three, gets off the train one stop before Yoyogi Uehara. He walks to the exit at the back of the train – he still remembers – and emerges opposite a frozen, abandoned Yoyogi Park.

The man pushes through a hinged wooden gate. He enters a small lane. He gazes up at the back of a building to find the glass door he once knew at a glance. Now he has to count up and over. There's a new washing machine on the narrow balcony and some female undergarments hanging from a plastic device with a red claw, which grasps a peeling bamboo pole. The panties sway gently in the winter breeze. It's Craig! Pursuing his hormonal, holy grail.

The ends of these various strands are much harder to grasp. Last heard from, Ted was in Sigiriya, Sri Lanka. But rumour insists his exile has shifted several times since. Anton Vavasour vanished into thin air, a considerable feat for such a corporeal man. His reputation lives on, however, and nowhere more than at the Hong Kong Foreign Correspondents Club, where newcomers are given full briefings on the night he appeared at the bar in grey curly wig and a massive white sailor suit, replete with ribboned hat.

Craig has gone missing in that compelling land to the south, the Philippines. I imagine him in a tiny boat, traversing the humped islands of the South China Sea, on a romantic quest that, as far as I know, has yet to be fulfilled. There's one more character to my story and . . . No – I'm not prepared to bring him on. He also went missing in the Philippines, to return, in a fashion . . . Give me time. For all things, and all fates, there is the proper time.

Shall I show you myself? To see me, you'd have to take the Peak Tram from Central and then a taxi, or, if you were really determined, you could swoop up from the harbour in a clattering helicopter. Even better: you could drop in a hang-glider from Hong Kong's ultimate peak. Is hang-gliding as wonderfully silent as it seems? I imagine it thus, with just the sweet sound of rushing air and, perhaps, an occasional car horn, the roar of a jet engine, an amplified snatch of music escaping a bedroom window. If you twisted towards Wanchai, weaving in and out of Hong Kong's brilliant stalagmites, you'd have to aim for the dark hillside near the power station. If you got lost, you'd look back to my glittering harbour, fix the tubular Goodwill Centre, and then proceed directly south.

There you'd find my lovely little house, high on the dark hillside, a tiny flicker in the autumn Hong Kong night. Can you see that silhouette in the window: that tall, stooped woman, no longer young, more than slightly frail? Imagine the people asleep. And all of us awake with our memories and our music. Idle, if possible. Let the rush of the Hong Kong wind be calmed. Listen carefully. The walls in Hong Kong houses are thick. But I like my music loud at night. A tune will waft your way, floating towards the mirrored harbour, with its crimson and royal and aquamarine highlights. A tune that suits the mood like few others at 3 a.m. A tune that lifts me to the stars. Perhaps the silhouette will gyrate slightly, clumsily, in time with the music. A frail arm might exuberantly slice the early-morning air.

> *I didn't know if it was day or night.*
> *I started kissing everything in sight.*
> *But when I kissed a cop down on 34th and Vine,*
> *He broke my little bottle of*
> *Love Potion No. 9.*

Life Cycle of the Foreign Correspondent (Male)

1. Cub reporter.

2. Newly-divorced.

3. Hopeless alcoholic.

4. 'Old fart'.

5. On his fourth wife (constantly!)

6. Foreign Editor.

7. Doyen.

Life Cycle of the Foreign Correspondent (Female)

1. Does adequate work, but needs a good man.

2. Did great work. Still can't find a man.

3. Continues to crank them out. Never found a man.

THE RAIN FOREST

I

Ted Augenstein sped across the deep green hills of northern Malaysia in a rented Toyota. The roads were fine, with rich Malaysian loam at each shoulder. It was an old landscape with lovely new features. There were no wretchedly poor farmers: not in this prosperous land. Just the bulging crops and the occasional mild-menacing truck on its way to market.

That peculiar joy that accompanies new travelling overtook Ted Augenstein.

This is a country I've never quite understood, he thought to himself, whizzing imperviously through it. *It's a place and a people I've never much liked. So brown. So ugly.* Ted had never had a Malay friend, never written an original story from Malaysia, never really penetrated the copse-shrouded Malaysian *kampong* or the Malaysian mind that takes root among its stilt houses and shadowy spaces.

Ted took a deep, satisfied breath and joyfully stepped on the gas. He was aware of the strange and exclusive country outside and felt content within his sealed, hurtling shell of iron. He decided Malaysia was the perfect country to restore to him his expatriate sensibility: that heady blend of alertness, excludedness and a heightened sense of personal sovereignty. He felt at home for the first time in months. A tiny thought buzzed in his brain – it said 'underpants' in a harsh, New York accent – and he dismissed it resolutely. That kind of dignity was far behind him now. *For*, Ted thought as he traded obscene gestures with a happily reckless Malaysian truckdriver, *I am back abroad.*

2

On that fateful week in which the hoax was exposed and universally condemned and corporately lamented, Ted complained to his bosses: 'What's the unholy rush? Why not wait until the paper's investigation is complete?'

And, by handing him a ragged brown envelope and a folded sheet of letter paper, they signalled that the investigation was complete. The ombudsman had yet to start his probe, it was true, but the salient facts were already plain. The bogus story in the Sunday magazine had been accepted by the *Tribune* on the basis of one letter and, in that, on the strength of a single, fraudulent half-sentence.

It read: '. . . and I once worked with great satisfaction as a stringer in Indochina for your Bangkok bureau chief, E. G. Augenstein . . .'

'Why didn't someone check Vavasour with me?' Ted asked incredulously.

The bosses looked shamefaced. Several of them had no place in the meeting to begin with. Even an ad man was present. With much displacement of phlegm, one solemnly stated, 'Ted, you know how the magazine doesn't like interference from the news pages. The foreign section in particular.'

Ted looked down at the letter's florid signature. His meaty hand made a check of his honey-coloured hair. Then he looked at Alexander Postlewaite III, the *Tribune* magazine's pampered, high-profile editor, whose horn-rims were perched atop his prematurely-white mane.

'Yes, I know,' Ted said in a carefully neutral tone. 'We on the foreign desk, on the other hand, have this thing about our writers actually visiting the places they report on.'

Alex Postlewaite didn't see the need to reply. He was examining his gracefully-thin wedding band.

'Alex,' Ted said, confrontation crreeping into his tone, 'excuse the interference. But you above everyone else know I was never the Bangkok bureau chief.'

Alex failed to reply again.

'Because *you* were the Bangkok bureau chief.'

Alex said he had full confidence in the ombudsman's followup investigation.

Ted erupted: 'I've always said this "One Country, Two Systems" arrangement would get us in trouble, and if the magazine doesn't think this hurts our reputation as well as its – '

Alex Postlewaite leapt to his feet, whipped off his glasses and embarked on an obviously rehearsed rampage. His hair had a Beethoven-esque quality that was so striking it nearly looked natural. 'You bloody well know, Ted, that our foreign coverage is often better than your reporters' straightforward, some might say *unimaginative*, files.'

'Alex, imaginative journalism is our *problem* right now, not our aspiration.'

'He was a nut, dear heart,' Alex said. 'He had something against the paper, something against the world. It's impossible to guard ourselves from that kind of nut.'

'Your staff – ' Ted said.

'Your reporters – ' Alex countered.

' – doesn't have the experience necessary,' Ted continued.

' – are addicted to the spot story,' Alex persisted. 'They don't ever get the big picture – '

' – and wouldn't know their way to – '

' – the foreign policy implications, the ideological drifts, the things people really *need* to know in Washington and – '

' – New Jersey and that's the reason why – '

' – I, just between us girls, am in favour of a total rethink of how – '

' – Frederic Prokosch, twenty years later, gets some unexpected copy in the Sunday magazine, the paper gets in deep shit and – '

' – we look at the world – '

' – makes believe nothing is happening – '

' – and write nothing of pertinence to our most important readers – '

' – because we are – '

' – the rich, the influential, the powerful.'

' – The *New York Tribune*!'

The two men ceased their confusing duet at exactly the same moment. The business-suited executives were thrown into worried befuddlement. Except for the excited ad guy who, at the mention of New Jersey, had raised his voice in a hearty, 'Absolutely!'

The two men tried to present concise closing arguments.

'You have a point, Ted,' said Alex hurriedly. 'But, dear heart, let's step back a bit and think of the paper.' He deposited his glasses back in his mane and dropped into his chair in a posture of quiet triumph.

Ted smoothed his own hair, glanced murderouly at the magazine editor, and was about to reply when Abe said, 'Yes, gentlemen, the paper.'

Ted recognized a battle narrowly lost and said, 'All right. But Abe, how do we know he's still at this address?'

A relieved rustle rushed through the room. Lunch dates were approaching, the traffic was likely to be killing, and most of the men had long passed the age when editorial squabbles worried or even entertained them.

But Ted still had the floor. In his hand was the envelope. He waved it aloft. It was a cheap envelope that somehow managed to embarrass all the people seated in the room. Alex Postlewaite averted his gaze.

'And,' Ted said, 'what do I say to Anton Vavasour, even if I do find him?'

The business-suited men had no reply. They all had watches, however, and although thin and expensive, they all seemed to have something wrong with them at the moment. Then, as if reacting to an invisible signal, the men rose in a body. Ellie, Abe's famed super-secretary, opened the door to the conference room just in time to let the first executive out. It was all quite magical. Ted was the only man not moving towards the door.

'Alex,' he called, penetrating the noisy bonhomie that had filled the room. Alex halted a few paces short of the door. He looked back with ostentatious courtesy.

'Was the manuscript, like this letter, written in longhand?'

Alex replied breezily, 'Why, yes, dear heart, I believe it was. In fountain pen and in a clear hand. It is now with the ombudsman.'

He addressed the entire crowd around the jammed doorway. 'Obviously' – he could barely restrain a charming grin – 'we are dealing with a faker of the Old School! A man of imagination, daring and . . .'

Ted interrupted in a quavering voice. 'You often accept manuscripts from strangers, from half a world away, written in fountain pen?'

But Ted was too late. The exodus was on. Alex, with a startled expression, was swept through the conference-room door. Soon, the only person remaining was the ad man, who wished Ted the best of luck 'over there.'

And Ellie, who held tickets, a passport and an envelope plump with cash.

'Ellie,' Ted said, 'why me?'

Ellie patted him comfortingly on the back. 'You'll enjoy yourself,' she said in a motherly tone. 'You're the best. Your bag's outside. The copy boy said he couldn't find any underpants . . .'

'Underpants?'

'. . . so you buy some over there. If they even wear them, that is. He liked your apartment. Said it looked like a shop. I told him not to rummage through the hamper.'

'A shop? My hamper?'

'A nice shop, I'm sure he meant. And there's a little more money than usual since your trip is an unusual one.'

'And for the underpants.'

'Oh! Poo!' Ellie made dismissing motions with her pudgy hands. 'Go bareback if you have to.' She laughed raucously. 'And Ted,' she said, in as confidential a tone as a native New Yorker can accomplish, 'that reminds me. If you need Kaopectate, Abe has half a bottle in his john from Rio.'

'Half a bottle?'

Ellie laughed her short laugh. 'It was only a weekend trip. Hey – lucky I don't have to worry about *his* shorts.'

3

The fluorescent lights of Asia impressed Ted when he first moved there, and they struck him anew on his every return. On this trip they seemed a beacon of all the brightness and plainness he had left behind when he had returned from abroad. Ted's heart soared when the sun finally set and the first rickety, illuminated Malay house came into view. *How long it's been*, he thought, watching a stooped Malay grandmother balance an infant in her arms and fiddle at a gas burner. *Too long*. He passed a succession of houses, mere shacks on stilts, and gained quick glimpses of each brightly-lit interior. His travel numbness dissipated and his mind raced with euphoric and desperate thoughts. *How can I escape New*

York? How can I return to this? He sped by a house with darkened windows. As he passed, sparks flickered in the cracks of the slatted walls. The fluorescent spear was starting to throw its artificial moonbeams. Chameleons were scattering to cobwebby corners. The night life of one Malay house was beginning anew. Food, family, talk, a cuff on the ear for the mischievous brown boy, endearments for the baby. The good life. *Where have I been these past eighteen months?* Ted thought. Dusk in lower Manhattan summoned for him the image of plastic Tiffany lamps hanging in his neighbourhood Brew 'N Burger. The waitress: 'Alone again?' Unconsciously, he stepped on the gas and raced even more recklessly into the darkening Malay interior.

He had once thought the fluorescent lights ugly. *Why don't they use normal bulbs? Where are their curtains?* But he soon came to rely on those cool white tubes for the unusual access they gave into Asian lives. Thanks to the ubiquitous fluorescent coil, the serene rituals of the Japanese home were exposed to him on his long strolls through Tokyo. On cab rides through the high-rise corridors of Hong Kong, he could enter the slovenly Chinese flats, with their barking housewives, their dervish children, their magnified sea sounds of mah jong tiles. And then, as his years abroad stretched on, fluorescent lights started flickering on in the other countries on his beat and Ted was drawn into the austere cubicles of the South Koreans, the high-rise kennels of the Singaporeans, the bamboo pagodas of the Filipinos. They were his own moon, casting beams where he chose and illuminating the lives of brown and yellow people for his observation. At one happy time, that was his job, his pleasure – in essence, his life.

Ted Augenstein was a foreign correspondent through and through and an Asian hand down to his stubby, flaking toes. And in return for his years of devotion, Asia and its people had opened themselves to him. It began in Japan in the 1960s, where he witnessed men and women bathing themselves for the first time. It continued in the flesh-spots of Asia – there were so many – where you could watch men and women indulge in the sex act for mere nickels. You could reach out and assist, or join them, for a few nickels more. In India, where you could watch humans squat like cornstalks in fields to defecate for your viewing pleasure. (And it was a plain pleasure for Ted; he greedily absorbed the sight whenever it presented itself.) And there was Saigon, of course, where all of these were, at one odd time, combined. Where the girl would bring you home for the sex act, where grandmas and parents and, most disconcertingly, babies would shuffle noisily outside the thin partitions, ignoring your own moans and shudders. Where modesty seemed permanently and irrevocably suspended and where foreigners scaled the very peak of expatriate power. When one emerged from that cardboard cubicle, one could sit down and conduct an impromptu interview of the family on a timely topic, paying the girl a little extra for the quotes.

Over the years, Ted Augenstein's work, his solitary ways and his glorious Asia combined to produce more than an impressive, Pulitzer Prize-winning career. A particular life had hard-formed, built on two pillars: the newsman's freedom to ask what he will and answer what he chooses; and the expatriate's profound sense of separateness from – and superiority over – the society around him. He was ill-prepared for his new existence in Manhattan, where the tables were yanked around and he found his tender, close-guarded life open to public scrutiny.

It began on his first day back, as he waited for Abe to finish jawboning with a visiting Arab minister. Ellie welcomed him with her usual New York sassiness. She made an unflattering remark about the Arabian's scent and chatted in her telegraphic style as she prepared for Abe a dossier on a disappointing reporter in the Los Angeles bureau.

'Ted,' she remarked, 'you're the only one of our boys not to come home with an Asian girl.' Her freckled, pudgy hands worked quickly to attach the bureau chief's lengthy memo – length was a negative sign – to a sheaf of clips: a man's worth in a small pile of Xeroxes.

'Don't tell me they're not making them beautiful anymore,' she continued. 'They must be. Remember Arthur Ecclestein's wife? The Vietnamese?'

'Laotian,' Ted corrected.

'Yeah, Laos,' Ellie said. 'He met her during The War. Now, she was beautiful.'

Ted suppressed his disagreement about Mrs Ecclestein's beauty and charitably failed to remind Ellie that Arthur Ecclestein had met his wife over a mop. He had married his maid.

'And so slim. Jeez.' Ellie paused to reflect. 'Maybe all that housework.' She remembered.

'They're divorced.'

'Yeah,' Ellie agreed, still busy with her paperwork. 'But he remarried on his next assignment. A girl from Mexico.'

'Costa Rica.'

'Yeah,' Ellie said. 'Now, she's really beautiful too. Black beauty. What happened with you? Didn't you like the Asians? Can't blame you really. They're graceful, but. Now you're home, you can settle down with someone more like Mom. You're not too old still. I don't think so. It would be good for you. Where's Arthur Ecclestein these days, anway?'

'South Africa.'

'I mean – '

'*Christian Science Monitor*.'

Ellie shook her greying head. 'Imagine that. *Christian Science Monitor*.' The grey head shook again, with sadness for all the poor journalists who found themselves having to leave the *Tribune* for jobs with papers like the *Christian Science Monitor*. She hesitated to put the dossier in Abe's In-tray: the qualms of the executioner.

'I hear you can't drink coffee or tea when you work for them,' she said. 'Or smoke. Imagine that!'

And Ellie was just the first. Before long, Ted encountered the impudent Brew 'N Burger waitress. 'Alone again?' How many times had she said it? Her extraordinary smirk!

And the news assistant from the Bronx, with his hideous running joke: 'How are the vases today, Ted? Don't tell me the Mings are diddling the Dings!'

At times, Ted felt he had been thrown into a world where the dandy's rule held sway: everyone in Manhattan was expected to live a life that, in itself, was a work of art, and, as such, was open to admiration or criticism from the world at large. He wondered when and how this ethic had arisen. He saw his fellow-countrymen behaving as if they were on continual display. He listened in subways and on buses as they disclosed the most personal details to caasual acquaintances: about hypoglycemic children, tumoured parents, aborted cousins, about diets that had done wonders to thighs, psychologists who had failed whole families, mortgages that had fallen through, inheritances (and relatives) that had finally dropped, articles of clothing that had cost less than they appeared to, appliances that had been affordable because they were stolen. He couldn't stop people from stating their philosophies on salt, sugar, butterfat and caffeine. Pride and shame seemed to have gone out of fashion at precisely the same moment, apparently by mutual agreement. Everyone was constantly burnishing a public self-portrait – replete with warts, pimples and scars – and making meticulous efforts to keep it up to date. The morning chat in the office was wholly dedicated to this daily updating, and each social encounter had to end in the same tacit truce: you tell me everything about your divorce and I'll tell you about my recent liposuck treatment. The reason the voyeur was the era's least favourite figure was that he wasn't holding up his half of the bargain.

Ted moved back to New York at the end of a summer and he took possession of a coop in the Village on a balmy September Saturday. His first chore was to paint the trim on the peeling windows. He opened a window as far as he could, looked out at his new view, and saw, on a low tarpapered rooftop, two nearly-naked people in a fierce, familiar embrace. The woman, who was underneath, wore only a flesh-coloured, sleeveless T-shirt pushed up to expose two freckled breasts. The man, who was having trouble choosing a tempo for his thrusts, also wore a shirt. Two pairs of bright running shorts were intertwined on the tarpaper and the man's tan briefs were caught on his left calf. Both the man and the woman were wearing their running shoes. As the act progressed, the woman increased the thrust of her hips from what appeared to be a rumpled Indian bedspread. The man matched her tempo. The two were curiously silent, as if content to be watched but shy about sharing sounds of pleasure. Finally, the man burrowed his face into his partner's neck, grasped her pale, frantic buttocks from underneath, and started pumping rapidly. Ted counted the windows in the buildings of the neighbourhood. When the couple ardently climaxed, more than one hundred of his neighbours were in a position to witness. And at that strenuous moment, inevitable cheers and whistles issued from a neighbouring building.

That evening, Ted returned to his empty apartment and gazed out at his one hundred neighbours. Some of the windows were dark. Behind others, life was going on. But thanks to the dim yellow lightbulbs of the West, Ted couldn't perceive what kind of life. In one window, Ted noticed the frozen silhouette of a sturdy man wearing a T-shirt and looking in his direction. Ted wondered if the man was watching him. Unexpectedly, the man lifted his arm and waved. It wasn't a wave of recognition or of voyeuristic solidarity or of passing friendliness. It was a wave of invitation. Ted could barely see other men in the obscure light of the stranger's room.

Ted abandoned his plans to use Japanese paper screens in his living room and billowy Indian blinds in his bedrooms. He ordered heavy drapes for all the rooms, which shut out all light and most of the sounds of the streets of lower Manhattan.

4

The car continued its flight through coconut groves, bluish forests of rubber trees and tall, irregularly-shaped hills with strange, lacy trees: nature's own permanent wave. Quite gradually, Ted entered the rain forest. Along the way, he peered into the illuminated Malay houses. At one point, the road deteriorated and he slowed. His car captured the attention of the occupants of a particular house. They were standing together at a side window facing the street: husband, wife and adolescent child. The house was on graceful, slender stilts. Through a light drizzle, the bare-chested father and son and the sarong-wrapped mother stared out at the passing car. Ted couldn't tell what had captured their mesmerized attention. He presumed it was the 20th century, fixing the simple savages in its fantastic beam. Instinctively, Ted waved his substantial arm. He caught a glimpse, as he passed, of the boy hesitantly returning the wave. And then he was past, on his way to the town beyond. The small kampong was left in its timeless drizzle. When the sight and sound of his car were finally gone, Ted wondered: *Will they even remember I passed? Or did the swift encounter with the future throw them into a moment completely lost in time and destined to be forgotten?*

In only one sense was Ted correct about the watchful Malay family. When the drone of his Toyota had faded, the family resumed its nightly routine. The mother went back to her cooking. The father paced about the room before settling down at his place on the floor. The son watched him with concern.

The family was not, however, dazed by an intrusion from a different century.

'Foreigner!' The boy used an awed tone.

'He didn't stop,' called the mother from the cooking area. 'He kept going!'

The father remained silent.

The mother entered the room wiping her hands. She said soothingly, 'He's gone. He's gone to Selarma.'

The father looked up stonily.

'He's coming back.'

As if attuned to secret music, the family rose and went to the window of their brightly-lit room: not the window that faced the road but the one that faced into the jungle. They gazed into the drizzling, darkening rain forest, awaiting the strange sounds that were becoming a part of the kampong's night. The raucous shouts, the unpleasant music. But it was too early. The sun had just set and it was the peaceful part of the evening. Trouble occurred later, when the dinners were done and the regular inhabitants of the kampong were falling asleep. That was when tumult could be expected from the house at the end of the path.

5

When Ted Augenstein reached Selarma, the open-fronted restaurants, in which everything, including the customers, looked flyblown, were doing a brisk business. The fruit and vegetable stalls were still blindingly lit with large, exposed lights, but the customers had finished their shopping. They would soon be dark. The padlocked shops along the road were filled with ghostly washing machines and plastic-wrapped television sets, dim visions through plateglass windows. Ted realized that his plans had gone amiss. The drive from Penang had taken hours longer than he anticipated. Vavasour's village was not beyond Selarma but before it; he had unknowingly passed it on the road. The larger town he had planned to spend the night in, Gerik, was still three hours in the opposite direction. Ted examined the only hotel in Selarma, the Phoenix, but when he detected a scared movement beneath the bed, he decided Vavasour could put him up.

It had been years since Ted had kept a foreign correspondent's schedule but the lack of sleep didn't affect him. It was one of those trips on which a feeling of momentousness prevails. One of those trips when the plot of the novel begun in New York seems ages old when returned to; when the razor blade is changed the first morning out, even if it is almost new. When Ted drove the Toyota onto the first ferry to the mainland that morning, he had already been awake for hours, sitting on the E & O's sea wall, soaking up the smells and the sounds of the tropical dawn. A sleepy waiter had brought him an unsolicited pot of tea. Ted half-expected him to say, 'Alone again?' To which he could have happily replied, 'Yes, indeed!' But all the waiter did was bow his dark head and silently depart.

The policeman said seventeen kilometres, so when Ted's odometer revolved to show 17, he stopped to ask directions. It took him several moments to recognize a forlorn house on the roadside. It was the home of the staring, 'Malaysian Gothic' family. The adolescent boy scampered down the steps from the gallery and timidly approached Ted's car.

Ted showed him the tatty envelope. The boy looked at it with wide eyes and a fearful expression.

'Is this – ' Ted began, but the boy stepped backwards and looked anxiously to the window of the house. The bare-chested father stood there, materialized from thin air.

Ted stepped from his car. 'Excuse me,' he said, 'but I'm looking . . .'

The Malay man folded his arms and glared at Ted.

'You see, I'm looking for . . .'

The Malay man unfolded his arms and pointed. Ted noticed a small dirt lane going into the dark trees behind the house. He pointed in the same direction.

'. . . that . . . ?'

The man continued pointing rigidly.

'Are you sure . . . ?'

He moved neither his arm nor a muscle of his face.

'. . . the foreigner who was here about . . .'

The man shook his arm sternly, as one would repeat a silent command to a dog or a dim child. The boy had somehow transported himself: he stood next to his father, looking down at Ted with undiminished fear.

'Thank you for your kindness and hospitality,' Ted muttered as he climbed into the Toyota. 'The warm Malay spirit. If Mom comes to the window, I'll thump my chest and holler like Tarzan!'

But as he manoeuvred the car into the lane, he found the boy at his front bumper guiding him on. Ted gestured for him to get inside the car, but the boy kept running. The car moved slowly through the dusty-looking trees and the widely-separated stilt houses. They had varying amounts of decorative trim on their wooden lintels and baseboards, but each had the same living snapshot of Malay life, brightly lit, cut from its side. The boy hurried Ted on, his skinny legs occasionally darting from the slit of his dark sarong. His eyes, when caught in the headlights, no longer looked alarmed; running seemed to have restored his boyish spirit.

Ted wondered: *How far are we going in?*

But the brown boy kept running. He made a puzzling, extravagant gesture with his thin arms. Then, in a flicker of headlights and at a slight turn in the path, he vanished into the black of the forest. Ted's headlights shone on a small house squatting at the terminus of the path. He instinctively flicked them off and rolled the car to a stop a distance from the house. He leaned out of the window and hissed: he wanted to bring the boy back for a tip. But only the forest responded with its inky rattles and unexpected yelps.

He shut the car door gently and slowly approached the house. It sat on an unkempt lot, and the structure appeared abandoned except for lights and the signs of motion within. There was also the sound of a voice. And, abruptly, an English word, hissed with odd vehemence.

'*Magic!*'

Ted gingerly ascended the wooden steps, moved across the rickety gallery and entered an open doorway. He quickly took in the scene. The room was unfurnished except for a reed mat and some scattered, ancient-looking pillows. Books were thrown in a corner. All was illuminated by a single strip of fluorescent tube across the ceiling. The room was empty of people except for an enormous man dressed in black and white, who leaned on an interior doorway with his back to Ted. He was waving a glass tumbler and talking into an adjacent room. His voice was English-accented. It was a good accent and the voice was melodious, perhaps trained.

'It is the death of the father, dear boy, that assures the life of the son. It's as simple and inevitable as that. Look it up! Go to the God damned British Museum if you must!' (The tumbler waved like a heavy flower in a storm.) 'It's written everywhere. The Killing of the Divine King, it's called. And that's exactly how it inevitably transpired in my quaint, less-than-regal English family, although I was the only one gathered around the bedside who recognized the process. My pitifully ambitious father, with his miserable premature death of a disease I refuse to have named in my presence. Oh, what plans he laid for me! When I saw him lying there, Ramse, with tubes that changed hue as their blood gave way to pus and then back again, I thought to myself: "Ta, Dad. You give me life. You poor sod." I upped, quit and clambered onto the first bloody banana boat I could rustle up. To carve out a new life: the life of a killer!'

There was a murmur from the room beyond and the sound of a utensil scraping a pan.

'I told you, coconut-head, it's not custom. It is magic, plain and simple. Magic! You bloody *bumis* think the *tunkus* invented magic and that's what you have up on the English. But here's the surprise. Don't laugh, don't laugh, boy . . .'

There were giggles from the far room, more cooking sounds, a large crash. The fat man was now standing with his legs apart, his tumbler held majestically high.

'When I'm on – and, boy, these rough patches never last that long – when I'm on, I'm one of the most talented scions of that ancient land of magic. The magician of choice, the magician of power, the renowned, some might say infamous (in particular, some asses in Philippine industry), the indomitable, the lethal – '

Ted said, 'Anton Vavasour?'

The huge figure froze. It didn't turn round. First, the tumbler was steadied and lowered. Next, a subtle adjustment of weight and balance was affected. Only then, and with a kind of grand slowness, did the broad shoulders and giant head twist to present to the brilliant room a fleshy face with a shiny bald head streaked with a few grey hairs. Only the small eyes held a trace of youth. He was a monster of a man, thick from his neck to his ankles, shining with sweat and an alcohol glow. Craters on Vavasour's neck gave him the puckered jowls of a hog. Ted was taken aback. The tiny house accented his size and for a moment Ted wondered whether the flimsy structure would give way beneath their combined bulk.

He should be chained beneath the house!

Vavasour, twisted in the doorway, squinted theatrically at the newcomer and raised a single, heavy eyebrow to convey the idea of restrained curiosity. 'Ah, Mr Bond!' His voice was rich and facetious; his smile was pus-colored. 'We have been expecting you. Haven't we, Ramse?' He made two graceful steps and his entire bulk was facing Ted, in its sack-like trousers and sweat-yellowed shirt.

A large smile in a brown face appeared adjacent to Vavasour's waist. It giggled and disappeared. Vavasour beat the air behind him with a puffy hand. 'Hush, Ramse!'

He returned his attention to the newcomer. 'Please,' Vavasour said grandly, gesturing to the furniture-less room. 'Come in. You must be . . .' He left the sentence heavily incomplete.

'Thank you.' Ted stepped in and settled himself neatly on the floor. He smoothed his hair.

Vavasour paused thoughtfully. '. . . tired. You must be tired. From your journey. Our village is undeniably out of the way. Some might say charmingly so.' The puffy hand gestured theatrically. 'I wouldn't, but some fool might. A goblet, Ramse, for our visitor. And vino.' He smiled generously and Ted saw a mouthful of cramped, stained teeth.

The brown boy appeared. He was slight and wore a pair of satin gym shorts. With a smirk, he handed Ted a tumbler half-filled with a milky liquid.

Vavasour raised his glass and said, 'A toast!'

'*In Vino Veritas*,' Ted proposed.

Vavasour accepted the suggestion with a forced chuckle. 'So they say,' he replied, raising his glass and taking a delicate sip. 'The non-drinkers, that is.'

Ted suffered an involuntary grimace. 'Sweet,' he coughed. 'What is it?'

'Our local vintage. Toddy. From coconut. One get accustomed.' Vavasour looked at his own glass reproachfully. 'Or one dies.'

'Of stomach cancer?'

'Of boredom.'

The two men fell silent as they sipped their viscous drinks. After the long drive, Ted was content to sit silently in the bright, unadorned room, feeling the initial stir of alcohol through his body. Unfamiliar sounds intruded from the forest and the opaque, paneless window-frames seemed to pulse with the life that lurked outside. Insects casually swept through the room: the forest's scouts. The muggy, submerged feeling comforted Ted. The jungle seemed a buffer between him and the looming Vavasour. His escape routes were clearly marked; his voice, if raised, would boom through the trees. Ted realized instinctively that it was Vavasour, not he, who was afraid of the jungle. Whatever the debacle that had driven him here, he was merely in hiding, awaiting his next battle. He wasn't taking on this forest or this kampong: apparently, he barely survived on their slim tolerance.

Vavasour, with an involuntary groan, settled his bulk on the reed mat. Ramse refilled their glasses, leaving the dirty, green toddy bottle between them.

'When you arrived so dramatically and unexpectedly, I was instructing my friend Ramse in the history of magic in the West, which, as a good son of the soil, he was trying to – '

'I am from the *New York Tribune*,' Ted stated.

Vavasour accepted the interruption with a nod. He looked thoughtfully into his drink and nodded a second time. 'I've done your crossword puzzle,' Vavasour said. 'Quite good, actually. First rate, I'd say.'

Ted was astonished by the silly reply.

'Of course that was a long time ago.' Vavasour sipped his wine meditatively. 'But I'm sure it remains challenging. American papers, as you know, aren't known for their crossword puzzles.'

Ted wondered how long he would prattle on.

'Now, the English papers – '

'I've flown from New York,' Ted interrupted, 'just for this trip.'

Vavasour accepted this information with equal equanimity. 'You're early for the turtle eggs.'

'Mr Vavasour – '

Vavasour was finally shaken from his massive calm.

'Of course. You spoke my name earlier as well. How do you know my name?' The yeasty face glared darkly at Ted. The little mouth, set in an ugly snarl, showed an ugly ribbon of bumpy yellow. 'Identify yourself,' commanded Vavasour. 'Who are you?'

'I am E. G. Augenstein. I am foreign editor of the *New York Tribune.*'

Vavasour seemed confused. 'You brought a cheque?' he asked. Ted shook his head.

'My Cambodia piece. Yes, of course: my little literary experiment. On Pol Pot, wasn't it?' he asked, as if recalling a distant, naughty adventure. 'From the Thai border: "I fix my binoculars on the rebel camp. And Mr Pot" – is that what I called him? *Mr Pot?* – ". . . strides forcefully from his tent, older and wanner than in pre-revolutionary photos, but still hearty. I am the first Westerner to set eyes on him in six years. It's obvious he and his band of rebels have seen better days, blah blah blah." I thought it was pretty authentic. And amusing. I had to crib a little from Prokosch to get myself in the mood. Some clever sub-editor must have picked that up, some female who read literature no doubt. Asia is wonderful in Prokosch, you know, and he never got out of Connecticut. Clairvoyant stuff. One of your best writers and one of the least appreciated, I understand.'

Ted watched the fat man across from him, rambling on senselessly as insects circled the room and Ramse served the dinner: rice in battered tin plates, accompanied by a weak vegetable curry. He wondered if the business-suited men could conceive of his situation. He thought of Ellie and her preoccupation with underpants and diarrhoea. He recalled the words of Alex Postlewaite III – 'Think of the paper, dear heart!' – and Abe's mindless echoing of the words. He thought of the jubilant and nasty editorials that the competition had rushed into print, drum-thumping the big issues: Truth! Credibility! Vigilance! Ted looked at the man who had violated these mountainous virtues and saw him shovelling food into his feminine mouth. A wasp hovered over Anton Vavasour's curry – they were exactly the same shade of yellow – and he continued to eat, paying it no mind.

'. . . although his Byron novel I consider nothing more than high camp,' Vavasour continued, through abundant mouthfuls. 'Ramse, get me that Prokosch over there. Not the Naipaul, nincompoop, the Prokosch. That green book.'

He addressed Ted in a conspiratorial stage whisper. 'He's no litterateur and a Chinaman could cook rings around him, but I assure you, in a pinch, he's a godsend.'

'In a pinch?' Ramse squealed. 'In a *pinch?*' He erupted in a shower of giggles.

It became clear that Vavasour was ignorant of the uproar that had accompanied the publishing of his bogus story. He hadn't known the story was printed. 'How extraordinarily easy,' he commented, and Ted could only nod his agreement.

Vavasour inquired several times about payment. Ted explained that no payment was forthcoming. Vavasour puzzled over this.

'I fully understand your point, what with scandal and all, but surely there must be some copyright issue involved. You admit the story was printed. Surely payment must be made, even when . . .

Or could I sell my story to the tabloids: "How I Faked the *New York Tribune*." Now there's an idea, Ramse.'

'Mr Vavasour,' Ted asked wearily, slowly recognizing the ridiculousness of his quest, 'may I ask you: what is your profession?'

The question drew Vavasour out of his puzzled stupor. He seemed to enjoy talking about himself. 'I'll spare you the silly joke about being "between successes," Mr . . .'

'Augenstein.'

'Yes, Mr Augenstein. I have heard of you before, you know. Your name stuck in my head. In fact, I believe that in my letter to your newspaper . . .'

'That's correct.'

'Anyway, what's past is past. Too bad that didn't work out differently. One can't live in the past. To the present.' He refilled his glass and called for a refill of the dirty green bottle. Ted wondered about the vat that held the main toddy supply.

'Over the years,' Vavasour continued expansively, 'I've answered your question in many different ways. With pistol. With stiletto. But tonight' – he waved at the buzzing windows – 'or for these past few weeks, to be more precise – '

'Two and a half months,' Ramse amended, depositing the refilled bottle on the mat.

'Shoo!' Vavasour said. 'Suffice it to say I'm a professional expatriate. I live abroad. And make of it the best I can.' He was flipping through a book. 'Here,' he said. 'Listen to this: "*They were the ugly ones whom no one loved . . .*"'

'Expatriates?'

'No,' said Vavasour. 'These are Prokosch's toilet queens at Benares. Benares, I should add, as envisioned from New Haven. '"*There were many of them, making this place their resort, habitually excited by the smell and the wandering glances, noticing each newcomer with a quickening of the breath, but nevertheless repelled by one another. There was nothing else for them; that, of course, was the reason for it all.*"'

Ted decided the grotesque fat man was harmless and he dimly perceived that if there was any understanding of Vavasour to be accomplished, and the forest night offered few better challenges, it would come in a descent to his level through alcohol. He decided to match Vavasour drink for drink. Ted was a man who could descend into many levels of drunkenness without causing or bringing upon himself trouble. He refilled his glass, draining the green bottle, and drank deeply. The hypnotic forest called and he chose to surrender.

'*"Shabby, indefinable creatures, peering and shifting slowly from side to side like pariah dogs, never uttering a word, unless perhaps a monosyllabic whisper. Lost altogether, quite incurable."*' Vavasour's trained voice whispered the last few words.

'You like our local vintage, Mr Augenstein?'

Ted shook his head.

'Ah!' Vavasour said. 'Like spirits! Soul brothers! May I refill your glass?'

Ted's watch said 9.30. Night in the jungle came quickly and, it seemed, lasted long.

And so they drank.

'But Vavasour,' Ted persisted. 'Surely money alone – '

'Don't underestimate,' scolded Vavasour, wagging a bratwurst finger, 'the difficulties an expatriate can face in visa matters.'

'Visas?'

'And passports, of course.'

'What do visas have to do with anything?'

Vavasour goggled at him. 'What do visas have to do with anything?' He mocked Ted's accent. 'Visas are everything!'

Soon Vavasour was paging through Ted's worn blue passport, reading out the visas to Ramse, who hooted and giggled at appropriate moments. Vavasour made it a theatrical exercise.

'Sorry, Mr Augenstein, but Indonesia is finished, kaput! One entry. Who would want a second, I ask! Wretched, intolerant place. The region's most humourless tyrant.' He rose unsteadily, feigned the ripping of a page from Ted's passport and then drew an old cloth around his bulk to imitate, in turn, Javanese men and Balinese women.

Certain visas made him furious. Others threw him into a kind of reverence. '"Multiple entry Thailand, valid for five years from date of issue." Five years, Ramse! And the same for Japan. Hong Kong four years. What I could do with four years.'

Vavasour pushed his face towards Ted. He snarled at him under the relentless fluorescent tube. 'How much would your damned magazine have paid if bloody Prokosch hadn't exposed me?'

'It wasn't the Prokosch.'

'How much?' Vavasour demanded.

Ted told him.

Vavasour flung Ted's passport at the opposite wall with theatrical disdain. It startled two chameleons competing for a fluttering winged creature.

'For that kind of money,' Vavasour sneered, 'I could have two passports from any country in the world. Ramse here could be a fucking Swiss.'

Ramse made repeated trips to the kitchen with the dirty green bottle.

'I believe you're drunk.'

'I believe I am,' Vavasour giggled.

'And I wonder if you're not mad.'

'Mad?' Vavasour asked. 'Mad? Oh, I wouldn't say that. It's been my motto for many years. "Don't get mad . . ."'

'". . . get even!"' Ramse howled, and the two jumped up and did a clumsy, impromptu dance.

'You know what I mean.'

Vavasour, standing and holding Ramse's two slim hands, became pensive. 'I know what you mean? Why, my good man, how can anyone ever know what another person truly means? With all these façades, these dreams, these masks.' He was stimulated by his own comment and he rummaged noisily through his stack of books.

'I gather you journalists don't read much. Have you read Von Rezzori? Listen: *"The thing that made them all one and the same person was: dreaming. When he thought I, he felt as if he were dreaming himself up:* Somnio, ergo sum – *I dream myself up, therefore I am."*'

Ted's expression was blank.

'It's all semiotics, I am convinced,' Vavasour proclaimed. He flung the book over his head and it hit a wall with a large noise.

He fixed upon Ted a stagy squint of menace.

'I could kill you, you know,' Vavasour said. 'Here in the forest, no one would tell. Here in the forest, I am king. They are afraid of me. And I have killed before.'

'Liar,' Ted said.

And later, when the men were drunk and the boy-man was asleep with his head in Vavasour's lap: 'I always desired to be a master of disguises.' Vavasour spoke wistfully.

The two men, in the moist night, had grown to resemble each other. One was still more monstrous than the other. But both were shiny with sweat. Ted, normally so concerned about his honey-coloured, blow-dried hair, had abandoned it to the elements. It was slickly pushed back from his face. The men's shirts were equally sweat-ruined. Both held their tumblers in the same laconic droop.

'You laugh,' Vavasour said with drunken petulance. 'You think me too fat to be a master of disguises. To change my skin.' Vanity prompted him to gingerly rearrange the thin strands of hair on his glowing head. His face loomed in the night. 'Or too – *ugly*.' The last word was pronounced with a prissy shudder. 'But there was a time, not too, too long ago . . .'

Ted looked at the brown boy asleep in Vavasour's lap. The jungle and the native wine had brought a change in Ted's attitude towards the couple. However grotesque they had seemed, however easy came the sneers about gay couples in general, he now wondered whether they had something lovely to them: something born from their inevitable exclusion from the world. He saw, for an instant, a tableau of odd but essentially content domestic life, away from the eyes of the world at the bottom of a rain forest. He meditated on the idea dreamily and happily.

Vavasour noticed Ted's gaze at Ramse. His topic changed abruptly. 'One can be surprised at what lurks behind certain façades, Mr Foreign Editor. Let's take a random case.' Vavasour pointed with his tumbler. 'You.'

'What hides behind that chinkless, official attitude of yours, Mr Augenstein? You have everything in place, it seems, and the world opens its arms to you, beckons you, throws visas in your path. "Fee: gratis" – don't think I didn't notice. For when you come, you also go. You are nothing more than a professional interloper. But down deep, the core can conflict with the façade, can't it Mr Augenstein? I have said in the past, we all suffer from terminal culture shock, even those who never leave home. And emotional jet-lag. The world is always on another clock – isn't that how you feel? The only way to consider that is to keep on travelling. Is that what you think? Do I capture your hidden sensibility?'

'You're drunk.'

'I've learned the difference between the heart and the masks of men, Mr Augenstein. I have been compelled to in my kind of life. Consider the world as a place of signs. *Semiotics!*'

'What time now?' Ted looked towards the sleeping boy, and then to Vavasour.

Vavasour smiled his pus-coloured smile. 'You like him, Mr Augenstein?' He nodded at the brown boy.

Ted, after a moment, shook his head.

A peculiar thing happened during the night. Ted awoke, disoriented and thirsty from the raw native liquor. Someone had turned off the fluorescent light but the room was oddly bright. It was the moon, which somehow penetrated the forest cover. Ted saw Ramse, bathed in silver, asleep in the arms of a figure that looked like himself. The moonlight was kind to the monstrous Mr Vavasour.

But when he awoke again, the fluorescent light was ineffectually burning. Dawn was chattering through the trees. The forest outside looked like any other shady grove, so different from the forceful presence that had eavesdropped, with heavy breathing, all evening. Ted stood up quietly, felt for his passport and walked to the door. He avoided looking at Vavasour, sprawled violently on the mat. Ramse was nowhere to be seen.

At the main road, Ted looked to the roadside house expecting the usual signs of life that daybreak brings to a native village. But the house was still, with windows of black where the illuminated snapshots had glowed the evening before. He wanted to see the boy and to thank him with, at the very least, a wave. But the house looked asleep.

Ted pulled the car onto the main road and headed west. He would stop at Buttersworth to enquire about flights, or, if need be, get back on the ferry to Penang. It was Friday morning. He wanted to get to Hong Kong as soon as he possibly could.

THE PILLOW BOOK OF ALICE GILES, FOREIGN
CORRESPONDENT (CONTINUED)

Three Little Words

Three little words. Everybody knows them. Everybody adores them. Ask a poet and he'll respond, *con amore:* 'I *love* you!'

Ask an engineer and he may blink a bit or play a round of pocket billiards, but finally he'll come out with it: 'I *love* you?'

Ask Adam Fendler, journalist, to state the three famous words and he'll say, with the special forthrightness of the journalist: 'By Adam Fendler.'

The Byline! Remember this particular byline – 'By Adam Fendler' – for Adam is the fool of this story. Every story must have a fool; in any case, most stories end up with one. If the byline escapes you, just think of a brown fedora, the only one in town, set at a rakish half-tilt above a pasty, beady-eyed face. For Adam, the byline and the fedora served the same purpose.

The Byline: the three little words that attract normal young people to the trade of journalism and keep them enslaved for the rest of their lives. Much of journalism is dreck, as every journalist's mother knows. But the byline is always wonderful: short, never ungrammatical or inaccurate, always crystal clear.

So wonderful is the byline that, like a newborn infant, its faults are never recognized. And bylines have distinct, characterizable flaws. Take the middle-initial bylines, used by hopeless stick-in-the-muds; the 'John Jones Jr' bylines, for confirmed father-haters; the double byline, inevitably a reporter who can't write paired with a writer who can't report; the byline so long it can't fit in one column (usually ethnic); the female disguising her gender ('By M. J. Andersen'); the overly musical ('By Manuella Coppalecchia'); the Chinese 'Dings' and 'Lings'; the plain laughable ('By Patty May'); and the truly pitiable ('By Gary Fish and Al Pain'). The world can pick up its morning paper, stare at a byline and laugh so hard its coffee spills. But the journalist won't mind.

I will share with you one of journalism's greatest secrets: it is the journalist who doesn't treasure his byline who departs for public relations, securities analysis or academia. If a test was done in J-school, that question alone would determine which of the class will run the entire course, down to the last tearful column that begins: 'When I first started banging an Underwood typewriter some 35 years ago, the world was a very different place . . .'

Adam Fendler's first byline read: 'By The Old Grouch.' He would have passed that J-school test, had he gone to J-school. But I should start at the beginning. I should start at the Hong Kong Foreign Correspondents Club, where Adam Fendler first gambled all by standing on the peeling bar of the fourteenth floor. Any discussion of journalists in Hong Kong must begin at the FCC. In journalism, legends are not merely born. They are worked at. And there is no greater centre of legend-mongering than the Hong Kong Foreign Correspondents Club.

The FCC is an organization that satisfies mundane demands of its several hundred members – food, drink, companionship – but which, at the same time, labours to sustain its own slightly chimerical reputation of an exciting past. Vital pieces of news were first related at the FCC. Not this FCC, old bean, but in that building in the mid-levels. Uproarious practical jokes were hatched at its bar – not this bar, exactly, but the more intimate bar in that building in Kowloon. In one of its most wonderful locations, FCC members could dance in gardens with the twinkling lights of the harbour just a magnificent hand-gesture distant. The weather seemed better in Hong Kong then. In other locations, when the weather seemed quite dismal, the club's carpet was damp and the doors of the old wooden elevators jumped nervously, endangering ladies' hands.

In the late 1980s, the club was located in a particularly unglamorous site – ladies watched their hands and gentlemen wiped their shoes upon *exiting* the club – when the landlord decided to redevelop his property. The FCC was, once again, on the move. A Relocation Committee was convened, which decided on new premises on Ice House Street. Comfortable premises, the committee promised its members. Affordable. A bit of a walk, but suitable. Definitely suitable. A home? A home at last for the wandering journalists of Hong Kong? So it seemed.

Until Adam Fendler stood on the club's peeling bar and announced, at a well-attended gathering of members, that he had a statement to make 'of import to all the members of the Fourth Estate hereunto gathered.' His fedora was perched at its usual half-tilt. He had the air of a little boy dressed up in Daddy's clothes and mocking Daddy's mien. The interest of the jaded members of the FCC was temporarily piqued.

Anthony Lawson, who chaired the meeting, went into a huddle with his committee. The entire membership could read the question on his thin, passionless lips. *'Who?'*

The answers were hidden behind cupped hands, but everyone knew what they were.

– Fendler.
– American.
– New boy.
– Starting a column at the *Post*.
– Energetic. (An ambiguous term at the FCC and, indeed, in all of journalism.)
– Spent time in Taiwan.

Were the other things stated? *Jewish? Every night at the bar? Seems anxious for a better job?* Nobody could tell.

Refreshed with information, Anthony Lawson recovered his particular brand of oily cool. He sipped a tiny glass of clear liquid. 'Yes Mr Fendler, the floor is open. Or the bar. Whichever you prefer.'

Adam drew a sheet of paper from the pocket of his baggy trousers, shifted uncomfortably, nodded formally to the chairman and began in a querulous voice. 'Ladies and gentlemen of the Fourth Estate, tonight, we meet not to discuss land prices or budgets or dues or relocation bonds or even the quality of the club's Singapore noodles.' He stared hard at the audience. His chin quavered. 'Instead, we decide the fate of one of the great symbols of this continent's greatest hope. And I mean, I'm sure you realize, a free press.' Adam continued to stare uncomfortably. Anthony Lawson resumed his whispering with his neighbour. Was it the Jewish question this time? Or, perhaps: 'Every night at the *downstairs* or the *upstairs* bar?'

'Asia is rising,' Adam continued, half-ringingly, 'and we already tower above it. We here on the fourteenth floor are, in journalistic terms, the guiding light on this wide, diverse continent. This, the Hong Kong Foreign Correspondents Club, is where some of the most incisive reporting from Asia pours forth. Reporting that can bring change. Our brethren in Korea, Japan, the Philippines, Indonesia, Malaysia and Singapore look to us, as children gaze upon – '

'Japan?' roared a voice from a far corner. 'Get off it!'

Adam's tenuous hold on the group, borne of shock more than respect, gave way suddenly and crashingly. The room came alive. Someone sang a Japanese folk song in a discordant falsetto.

Adam tried to recover his command. 'Okay,' he shouted, 'but the truly underdeveloped countries, the dictatorships – '

Another voice shouted: 'In Singapore, they're not looking to us. They're facing the other way. We're looking at their *arses*.' Laughter broke out, animated chatter rose from the tables and a few matching falsettos screeched Chinese opera.

In short, there was the usual FCC ruckus. The members, whose interest in the meeting had never been keen, abandoned themselves to their nightly gossips and intrigues. A high and false female laugh floated from one of the tables facing the harbour. It signalled the evening's proper beginning. Lawson downed another shot of gin. The rest of his committee laughed and ordered drinks from a waiter.

It was a fact that there was an acutely uncomfortable man in a baggy business suit standing atop the bar, a folded speech in his hands and a stricken look on his pasty face. But at the Hong Kong Foreign Correspondents Club, attention is bought in much harder currency.

To the man standing on the bar, in his baggy brown pants, his formless white shirt with the carefully frayed collar, the emblematic fedora pushed back on a prematurely-balding pate, the view must have appeared a painful rout. Adam Fendler knew that first, sweating feeling when failure has you in its grasp. He remembered it from boyhood, when the hand slipped. 'Oh my God,' you thought, as time stood still. 'Surely *I* can't be falling off this roof. Other people fall of roofs. Not me.' He knew that blissful wave of relief when balance was regained. He also knew the feeling when the hand refuses to catch and when one's balance betrays. He discovered that feeling when he was an overconfident, twenty-two-year-old fact-checker.

Standing on the FCC bar, he wondered: *Is this my second fall?*

The world had been unkind to Adam Fendler. Childhood had been a lengthy ordeal. Adolescence was worse. College started off unpromisingly until, in an unrecorded moment of nerd's inspiration, Adam returned to his dormitory after Christmas vacation dressed in his father's oldest, shiniest suit and a pair of scuffed brown Oxfords. Gone forever were the tan corduroys and sneakers. Within a few weeks, no one could recall his first-semester failures: the unsuccessful tryout for the freshman revue – brightly singing 'The Seven Deadly Virtues' – and the unaccepted dates. With a simple change of clothes, Adam became recognized as a campus eccentric. In sophomore year he began lecturing at the Student Union – which he called the Student Gathering Place, 'because I don't believe in unions' – and the amusingly pompous newspaper column, 'The Rambler,' which bore his photo (before the fedora) and his first byline: 'By The Old Grouch.' At the start of junior year, he revived the Young Republicans Club, only to abandon it by November to what he called 'inflexible doctrinaires.' Senior year was his zenith, as founder and president of the Madeleines, 'conservative *bon vivants* dismayed by the decline of gracious living and interacting.' The *Alumni Magazine* printed his photo on its cover: Adam, hatless, with a sombre expression, a determined glass of champagne in his stubby hand, wearing a worn pair of tails. The black-and-white photo failed to show the brownness of his shoes.

He was elected to speak at his graduation and his address – 'Platitudes On Parade' – earned him wild applause and his first and last hello from Lydia, the prettiest English major. And then, Adam Fendler's college career was over. One can only wonder how he felt after four years of perfecting a self-image. Did Adam feel like a famous actor dying at the apex of his popularity? An exiled emperor, forever separated from the people foolish enough to have tolerated him? Or, perhaps, did Adam look patronizingly at the little nest, containing the cracked shell of his transformation, from which he could now soar into the world with his Oxfords, his frayed collars, his sagging crutch? Please note: he still wore no fedora.

He applied for a job as a fact-checker at a famous national newsweekly. His interviewer, the chief of the checkers, had the unusual name of Flora Jew, which caused confusion when Adam arranged the appointment by phone.

'Then I simply ask for . . .'

'Miss Jew,' replied Miss Jew.

'Miss Jew?'

'Yes, Miss Jew.'

'Just Miss Jew?'

'Yes,' she said impatiently. 'I will come to the security desk to get you.'

Only when Adam saw her black hair, puffy cheeks and slanted eyes did he comprehend.

Why didn't she spell it out?

Flora Ju explained that if Adam was hired, he would be assigned to the business and economics section.

'I think American business is still the greatest success story in the twentieth century,' he told her. 'Don't you agree?'

Flora wasn't the kind of woman who agreed with much, or many. She was blunt, fat and the only fact-checking she did was for the People section. Each Monday her staff combed the section, hoping to find Barbra Streisand referred to as 'Barbara', which would have cost Flora her job.

'In fact,' Adam continued, warming to the interview process, 'I was reading a very interesting editorial in the *World Business Journal* on competitiveness. Did you see it on Saturday?'

Flora's pudgy face shook inscrutably.

'It said that American industry still, despite what everyone says and despite the challenge from the Japs, is the most innovative in the world. I'm surprised you didn't see it.'

Flora said nothing.

'The Japanese, I mean.'

Flora, in her flat Californian accent, commented, 'There is no *World Business Journal* on Saturdays. And that reminds me.' She laboriously rose. (The interview was ending.) 'The rule says you get one published mistake. A second mistake gets in the magazine and you're out. Mistakes that are caught before deadline don't count – unless I catch them.' Her moon face folded upwards. She had made a joke. At that precise moment, Adam devised the nickname that would score him his first points among Flora's staff. From then on, Flora Ju was known as 'Fauna Ju.'

'In journalism,' Adam told Flora loftily, 'the details are extremely important. But we should also keep an eye on the big picture.'

Flora stared at him. 'You,' she said. 'Forget about the big picture.'

Adam's first checking mistake was in a trade story. He confused billions of dollars with millions. The error was caught by a proof-reader before publication. Another time, he used the word 'and' instead of an ampersand in the name of a certain public corporation. The tiny error was published. Luckily, no one complained.

'This business is trickier than I thought,' Adam told a colleague. 'What ever happened to Investigative Journalism and Muckraking and Digging Deeper. Who's monopolizing the Truth beat?'

Soon enough, figures, spellings and mathematical computations caught up with Adam. A film producer complained that a story misstated his age by one year. Adam was outraged, for he had checked the fact. But the producer's birthday had occurred between the checking of the story and its publication. Adam was debited for his first mistake.

Adam's life became a race: he had to get promoted out of the checking pool before his next published error. He lurked around the international section, trying to impress the editor with odd clippings from North Korean newsletters. But the foreign section had no openings – yet.

Enter Mr Peter H. Leman, a 41-year-old wunderkind in the disc drive field (or so the magazine reported), a businessman with the kind of international flair necessary in the increasingly complex global marketplace of the 1980s. Mr Leman was handsome, as proven by the black-and-white photo showing him at the Great Wall of China holding aloft a disc drive. He had automation, a positive genius for currency risks, production in Taiwan and Singapore and nascent sales in China. (Or, as the headline said, 'Sales Up The Yangtze.') He seemed to have been created for *Time Magazine*.

He also had an 'h' in his surname and no middle initial.

'Yes, Mr Lehman, I understand,' Adam said, shouting to overcome a bad line from Taipei. 'It's entirely my fault and I want to extend my sincere . . .' As he listened, he felt the hand slip on the rooftile.

'But I don't think, Mr Lehman, that a correction is really necessary. Your company's name was spelled correctly, your age was correct . . . Yes . . . Yes . . . I know, Mr Lehman . . . No, I am not married but I fully understand how wives . . . Yes, I do have a middle initial but I don't use it . . . Yes, two mistakes in one name is disgraceful but a correction . . .

'I propose, Mr Lehman that I inform my editor and we here at Time Inc. will decide whether a correction . . .'

Adam's face settled stonily.

'Yes, Mr Lehman, I can transfer you. Her name is "Ju." No, no, not a Chinese name. The precise spelling is J.E.W. What's the matter, Mr Lehman? You have something against Jews? Her first name is F.A.U.N.A. The middle initial, Mr Lehman, please note the correct middle initial, is U.'

So Adam, for a missed birthday and a misplaced H, was canned from a job at the age of twenty-two. Those who have never been fired cannot understand the effect, especially on the young. Adam would never feel secure in a job again. Whether he could even get a job in the fraternal world of journalism was doubtful. He imagined his dismissal as instant news in newsrooms across the country, the journalistic equivalent of a war crime. He pictured Flora Ju on the WATTS line, spreading the word.

Through some combination of luck and panic, Adam did the right thing. He fled. Within weeks, he was working on an English-language newspaper in Taipei. Two months later, history stepped in to boost Adam Fendler's fortunes. Taiwan's aging premier croaked. Adam received his first professional byline atop a story in Hong Kong's *South China Morning Post*, a newspaper that sounded to him like a breakfast cereal. It took only a few months more, and several expensive flights to Hong Kong, before he clinched a staff job on the paper. Its dirty eight-storey building next to the pungent Hong Kong harbour became his home. It was where he worked eighteen hours a day, and where he slept, either on his desk or beneath it. It was where he hung his hat. For yes! Adam now sported his trademark fedora. On his first day at work, he installed a scarred hat-rack in the newsroom and generously offered its use to the whole hatless staff.

(The debate was never resolved as to when Adam adopted his fedora: on the way to Taiwan, in the middle of his short career there, or five minutes before he entered the newsroom of the *South China Morning Post*. No one at the paper could recall him prior to the day he pushed through the newsroom door with an ancient hat-rack in his arms, puffing like an exhausted but happy dance partner.)

Adam bought a comically dilapidated car, festooned it with *South China Morning Post* stickers and scattered banknotes of various currencies on its seats and floor. (Adam feigned a distracted attitude towards money.) On the rare evening he returned to his tiny warren in the mid-levels, he would hang his *Morning Post* ID card on a nail on the front door, suggesting, *The Newsman Is In.*

And he joined the Hong Kong Foreign Correspondents Club with a blissful thrill. The same day, he went to Lane Crawford to price raincoats with epaulettes.

Adam hovered five feet six-and-a-half inches above the peeling bar of the Foreign Correspondents Club. The woman by the window continued her peals of false laughter. The relocation committee made no attempt to bring order to the meeting. He had gambled with a theatrical gesture, and the members of the FCC were showing him how demanding an audience they were.

Desperately, Adam squatted to the bar and grasped a large book with a faded black cover. From a distance, it looked like a Bible. He raised the book before him like a preacher.

'Journalists and journalistas,' he announced vibrantly. 'Reporters and reporteras. Hacks and Mrs Bloody Hacks. And you fellers hiding in the back.' The crowd began to settle. Adam realized that this was his last chance.

'When we decide this evening whether to move this august club from these fabled premises, let us turn from considerations of price and square footage. Let us consult the great book. The book of Hong Kong. *Our* book.'

He held the book towards the crowd as an offering. He opened it, flipped several pages and started to read.

Adam raised a portentous eyebrow. 'And I quote! "The crown colony had become for Luke what it was for the rest of the journalists: an airfield, a telephone, a laundry, a bed, occasionally a woman and, most importantly, a club: *The* Foreign Correspondents Club."'

Adam announced gravely: '*The Honourable Schoolboy.* By John . . . Le . . .'

The membership joined Adam in the last syllables, lustily cheering: 'Le Carré!' There were whistles and hoots.

Adam raised his hand again. 'Brethren,' he said. 'Fellers! Wait!

There's more.' He flipped a few pages. ' ". . . and in the FCC men's room, one encountered the finest view possible of the glorious Hong Kong harbour!" '

There were more whistles and hoots. The woman by the window cheered, 'Jolly good!'

'Fellers,' Adam implored, the black, worn novel held above his fedora, 'are we gonna abandon a club that has, since the year nineteen hundred and seventy-seven, gone down in legend? Does Ice House Street boast a better view of the harbour? A better men's room? Anyway, where the *hell* is Ice House Street?'

'It's near Kelly & Walsh,' someone shouted helpfully.

'Too bloody far!' yelled someone else. The club erupted boisterously.

'Why don't we move to North Point!' shouted another employee of the *South China Morning Post*, which was located beyond North Point.

'To the men's room!' proposed a female member and an *ad hoc* View Committee, entirely women, rushed off to inspect. There was even a moment when Adam thought he would be hoisted from the bar and onto members' shoulders. He was mistaken. It was simply a rush for more drinks.

That evening the members voted unanimously to move the club's premises to Ice House Street. Financially there was little choice. No one accused Adam of cunningly misquoting Le Carré. (The novel's exact words: 'And in the men's room, which provided the Club's best view of the harbour . . .') But the evening was a triumph for the previously-unknown Adam. That evening, by another lusty vote, he was elected chairman of the Decoration Committee for the new premises.

'And we'll have no candy pinks nor earth tones, neither,' he pledged.

Adam's first Sunday column – 'Ramblin' Again' – was printed the following week. He was present when the first copies flew off the press early that Sunday morning, his face atop the column in a high-contrast photo. It was a facetious column, full of wry ruminations on Deng Hsiao-Ping's bridge playing and Imelda Marcos's shoe fetish. A column designed for a *nom de plume*.

The same morning, he was on the water: he had scored his first invitation to a launch picnic, an important institution among Hong Kong expatriates. He spent six sunny hours on a teak junk with four foreign correspondents, two bankers, one Indian public relations man, six wives and five bulky copies of the Sunday *South China Morning Post* in twenty-five sections. The talk was a captivating mixture of Hong Kong gossip, journalistic sniping and strange placenames, like Afghanistan and East Timor. Adam had trouble concentrating whenever a guest opened up the third section of the paper, which contained 'Ramblin' Again,' by 'B. G. Deal.'

'Who's this B. G. Deal?' asked one wife disapprovingly.

Adam gulped.

'Is it Brian Diel? What happened to that *TV Week* woman? Who did the social column?'

'The one in the soap commercials?' asked another wife.

'Yes, who was the nun in "Agnes of God" last year,' said the first.

'The psychiatrist,' contradicted another wife in an intolerant tone. It was the Indian matron who had unpleasantly refused to swim.

'I'm sure it was the nun,' replied the first wife. 'Which character threw up on stage?'

Later: 'The *Post* is getting a bit thick, isn't it?' said a wife, staring straight at Adam's photo.

Finally it was revealed that Adam was the new columnist. There were polite compliments and scoldings for improper modesty. One wife asked: 'What happened to that *TV Week* columnist who threw up on stage during "Agnes of God"?'

And a husband replied, 'That was me,' to hearty laughter from all.

And another wife said, as she gaped at the column's photo, 'What's wrong with your hair?'

'It's a fedora.'

But none of it mattered. Adam was arriving in Hong Kong. He could feel it. His foot was in the door and all he had to do was keep pushing.

If Hong Kong Didn't Exist

If Hong Kong didn't exist, it would have to have been invented by journalists. The salient question is: would they have had the imagination?

It sounds flippant. But believe me: if there's one thing I am not flippant about, it is Hong Kong. My harbour. My strength. My tower.

What is Hong Kong? And why does it attract such droves of professional truth- and lie-tellers, my meandering, bent tribe, the foreign correspondents?

The histories of Hong Kong start out with words like 'Lo!' and 'Hark!' and concentrate on the treaties of 1842 and 1898, the Boxer rebellion, the opium trade. You read about taipans and typhoid and expatriates being borne to their Peak homes each evening in sedan chairs.

At the risk of appearing grossly self-centred, may I suggest a more appropriate history of the place called Hong Kong? Your guide is a tall, still young, only slightly-frail woman in a handsome, aquamarine $90 raincoat from Lord & Taylor's. The year is 1966 – a much more sensible starting point than 1842. Watch as the woman steps off the Pan Am Clipper, stooping nervously, grinning, sweating profusely in the July heat and wondering why. The problem is her handsome raincoat, which she should strip off and throw flamboyantly into the glistening harbour. A first offering! For only newcomers wear raincoats in steamy Hong Kong. But she is a newcomer. Let us indulge her the raincoat. It is pretty, after all, and new, and it did cost $90.

What was Hong Kong in 1966? In many ways, it was the same Hong Kong as today. There was that same dichotomy between

Hong Kong at a distance and the greasy peasant embrace of its streets and alleys.

There she goes, still sealed in that silly raincoat, up the funicular railway. Imagine the shivers she feels – despite the raincoat – at the majestic, miraculous jigsaw puzzle she sees, complete save for a few pieces still moving across the board: the junks and ships slowly traversing the harbour. And then, as the sun dims, imagine her awe as the lights are switched on. Those Hong Kong lights! How indescribable they were! How indescribable they remain today! (An update: no season goes by that doesn't find me at that same towering spot, at the same time of the evening, gazing down at my Hong Kong. I accompany the most obscure and unpleasant acquaintances, rearranging their schedules to reach the Peak at sunset.)

And down she comes. She totters through the market lanes, her hand clasping her raincoat collar, too timid to look into the interiors of the straw baskets filled with green, writhing reptiles, ready for the soup-pot or wok. Imagine her amazement on the tram when her gaze meets that of a blinking hen, trussed beneath a wooden-slatted seat and behaving more politely than the shrieking Cantonese who will butcher her that evening and nibble on her rubbery toes. Watch her recoil from the oily winds that explode from every sidewalk restaurant. She runs her hand through her hair: it feels sautéed.

See her at work, in the tiny office with the portable Olympia typewriter, studying yesterday's Hong Kong and chronicling today's. Hong Kong was jammed to the rafters in 1966 with immigrants from China. So the people were put to work making nasty toys and hideous Dynel wigs. The rafters grew. Factories sprang up, apartments followed the factories, and in many parts of the city there was no distinction: sewing, sleeping and slaughter of pigs were done on the same premises. More immigrants came and the rafters grew even higher. The toys became less nasty. Dynel wigs gave way to electronics. Miraculously, Hong Kong became the regional centre for that weird entity named 'Asia,' a continent with as many faces and arms as an Indian goddess. And just as suddenly, Asia, once a word for poverty and temple bells, became a synonym for success and synergy. More towers; more wealth; talk of a century that bore Asia's name. McDonalds arrived and taught the Chinese to eat hamburgers. Then McDonalds caught the greedy, local spirit and taught the Chinese to eat hamburgers for breakfast. And they ate them.

The office expanded. It moved premises. It installed computers and a succession of bureau chiefs. Soon an entire edition was being printed from Hong Kong with the help of that old warhorse with the little girl's voice, whose first piece of whispered advice to newcomers was to chuck their raincoats and buy cheap, made-in-Hong Kong umbrellas.

Inevitably, the newcomer would knock, close the door behind him, and ask her: 'Alice, I don't get it. Hong Kong I mean. It doesn't seem to make sense!'

How could she explain? Could she refer to the towering bank buildings? Shouldn't 'world financial centre' refer to a collection of real banks in real cities in solid nations, not to a house of cards stacked perilously in decidedly windy seas?

Only she could reconcile the celestial grandeur with the slimy streets, the towering insecurity of the place with its continuing growth. Only she, after eighteen and a half years, seemed able to accept Hong Kong for the senseless wonder it had become. They had, after all, grown up together.

Meanwhile, most journalists clung to the rational. Which brings me back to my opening question: could journalists have created such a fantasy land as Hong Kong? By trade, they possess the necessary skills. Each time a journalist touches down in a new place, he measures it against places he has written about in the past. He clings to similarities and grubs for distinctions. Then he sits down at the typewriter and creates a new country. It resembles the country he is reporting on, with occasional variations: a hopeful turret that will never be erected, a slightly deeper foundation, the occasional fabricated wing. In other words, a lie. Our dirty little secret! One of those lies that smooths out a troublesome story. A lie that hurts no one. A lie that is inevitable, because the truth isn't in the notebook and the government spokesman isn't answering his phone. To a layman, 'truth' and 'lie' sound so contrary. But to the working journalist, alone in a country he's never been to before and faced with a *coup d'état* or a catastrophic earthquake, they have a compelling resemblance. I've long called them twins. And we are their nannies. Loyal nannies: loyal to the one as we are to the other.

But even a journalist can't accept the monstrous lie on which

Hong Kong is built. Hong Kong is simply too implausible. So Hong Kong, the metropolis built on illusion, has become the home base for those master illusionists, the journalists. They make their nests here, deposit their families here, take their R & R here between elections and famines and floods. It's a soothing place for journalists. They don't understand it and don't care to. The journalist can switch off his harsh searchlight of inquisitiveness and bask in the preposterous colours that Hong Kong washes over him as he strolls its neon streets.

I am looking down on that light-show from the large window in my bedroom. I am alone: Yrlinda has been asleep for hours. The stereo is, for the time being, silent. For Hong Kong is its own symphony. And I wish to sing.

Nature has been unkind to Alice Giles, both in health and in beauty. Time is no friend. God and Man both left me at the altar. Literature, Music, Art, Cinema: they are nothing but fond acquaintances who, like all acquaintances, I occasionally can't abide.

Who has been a better friend to me than Hong Kong? My old pal: don't desert me. For you, I took off my raincoat and became your slave.

Words Always Used in Journalism

1. *Burgeoning*, as in forests or woes.

2. *Woes*, as in intractable or mounting.

3. *Notwithstanding*, as in 'notwithstanding its current, burgeoning woes, Haiti's people remain . . .'

4. *Vex*, as in 'Vexed by his mounting woes, embattled Haitian leader . . .'

5. *Discomfit*. I have rarely seen this word used properly. It is most certainly not a synonym for 'discomfort.' Why would anyone think synonyms would also look, sound *and* be spelled alike?

6. *Bemused*. This word is only misused in nine out of ten cases. Journalists think it means 'amused.'

7. *Elaborate*, as in 'elaborate security system.' Some words are best known in the trade for being innocuous and incontestable.

8. *Very*. Ditto.

9. *Draconian*. The original meaning of this word is lost. It now means 'South American' or 'Chinese.'

10. *Cacophony*. For sound, usually a language the reporter can't speak.

Words Never Used in Journalism

1. *Snot.* In any context.

2. *Douchebag.*

3. *Mucous Membrane.*

4. *Pleasant.* A word rejected by the trade because of its mildness. And yet most interview subjects, if not flaming assholes, are little more than pleasant. Inappropriate synonyms are usually employed: 'agreeable,' 'charming' (rarely an accurate description), 'well dressed,' etc.

5. *Lest.* Lest sentences trip too rapidly and lovingly across the page.

Words I Long To Use In Journalism

1. *Boo*. In a lead. 'Hong Kong – Boo!' (The second sentence has long eluded me.)

2. *Bunfight*. To describe a governmental dispute. 'Analysts say the situation has deteriorated into a typical bureaucratic bunfight . . .'

3. *Cat-fuck*. Ditto.

4. *Salivary festival*. In coverage of a US primary or an AIDS conference.

5. *Transude*. A word with the most horribly appropriate sound. Definition: to ooze blood or pus through pores or stitches.

6. *Glorious*. So few events or persons deserve the term. We journalists are mired in the mundane. Witness those newspapers who actually have United Nations correspondents!

7. *Lonely*. But no one is lonely in the newspapers!

8. *Evanescent*. But what in this world is not?

The First Annual Hong Kong Foreign Correspondents Club Chilli Chompin' and Beer Guzzlin' Contest

'The First Annual Hong Kong Foreign Correspondents Club Chilli Chompin' and Beer Guzzlin' Contest – Gals Invited – Bring Your Own Endorphins' (for this is how Adam Fendler advertised the event) was held at the club on a perfectly rainy Saturday afternoon. Adam's timing couldn't have been more superb. Hong Kong had reached its dreariest, with the clouds and buildings and cars and people all washed in identically grim, yellow-grey tones. It was a day most suited to hot foods and obliterating drinking, if one was so disposed, or, for the chronically indisposed (like me) the spectacle of such foolishness. It was the kind of day on which women look poorly and men fail to shave; ill-advised affairs begin; gossip turns vicious and quarrels are later described as unprovoked. It is the day that drinkers can't quite recall on Monday. And no one recalls without a twinge of regret.

This particular Saturday had a second claim to fame. It came less than a week after the hoax scandal had broken in New York. A newspaper scandal: that rare, wondrous occurrence! A faked story – The Big Lie – set in Asia, no less! One that humiliated that Venerable Publication and elicited a notably bitchy editorial from the competition, which happens to have been my untrusted employer for the past aeon or so. A story that was condemned throughout the First, Second and Third Worlds, and finally, officially, gravely, but at the same time arrogantly, regretted. (It's hard to pinpoint the arrogance in the paper's statements or in its follow-up articles. Perhaps it was the smug assurance that the episode was being investigated by the paper's official ombudsman. The ombudsman! Was the world supposed to breathe a sigh of relief? One pictures the ombudsman in velvet robes and a collar that resembles an automobile air filter, with a tasselled pillow on top of his head. One can almost hear his tinny, disregarded voice.)

The chilli contest was to be attended by the man of the hour himself, Ted Augenstein – E.G. to his faithful readers – fresh from the scene of the crime in the northern jungles of Malaysia. I was almost out of my door and headed for the 218th step when I learned, by frantic long-distance call from Florence in New York, that Ted was in Hong Kong. As I placed the phone in its cradle, Sue Philipps called with the stunning news about the chilli contest. I was forced to cancel a doctor's appointment, for suddenly even Alice Giles couldn't miss Adam Fendler's Chilli Chompin' and Beer Guzzlin' contest, despite my natural antipathy to Adam, chillies and beer. A raspberry-eating contest! Is the world too jaded? Raw chocolate chip batter! Heath Bars! Am I the only one left behind in the gingerbread house?

An endorphin, incidentally, is a chemical released by the brain to dull pain. Chillies pain the tongue; when the heat gets too high, the brain oozes its endorphin, which masks the pain and can even cause euphoria. Leave it to foreign correspondents to become addicted to them!

Adam's chairmanship of the decoration committee had yielded him little glory. The club was all potted palms and ostentatious ceiling fans; a big surprise was how *little* attention Adam could draw to himself when a risk was involved. From decorating, Adam wormed his way onto the entertainment committee, but his series of movie nights, showing movies about journalists ('WITH FREE POPCORN FOR THE ACCREDITED') were ill-attended. In contrast, his chilli contest seemed charmed. The infuriating rain; the scandal in New York. The only news in the region was a tragic hotel fire in Pusan, which the entire membership was poised to cover until the good news was flashed across the wires: the 126 victims were, to the last charred corpse, Koreans. The wailing widows who graced the week's magazines, faces plump with grief, were Korean widows photographed by Korean journalists. The foreign correspondents remained in Hong Kong, where they criticized the photos, the dispatches and even the widows. 'They're so plain,' groused Matt Mell, my workmate and the club's most accomplished sourpuss. 'Don't they have make-up in Pusan? Can't they smile?'

Adam pushed through a motion that clinched a heavy turnout: spectators got free beer for the duration of the contest and contestants could drink unlimited beer before the event and afterwards. During the contest itself, of course, they were denied all liquids.

'No feller I know needs beer with his hot chillies,' Adam drawled as he patrolled the bar before the contest. 'No real feller, anyway. Gals are different.' He hoisted a right eyebrow.

When I arrived, my white hair crowned with a halo of dirty mist, I found Craig Kirkpatrick sitting alone at the bar. He was shaking Tabasco sauce into a Bloody Mary.

'Warming up?' I inquired brightly.

His cheeks were full of drink, so he simply shook his head. When he spoke, his first words seemed to have been swallowed along with his first gulp.

'. . . like my food hot, but . . .'

I detected the etchings of a hangover in those recessed, mysterious eyes.

'But you like your hot with some food?' I tucked myself into one of the bar's uncomfortable moulded-plastic chairs.

'Rotten day.'

The conversation needed leavening.

'This contest defies a clever comment,' I whispered in a warm, confiding tone. 'What line are the others taking?'

'The *Review* folk are disapproving.' He gestured with his chin.

'They always have the corner on petulance.' One member of the group was morosely flipping through *Foreign Policy*.

'AP has assembled a cheerleading squad.'

'Pee Yew,' I said. 'Leave it to the Texans.'

'Jabbah the Hut – Nigel Harris – says the event is "jolly" and that group over there, at last sounding, was talking about diarrhoea.'

It was the single women journalists, known collectively as 'Les Misérables.'

'All talk, no action.'

'And, of course, the PR types are peeing in their pants with excitement.' This was a loud comment aimed at a cluster of business-suited men beside us.

'What about this crowd?'

Craig shoved his chin in the direction of a man at the contestants' table, who was greeting what appeared to be his long-lost brother.

'*Ted!*' I said. 'We've *got* him. Has he said anything?'

Craig shook his head.

I squinted across the room. He looked much the same as I recalled: the thinning, honey-coloured hair that was never out of place. The modest but unflappable smile. The firm hand deflecting awkward questions and grasping a frosted beer mug. His was the kind of professional ease that, in our business, men monopolize. Especially men with Pulitzer Prizes (won in 1973 for reporting on martial law in the Philippines). He was older, of course, and slightly stouter. I was surprised to see him at the contestants' table. One associates bulky men with long hours on the pot and strange disappearances towards the end of dinner parties. Chillies, tabasco, jalapeños are the food of the lean, hungry types with unfulfilled ambitions and cast-iron constitutions.

We were joined at the bar, fortuitously, by Christopher Smart, the only man at the FCC who called Ted Augenstein his boss. Greetings were exchanged and Chris stared disapprovingly at Craig's drink.

'That looks . . .' he paused uncertainly, '. . . *refreshing*. And so suitable for this morning.'

Craig glared at Chris, whom he despised.

'Waiter,' said Chris, 'may I have a Virgin Mary please? *Virgin Mary*. Understand? Not too hot.' He returned his attention to us and smiled charmingly. 'I'm not here to win any awards.'

'Is your boss enjoying his trip?'

'He says he's had more fun at war.'

'Real war or the kind that occurs in your New York newsroom?' As I spoke, Chris's Virgin Mary was placed on the bar. I watched over his shoulder as Craig shook several teaspoons of Tabasco sauce into it.

'Oh Alice,' Chris said, turning back to the bar, 'I've always admired your piquant wit!' He picked up his drink, sipped it and coughed.

'Refreshing?' Craig asked.

Chris, holding his chest painfully, nodded his head.

It was most common to denounce Christopher Smart for pretentiousness – that misused word – for ostentation, for pomposity, or, among the acutely insecure, for snobbishness. I thought everyone was on the wrong track. Chris Smart merely had ideas above his station and a profound laziness that propelled him out of the office and onto the squash court each evening at 5 p.m. He also had a passion for clean shirts – he favoured a blue shirt with a white collar and a tiny 'CSS' embroidered on his cuff – which prompted the inevitable nickname, 'The Man of Many Shirts.' In short: he was the typical *New York Tribune* reporter.

'I like your Singapore piece, Chris.'

The false compliment gave him a bridelike glow.

'Thank you, Alice. That's decent of you. You know, I was amazed that nobody had done that story. It's really a good story.' (These too were lies.) 'I always said that . . .'

'Harry wouldn't see you?' Craig interjected.

'Harry this, Harry that,' Chris snapped. 'Harry Lee's not the story anymore in Singapore. It's the technocrats.' He jabbed a finger in Craig's chest. 'The technocrats have got the ball now.'

Over Chris's head, Craig gave me an imploring look. I widened my eyes, opened my mouth in a mute gasp and threw my hands to my chest in mock-alarm.

'When did Lee Kuan Yew resign?' Craig asked. 'Help me, Alice! Have I missed something?'

'Well,' I said. 'You heard about Krakatoa . . .'

We were interrupted by the grand entrance of the *Chicago Tribune*'s Carl Rolla, also known as 'La Rolla,' 'Mr Scoop' and 'The Best Journalist In The Whole Wide World.' As was his custom, Carl swept into the bar with his head held high, his chest thrust forward, his hand half-way to a pocket of a fishing vest in search of his worn Zippo lighter. His sharp blue eyes were wrinkled in a picturesque squint: he scanned the crowd for worthies. Carl Rolla considered himself the region's number one reporter. The nicknames were backhanded tributes to his energy and his ego. He had plentiful detractors. Less vocal, though no less numerous, were his supporters: the boys at the bar, the correspondents on the story, men hungry for companionship, help and counsel when exiled to strange and turbulent lands. They were nothing less than Carl's constituency and as a matter of policy he treated them well. Carl shared with them his wisdom, contacts, quotes and rental cars. In return, when Carl Rolla burst into a hotel lobby in Kuala Lumpur or Islamabad or Seoul, he rarely found himself without a dinner partner and a professional ally, someone to fill him in on the quotes and events of the past 24 hours and to show him the Xerox of his latest file.

It was a neat and fair system except in one way. While Carl helped himself to others' reporting, only the bravest reporter would print an unchecked fact from Carl Rolla's notebook. Several had done so under duress and been burned. It was even rumoured that Carl's personal history had some fictional underpinnings. The crazed lawyer wife in Denver apparently wasn't so crazy. The son Carl missed so tearfully: he didn't exist.

La Rolla spotted Chris Smart at the bar. He waved ostentatiously, stopped to light a cigarette and take a manly drag, and strode to the bar, fishing vest swinging heavily.

'Chris,' Carl barked. 'What happened in Malaysia? Did you guys find that guy? I heard he was hawking that manuscript all over the place. No one would take it but you guys.'

Craig, who had coined Carl's nickname of 'The Greatest Journalist in the Whole Wide World,' closed his eyes as if in pain, and prepared to leave.

'That's untrue,' Chris whined. 'But if you want information, you have to ask Ted himself. The paper's keeping a lid on the clean-up. I'm not involved. I haven't been able to get a call through to my bosses in a week.'

'Wish I had bosses like that,' I said.

'You do,' Craig said. 'Bye.' His exit went unnoticed in the escalating hubbub.

'You should have told the secretary,' suggested Kathleen Powell, a radio stringer, 'that it was Anton Vavasour calling.'

'From Ipoh,' suggested Benjie Kwok, Kathleen's temporary companion. (Her favourite kind.)

'Collect,' I added.

'Chris,' persevered La Rolla. 'Did he find him or not? That's all we want to know. Just that one fact. Was he still in Malaysia or was he not? And where in Malaysia was he? What did he have to say for himself? Are charges being – '

At this moment, the voice of Adam Fendler welcomed everyone to the First Annual Chilli contest. There were ten contestants, he announced, which elicited cheers from the AP table and excited applause from the public relations executives at the bar.

'All are accredited,' Adam continued, to lesser applause from the bar, 'but only one will walk away – or crawl away – as the first winner of the FCC Chilli Chompin' Contest.' There were vulgar whoops and clinkings of spoons on beer glasses. Someone from the AP table bellowed: 'And the winner is . . . Anton Vavasour!'

'. . . because there's no extradition treaty between Malaysia and the US,' lectured Benjie Kwok in his harsh Singaporean accent, 'and even if there was – '

Adam struggled to make his voice heard above the crowd. He proclaimed that the Hong Kong FCC was ahead of the region's other foreign correspondents clubs. No other club, he barked, not even Bangkok's, had thought of a chilli-eating contest. A slimy Chinese dumpling rose through the air and landed on the brim of Adam's fedora. A woman laughed.

'Hey, people!' Adam whipped off the hat and brushed at a grease stain. A dinner roll bounced off his bald forehead. 'Hey, c'mon!' Tears welled in his eyes. 'For the contest's sake!'

Kathleen Powell barked at Chris Smart in aggressive, radio tones: 'Isn't the prestige of the paper irreparably damaged by the scandal? Especially in the Third World?'

The impressive prizes, announced Adam, rubbing his head, included one 1922 Underwood, 'a classic journalist's machine,' a box of rare Underwood ribbons . . .

'New York is very uptight,' Chris repeated patiently. 'The editors are going apeshit over the media attention. Japanese TV is camped outside the building on 43rd . . .'

. . . one fire extinguisher, twenty-four cartons of Rollo-brand mints donated by Park 'N Shop, a Red Flag-brand ice bucket 'straight from our very own China Products' . . .

'Chris,' implored La Rolla. 'Come on. Did he find him?'

Chris sighed wearily. His dirty Virgin Mary glass was now empty.

. . . one six-pack of Tiger Beer, one six-pack of San Miguel – 'Manila San Miguel,' Adam clarified, 'not the headachy type' – one six-pack of Kloster, three large bottles of Tsing Tao, three bottles of Sapporo Black Label, one bottle of Taiwan Beer, 'Please note: the smallest we could find . . .'

Four more journalists had edged into our group. The conversation threatened to turn into a press conference. It had attracted Adam's pained attention from the dais.

'Please, Chris,' I said in a motherly and unjournalistic tone. 'Please? Pretty, pretty please?'

'What about the Third World?' barked Kathleen.

'. . . and a free draught Carlsberg,' Adam continued, 'donated by the gracious fellers at Carlsberg Hong Kong, to be drunk at the FCC bar each evening for one year or until a Pulitzer Prize is won, whichever comes first . . .'

'Yes,' Chris admitted wearily. 'Ted found him. In the north of Malaysia. In a god-damned rain forest.'

The rules of the contest were laboriously expounded by Adam with the maximum number of puns on the word 'hot.' The ten contestants would, in succession, partake of eight types of chillies, each hotter than the last. The first was an ordinary thumb-sized chilli from China. The final chilli was a pale, innocuous thing from Thailand, as small as a peppercorn. The contestants were allowed no fluids. Their relief was limited to a large plate of cold rice, one per contestant. At either side of the contestants' table were rice, crackers, Wonder Bread, iced water, beer, cola, Perrier, iced tea and Tums, for the relief of the contestants who were forced to bow out. (For the sake of those who had to literally bow out, Adam announced, the FCC men's room had been especially tidied.)

I detached myself from the impromptu inquisition of Christopher Smart. Ted Augenstein was laughing uproariously at some remark passed at the contestants' table. With my eye, I traced the path from the contestants' table to the bar. Then I picked my table. There were two vacant seats; I hoped the second would remain unoccupied.

The conversation at the table halted. When I saw my table-mates, I realized why there were vacant seats. The table bore many beer bottles.

'Don't let me interrupt,' I said in a stage whisper. 'Please continue. Why do you and Kelly have separate bank accounts?'

Sonia Plant had a startled, put-out expression on her pale, pert face. It was an expression one rarely saw when she read the evening news – she preferred a benevolent, grimace-like smile – or when she went out on assignment. Sonia was Hong Kong's Happy Talk correspondent. Each evening you could see her windsurfing with the Royal Navy or attending the governor's annual tea party or interviewing a visiting lion-tamer. Inevitably the lion-tamer would say: 'And now, little miss, it's *your* turn!' And Sonia would stare into the camera with blue eyes wide, long blonde hair falling on her shoulders and a petite hand thrown up to her mouth. I was surprised she wasn't covering the contest. As we would say in our trade: 'Sonia, this is *your* story!'

'I was just saying,' she continued hesitantly, 'that I wouldn't feel truly independent without my own bank account.' I noticed a few glazed expressions around the table. Husband Kelly was shifting uncomfortably in his chair. I had known Kelly in all his various incarnations as newsman, academic, public relations man, horny old goat.

'Especially since Kelly is older than I,' Sonia continued happily. 'Much older, as you all must know. I mean, he has money from all those years working and investing when I wasn't even born.' She directed an incandescent smile at Kelly. 'And I, well, it wouldn't be fair and I . . . like to have my . . . my . . . independence.' The group failed to react and Sonia stumbled on aimlessly. 'I mean, what happens if we break up?'

'Why don't you split?' I asked. '. . . Expenses.'

Kelly looked at me warily.

'Oh, we already do, really!' Sonia graced me with her sunniest smile. 'It's my idea. Kelly pays for the dull things, like rent and travel and his clothes. And I decorate the house, buy the food and the presents for Kelly's wonderful family when we go to the States. And the compact discs . . .'

'And the baby?' I asked perversely. I had heard about the baby and even seen it – or a shimmering cave painting that was reputed to be it – on the news. The TV cameras had followed Sonia to her first ultrasound examination. 'Who's paying for the baby?'

'Alice,' intoned Kelly. 'For God's sake.'

'Wait,' Sonia interrupted. 'That's a good idea, really. If I paid for the baby, or say, most of the baby, then, if we broke up . . .'

'The Entertainment Committee,' Adam announced, 'has thought long and hard about the final rule. The winner is not the final contestant to stay seated at his table. The winner is the last person to sit at this table after sampling *each* and *every* one of the eight grades of chillies. In the event that more than one contestant lasts into the eighth round, the winner is the person who consumes the greatest number of these hot little fellers from Thailand.'

Adam caressed a jar of the small, grey chillies. 'Eat one!' shouted someone from the AP table.

'They're my personal favourite,' Adam said. He grinned horribly. 'Translating from the Thai, they're called "Old Chernobyl." Good for asthma.'

'I just returned from Bangkok, Alice,' said Milo Schindo, an Italian freelancer. (Sonia and Kelly were conferring in low, urgent tones.)

'Have they really shut down Patpong, Milo?'

'It's pretty dull.'

'Can it last?'

'Nah.' He gave an expressive Italian hand gesture. 'The economy!'

The contest began. With much mugging and hogging of attention, the ten contestants ate the first fat chillies from China. None of the contestants even touched his plate of cold rice. The second round was much the same but the chillies were red. Some contestants acted macho. Others feigned fear. Ted Augenstein smacked his lips after his second chilli and opened and shut his mouth in small, fishlike motions. Then he brought pinched thumb and forefingers to lips and announced to the crowd: '*Magnifique!*'

'What are all the girls doing in the meantime?' I asked Milo.

'Walking the streets.'

'Crowded streets.'

'It's not easy to walk,' he said. 'But who goes to Bangkok to walk? You can get a blowjob for thirty baht.'

'I wouldn't pay more than twenty-five,' I said. 'Senior citizen.'

Truman Toto from *Business Week* told a vulgar tale about a certain correspondent, a Thai prostitute and a concealed tape recorder.

'They play the tape over the music system whenever the guy walks into the bar,' Truman concluded. 'He doesn't go to that bar very often anymore.'

'It serves him right,' said I, 'considering what he did to his wife.' There were inquiries and I was propelled into the tale, to which I added an embellishment or two before I reached its climax, which I whispered in my primmest, girliest tone. 'He swivelled his neck, looked back at poor Louise clutching the neck of her granny nightgown, and said: "What does it look like I'm doing? I'm fucking the maid!"'

In the third, fourth and fifth rounds, the chillies were Sri Lankan and Indian. The heat was definitely on: the cold rice, first nibbled at, was soon gone from a few contestants' plates. In the fourth round, a vain network producer and two goofy Japanese photographers abandoned the contest. The TV guy rushed to the bar; the Japanese stood at the sidetables gulping water and grimacing comically. Ted Augenstein, still competing, laughed until tears came down his cheeks. Three more contestants bowed out in the fifth round. The crowd was exultant and the Wonder Bread was disappearing fast.

'You can't expect anything different in countries with such poverty,' Kelly explained in patient tones to his wife. Sonia had a puzzled and hurt expression. A delicious feeling of tension had descended on the table.

'But that's not my question,' she persisted, appealing with hungry eyes to the table. 'I'm asking: how can the man sleep with the prostitute? Any man, or, let's say, an American man. An educated man. It's so degrading to her *and* to him.'

'Especially if all he does is sleep,' joked Milo.

'And she goes back and informs his friends at the bar,' said Truman.

'I'm serious,' Sonia insisted, her face dark with agitation. 'I really am. I mean, I don't see how any educated man could pay a woman for sex. Even once. Not even once.'

'Oh, Sonia,' said Milo, in a shrugging, continental tone. 'It's a fact of life. Come, you face it.'

'With American men?' she raged. 'With married men? Who should *know* better?' She glared at Kelly.

'Sonia, it happens,' said Truman. 'With any kind of man. Every kind of man. Every man in pants.'

Kelly interjected sagely, 'As the saying goes, the oldest profession.'

'And a better-paying profession than journalism,' I said.

'Less running around,' blurted Kelly.

'Smaller phone bills,' said Truman.

'Colleagues you can talk to,' I said.

'Who fuck,' said Milo expansively, 'but don't fuck each other.'

Poor Sonia, abandoned and vanquished. The conversation had taken a maddeningly safe turn. I decided to return it to its greased, downhill rails.

'Remember the Literary Club in Peitou, Kelly?' My tone was falsely innocent. His wary look returned.

'That was where the two professions mingled most intimately. It's closed now, but it was the rage in the 1960s and the 1970s. Remember, Kelly? I seem to recall you being most literary in those days.'

The sixth chilli was from Thailand. It was fresh, red and the size of a bullet. The four remaining contestants ate their chillies and instantly turned to their plates of rice. Their expressions were inward: they could have been experiencing visions.

'I demand to be told, Kelly!' Sonia shouted. Then she stopped, with a rigid look on her face. Her hands held her belly protectively.

'Labour?' whispered Truman.

'Get the minicams,' I replied.

A contestant bowed out and the crowd cheered.

Sonia rose dramatically. She stormed from the club. Kelly, who had been making desperate, soothing sounds, clumsily rose. 'Alice,' he said with emotion. 'You've had your last fun with me.'

I reacted with mock surprise. 'Kelly, give an old lady something to look forward to!'

'Fuck you, "old lady,"' he spat savagely. He chased after Sonia. I looked at Truman and he shrugged sympathetically. Milo said, 'Silly bitch.'

The three remaining contestants were presented with their seventh chilli: a green Thai chilli the size of a pencil-point. Two began to eat. Ted stared at the chilli darkly. He looked at the crowd. Finally he stood. He announced in a weakened voice: 'Ladies and Gentlemen. Thank you. Goodnight.'

He walked from the table to cheers and huzzahs. He drank a huge draught of water, held it in his bulging cheeks for several seconds and then swallowed.

As I anticipated, he passed my chair on the way to the bar. People were patting him on the shoulder. At exactly the right moment, I whispered, 'Ted! Sit here!'

He looked down at me. Puzzlement flashed on his face. 'Alice? Is it Alice?'

'What's left of her!'

He took the offered chair. 'I'm sorry,' he said. 'For some reason, I didn't recognize you. So many old faces.'

It was an unfortunate remark.

'I recognized you,' I said, using my mock-bedazzled voice. 'The famous E. G. Augenstein. Welcome back to your happy hunting grounds.'

'Enough formality,' he replied. 'You can call me "E." Or even "G."' It was an old line, but he delivered it with charm. 'How are you, Alice? How is your health?'

'Never better,' I lied, flashing what could be called a brave smile.

'Alice Giles. The best damn business reporter in Asia. I'll never forget that time with Run Run Shaw – '

'*Sir* Run Run.'

'Wasn't he apoplectic? I met him the day after the story came out. I've never seen a Chinaman so mad.'

'And his brother too.' (My memory is precise about my own stories.)

'Yes,' Ted laughed. 'Both of them. How they quizzed me about you. "A woman?" they asked. "Are you sure she's a woman? What does a woman know about stock options?" I thought of you when that film of theirs flopped in New York.'

'Their stock options were a cinch,' I said. 'It was the damned dummy companies.'

'And that swindler in Indonesia . . . what was his name?'

'You mean the "Rising Star of the Year of the Dragon?"' I felt a bone, long-stuck in my throat, dislodge.

He laughed uproariously and nearly upset a bottle of beer. 'Don't remind me,' he yelled. 'Please don't remind me! If New York had really read my pieces, I might not be here right now!'

Or, I thought, *if they had read mine.*

'How is the Asian edition, Alice?'

'Lots of eager colts. Luckily they still need one old grey mare.'

'A war-horse,' he said. 'And they couldn't have a better one.' His voice had a winding-up tone. The bar beckoned, I knew. It was hard to pry Ted Augenstein away from the bar talk and the bar camaraderie. It always had been.

'Ted,' I said in an urgent whisper. 'You found him. In a rain forest, no less.'

'Surely, Alice, *you* can't be writing anything . . .' The prim hand smoothed the perfect hair.

'Ted,' I said in a schoolgirl tone, 'I'm just interested. I'm fascinated! Obsessed! You would be too!'

He succumbed. 'In your travels,' he asked, 'did you ever, by chance, meet this Vavasour?'

'We were engaged. But it was a silly, girlish fling.' I batted my eyelashes facetiously. 'Has anyone met him?'

'None,' Ted said.

'Was he once a journalist?'

Ted shook his head.

'Did he do it for the publicity? To embarrass the paper?'

Again, he shook his head.

'Did you get an apology?'

Ted shook his head differently now, with amusement. 'You are a good reporter, Alice Giles. I had forgotten how good. You never ask a wrong question. What you must be able to do in an hour-long interview!'

'I peer right into a person's soul,' I replied. 'Provided they have souls, that is.'

'Well . . .' Ted said, rising inexorably from his chair. 'If you want to see a strange soul, keep an eye out for my friend Anton Vavasour. You could do a real number on him, Alice. Yes you could.'

'An evil soul?' I blurted.

He placed his hand gingerly on my shoulder, as one might touch a frail, maiden aunt. 'A silly soul, Alice. A careless soul. A ricocheting soul. If the world is as small as we keep saying, we had all better watch out for Anton Vavasour.' He looked to the door, as if he expected the counterfeiter to make a surprise appearance. 'He's an enormously fat man, you know – '

'But Ted,' I interrupted. 'The fake story. Only an evil man would lie . . .'

He leaned down and whispered, thrillingly, in my ear, 'Lies and truths are the same to Anton Vavasour, Alice. They're like rice and bread. Anton Vavasour wasn't doing his worst when he faked a story for the *New York Tribune*. No, no indeed. I don't think I've seen Anton Vavasour at his worst. It's possible I've seen him at his best.'

The chilli contest was over. There was a victor and a loser. Both were at the side tables, gulping fluids in huge draughts. Adam tried to capture the crowd's attention, hoisting the winner's arm in the air, but the afternoon had gone on too long. Everyone was too drunk, or too engrossed with Ted Augenstein, or plain gone. There were arguments later as to who had actually won, and, when they continued unresolved, the list of claimants to the title grew. Up sprang a genuine need for the Second Hong Kong Foreign Correspondents Club Chilli Chompin' And Beer Guzzlin' Contest – Gals Invited – Bring Your Own Endorphins. This was good news for the Entertainment Committee and for Adam Fendler, who had survived the whole afternoon without ingesting one chilli, or, for that matter, one beer. For Adam was a secret teetotaller.

I left the club that evening without a burnt tongue or an aching head. But I buzzed with another, familiar feeling that obliterated Hong Kong's chill and its dirty drizzle. It was the stimulus of my life, my one, constant high. I was onto something. I had been, unwittingly perhaps, tipped off.

A scoop!

I bumped into Craig at the kerbside. He was scowling at the day, at the taxi-less street, at chilli contests, journalists and Hong Kong in general. I offered him a lift to Cloudview Road. As we glided through Hong Kong's grey melting streets, a slow flash of aquamarine in a monochrome cityscape, he gave me an impassioned critique of everyone involved in the contest, saving his most piquant condemnations for Adam Fendler.

But I could barely listen. I had my own high, and it was lifting me more than any chilli or alcohol could.

I thought of Ted's words about a silly, semi-evil, 'ricocheting' man. A man with a preposterous name. A man at his best at the bottom of a rain forest.

Was *this* a scoop?

Of course it was! Alice Giles didn't know what was going on, but she has an infallible sensitivity to the vibrations that ripple through her region when goings were, in fact, on.

A scoop! Craig griped on, and my car glided through the ugly Hong Kong rain. *How long it's been!*

I LOVE NEW YORK

I

'I bought a car,' Ted Augenstein announced one Monday morning at the office. It was one of those days when a grey battleship had nestled outside the office windows and the carpet showed snail-tracks of slush.

Florence, a news assistant who wore a skirt and running shoes to work, rolled her eyes voluptuously.

'Why, Ted?' asked gentle Nobuko, the secretary. 'You live so close.'

'I've decided I should travel more. Get out of the city.'

'People are irresponsible,' Florence announced as she brushed croissant crumbs from her tweedy skirt. 'You do your share for your gridlock. The subways get more crowded. And then it becomes my grind every morning.'

My gridlock?

'Where will you park it Ted?' asked Nobuko.

'There's a garage on . . .'

'$350 a month,' Florence barked. She was stirring what looked like sand into a container of purple yoghurt.

'$375,' he replied with satisfaction.

She nodded. 'That's where they make the crack, you know.'

The crack? They don't make enough on $375 a month?

'Don't you have a car, Florence?' Nobuko inquired meekly.

'My husband,' she replied. 'A van. I told him he was a douchebag but he had to have it. He said, "You have your manicures, I have my van." It's customized.'

'But he works – '

'Even closer than me. He gets his rocks off washing it and putting radios in it. First it's Blaupunkt. Then some Japanese make. Then we have to get a compact disc player. Although even I must admit, the sound is excellent.' The fat hand with the beautiful claws crushed the yoghurt container and tossed it towards a waste bin across the room. It made it.

Douchebag? Ted marvelled. *Gets his rocks off?*

'My husband has a computer.'

'IBM?' Florence demanded. 'Or pirate?'

'Apple II.'

Florence failed to respond.

'"Enhanced,"' the secretary added. This satisfied Florence. As if by preordained truce, the two conversationalists went quietly back to work.

At the end of the day, Florence, with grudging generosity, told Ted of a cheaper garage in his neighbourhood.

'No crack?'

She raked her claws through the air. 'They just chip your paint. My cousin-in-law owned it. 'Til he died of AIDS.' Then, as the clock hit 5:02, she departed in the scuffed running shoes that had never experienced more than a weary shuffle. Her body heaved from side to side, ready to give hell to the New York City subway system.

Ted drove home that evening for the first time. He thought of the term 'douchebag.' He thought of the Beatles and Beach Boys and Country Joe songs he heard at the houses of middle-aged friends. The slang, the songs, the mentality: they weren't only artifacts. They were cultural preserving fluid, which New Yorkers steeped themselves in to ignore time and the world around them. He swerved to avoid a pothole and nearly hit another Florence in skirt and hefty sneakers. She hardly noticed her near-demise. She was plugged into an orange waterproof Walkman.

Ted had looked up the friends who had preceded him home from abroad and was amazed at the change in their characters. People who had revelled in strange cities and new experiences had become shrunken impersonations of their personalities overseas. Broadminded people from Bangkok had turned stuffy in Brooklyn Heights. The hypersexed husbands from Manila now shook their heads unbelievingly and talked about jogging. It seemed that Manhattan drew its famed energy straight from its inhabitants: all of Ted's friends appeared paler and thinner, near-convalescents in flannels and tweeds. (Their oriental silks were never seen.)

They viewed their sojourns abroad as silly flings, something to be embarrassed about, like getting tipsy and keeping the babysitter up until 3 a.m. A few items bought abroad were displayed in their homes, but many more were stuffed ashamedly in deep closets: lamps made from abacuses, Indian hangings that dwarfed the apartment walls of New York. For most of them, being abroad may have been the liveliest time of their lives, but it was hardly life. Not to the New Yorker who knew that life was led in a living-room; who knew, from venerable American tradition, that once night fell, one wasn't allowed out in bright or smoky rooms. Even standing after dark was a kind of cultural transgression. After eating, Americans chose a position of rest and, as the night progressed, the rooms they occupied got progressively darker to minimize diversions from any of a number of small screens. One could not talk nor drink, in case the drink prompted talk. (Warm, soothing drinks were an exception.) People actually shuddered when it was suggested they stray from their cramped domains. And when Ted joined friends at their homes, he found New York conversation to be little more than an impatient exchange of opinions on new films and plays, which most had yet to see, followed by a quick capitulation to one of those small screens.

Ted, refusing to turn his back on his exotic past, engulfed himself in sumptuous Indian silks and hand-knotted carpets from Iran and Afghanistan. He replaced a door of his apartment with the crusted gates of a Korean temple. When set for twelve, Ted's 19th-century Visayan dining-room table glinted with silver, brass and a touch of gold on his Japanese dinnerware.

And then there were the ceramics. Ted had poured his time and his single man's salary into the vases and bowls of the East. His expertise had sharpened over the years and his collection was envied in Hong Kong. In New York, spread out in its entirety, it couldn't help but dazzle. For Ted had also dedicated his energies to the art of display. He had installed a graceful array of cherrywood shelves, custom-made and 'antiqued' by Hong Kong's expert illusionists. Each tier and stair had been precisely designed for the exquisite piece it would display. Above them, Ted installed a bank of sophisticated spotlights in a false ceiling, which he demonstrated for his guests. His hands would slowly manipulate a hidden bank of dials and a particular vase would glow with sublime brilliance. With another manipulation, the guests would notice a more arresting vase they had previously ignored. And then, the pink bowl with the venerable crack. And there – that charming green piece with the faint little men! This performance always elicited admiring gasps and the inevitable comment, 'Then if your lights are good enough, the vases themselves don't have to be . . . ,' which Ted would good-naturedly refute. The living-room held the colourful pieces from the Ming and Shun dynasties. A similar display of blue-and-whites was in the guest room, where other returned expatriates consigned cracked bestsellers.

At the foot of his front hallway, Ted placed the teak table he had found in a home in Peking. Guests gaped at its tiny top – as small as a paperback book – and its long, delicately bowed legs. Atop the table sat Ted's prize Ming vase. It was small and round and shining with spring greens and labial pinks. A dealer had once said to Ted, 'This is how the piece looked when it was pulled from the kiln in 1450.' A stark scroll with a single black character hung behind the vase. The vase was the first thing visitors saw when they entered the apartment. On their exit, most guests would turn back to admire it a last time.

It was Ted's custom at that precise moment to flick a switch and speak some Manhattanesque words about 'a big day tomorrow' or 'how did it get so late?' The brilliant vase was thrown into dull, intentional shadow. This was Ted's way of bringing his parties to a desolating close: to leave his deadened, unsatisfactory friends with an image of beauty fading on their dulled retinas. The last thing guests would see, as they waited for the doors of the befouled elevator to shut, was an artfully back-lit Ted, standing in a haze of oriental hues, exiling them to the grey, lustreless Manhattan below. In any case, that was Ted's intended effect. And he had worked hard, and spent a lot, to achieve it. One particular German spotlight had cost $190 and taken two weekends to properly install.

2

Like all Americans who turned their backs on their Midwestern origins, Ted Augenstein had considered Manhattan a peak he must scale or forever admit his unworthiness. New York was a notoriously difficult language and he was set on fluency. During the years he visited the city, he learned its districts and their different reputations. He walked the more interesting ones, like Chinatown and Little Italy. Abroad, he hungrily read of the changes in those neighbourhoods and altered his inward map accordingly. In his first few months as a resident, he delved into the city's lore and its arcana. Finally, he knew more about New York than the natives – a common plight of the immigrant – and his friends' laughter made him feel foolish and Midwestern all over again. They'd laugh when he could find the new theatres, or give train advice to visitors from New Jersey. He soon felt he had studied the archaic, polite form of that notoriously difficult language. Or the wrong language altogether.

But Ted didn't know the suburbs until he bought a car. After several weekends, he felt he knew them all: the grey strips of highway flanked by deserted factories and garages; the Burger King to the side of the exit ramp; the tawdry row houses occupied by blacks, which slowly gave way to postage-sized plots sold to young yuppies with budgets and children and vans. Then came the fancy neighbourhoods, heralded by ugly stone columns with cement balls on top. Finally, the pattern reversed itself: the children's toys in the grey snow, the bashed cars of the blacks, Pizza Hut, and back onto the highway only one or two exits from where he began. Ted could distinguish whole blocks of Spanish Harlem by a detail or two, but he found it impossible to distinguish Ridgewood from Rockville Centre or Mount Vernon or Mineola. His only enjoyment came from the towns' pretentious and preposterous names: Tuckahoe, Sayville, Rye, Pleasantville, Rockaway, New Rochelle.

Angelica Augenstein, Ted's sister, lived in a worn brick apartment complex in Rye bearing the forlorn name of 'Blind Brook.' The two met on most holidays and Ted invited Angie to his bigger parties. When he called to tell her about his car, he expected her invitation to dinner. He was startled, however, by her closing line: 'Bring someone, if you like!' Never had she said such a thing to Ted before.

Angie was the buoyant kind of woman that America produced with no shame but without much pride either. She was fun to chat with in the produce aisle, but the neighbours couldn't help but wonder about her parking-lot grimace. She was a dutiful committee worker, if slightly over-determined when elections for committee chairmanships came around. She was single, of course, and always had been. (Nothing infuriated her more than the question: 'Not divorced?' with its implication that even that would be preferable.) Luckily, America provided lots to do for buoyant single women like Angie Augenstein. She was the chairperson of the human rights committee for the City of Rye Democrats. Every Saturday morning, she did Meals on Wheels, as she had in Sherman Oaks, California before Rye and Eugene, Oregon before Sherman Oaks. And lately, she had developed a passion for aerobics.

'I'm being paid for it, now,' she said to Ted with pride, handing him a glass of sweet, over-refrigerated white wine.

'They pay you to exercise, Angie?' He was gazing, with satisfaction, at the exotic artifacts he had given Angie through the years. Some he wished he had kept.

'Silly, I'm a teacher.' Angie smiled proudly. Her teeth were a bright shade of yellow. 'Why, Ted, say goodbye to the old Angie. I'm an athlete now!'

They ate at an Italian restaurant owned by an immigrant from Thailand. Angie had hoped the Asian connection would appeal to Ted and she was delighted when her brother greeted the owner in rudimentary Thai.

'I'll never know how you remember all those languages,' she giggled. 'And the way you screw up your face! It's hysterical!'

Angie ordered a large portion of angel-hair pasta and Ted ordered veal.

'I'm carbo-stuffing,' she explained to the waiter, the owner's son. When he had taken their order to the kitchen, she whispered to Ted, 'He's sexy.'

Ted was astonished. He had never heard Angie talk about men, or sex, or marriage except in a befuddled, self-pitying way. Angie had not, like many single women, endured a series of painful, unfruitful relationships. As far as Ted knew, she hadn't had a date since college.

'He must work out. Or are all those Chinese men like that?' She smiled aggressively when the waiter returned to remove their knives.

'Thai,' Ted reminded her.

'Tell me, Ted,' she whispered. 'After all these years, can you really tell the difference? I mean, just by looking?'

Like most middle-aged brothers and sisters, Angie and Ted

talked about insignificant things. They spoke of car problems and cable television. She held forth on a land development that the democrats were opposing. He gave her an abbreviated account of his Malaysia trip.

'It sounds anticlimactic to me,' she said. 'After all that press. I've never understood all this talk about truth and the press. Can everyone in an entire profession be truthful? Think about the priests.' She took a large forkful of orange pasta. 'Was he, you know, gay?' And that reminded her of her aerobics friend, Matthew and his ex-friend, Ramon.

Later, she said in a pouty tone, 'Ted, you haven't even commented on my new body.'

And with this remark, Angie was propelled into a discourse on her 'new' life. Ted sat through it uncomfortably, for he and Angie rarely discussed themselves. As she talked, he tried to take in her 'new,' thinner body. But all he could focus on was her ruined face: the pouchy eyes with too much black make-up, the vulnerable chin, the big, exposed yellow teeth, the hair streaked with businesslike grey. He wondered why she hadn't yet dyed it.

'You know, Ted, when Daddy died, I almost packed up and moved in with you in . . . where was it then? Saigon or Hong Kong?'

'Hong Kong.'

'It was Hong Kong,' Angie agreed. 'I remember thinking, "At least the 'Cong won't get me." '

Ted noticed tears gathering in her eyes.

'I even called some moving companies. I was so depressed, you know. And not just about Daddy.'

'But how . . .'

'I thought I'd get a job at the American school. I'm qualified, you know. Say a two-year contract. You were single. You enjoyed visitors and I told all my friends, "My brother is always saying how nice it is living in Hong Kong. I don't believe him, but he always says it." I came this close to doing it.' She exhaled noisily and relievedly. 'Who knows? Maybe I should have.'

'You never said anything to me.'

'Maybe it *was* when you were in Saigon,' Angie said, her face rumpled with the effort to recall. 'Or maybe it was then that I thought about it first.'

'In Saigon?' Ted said with amazement. 'Why, my apartment – '

'Oh Ted. You and your apartments.' She looked at him with fondness. 'That's so long ago now, Ted. Your apartment! Lordy! You and your darned apartments!'

Over dessert, Angie returned to the topic of her 'new' life. 'Yes, I admit that aerobics started me thinking,' she said, 'and I know you're sceptical. But Ted. My whole mindset has changed!'

What comprised Angie's 'new life' wasn't clear. She was going to pay more attention to her hair and wardrobe, she said, as Ted took a farewell glance at her grey streaks. She was thinking of getting a roomier apartment and was definitely planning on quitting the human rights committee. 'The democrats only use me,' she confided. Ted wondered about the fate of Angie's Meals on Wheels patients. This was the first dinner at which they hadn't shuffled onto centre stage. He was curious about the Parkinsonian woman in Port Chester with the significant holler. At Christmastime, it was down to a sad yelp.

'And love,' Angie stated in a queer tone.

Ted waited for her to explain.

'You know what I mean, Ted Augenstein!'

'What about love, Angie? I do know what love is.'

'Ted,' she cried, 'this is no way to lead a life. For a woman or a man. When I began aerobics, I thought I was a used-up, middle-aged lady. Wasted! Now, I've realized I'm young. I'm fit. I'm attractive. Yes: I'm attractive! I've started meeting people – did you know that? There's no reason to live in such loneliness. I worry about you. I know you suffer in the way I used to. Psychically bound and gagged.'

She reached across the tablecloth, past the demolished desserts, and grasped his thick, frozen hand. 'Ted,' she implored. 'It's no good hating yourself. It's – '

'Hating myself?' Ted withdrew his hand.

'You can resurrect yourself. You owe it, we all owe it . . .'

'Owe it? To whom?'

'To life!' Angie cried, attracting stares from people at surrounding tables. But the attention was short-lived, for Ted and Angie Augenstein weren't the type of couple that held people's attention for very long.

Ted drove back to Manhattan with care but later he couldn't recall the bulk of the journey. His mind had raced. He had marvelled at the unsettling power of Angie's silly outburst. He wondered if it was the residual emotional bonds between siblings, flowing with current for the first time in decades, or whether it was the words she had chosen. Did the terms 'wasted' and 'psychically bound and gagged' and 'resurrection' pluck strings that, for Ted, were pulled unusually tight? He thought of Angie's most telling admonition. 'It's no good hating yourself!' Poor Angie. Had she really hated herself all these years? Is that what extra pounds, yellow teeth and an angry face do to a woman? And he wondered about aerobics and whether it taught one to love oneself. He thought briefly of Ramon and Matthew and the slim Thai waiter. He was reminded of how attractive he had always felt on business trips abroad, when yellow and brown people desired to talk with him, wanted to know where he came from, were desperate to relate to him such fascinating facts as 'This is a ball pen' or 'New Delhi is the capital of India' or 'Michael Jackson is a *Christian* black man.' He was reminded of the old days as a foreign correspondent, when he was the one who always said, 'Where shall we eat?' He contrasted this with his business trips within the US, where he was just another unattractive, overweight middle-aged man eating dinner alone. When a black boy leapt forward to wipe his windshield with a greasy rag, Ted came out of his reverie. The black boy, denied a tip, spat on the window and Ted's mind cleared. The suburbs were long gone and he was approaching his new home.

3

'Thanks for coming, Ted. Nice paper today.' Abe always said that. He couldn't talk about the weather because he had no control over the weather, and that upset him. 'Busy?'

Ted shrugged. 'Philippines,' he replied. 'Mexican politics. Poor jute farmers in Bangladesh. Welfare problems in Finland.'

'The more things change,' Abe said distractedly. 'Ted, we haven't had a chat since you've been back. I want to thank you for taking that Malaysia trip. The whole thing seems to have died down, thank God. That *Journal* editorial still burns me. They would have been right, of course, if it had been a staffer. I saw your rumination on the affair in the *Columbia Journalism Review*. Very clever.'

Ted said nothing.

'A newspaper's reputation – no one knows what a fragile asset it is until. And what are we supposed to do? Hire choirboys?' Abe glowered at some papers on his desk.

'So,' he said ultimately. 'How are you doing in New York?'

'Haven't been burgled yet.'

Abe stared hard at him. He was a New York chauvinist and he denied all of the city's faults.

'My breakdancing is improving.'

Abe still failed to smile.

'Only the usual language problems.'

'Ted,' Abe said, 'we have this problem with London.'

'What problem with London? Coverage?'

'No,' Abe said. 'Don't be silly. The coverage is fine. The problem is that Talat Ali wants a promotion.'

'He was named bureau chief only – '

'I know, but he's talking with other papers. I'm in a corner. He's our best guy on OPEC. And he's, you know, Muslim. I told him to take an expensive vacation with his wife. On the paper. He didn't go.'

Ted remained silent.

'To Greece. I even recommended the hotel!' Abe shook his head with puzzlement. 'Great hotel.'

'I don't know what to say, Abe,' Ted said. 'His organization of the bureau itself isn't all that popular, and – '

'Ted, I can't lose an expert on OPEC. I know he's talking to the *Post* and to the *Chicago Tribune*, although God only knows why. He refuses a trip to Greece – that says it all to me. I don't care about bureau reorganizations. I can't lose Talat Ali.'

'So?'

'I'm going to announce a reorganization of the foreign staff. London is going to report directly to me.'

Ted reacted angrily. 'There's no point in having a foreign staff . . .'

'And,' Abe continued. 'Hong Kong.'

Ted looked at him with amazement. 'Why Hong Kong?' he asked. 'What's the problem with Hong Kong?'

'Chris Smart won't accept Talat Ali in a position higher than himself. They started together on the desk and hate each other's guts. I don't want to lose Smart either. It's a one-man bureau, Ted . . .'

'Almost all my bureaus are one-man bureaus, Abe!'

'You won't miss him or London. You can still visit, as a genial older colleague, say. Just not as boss.'

'Abe, why have a foreign editor . . .'

Abe stood up, came around the back of Ted's chair and put an unconvincing, fatherly hand on his shoulder. 'Ted,' he said soothingly, 'the foreign editor's job is a . . . *reward*. A job to enjoy. It's often the case in journalism. You have your Pulitzer, Ted. Now, let someone else get the spotlight. Your task – and it's not an easy one, I know – is to make sure the spotlight is on him and not on the guy from the other paper. Help us get some more Pulitzers, Ted, for the other guys.'

Ted suppressed a groan.

'Administer. Start a family. Write some more for the *Columbia Journalism Review*. That's good – it keeps up the image of the paper. Or work on your hobbies. Your . . . knicknacks. Heard a lot about them. Some good buys out East. You ought to get a computer at home, Ted. I spend a lot of time at mine. Salaries and all, I have them all at my fingertips. IBM with a hard disk. Fast as a demon. You have your Pulitzer, Ted . . .'

'You said that already, Abe.'

'We all have to move with the times.'

Ted struggled to say it, but he couldn't. The words were just too painful. *Abe, if this is how it plays, why on earth did you bring me back? Why does anyone come back?*

'It's their turn now, buddy,' Abe continued, as the two men walked to the door. The door opened of its own accord. There stood Ellie, smiling at Ted. He realized: she knew.

Abe's hand gave Ted's shoulder a last pat, which was meant to impart fondness, but felt like a shove through the door.

'Relax and enjoy. You're home now, buddy. You're back home!'

4

A week later, Ted Augenstein announced some unexpected vacation plans.

'Back to Malaysia?' Nobuko asked with wonder.

'The east coast this time,' Ted replied with carefully rehearsed words. 'I had forgotten how wild the country was until my last trip. And beautiful.'

'But why the rush?' Nobuko asked. 'Next week?'

Nobuko always made Ted's travel reservations. Had he arranged it any other way, he would have invited suspicion.

'I want to beat the monsoon.' Ted hoped no one would check.

'You should drop in and see our famous contributor,' wisecracked Anthony Pasquale, one of the livelier screen-starers in the foreign section. 'What was his name again? Something Frog.'

'Anton Vavasour,' replied Florence, as she unwrapped a yellow croissant with some brown greasy meat stuck in its middle. Her reply surprised Ted. Never had he perceived in Florence the slightest interest about the paper, its politics, its success, its failure or the world outside lower Manhattan.

'And he was closer to Penang,' she continued, to Ted's further astonishment. 'Ted's going through Kuala Lumpur.' Then her attention seemed to swing completely to her sandwich.

'You never told us much about him,' said Anthony, 'or that trip.'

'Ancient history.' Ted's tone was meant to quell conversation. 'Corporate secret. For Abe's eyes only.'

'Should I message Chris Smart about your trip, Ted?' Nobuko asked, averting her eyes shyly. 'He's in Singapore. At the Goodwood Park.'

'No, don't bother.'

An uncomfortable silence engulfed the foreign section.

They know, Ted thought. *They all know. And Abe won't make the official announcement until next week.*

To thaw the silence, Ted said, 'I'll bring you all back some durians.' He waited for the usual questions and looked forward to explaining.

But Florence surprised him once more. 'Oh no!' she said, with appropriate horror. 'I've read about those things. I don't want one of those near me. They say it's like eating a trifle in a sewer.'

Ted explained the durian to the rest of the staff. 'Where did you read about the durian, Florence?'

'Oh, I don't remember. I've read about it more than once. Didn't Chris Smart do a piece last year?'

Florence asked Ted about the size and color of the durian and Ted was forthcoming.

'I've got a good idea,' she said, as her fanged hand crumpled the Burger King wrapper into a tight ball, and the greasy, orange projectile flew across the room into a distant wastebin. She spoke without a smile but Ted detected an unexpected note of sympathy in her tone. 'Why don't you bring a whole crate of durians back for Abe?'

5

At the airport, Ted exchanged Nobuko's ticket to Kuala Lumpur for one to Penang. He returned to the kampong on a damp afternoon. The keeper of the gate – the stern, bare-chested Malay – had apparently been visited by the state tourism board. He deigned to nod as Ted manoeuvred his car down the narrow forest path. There was no sign of his lanky son.

The stilt house at the path's end had lost its desolate look. Cooking-smoke curled above its roof; orange metal farm implements blocked the car's progress. Ted walked to the base of the house and found, at the top of the plank steps, an old woman with a frightened look.

'Mr Vavasour,' he called with slow enunciation, his abroad voice. 'Anton Vavasour.' Involuntarily, his hands formed a large, diffuse shape in the air above him.

The woman shook her head fearfully.

'Anton Vavasour,' he repeated patiently. *How could this woman, living in this house, not know the name of Anton Vavasour?* '*Farangi*. Foreigner.'

She shook her old, worried head and scurried back into the house.

'A big fat pig!' he called after her. 'Jesus!'

Ted paced back to his car and found its door ajar. Sitting in the front seat was a smiling, brown boy-man.

'Boo! Going my way?'

'Ramse!'

Ramse wore a faded sarong. Ted pictured a pair of satiny red gym shorts being buried in the damp, black forest soil by a scared-looking old woman.

Vavasour was gone, Ramse related, and with him the cloud that had blackened the entire village. Ramse's family had been able to return to its house. With Vavasour's departure, the attention of several government departments had been retracted, which was appreciated by the other villagers.

Vavasour hadn't taken Ramse with him?

Ramse laughed good-naturedly. 'Not Anton,' he said with another giggle. 'Oh no. As he would say: "I like to travel light!"' Ramse did an impression of Vavasour, hoisting one delicate, pencil-line eyebrow in imitation of Vavasour's fuzzy grey caterpillar.

Ramse thrust his hand at Ted. A new, gold ring glittered on his brown pinky. It held a candy-pink stone.

'Is it real?'

Ramse withdrew his hand in mock-outrage. 'I wouldn't dare check!'

When Ted pulled his car onto the main road, he caught a brief glance of his true friend, the skinny Malay boy, suspended above the road in a tree with lacy branches. Ted waved and watched as long as he could, until his image in the rear-view mirror vanished with a bend in the road.

At Selarma, Ted turned onto a highway that led into green, mottled mountains. He was headed north. Vavasour had stolen illegally across the Thai border.

'Try Songkla,' Ramse suggested. 'Anton's stayed there before. It's his kind of town.'

He continued wistfully, 'Tell him to come back someday to visit. I could meet him in Georgetown if he didn't want to come back here. Or even KL if he sent me the busfare. Anton always was a lot of fun.'

The comment reminded Ted of his night in the rain forest and of Ramse asleep as the hideous fat man blabbed drunkenly about façades and semiotics and Frederick Prokosch. And later, how the tableau had been strangely transformed by the cool beams of the moon: Ramse in Vavasour's arms, a scene no longer hideous but oddly admirable. Ted had summoned to mind that tableau many times in the weeks past. He had thought about it constantly on his journey back to the forest.

'And when you find him,' Ramse said with campy fury, 'tell whoever he's with to keep on *his* side of the border!'

6

Ted found Anton Vavasour in a Songkla brothel. It took few enquiries to trace him down. Songkla is the border town of all border towns, a shore that floods regularly with Malays and Thais hungry for vice. When the tide goes out, the region's most debilitated human debris is left behind. The brothel was a five-storey apartment house on a back lane. It was made of crumbling, yellow-painted cinder blocks. In the heavy tropical sunlight, its exterior had a sleepy, collapsed attitude. But within, with the tropical sun safely shut outside, it was midnight all day long.

The building was formed around a gigantic inner well. The girls, representing several races and hundreds of skin shades, gathered in the corridors around the well. They shouted to each other from floor to floor and kept continuous watch on life on all levels. They had the quick eyes necessary to spot potential customers: dark blurs darting between dusky girls in pink and fuchsia and baby blue. As Ted entered, he was reminded of a penitentiary taken over by the inmates. It was the least organized, most terrifying whorehouse he had ever seen. Ted climbed the stairs. At each level, the eyes of the girls followed, as they wondered when he would make the noises that all males in the building made. Or nearly all.

He found room 515, a scuffed, yellow-painted door with a sliding bolt on the outside fitted with a space for a lock. He knocked and heard a yell. The door was opened by a young Thai man with thin, cold eyes. Ted could hear Vavasour muttering impatiently within. He decided he couldn't, wouldn't, enter the room.

A few minutes later, the three men were settled in a local drinks shop.

'How perfectly lovely,' Anton Vavasour said, after an enormous swallow of beer. 'It's cold as well.' Vavasour's shirt, the same one Ted had seen in Malaysia, was deeply shadowed with sweat. His bald head shone.

'When one resides in a town like Songkla, Mr Augenstein, one starts to appreciate what most of our compatriots take for granted. Like refrigeration.' He took another gulp of beer. 'And regular meals.' He snapped his finger at his companion. 'Ek,' he said, 'get Mr Augenstein and I a few curries. *With* meat.'

When he had gone, Vavasour said 'He's a nice boy. And he has a room.'

Ted nodded.

'You'll notice,' Vavasour continued chattily, 'he rarely smiles.'

Ted said he hadn't noticed.

'He has no front teeth, you see. The hygiene in these parts is appalling. I have promised to buy him some dentures. And I will some day.'

Ted said he had seen several dentists' shops, with gaudy signboards painted with cartoon mouths.

'*Some day*,' Vavasour replied, lowering his voice confidentially. 'Not yet. Once he's got the teeth, who knows what he'll do. With *me*. Loyalty is not his strong suit.' The fat man drained his beer glass.

Ted told him, precisely and dispassionately, what he wanted him to do.

Vavasour leaned forward abruptly. To Ted's astonishment, an utterly new man faced him, bearing a look of excited, handsome youth. Later, when he pondered it, Ted decided the effect came from Vavasour's eyes, which somehow, fleetingly, denied the greasy skin around them, the mottled, bristly neck flesh, the fleeing strands of hair. From what trapped cave, what rock bubble, had this new Vavasour emerged? It was a man who, unlike all the other public Vavasours, could be imagined to love, weep, elicit pity, recall a boyhood. Over the succeeding months, Ted would think of that transient Vavasour at odd moments: in front of his computer terminal, on his grubby drive to work. He thought of him when the workmen came to install the telex.

'Like your vases,' the workman said, wiping his brow with his sleeve. 'You know, we don't install many of these babies anymore. Mostly we're taking them out. You ought to get a computer. Cheaper, and your kids can play the games.'

Ted assured him that he was happy with the telex machine.

'And we've never put one in a closet before. But like I say, the customer, however screwy, is always right. Especially in New York.'

This Vavasour was a man one could be drawn to, one could love. Then some inner globe spun, or clouds gathered, for his brief moment of youth was eclipsed. He resumed his lump against the stained shop wall and squinted.

'What you are asking me to do, Mr Augenstein, is nothing short of . . .'

'Nothing short of what? Appalling? Disgraceful?'

Vavasour paused. His eyelids rose and fell. He gave a crocodile smile. '. . . short of miraculous! You have come to exactly the right men. I know this part of the world so well, and I have so many acquaintances in all the countries you have mentioned. And, as you have noticed, I am available. There is so little work of any sort, safe or risky, in Songkla these days. All I need is a passport, Mr Augenstein, and I am at your service. At the rates we've been discussing, that should be no trouble at all.' He hoisted a heavy eyebrow at the paper in front of him, which was filled with figures scrawled in his own flamboyant hand.

'I would almost think of getting two,' he mused. 'I've always wanted to be a New Zealander. Actually, I've always wanted to be a Zulu, but that seems too frivolous.'

Ek returned with loose yellow curries and he and Vavasour set to eating. The conversation began again when Vavasour was sated. It hit a second lull as his doughy hands slowly flipped through the photos of Ted's ceramic collection. He looked Ted in the eye, flipped back to two particular photos, and bowed in ostentatious tribute. Then the men discussed communication techniques.

'No computers, please,' Vavasour pleaded. 'I couldn't handle such a dehumanizing machine. I would break it or it would need cells in the most inconvenient situation. Please. Something simpler.'

After his feed and three large bottles of Singha beer, Vavasour leaned back once again and fixed upon Ted content, half-closed eyes. 'You're more interesting than I thought, Mr Augenstein. Last time we met, you were such a boring company man. Although even then I said to Ramse, "He amuses me, Ramse. There's something lurking beneath that hard-gloss exterior . . ."'

Ted didn't feel compelled to reply.

'I should mention, Mr Augenstein, there are more satisfying forms of revenge. More satisfying for you and for me. Ek can tell you how restless I've become in the last few weeks. For a small premium – almost nothing – I can accommodate more violent requirements. *Real* violence. It would be a treat for me. If you don't like your boss, suggest he take a vacation in Thailand. Or the Philippines. Anywhere. Even the Caribbean. We recently met the most interesting person from Haiti. Right here in our little Songkla. Didn't we, Ek?'

The Thai boy sat sullenly.

'It would be much simpler than what you are proposing. Simpler, cheaper and . . .'

'I'm not interested in revenge, Mr Vavasour. Think of this as a little game on my part. And to you, it is a mere job. Nothing more.'

Ted handed Vavasour an envelope filled with cash. Vavasour graciously declined to count it. 'In Songkla, Mr Augenstein, it's not safe even to think of money in public. And don't bother seeing us home, Mr Augenstein. We will meet again.' Vavasour rose unsteadily to his feet, leaning briefly on Ek's arm. 'And, as we agreed, I will choose the most sensible venue. I should ask: do you know Calcutta very well? I have a friend in Calcutta.'

Walking back to the brothel, Vavasour said, 'A fool, Ek. Perhaps one of the biggest fools to ever leave Songkla alive. And only because he met *me*.'

'You are leaving,' Ek said gloomily.

'Ek,' Vavasour said. 'No histrionics, please. This is the life we have chosen: strange couplings, separations, masks and evasions. I will be back, some day, in Songkla with luck.' Vavasour's voice dropped. 'Extremely poor luck. But Ek,' he continued, regaining spirit, 'this Mr E. G. Augenstein interests me. I think he really is trying to play a game. A foolish game – with life itself. What life is he trying to abandon? And what life is he trying to woo?'

Ek pulled the fat man aside to avoid a decomposing dog on the broken sidewalk.

'An unusual fool, really. Is he so foolish as to think that Anton Vavasour takes "mere" jobs? I don't like that term. I despise it. When a game is played, Anton Vavasour likes that enormously. But I doubt that Mr Augenstein's game is a very good one. And I suspect we'll have to play our own little game with Mr Augenstein. A game with our own rules.'

'*We*,' said Ek doubtfully.

'Buck up, young man,' Vavasour replied. 'You're part of the game! Your job is to get me my new passport from that fat thief behind the market. And I expect a fair rate, a local's rate. I'm an honorary citizen by now. Come on. Snap out of it. The two of us have work to do! And yes. I had almost forgotten. Let's think about which dentist, if any, we trust to make you even more handsome than you currently are.'

The two men approached their brothel home, crumbling in the early afternoon glare.

'And let's get a bloody hotel room – *with* air conditioning.'

THE PILLOW BOOK of ALICE GILES, FOREIGN
CORRESPONDENT (CONTINUED)

Presents I'd Rather Not Receive

1. Japanese sweets (with bean paste within).

2. Indian underwear.

3. Taiwanese automobile brakes.

4. Dentures from the Philippines.

5. The newest novel from Malaysia.

6. Eye medicine made in Indonesia.

7. Barbecued chicken's feet from China.

8. More Korean ginseng (the things people present to old women!).

9. The soundtrack of a Cantonese opera.

I Once Remarked

I once remarked to Bob Kingsley, 'Who could imagine what it's like to be Craig Kirkpatrick?'

Bob lowered his *Time* magazine, puffed on his pipe and looked at me with sublime puzzlement. He was always disappointing me in that way. I love Bob for his subtle grasp of international politics, his patience with diplomacy (and diplomats) and his up-to-date, if maddeningly dry, recitations of office politics. But his perspective on human beings is shockingly sanguine. In the view of Bob Kingsley, people with babies were happy. People with good jobs were successful. And people with talent: what more could they want? It was useless to argue with him: him with his talent, his Editor-in-Chief job, his new baby (by his third marriage). He was the reporter who sent Christmas cards reading 'Peace on Earth' from Saigon in 1969 and had to have the irony pointed out to him. (By me. 'Alice, please,' he replied, 'it's Christmas.')

Having known Bob Kingsley for twenty years, I believe that one can live without acknowledging the more troubling aspects of existence if one tries very hard, switches wives periodically and reads *Time* with regularity and complete credulity. But I have also learned that highly intelligent people with pipes frequently make the most superficial observers of life around them – in short, the worst reporters.

Before Craig arrived from Chicago, there was the predictable preparatory talk.

'What? You don't know Winn Kirkpatrick? Those famous photos of the GIs from World War II? The special Pulitzer? Dean at Columbia? "Foster-father" to two generations of foreign correspondents? Yes: *his* son.'

(. . . and on the other side of the newsroom . . .)

'What? You don't know Ai Kirkpatrick? Ex of Winn? From high Japanese society to the trenches of Korea? Where she engaged Winn, shutter to shutter, in a battle that has yet to be called? The famous fights? The custody battle? The marriage to the flush-valve king and the rapid, fortuitous widowhood? *Her* son.'

Naturally, everyone mentioned the famous photo from the Columbia graduation: 'Kirkpatrick and Kirkpatrick by Kirkpatrick.' (Ai never relinquished her famous professional name.) Appearing in newspapers around the world, it implied that the Liza Minnelli of journalism was being debuted. Poor Craig. Even he didn't look very happy being Kirkpatrick by Kirkpatrick and Kirkpatrick. Commented the *Daily News* about his appointment to the *Journal*'s Chicago bureau 'What? No mailroom? For a couple of editions at least?'

Craig received no particular pampering in Chicago. He wrote the required number of clever features on odd vegetables and obscure animals, all snapped up by Page One. A big bank failed and his coverage succeeded. And then came the front-page story that made his name – that already over-made name – disclosing the peculiar concerns of corporations launching new products. The famous anecdote: how McDonalds Corp nearly cancelled its breakfast menu when it realized the toilets in its franchises were designed for light, afternoon traffic and not heavy, post-breakfast dumping. Egg McMuffin was almost a wipe!

The wandering Hong Kong post was a plum and Craig's appointment garnered even more snide attention from the ink-stained brethren.

'If any foreign correspondent has ever had to worry about tripping in large footsteps . . .' wrote Page Six of the *New York Post*. The *Columbia Journalism Review*, in its 'Assignments' column, printed a baby picture of Craig holding a Leica, which *Life* magazine had had the bad taste to print two decades before.

Craig cut a relaxed and professional figure when he entered the newsroom the first day, disappointing those who had hoped for a rookie they could bait and mock. He secured a private office in a major interdepartmental war. And there was that face: everyone enjoys examining the faces of mixed bloods. But there was something especially intriguing about Craig's. I kept going back to those dark, handsome eyes, examining them over and over again, but I never discovered their shadowed mystery.

And Craig's stories: from the first day they were good. A floor-by-floor profile of a Hong Kong industrial building, which said it all about my slimy colony. Singapore's enfeebled opposition, which made him friends with neither the government nor its foes. A jolly piece on Taiwan's umbrella king. He had no trouble easing into his job: no cultural jet-lag, no tenuousness in countries he had never visited. And to an experienced journalist like me, it was obvious why: he saw everything as a story. Not news. Not important information that readers needed, whether they wanted it or not. He made no crusades and waved no flags. Every piece was a yarn, a mere tale to be told. Was the passion so completely lacking from even those early tales? Yes, I guess it was. But journalists, however handy they are with passion in the brothel or at the bar, rarely employ it in their work without getting into trouble. Perhaps Craig had the right idea from the start.

What friendship could arise between me, the Ancient Mariner of the office, and Craig, the bold loner, who strode into the office with a famous past and a Brahmin's approach to journalism? Perhaps we never would have found out, were it not for Craig's irregular hours and Yrlinda's ill-timed visit to the Philippines.

'Hello.' He never answered with the newspaper's name. It was as if each call was for him.

By then I could barely speak.

'Alice?' he said. 'Is that you? Are you all right? What time is it . . . it's past midnight.'

He arrived at my door in nine minutes, breaking all previous records from Quarry Bay. I was weak but not so ill as to ignore the social awkwardness of the situation. I'll never forget his terrible hesitation. My strongest instinct was to block his ghastly pity.

'Craig,' I croaked. 'Don't be alarmed. I think it's dehydration more than anything else.'

He guided me to the car, down 218 stone steps with an iron arm and a wonderfully gentle step. At the bottom, I whispered to him hoarsely, 'Oh Craig, you give such good arm.'

Our eyes met for the first time that dark Hong Kong morning.

'Alice,' he said, refusing to joke in such a grave situation. 'Get in the taxi.'

We started having regular dinners together. We went to the Vietnamese restaurant near the Palace Theatre and to Lindy's for corned beef and to the Beverly Hills Deli for chilli dogs and to California for hamburgers and once, on my request, to the tacky, tourist restaurant at the terminus of the Peak tram, where Craig mercilessly teased the Cantonese waitress about her unfortunate Vs.

'Wegetables?' Craig asked flintily. 'Yes, we would like wegetables. Vot kind of wegetables do you have?'

She looked at him grumpily.

'I would like,' he announced, 'to wiew the wegetables. I would like to wet the wegetables I order.'

When she had been humiliatingly dispatched, I asked him why he gave the Chinese women such a hard time. I had noticed it before: with waitresses, the girls at the office, even strange ladies waiting for taxis in the rain.

'I don't know,' he said defensively. 'I don't like them much. I think they're vulgar.'

'More vulgar than the navy wives with their accents and their wobbly baby strollers?'

'The ankles,' he laughed. 'Don't forget those thick ankles.'

He considered again. 'They're different, the Cantonese girls. Not good enough. I think I consider them cheap imitations of Japanese women.' Below us, Hong Kong was ranged in all its illuminated busyness. It was somehow easy to view the Hong Kong Chinese as a race reduced to scavenging for coins and scraps of paper at the foot of skyscrapers. It was easy to see ourselves at the top of those skyscrapers, looking down with pity and unavoidable disdain. 'Corruptions of the breed.'

'Mixed wegetables,' the waitress announced. The dish was deposited on our table with a crash.

'Wery nice, Wiolet,' Craig called after her. 'Alice, her name is Violet.'

'Craig,' I said, 'it is not.'

Another night, at the Pine and Bamboo, we traded our binary theories of people.

'Everyone I know,' he proclaimed, 'can be divided into two categories: those who insist you come to their place, or those who will agree to meet at a restaurant.'

'I think people can be split by their food preferences. They are either cheesecakes or they're vindaloos.'

'They're thousand island or vinaigrette.'

'Scampis or Newburgs.'

'Newburghs or Danburys.'

I looked at Craig with puzzlement.

'In college,' he explained, 'I used to hitchhike to visit a strange girl at Manhattanville. There was a junction off the Taconic where I waited for a ride. A sign gave motorists two choices: to Newburgh or Danbury. Now, I've never been to either Newburgh or Danbury. Each time I hit that junction, I would panic. I'd forget which direction was mine: to Newburgh, which sounded almost midwestern, or Danbury, which evoked trees and hillbillies. Yet the sign made the choice seem so clear. And the cars, as they zoomed up the ramp to Newburgh, or around the clover-leaf to Danbury, suggested that everyone in the world was headed towards Newburgh or Danbury. I used to think: am I the only one who doesn't know my destination? The only one who doesn't like the choices?'

He looked at me a bit sheepishly. 'I bet your brother lives in Newburgh.'

'He would,' I replied, 'had it been in California.'

'Does he dry his toes after his shower?'

'Frank? Of course.'

'Do you?'

'No!' I made my admission with girlish glee.

'Do you wash your legs?'

'Of course!' I adopted a scandalized tone.

'A waste of precious morning minutes.'

'Do you,' I parried, 'pee in the shower?'

Craig looked at me with shock. 'Don't tell me . . .'

I nodded seriously.

Craig's face was comically crestfallen. 'I got you that time, unshockable Craig!' I crowed. 'How I got you!'

Mostly we talked office gossip, of course. I related over Mongolian hotpot the history of the Hong Kong bureau and, after it, the Asian edition. He told me about the affair between Norm and Giselle, which occurred, long-distance, while he was in Chicago. I filled him in on their breakup and Giselle's new job.

'At "Inc.," poor dear. But it could be worse. It could be *Fortune*.'

'*Fortune*'s not that bad,' Craig said. 'Just because you work there doesn't mean you have to read the magazine.'

'Or *Forbes*.'

'That,' Craig conceded, 'would be the worst.'

At the Excelsior coffee shop, Craig told me of his parents and their opinion of his stories from Asia. 'You know what Dad calls them?'

I shook my head.

'Girl stories.'

'Craig! They're wonderful! You're our best writer.'

Craig and his mother had rendezvoused in Bangkok, at the Oriental, on the occasion of an exhibition of photos by the famous couple. It was called 'The World according to Kirkpatrick and Kirkpatrick.' Ai had a bee in her bonnet, Craig said. 'A review in the *Bangkok Post*, of all places, called news photography middle-brow. She howled for days!' Craig mimicked a Japanese accent overwhelmed by American tones and slang. '"Journalism may not have the beauty but what is so beautiful about the art? The shit on the floor. TV sets smashed in. It's all boring."' I could picture old Ai: that long, girlish hair, with those signature bangs, that pudgy middle-aged Japanese face.

'She's full of poo poo,' I whispered. 'Who says journalism doesn't have the beauty? The perfect lead? The artful quote? The throat-catching ending?'

Craig took an enormous swallow of beer. 'Alice, I realized my problem that night – my life problem. It's my writing. Since I was a kid, I thought my writing set me apart from them. I clung to it, through the high-school newspaper, through my college column, through Japan. I thought writing was my calling and my salvation. Mom can't write a letter. Dad, despite those famously blunt letters to the *Tribune*, is a terrible writer: disorganized, unstylish. When I got this job – *the* writing job of the profession – I thought I was free of them. But this was what they were waiting for. *This* is where it all led in their eyes. Their goddamned friends are watching. And they think I'm writing . . .'

'. . . girl stories.'

Craig nodded.

'Do they read them?'

'I asked her if Dad saw the Marabar Caves story. You know what she said?' (The queer transpacific accent resumed.) '"When I saw him, all he could talk about was the *Tribune*'s Ethiopia coverage. You know how he watches the *Tribune*. I tell him he's obsessed."' Craig made a flicking motion with his hand – his mother's toss of her girlish hair.

And over dim sum at the Lee Gardens, I heard of Craig's year in Japan. The job he got through a college connection, not via Winn or Ai. The tiny room he inhabited. The strange months of working, wandering, drinking. The time he opened the letter addressed to Ann Landers and discovered it was from the proofreader at the adjacent desk, asking Ann's advice on a girlfriend with brain cancer. The summons home to Columbia and a more serious life. Because 'only a fool stays in a job like that for more than one year.'

'Winn may have been right,' I said.

'I know. He *was* right, in a way. "You've paid your dues," he said. "Now go out and become a real writer."' Craig swigged his beer. 'It didn't feel like dues, Alice. *This* feels like dues.'

It was only later, over a very late dinner at the Korean restaurant in Causeway Bay, that he told me about the woman. We were the only patrons and the waiters had put the chairs up on the other tables. When I heard her name, I said: 'Craig, no!'

He gave a shy, proud smile. 'It was a completely different character, of course.' He traced it for me on the unclean tablecloth.

'"Aya,"' I repeated. 'It's pretty. Did Ai ever find out about her?'

He shook his head.

'The name didn't attract me.' Craig was talking to me but he was looking away into memory. I felt for a moment like a mother gazing at a sleeping child. Those eyes: so placid, so clear, so deep and so hidden! I had never seen him so tranquil.

'It was her singing. We were in a tiny bar in Shibuya. Her voice was low and husky, so different from the squeak of the typical Japanese woman.'

'It was a Japanese song?'

Craig focused on me with a start. 'You won't believe it Alice. She was singing "Fly Me To The Moon." With perfect seriousness.'

'Cor-neee!'

'No,' he said. 'That's Japan. It doesn't seem so corny there. I had never paid attention to such songs before. "Red River Valley." "Fly Me To The Moon."'

Craig fixed me with a wicked glint.

'And she had her own, peculiarly Japanese version of the lyrics . . ."

(. . . I knew in an instant . . .)

'Yes,' Craig replied. '"Fry Me To The Moon."' We both laughed and I whispered: 'Was she beautiful? She must have been beautiful!'

'I don't know,' he continued. 'She didn't have that pinched look so many Japanese women have, or that rigid, powdered mask. She had a big face, with strong features. A high forehead. A very high forehead.

'I remember her best from a night when she was angry with me.' He laughed. 'God, was she angry with me! She deserved to be. She stormed out of the bar we were in. I paid the bill and followed. It was May in Roppongi. When I came up to the pavement, I saw her across the street, which was shiny with some rain. A small wind was blowing her hair back from her face. Roppongi is so bright, you know, even late at night. And though busy, it's quiet. Roppongi always reminds me of a scene from a dream: that artificial light, all that life going on smoothly and quietly, swirling around you. The cars: so shiny and silent. Cars from a dream.'

He turned back to me. 'It's the best place in the world to be drunk, you know. You move along, no one sees you, the night is clear and busy. I've never felt more my own person than when I was drunk in late-night Roppongi.

'Aya wouldn't look my way. I remember that big forehead, those maddened eyes, that furious, set face. I stayed on my side of the street and watched her. That's when I first thought she was beautiful. A taxi stopped; she entered it. The taxi made a U-turn directly in front of me. That marble profile sailed past and although it was night, and although she was in a taxi, and although I was drunk, the image was bright and utterly clear in my mind.'

Craig looked at me.

'It still is, obviously.'

'Yes,' he said. 'Yes, it is. I guess you can say she was, in a way, beautiful.'

'Is.' Mine was a schoolmarmish tone. '*Is* beautiful.'

'No, Alice,' he said. 'I think *was* is the right word. For me, anyway.'

Peoples Are Different

Peoples are different. They do different things in the same circumstances.

When a plane touches down on the runway, Chinese pop up from their seats like jack-in-the-boxes and lunge at the overhead bins to claim their carry-on treasures: packages of dried pork, herbal medicines, cassette recorders.

Filipinos cheer. They blab to their companions, to assure each other that all are alive.

Indians whip out combs and energetically attend to their hair.

When you are driving in a taxicab and the passenger door flies open on a turn, a Hong Kong taxi driver goes mad. He yells and screams and nearly loses control of his vehicle.

A Filipino driver shrugs and waits for you to close the errant door.

An Indian, usually a Sikh in a magnificent turban, raises his hand imperially in a call for calm. The ancient taxi swerves elegantly around the traffic circle, its door flapping like a broken wing. Still, the driver does nothing. 'Don't panic!' he suggests, with martial calm. Pavement rushes by. The heart pounds and one can almost hear hoof-falls and war shrieks. The Sikh calmly rides his charge through battle.

Some people prefer peoples. Others, the airy types, like places.

I prefer persons. At my age, I most regret the hundreds of people, from all lands on the planet (and a few from outer space), I have allowed to escape. I refer to those people whose lives are nothing more than half-remembered snippets of gossip. Late at night, in my aquamarine tower, I find myself visited with unnerving frequency by these people. The first in my aimless thoughts are, of course, my enemies, followed by a few loved ones. Then come the ghosts of the half-remembered people. The silliest stimulus brings them, half-formed, into my mind. And often, those limbless trunks or floating heads, plus the occasional hand or wrist – always wearing an exquisite piece of jewellery – are the hardest visitors to show the door.

Take the couple that used to fuck in his office at lunchtime in New York. I remember him quite well: a promising hire from *Newsweek*. She was a researcher who had been around for years. I can picture a black dress she used to wear, with a little yoke sewn on the front. I can't recall whether they were married to other people, whether they were a public couple as well as lunchtime friends, or whether they subsequently married each other. I forget why they fucked in his office; at the time, the act itself seemed of sufficient interest. What might they be like today? He eats lunch each day in Chinatown, under the naive impression that it's healthy for him. She, sadly, skips lunch altogether . . .

It's a pointless exercise, really. I've lost the connection between then and now. They exist in that one narrow moment, half-distracted by impending deadlines and the unenviable prospect of a hungry afternoon. She with her face among the notebooks, her hands ecstatically grasping the latest *Business Week*. He with his shirt-tail flapping, his piston pumping, reflecting on whether he grabbed enough tissues from the company latrine. They never move from that awkward position, except for the necessary gyrations of pleasure. The tissues are never required; the phone, ever-threatening, never actually jangles. The deadline never comes.

How strange, the ghosts of our past. And we, at the oddest times, are we half-summoned ghosts of another's past? Does a word, or a sundae, or a wedding cancellation prompt someone in New York to think: 'Alice.' And what does he see? An ungainly, intensely-shy young colt, with a whispery voice and a wicked tongue? What does the Alice Giles ghost do? Walk solitarily down an East Village street? Dash home from the office, by herself, in New York's spring rain? Cry in the ladies' room?

Oh, to be able to marshal the faded forces one leaves in one's wake. 'Smile!' I'd command. 'Chin up! No moping! We will not be seen moping around the globe and through the years.' I would make each ghost strong, brave, cheerful. Isn't that a fine idea?

Yrlinda Was Her Unusual Name

Yrlinda was her unusual name. How it differed from 'Linda' I never did discover. She once explained it to me, but as was common with Yrlinda, her explanation failed to clarify. I claim an uncommon and profound understanding of my Yrlinda; she, in her inarticulate way, grasps the essence of me. These I insist. But at the same time, I have to admit we have trouble understanding a word the other says.

I subscribe to the theory that every person has one great opportunity in his life: a totally suitable job, a move to the correct country, the perfect marriage. In the past, I considered Hong Kong my great opportunity. Now, after much pain and gallon upon gallon of her beef-marrow soup, I know better: it is Yrlinda.

I have always had maids in Hong Kong. I am so accustomed to the accompanied life that I have trouble comprehending how one faces the world – or, at least, the world of repairmen – without a maid.

In my first years, I hired Chinese amahs. A long chain of these wiry witches ascended my 218 steps and entered my life. But in effect, they were all the same amah. They wore the same Gloria Vanderbilt haircut. Their skinny wrists jangled with the same bangles of milky jade. They wore the same shiny pyjamas, the robes of a tribe of princesses or rejected widows.

These women led austere lives. Their cubicles displayed no possessions or mementoes. They received no phone calls. No visitors followed them up the 218 steps, by day or by night. I began to picture them as having mysterious other lives, either concurrent or in their pasts. And yet, I could never gather any proof. The amahs didn't linger at the marketplace to chat lengthily with their fellow-priestesses. They didn't vanish unexpectedly on turbulent nights nor moon over old scrapbooks. On Sunday evenings, search as I might, I could perceive no glow of happy family gatherings fading gently from their set faces. They appeared to spend their Sundays haggling over groceries – an experience that rarely leaves a glow on one's face, even for a Cantonese.

Some expatriates compared their demeanour to that of cats. But they had a rough devotion to the 'missies' (as we were called) and their occasional huffs were certainly un-catlike. Ah Chan was my last amah, and she once went five-and-one-half weeks without talking to me. I would find food on the table at night, the soup plate steaming silently in the empty dining-room, like a scene from *Beauty and the Beast*. My laundry would appear stacked outside my bedroom door on Sunday mornings. For five-and-a-half weeks, my bathroom went uncleaned and untidied – my real punishment. Then, as abruptly as it began, my punishment ended one Monday morning. The hairbrushes were aligned that evening. I could choose my meals again. In response, I added a tip in the monthly pay envelope and made unusual and intentional messes in the bathroom for five days running, including a daily scattering of powder on the difficult tiled floor. Calm descended on my house. Apologies were strictly unnecessary.

When I ponder my amahs, I locate them in another time and place. I see them picking across a desolate battlefield, stripping boots and armour from battered corpses. I see them in the desert, bangles hitched onto their skinny biceps, searching for iguanas. They present the plunder and harsh provisions to me. I always maintained one could do no better in the aftermath of a nuclear holocaust than to be cared for by a Chinese amah.

But that holocaust had best come soon. For the amahs, old and dying, are being replaced in apartments across Hong Kong by the cheaper Philippine maids: the priestesses ousted by the can-can girls. I wondered how they felt about this, but never found out. When Ah Chan's bony head, with those knobby, exposed ears, bobbed down my 218 steps that final day, I'm fairly sure she never shed a tear for herself or for the passing of an era. She didn't even look back. I shed a tear or two: for the era, that is. Ah Chan, with the iron fingers that ruined several of my favourite tunics, I never did miss.

My parade of amahs evolved into a parade of Filipinas. I

can still recall their peculiar names: Ghosing, Maybelle, Boobsy, LaLynne and Fely. The Philippine maid never just materialized or disappeared, as the amahs did. Each hiring was a betrothal. Each parting, as I discovered with Fely, my maid before Yrlinda, was an abandonment.

'My Ninong!' Fely wailed melodramatically one glary, impossible May morning. Tears poured down her sallow face and her hand held a crumpled, fearful-looking telegram. It told of a car crash that befell her ageing grandfather. There was a comical pair of mistakes in the text: 'He is near death, I sweat, but may survive, God illing.' (Even God seemed in dubious condition in Ilocos Norte.)

She would be gone only ten days, Fely vowed. Two weeks at the most. Her family needed her. With God's illing help, Ninong would pull through. (The sign of the cross was performed.) Fely refused my offer of financial help, which, I realized later, was Clue Number One. And as she began her descent down the 218 steps that bright, sticky morning, with those finger-like towers ranged conspiratorially behind her, Fely looked back. I immediately knew: the old telegram trick. I would never see Fely again. She hated, in her gentle way, my ways. This was her lovely, lying Philippine way of quitting.

So the following Sunday, early enough to beat the worst heat, I strode through a public park annexed by the maids on their days off, Statue Square, and accepted the greetings due a feudal mistress or an actual monarch. 'Hello, Mom!' chanted the brown women, 'Good Morning, Mom!' (Their pronunciation of 'ma'am' was ever disconcerting.) The greetings embarrassed me and called forth the unattractive hunch I strive to overcome during interviews and televised press conferences. I hunched in fear of encountering Fely, far from her perfectly healthy Ninong, strumming a guitar or, even worse, painfully relating to her compatriots the sins for which I earned my abandonment. The bathroom. My fits of unbecoming temper. The late nights. (I could picture her face, distorted into a theatrical mask of pain, as she laid it out for one and all to hear. '. . . and then, when you least expected it, at three in the morning, the stereo is blaring again: "Hello Young Lovers (Wherever you Are.)"' Here Fely would be interrupted by an impromptu performance of that captivating song by her natively-musical audience. Then she would continue: 'And the next morning, with all the dinner dishes washed and put away the night before, you know, are two ice-cream cartons in the sink! Two! And they are the big ones, you know. Scraped clean! *Talaga!*' There would be much sympathetic nodding of brown heads, several giggles, perhaps a few, lingering bars of that most perfect of songs, even, maybe, the climactic lines: 'All of my memories are happy tonight. For I've had a love of my own . . .')

How many of the maids knew of my secret habits, my dirty corners, my three in the morning songs? 'Hello Young Lovers.' 'I'm A Fool (To Want You.)' 'Oh, My Mysterious Lady' (in which I sing, *con gusto*, the parts of both Peter Pan and Captain Hook.) And, when pep is particularly needed, 'Love Potion No. 9.'

To my relief, Fely wasn't in Statue Square that day. Quasimodo receded. And then, next to an enormous bronze lion with a stretched, hungry mouth, I saw a woman in tight green pants and a loose, gaudy blouse. The woman was telling a tale before a cluster of Filipinas on a bench. Her arms were comically akimbo. The green legs were spread wide, tottering on fat, red heels. I couldn't see the face, but I couldn't miss its large, hilarious laugh. She was the kind of woman who couldn't talk and sit still at the same time. Speech equals action for my Yrlinda.

When I approached the woman in green, I realized her tininess: she was less than five feet tall. I towered above her. Her personality gave her height and breadth – although she hardly needed the latter.

I looked down into her round, brown face. 'I need a maid,' I whispered. 'And I could use a good laugh too.'

She looked up at me with a gasp. I don't know if she understood. She stared at me for a moment. And then the laugh began again.

The mechanics were accomplished easily. She would abandon her slavedriving Chinese employers and come to work for me. I gave her a lift in my green car and broke the ice with a question about her slacks. 'They're unusual.'

She hooted, as if they were a huge joke.

'Did you get them in Hong Kong?'

This produced a gale of embarrassed laughter. She explained, in her opaque fashion, how she had altered a pair of employer's trousers. Either the employer was a Japanese fishmonger or I misunderstood her. She said they never seemed to wear out.

'That's a pity,' I said sweetly. She misunderstood my sarcasm or was unconcerned by it. I suggested they must have been golf pants at one time and that brought us to our first verbal tussle.

'Golf?'

'Yes,' I said. 'Pants worn during the playing of the game called golf.'

'No,' she replied airily. 'I no play golf. They man's pants. From my old master.' And she laughed again, delighted with herself and my silly suggestion. She twisted her bulk in the bucket seat, hoisted her blouse and rolled the waistband of the pants so I could see the name of the designer. At the same time, I saw a charming roll of plump, brown stomach. In fifteen years – for this was three years ago – I had never seen the stomach of any of my maids.

When she finished her display, she was still chuckling. 'You play golf?' she asked. 'Those golf pants?'

I was to learn that Yrlinda got joy with extraordinary ease. When she salvaged a pair of rusty scissors she gloated over them for days. When she discovered a certain rare vegetable at the market, or a distinctive silver-skinned fish, she glowed! The oddest memories could bring happy tears to her eyes. She once told me, as we were both occupied in the kitchen, of the day her daughter was inoculated for smallpox. When I looked up from my cutting board, big tears were splashing down her proud face.

And then there was the name. She laughed when I inquired about it and began a long saga of her family and their tumultuous times in the central Philippines. Her hometown bore the musical name of Kabankalan. It was poor – 'very poor, very very poor, very *very* poor!' to quote Yrlinda precisely – and plagued by rapacious landlords, brutal communists, scheming politicians, slaughtering soldiers and, from time to time, natural calamities of unearthly destructive force. 'It's nice place,' she concluded loyally. 'Very beautiful place. You visit sometime.'

The name Yrlinda was the creation of a neighbour, or a distant uncle – this explanation too was unclear. It had something to do with Yrlinda being a skinny baby – 'very, *very* skinny!' – and this detail set her into a gale of self-conscious laughter. She danced around my kitchen. 'Me, skinny!' she shrieked. 'It's true. And pretty!' She nodded eagerly, trying to convince me of the unbelievable claim. Her eyes were wide.

'Yes,' I said. 'Very pretty.'

'We were seven.' Yrlinda's eldest brother had been ill and she performed a skit of his short, sad life. She strode across the room in a demonstration of fitness. 'First,' she said staunchly, 'he healthy.'

Then came the illness. It had something to do with his legs. 'He fine. Then he sick.' She began walking with a queer wobble. 'He healthy, he sick in the legs.' The legs got bandier until, suddenly, the wobble stopped altogether. 'Then he dead.'

Other children were born to the family and one was named Linda, spelled in the normal way. But something happened to that Linda, making the mother 'very *very* sad.' Subsequently, another sibling – either a sister or a brother – also contracted 'brain' disease. The sister (or brother) died (or remained an invalid). The next child was Yrlinda. And she was skinny.

When Yrlinda was baptized, the priest was perturbed, not because he himself had the unbiblical name of Father Jojo, but because the baby was nameless. Babies can't be baptized without names.

Enter the neighbour, or the distant uncle, who announced to the family that he had been visited by a *duena*, a Philippine fairy. The fairy told him that to stop the family's run of bad luck, the baby had to bear the same name as one of its siblings.

'Didn't the priest object to this?'

'No,' Yrlinda replied. 'My whole family is Catholic family.'

On the leprechaun's advice, the family named its child, once again, Linda. 'And that's how I got my name!'

It was a nice happy ending, if a bit incomplete. She never did explain her peculiar spelling. 'And then *everything* fine in my family!'

'You had more brothers and sisters?' I inquired. 'And they were all healthy?'

'No,' Yrlinda said. 'My mother die. She old, very old, very *very* old.' Yrlinda made a grossly puffed-out face.

I diagnosed the mother's complaint as goitre. But, as usual, Yrlinda contradicted me. 'She died on road.' Yrlinda laughed discordantly.

The story gave her immense pleasure and I heard it several times over the years, with numerous variations and plentiful enduring mysteries. That poor, polioed brother; that goitred mother, expiring 'on the road' as if she were a Philippine vaudevillian.

'Yrlinda, that's a nice story,' I said. 'Very nice.' (I was taking on some of her constructions.)

'Yes!'

'You know that we say in English? We say: You can pick your friends, but you can't pick your family.'

She nodded her head with unexpected vehemence. 'Yes!' she agreed. 'That is why none of us – none out of seven – ever married!' Pride shone on my Yrlinda's face: pride for her crippled, decimated, unmarried family, in her poor, abused, *very* beautiful Kabankalan. I do so wonder about the Philippines. Imelda Marcos used to believe in a hole in the sky above her country, from which spirituality poured unrelentingly. I have a different theory. Just as some think that Atlantis will someday be discovered in the East Atlantic, or Noah's Ark atop Mount Ararat, I believe in Pandora and her box. I think some bones and a twisted, rusted trunk will someday be discovered in the Philippines, perhaps in Kabankalan itself.

Since Pandora, the rest of the world has had its share of suffering. But there, in those six thousand chaotic isles, the furies continue to rage as they did when the box was first pried open: men are well, sick, dead; people pick their friends, but they're scared to choose a family; mothers die in the road.

A few weeks later I realized Yrlinda and I were somehow fated for each other. She, and her bone-marrow soup, saved my life.

Once again, I was checked into Canossa Hospital, my second home. The nuns there are even older than I am – by several centuries, at least – and they pamper us chronic visitors with touching little gestures: a slice of lime with the tea, a better television set, a deliberate rudeness with the self-engrossed young ladies on the maternity ward, who have no reason to make the racket they do, especially at night. (Or so says Sister D'Souza.) They always give me the same room – 'Here's *your* room,' Sister D'Souza announces – with its glorious view of the harbour.

But this time I wasn't recovering. Neither my dehydration nor my anaemia would go away. The doctors, ever embarrassed in the face of my elusive condition, said my life was in God's hands.

The next thing I recall was opening my eyes and seeing a pair of pudgy brown hands on my coverlet. 'Yrlinda,' I said, 'I want that soup. The soup you made last weekend in the kitchen. That yukky . . .'

Yrlinda laughed. That evening, she appeared at my bedside with the thick brown soup in a recycled Tang jar.

'Yrlinda,' I asked weakly, 'who drinks Tang?'

'I do!' She burst into inappropriately robust laughter. Yrlinda: the secret quaffer of Tang.

How the staff must have marvelled at my swift recovery, my new appetite. It was as if the hospital window had been left ajar by that careless night-shift sister. Some strange monster had managed to gain entry under the cover of night. And the next morning, Alice Giles looks a bit peculiar when she requests, in an alien voice, the marrow of a young calf boiled for hours with dirty herbs and pungent vinegars.

('How peculiar,' says the dietician. 'Just yesterday it was raspberry ice cream!')

Afterwards, I always craved Yrlinda's soup when I fell ill. The emblem of crisis in the house of Alice Giles became a line of Tang jars on the kitchen counter. My attacks continued, for whatever reason: a weak immune system, as the doctors claimed, or psychosomatic causes, as they actually believed. And through my later attacks, that thick, primitive stew, first simmered in the hills of Negros island using the bones of God only knows what creature, kept me alive. Once, when I had the notion to can the stuff and sell it commercially, I asked Yrlinda how she made it. She removed from the pantry a long, pointed kitchen instrument made of rusted iron.

'Stop, Yrlinda!'

'Sometimes it most hard,' she said. She pantomimed the slaughtering of an elephant.

'Stop right there.' I put my hand on her arm and forced down her rusty weapon. 'Please.' I realized the knowledge of the recipe might have killed me right there in my kitchen. Or put me off the soup forever – which probably would have had the same effect.

Why Are Some Song Titles (The Way They Are)?

I've always wondered about song titles with split personalities. Whenever I buy an album, I look for such songs. On one album, I found three!

I'm referring to the song title that is accompanied by a phrase, usually an adjacent line of lyric, mysteriously put in parentheses. The songwriter can't decide which line of lyric is the better title. Or, perhaps, the original title was superseded when the public started calling the song something different. This is undoubtedly the case with 'The Christmas Song (Chestnuts Roasting On An Open Fire).'

Which line, I wonder, gets exiled between the parentheses: the original title or the popular favourite? My research shows that sometimes the parentheses come first and sometimes after.

How do the proud authors of these songs refer to their creations in conversation? 'Hi! You don't know me, but I wrote the song, "Kicks" (Just Keep Getting Harder to Find).' Perhaps they hum a few bars.

Nancy (With The Laughing Face)
If You're Going To San Francisco (Be Sure To Wear Some Flowers In Your Hair)
(I've Got A Woman Crazy For Me) She's Funny That Way
(Ah The Apple Tree) When the World Was Young
Raindrops (Keep Falling On My Head)
Saturday Night (Is The Loneliest Night In The Week)
(I Don't Stand A) Ghost Of A Chance With You
(Anyone Can See with Half an Eye that) I'm in Love with You

No one has ever explained this phenomenon to me. But sometimes, I feel like doing something similar with my byline. 'By Alice Giles' can be so tiresome.

I can see this atop my big scoop: By Alice (Giles), as if I were a Renaissance painter.

Or, when I'm feeling formal and demure: By (Alice) Giles.

Or, on those days when things just don't work out: By ( ) ( ).

When You're An Older Woman

When you're an older woman, or just plain old, you gain a certain amount of public invisibility. I used to think I was growing less self-conscious. But the fact is that people don't notice the older Alice as they noticed my younger self. They don't notice me in restaurants or concert halls. I can sneak up on friends as I never could before. Or spy on them.

Age brings a magic shield and it's not the little old ladies alone who lurk: the big ones can too. Mata Hari should have been a crone. Instead of ending as mere legend, she could have written her memoirs, with helpful chapters on garrotting with arthritis or the importance of segregating your poison from your digitalis.

If the world at large sees old people fuzzily, we are utterly invisible to one group of people: those with lust in their eyes. On several occasions, I have sat patiently, a paperback book splayed on my lap, and watched full seduction scenes enacted shamelessly before me. Sometimes the couples will turn shy when another individual enters the train compartment or the bus or comes too close in the hotel lobby. They will feign indifference when a stewardess intervenes. When the stewardess sashays away, the courtship immediately resumes. With me in the middle all along, my book still face-down in my old lady's lap.

I have seen hands brush – it's a thrilling sight, really. I have seen eyes glow, wedding rings significantly fondled, and I have heard numerous conversations of mind-bending banality. The words don't exist at those times: only the tones and the flashing looks.

'Do you live alone or with your family?'

'You have a business card? This is home or residence?'

'It's too bad you're going on to Calcutta. Have you ever spent time in Delhi?'

'My wife – she's my *best* friend.'

Once, I watched an entire marriage, from first blush to divorce, transpire between two people seated beside me on a jumbo jet. The foreplay was subtle but obvious: the brushed knees, the 'Oh, I love China Products!' (hand placed heavily on forearm), the evasive replies to questions about domestic arrangements, the tense explications of phone numbers. ('It's best to call before 9 a.m. or after 5 p.m.')

The airline meal ended. The cabin lights were dimmed for the in-flight movie. I saw an arm slip under a lap blanket. A head sank back into a pillow, and eyes closed. I found my book less than engrossing. The man rose to excuse himself, begging my forgiveness and pulling at the front of his trousers. (I was on the aisle.) Three-and-a-half minutes later by my Seiko, the woman followed. She was ageing, I noticed, and her suit had a spot on the front. She reminded me so much of Bridgette! Twenty-seven minutes later by my watch, the couple returned, chatting in a more relaxed manner. The man chastised the woman. 'Oh come on, you can't believe that,' he said with a new harshness. Within a few minutes, he was asleep. Bridgette, sitting by the window, smoked pensively and frowned. The Chevy Chase comedy on the small movie screen flickered away soundlessly.

I remained on the aisle seat, unnoticed, my paperback book still on my lap, my white hair glowing brightly in the reflected light – a ghost. An old, invisible, inaudible ghost.

I Envy Married Persons When They Say

1. 'The next day, we did our usual post-mortem of the party . . .'

2. 'Both of us were sick from the clams.' (How preferable this is to having food poisoning alone.)

3. 'We're getting fat.'

4. 'We miss you.'

I Despise Married Persons When They Say

1. 'We're dieting,' or 'We're off salt.' (Or 'We're joggers,' 'non-smokers' or 'for all intents and purposes, vegetarians.')

2. We've been married four years. Four years! Imagine!'

3. 'I liked the film, but Vivian thought it pretentious.' (When asked, 'How did you (singular) like the movie?')

4. 'We can't come because I've got to work and Vivian's mother is visiting, but Vivian says we hope to see you soon if only I could finish these stories.' (This offends the grammarian in me.)

5. 'We're depressed.'

ONLY A FOOL

I

Craig Kirkpatrick was on the road so frequently that when he returned to his apartment on Cloudview Road, he missed the room service and the wake-up calls. When he went to hang up wet clothes, he instinctively reached for the 'EZ Line.' But it wasn't there.

In thirteen months on the beat, Craig had visited Thailand twice, Taiwan, Malaysia, Singapore, India and China. He would soon travel to South Korea or the Philippines or, if things got really hot, Sri Lanka. The one country Craig hadn't written any stories from was Japan.

And now, in his sparsely furnished dinette, he held a wrinkled air-mail envelope in one hand and a sweating can of Coca-Cola in the other.

Craig drained the Coke. The letter had propelled him into a long Wanchai debauch the evening before. He slid open the balcony door, stepped into the Hong Kong mugginess and made his morning appreciation of the harbour view: a vertical ribbon of water, with an occasional half-junk or container ship, glimpsed between two other apartment towers. He looked at the envelope, with its numerous, ancient-looking stamps and the large, ugly defilement across its face: RETURN TO SENDER. He desired to drop the letter, with the Coke can, onto the pavement 28 stories below.

At the office, nursing his third Coke, Craig scanned the messages on his computer. The first from New York stated: 'I had an extremely stimulating lunch Wednesday with the Pakistani ambassador, and on looking through the Pakistani clip file . . .' Craig closed the file. He opened another: '. . . trouble getting through to your home number over the weekend; please have it checked. Anyway, I'd like to have a talk with you soonest about Pakistan and coverage in general . . .' The stakes had been upped from Thursday to Monday. 'Coverage in general.' Then he opened up the feature story he had begun weeks before and groaned at his own, amateurish lead.

IPOH, Malaysia – *When the durians drop, watch your head. And hold your nose.*

'You know,' Craig said to Matt Mell, who sat near the Coke machine, 'I'm doing this ahed on . . .'

'Don't tell me,' said Matt, who was nicknamed, inevitably, 'Pell.' 'Feng Shui in Hong Kong.'

'No,' Craig said, 'it's on – '

'Thai kick boxing. Or is it Malaysian turtles?'

Craig had anticipated more Matt Mells: reporters who, because they resented his beat and his name, would brand him as an Asian neophyte. (Asian blood not quite counting.) Matt, so far, worked the theme most obnoxiously, even though he had slim claim to the title of old Asia hand. Young, loud and given to red sweaters and baseball caps, Matt had been at the paper five months. He had escaped from a newspaper in Hartford, Connecticut. Matt covered the most boring beat, textiles and shipping, with a thoroughness that made even shipping magnates and shirtmakers snooze. 'Nobody's had the stories I've had,' was his signature line, voiced frequently at the FCC. (And once, but only once, a guy from Reuters delivered the obvious reply: 'Yeah, Matt, that ought to tell you something.')

Craig said, 'No, it's – '

'The stock market in Katmandu.'

'No.'

'Monkey-brain banquets in Canton.'

'No.'

'Snake wine in Korea. Dogmeat restaurants.'

'Matt,' Craig said, 'give me – '

'The closing of Bugis Street.'

Craig turned his back on Matt and stepped to the Coke machine.

'The reopening of Bugis Street.'

'Forget it, Matt. You just wait . . .'

'Or,' Matt said in a crafty tone, 'could it be durians? The old durian feature?' Craig wondered whether Matt was smart enough to get into his computer file.

'If you were doing a durian story,' Craig said diplomatically, 'what angle would you pursue?'

'None. There are some stories that just can't be done anymore, Craig. Ever again. Like durians.'

Georgie Tam, the banking correspondent, strolled between the two men unawares. He was reading a copy of *Asian Banking* magazine. The newsroom's sudden silence penetrated his cluttered brain and he looked up with a blink. His glasses were, as usual, filthy.

'Georgie,' Matt called, 'would you ever want to read another story on a tired topic like, say, sinking Bangkok?'

Georgie answered the question with serious consideration. 'Actually,' he said, 'I've always been fascinated by that. I've never quite understood – '

'Georgie, it's been written to death.'

'But never very well,' Georgie said. 'For instance, what will happen to people when . . .'

Craig gave Matt a look. It said: *Done Well. Stories done well are different.*

'Georgie,' Matt pleaded, 'what about Bugis Street?'

'The government's attitude on that issue has been very interesting from both the angle of state puritanism and the sacrifices they are willing to accept in terms of tourist income . . .'

Craig continued smiling.

'Georgie, you know as well as I do that some stories are plain overdone. Like bride-burning in India. The Philippine cockfighting story. *And* the durian story.'

Georgie blinked with surprise. 'The durian story. Oh, that's different. Everyone has done the durian story. And I've never understood why. It's just a fruit. Who'd want to read continual stories on the kiwi? The avocado?' Foggy Georgie, oblivious to the interpersonal conflict he had stepped into, head swarming with complicated syndicated loans and state corporation borrowing needs, kept talking even after Craig had disappeared and Matt had returned his attention to that week's charter rates.

'Another example would be the bred tomato. Is it really tasteless? I've never been able to tell, myself. But you read so much about it, especially from America. I, personally, rarely eat tomatoes . . .'

Back in his sanctuary, with its door closed firmly behind him, Craig rolled a piece of stationery into his typewriter. The envelope on his desk, with its violent tear, was puckered with beer stains from the night before. He recalled reading the letter in the light of the streetlamp near the Empress Theatre and wanting to cry. He read his own, foolish, impotent words. And his failed, hand-scrawled, concluding plea. Then he pulled the blank sheet from the typewriter, picked up the phone and made air reservations to Japan.

For Craig Kirkpatrick, Japan had the smell, the taste and the climate of freedom. He had been there countless times with Ai and Winn, staying in exquisite inns and visiting grandparents, but never had Japan meant anything until that endless and fleeting twenty-first year. For the first time in his life, he was freed of his parents, his famous name and the demands attached to all three. Japan: it was as if a child, at the precise moment it grasped the concept of 'food,' had a sweet, bursting grape placed in its mouth. For Craig Kirkpatrick, freedom and independence tasted of raw pickled ginger and salted salmon on steaming rice. Happiness had the look of Yoyogi Park on a clear Sunday evening in spring. Life itself smelled of stewing oden, toasted squid, and, most of all, it smelled of frantically barbecued meats and vegetables on the sidewalks of Shibuya. Pleasure was the feel of a certain Japanese woman, with a certain name, in a maidenly silk dress with a girdle hidden underneath. How surprised Craig was when Aya wriggled out of a garment he associated with mothers and grandmothers. She begged him to look away but he refused. She continued wriggling and protesting until the waist showed, and the dark triangle. He said, 'Stop!' and, with the girdle around her thighs, she stopped and waited for his next command. For it was Aya's sexual custom to do as she was told. Craig fell under a heavy, Japanese spell. He was instantly disdainful of his sexual past with heavy-thighed, clear-eyed English majors who discussed Chaucer along with their post-coital cigarettes. Aya, in contrast, did what he wanted: when he awoke with a random erection, during her heavy periods, when she was late for work. Craig discussed with her the feminist gospel of his world and she shrugged it away with intoxicating charm. And Craig realized at that moment that life wasn't as set as it had always seemed. The accepted wisdom could be rejected if one tried. Life was not just merely surrendered to.

And then, on a crackly long-distance phone line, he surrendered, because 'only a fool stays in a job like that for more than one year.'

Only a fool, Craig thought, looking at the dimpled envelope and a pair of crushed Coke cans.

Matt Mell had abandoned the newsroom for some thrilling developments in the knitting sector. Craig, still worrying about his durian story, strolled to Alice Giles' office. The door was locked. He returned to the newsroom and approached Sue Philipps for advice. Sue had recently taken over the editing of the right-wing editorial page and was having trouble boning up on various ideological tenets.

'Did you know we are in favour of DDT?' she asked, glowering at her green screen.

'I think we disapproved of the banning of DDT.'

Sue raised her eyebrows sceptically. Craig explained to her his dilemma.

'Oh Craig,' she said sympathetically. 'It's such an old story.'

'Matt Mell made it sound like a profile of Peter Ustinov,' Craig said, 'Sue, I've already done the reporting.'

'Let's see,' she said brightly. 'Has anyone tried breeding a less-smelly durian? That would be a fun piece.'

Craig shook his head.

'A more smelly durian?'

Craig laughed.

'How about the smelliest durians? I read they were in the Philippines.'

'Where did you read that?'

'In *Asiaweek*,' she said. 'And I think in *Asia Magazine*. And didn't the *Review* have something?'

'And I went to Malaysia,' Craig moaned. She placed a consoling hand on his shoulder.

As he was leaving the office, Craig was halted by Bob Kingsley, who had his feet up on the copy desk and was absorbed in the current *Time*'s Publisher's Letter.

'I hear you're doing the durian story,' Bob said.

The durian story?

'Don't,' Bob wagged his pipe, 'get that quote wrong about the durian in the toilet.' He continued: 'Everyone does, you know. A month doesn't go by that a durian isn't compared to eating a raspberry pudding in a urinal. Or a blancmange in a men's room. A few months back, *Insight* had it as "Gumming a Softee in the Cumberland House comfort station." Incredible!'

Insight Magazine, Craig thought. *Even Insight!*

'The original quote,' Bob continued, 'which no one bothers to look up, of course, is in Anthony Burgess's Malayan Trilogy. I have my old copy at home. I could lend it to you . . .'

But by then, Craig was gone. It was dark. He was headed to Central to pick up his airline tickets to Japan.

2

It is in Tokyo's night-towns, and there are many, that Japan's neon present coexists most comfortably with its cobblestoned, rickshawed past. A master of the woodblock print, were he to be transported magically from the last century, would certainly be boggled by late twentieth-century Tokyo – daytime Tokyo in particular. But given time, he could start to feel at home at night. And soon, if he put his mind to it, he could begin once more to draw. The buildings would be higher, of course, and he would have to adjust his artistic eye to the effect of neon on concrete and human flesh. But he'd have little trouble recognizing his cast of characters even a full century later. One can only imagine what the resulting print would be like. The towers of, say, Shinjuku, shaded in lugubrious grey. A winding alley, bursting with light. A clutch of navy-blue office workers frozen in a perilous sway. Teenagers would be portrayed breaking into a bruising run. Along a venerable wall, men would be concentratedly, but unabashedly, pissing, and the steam would be caught floating up from the mossy stone. A girlfriend, as girlfriends always do, would be vomiting on the street corner, staining her blue and white school uniform. The scene would have the same frozen quality of the nineteenth-century *ukioes* – and the same feeling of life straining to go on to the next moment. After the shutter clicked, so to speak, the salarymen would recover from their sway; the adolescents would have vanished in a burst of noise and energy; the girlfriend would be squeakily apologizing to her boyfriend and he would consolingly wipe her uniform with his handkerchief. He would throw the handkerchief to the ground. And the river of humans would resume its flow, pushing those characters along and replacing them with another set, straight from another vision of another, full, eternal Japanese night.

Craig wandered through his beloved Tokyo night-town, Shibuya, taking little notice of the vomiting girlfriends and the 'steaming walls.' When he had lived in Tokyo, Craig knew all of Shibuya's alleys. The knowledge returned to him so rapidly he almost regretted it. He felt a wave of nostalgia for his initial few months of confusion. Back then, everything was new and notable. He could lose himself completely, try a new alley and then, unexpectedly, come upon an artery he knew – one that led back to Aya's apartment. For Shibuya was not Craig's neighbourhood. His apartment had been elsewhere. Shibuya had drawn him as Aya's back door.

He weaved in and out of the smoke that wafted from barbecue restaurants and waved it around him, as Japanese do with incense at a shrine. It was good luck and Craig needed it. For he had returned to the only altar he had ever worshipped at: the altar that held his lost, free life in Japan. And after two days of uninterrupted travel, on planes and trains, through airports and crowded train termini, to the bottom of the country and back, he had returned to Tokyo empty-handed.

Craig wanted to take Aya back to Hong Kong, so nothing else would matter. She had said: *After you, I'm through with this kind of life. I can't endure. I go home to open a coffee shop. Or a drinking place like my aunt.*

But Aya wasn't in her Kyushu hometown. Craig had taken tea with her hesitant, gnarled parents. They displayed for him a stack of unopened air-mail envelopes. His letters. He withdrew from a pocket a similar pack: the letters they had returned. They told him she had gone '*gaikoku*.' Craig was astonished to hear the word. *Abroad*. With excruciating politeness and regret, they informed him they had no address for her. They shook their heads, sucked air through their teeth, bowed, and said they didn't even know the country she was in. Such scrupulous lies, coming through such ugly gold teeth.

It wasn't long before Shibuya's neon lanes led him back to Aya's old neighbourhood. Craig passed Yoyogi Park and pushed through the rotting gate. There was no sign of life in Aya's old apartment and no laundry hanging from the red plastic claw on the peeling bamboo pole. He stood looking at Aya's old window.

The new occupant of the apartment opened her patio door. She held laundry in her arm. The woman saw Craig. Unexpectedly, she waved.

Later that night, Craig was watching *Seven Nights in Japan* on the hotel television when the phone rang.

'If you had told me you had a family engagement, we might have thought up some Japan stories for you,' said the offended voice from New York.

'It's not exactly family, Paul, it's personal. It's my trip. On my own ticket.'

'Yeah, Craig, I know you have family and all, but there's lots going on there. I read something interesting about the privatization of telecommunications and the editorial board recently had lunch with the Minister of Finance, I forget his name, who had several interesting things to say about – '

'I'm supposed to go to Seoul or Manila.' Craig blurted hastily. 'I could be in Seoul tomorrow.' There was silence from the other end, only broken by the celestial sounds of transcontinental phone lines. Craig thought: *'Coverage in general.' Here it comes.*

'. . . I mean, we all liked the Maharaja Caves story, Craig, it was a classy story and a pretty good read. And the umbrella king: good business angle, lots of bright writing. But it's the Pakistan-type stories that are going to make your name.'

My name!

'. . . I would just hate for you to turn into another Fonz Mackenzie . . .'

'Paul,' Craig protested. 'Fonz went home because his daughter drowned.'

'I know,' the voice said with a stunning lack of sympathy, 'and it was a great personal tragedy, but still, everyone knows his reputation suffered. Craig, some people are saying your beat is jinxed. Remember Rebecca Tirella?'

'She got cancer!'

'Of the colon. And Billy before her never really knew what New York wanted. He wrote all those DBIs.' (Dull But Important stories: the death of many a career in journalism.)

'He went on to become foreign editor.'

The voice chuckled. 'Yeah. Like Chernenko. Look at him now. "Special projects." Craig, I'm a friend of your father. I wouldn't know how to explain it to him if you sank in this job. Let's think seriously about this Pakistan trip . . .'

On the screen, Michael York was taking his Japanese co-star in his arms in a room decorated with plenty of tatami and paper screens. Craig had seen the film over and over again. It was terrible, and a favourite in Japan. There was a close-up of the Japanese girl. She looked out at the camera. Her eyes locked onto Craig's. They were identical.

The chuckle rattled across the phone line again. 'And how,' the amused voice asked, 'could I possibly explain it all to Ai?'

The next day, Craig Kirkpatrick went missing. He left Tokyo and failed to log in with New York. He didn't appear at the Hong Kong office. His home phone rang continuously. When New York inquired via long distance, they found he hadn't checked into the Chosun or the Lotte, so he wasn't in Seoul; the Mandarin, the Peninsula, the Intercontinental or the Manila Hotel, so that knocked out Manila; they tried the Galle Face and the Méridien, eliminating Sri Lanka.

'Call the Karachi Sheraton and the Islamabad Holiday Inn,' Paul commanded, 'but I'll eat today's *Post* if he's in Pakistan. The spoiled brat.'

They tried, and it wasn't easy considering the phone links to Pakistan. He wasn't there.

It's a worrying thing to a newspaper when a reporter goes missing. He could be dead. More important, when a reporter can't be pinned to the Karachi Sheraton or the Lotte in Seoul, there's a good chance he isn't working.

'There may be some Kirkpatricks who don't have to follow the rules in this business,' Paul warned the foreign staff after a long, boozy lunch. 'But as long as I'm foreign editor, Craig Kirkpatrick is not one of them.'

3

As his battered outrigger pulled away from the island of Culion, Craig thought to himself: *I'm at the end of the earth. And going beyond.*

Culion was a leper colony. At one time it was the largest in the world. Culion was in the middle of the South China Sea, miles from any other Philippine island. Its main characteristic, aside from an accidental beauty, was its perch at the end of the earth. In the old days, lepers were collected from other parts of the world and given one-way tickets to Culion. The first thing they saw –

Craig watched it slip from his own view – was a grand church on a rise overlooking the sea. It must have been a comforting sight as their glum journey came to its close. But when the lepers landed at Culion's docks, on the island's other side, that comfort must have fallen away. Even today, Culion carried the stench of exile. In 1913, the sanatorium authorities stopped importing currency from the outside world. They minted special coins with the words 'Bureau of Health' stamped on them. As a prophylactic measure, the coins were periodically cleansed with acid. Local histories report that when the coins were first distributed, the offended lepers flung them into the sparkling sea. Craig had several of the coins in his pocket. They were still in circulation in Culion.

In Craig's bag was a portable computer, wrapped in several shirts to protect it against the sea spray, and a notebook containing the raw material for a story about Culion. Craig had disappeared, it is true, but he had been working. The next logical step would be to head to Manila, call room service, type the words into the computer – the words that described the glaring sun on Culion's gravelled paths, the doddering French nuns in their white habits, the lepers themselves: 'Gorgons and Chimeras dire . . . such a population as only now and again surrounds us in the horrors of a nightmare,' as Robert Louis Stevenson wrote of another leper colony. But Craig's boat was headed in the opposite direction. It moved slowly through the placid, aqua sea. The trip would take all day and Craig had brought along food and drink for himself and the boatman. Had there been anyone to witness, he would have presented a strange sight: the well-dressed foreigner in the primitive craft, gliding slowly through the empty sea with a Penguin book hoisted before his face. But the only witnesses were the flying fish, an occasional fisherman, the endless sea.

And the islands of that sea, which, as Craig glided by them, began to grow. Gradually, they rose towards the sky and the strong sun, as if pushed from beneath with magnificent might. Sands and single palm trees gave way to boulders. And then rounded humps of charcoal-coloured sea serpents. And finally, towering cliffs of black limestone, bearded with ferns and orchids and pulsing with swinging monkeys and fluttering egrets. The Blue Lagoon gave way to a landscape straight out of myth. King Kong country. But Craig remained oblivious to the alteration. He read. Every once in a while he looked at his watch and shouted a question to the boatman, who would shake his head in reply. Occasionally Craig glanced at the islands, not admiringly, but searchingly. As dusk approached, an egret cried and attracted Craig's momentary attention. The egret climbed into the pale sky. Below it spread the sea, now a deep royal blue. Craig's boat was the tiniest of water bugs, winding its way around an oafish hump of rock. On the other side of the island was a large black shape, a complicated Chinese character drawn with an inky brush in the blue sea. The tiny schooner headed for the sandy swatch beneath the character's radical. If the egret had swooped, he would have seen Craig close his book, look to the brown boatman and receive the acknowledgement he had been awaiting. Craig was approaching El Niño.

El Niño was a resort, famously expensive because of its extreme isolation. Its guests flew by chartered aircraft to a landing strip located on an adjacent island. Occasionally they descended directly in private helicopters, scattering the resort's sandy beach in a picturesque whirl. The seas of El Niño teemed with exotic and endangered species. The air was thick with primitive birds and monkey sounds. El Niño's guests invariably treasured their stays, for few had ever experienced the luxury of total wilderness. And yet, for most visitors, El Niño differed from the beach paradises that prompt them to say, 'I could live here forever!' El Niño was a return to the life mankind left behind millenniums ago. That was the secret of its success; and, at the same time, it explained why travel agents rarely recommended a stay of more than three nights. For as they departed with superlatives pouring from their mouths, most guests peered back through the windows of their tiny aircraft, not for a last fond glimpse, but to make certain they were rapidly pulling away from El Niño's exile. How pleased they were to return to civilization. Japanese civilization, that is. For El Niño was a resort for rich Japanese.

Craig occupied a thatch-roofed cabin on stilts in the resort's bay. It was connected to the beach by a brightly painted boardwalk. He stepped onto the boardwalk and looked at the sea and the dragon humps that were fading with the twilight. He heard a boat and watched it round the last island before El Niño.

The guests were returning from an outing. Craig could recognize the types. There was the bulky, crew-cutted Japanese man with white pants, white belt, white shoes and a coarse companion with brassy hair: the gangster and his moll. There were a selection of rich

Japanese nerds with 'Wetmen' and diving equipment. There were the dough-shaped Japanese couples straight off some farm, always out of place and ever confident. As the boat drew closer, Craig left the boardwalk and entered the dark interior of his cabin. He stood at the window facing the cove.

The boat passed and on its prow, like a ship's enamelled figurehead, was Aya, her hair thrown back by the wind. Her prominent features led the boat in its passage. It was the face that had haunted Craig for months: a face neither happy nor sad, with chiselled features illuminated by the rosy sunset. She held one hand over her squinting eyes. The other grasped the boat's railing. He watched the face glide toward him until it was only a few feet distant. A mere whisper would have pulled that marble gaze towards his cabin window. Then it passed. Craig returned to the balcony and watched the boat land at the beach. Aya was the last to disembark. She lit a cigarette and turned to watch the sunset as she took her first drag.

That evening, Craig left his cabin and walked through the tropical night to the beach. He recognized the characteristic sounds of Japanese at play. The giggles were impossibly high-pitched; the male guffaws had a drunken, caricatured quality. There was singing of pop songs. He knew that the man performing the song was the singer in the group; every Japanese group had one. He would surrender his mike to the macho buffoon, and he to the office girl with the reedy voice and she to her friend, Miss Whispers. All the types were there, transplanted from inner Tokyo to a razor's edge of sand in the wilderness, covertly watched by a Noah's ark of strange fauna.

The group sat beneath a thatched shelter ringed by torches. Empty San Miguel bottles littered the sand. The music machine sat atop a bamboo bar and Aya, the resort's hospitality hostess, was its keeper. As Craig walked toward the shelter, a new song was coming on.

Aya had taken the microphone from her dull charges and started to sing. Craig remained outside the circle of torchlight. He watched as she pulled the words from inside – Aya always did. It was the best part of Aya's evenings at El Niño: grabbing the microphone, abandoning her boring guests and surrendering herself for a brief interval.

She sang:

> *Gone my lover's dream.*
> *Lovely, summer dream.*
> *Gone and left me here*
> *to weep my tears into the stream . . .*

Aya strained to reach the low notes and the gangster's moll, with impossibly long silver fingernails, applauded. Aya smiled, her eyes on the lyric book in her hands. That marble face glowed happily in the torchlight.

> *Whisper to the wind,*
> *And say that love has sinned*
> *Leave my heart abreakin'*
> *And making a moan.*
> *Murmur to the night*
> *To hide her starry light*
> *So none will find me sighing*
> *And crying all alone.*

The song ended to applause. Aya passed the microphone along and fiddled with dials. A new song began. She looked at the night. Craig stepped from the shadows and approached the bamboo bar.

'I'd like to request "Fry Me To the Moon."'

Aya regarded him emotionlessly.

'Please? For an old friend?'

'How?' She used her terse, telegraphic English. 'My parents? You went to Kyushu?'

Craig shook his head. 'Nakayama. I found her at your old apartment. By accident. I begged her and she told me.'

Aya took a gulp of beer. She said in a low, unforgiving tone, 'She is weak.' She turned to the machine, which had gone silent, and coaxed from it a song for the girl with the reedy voice. The girl shrieked away.

Aya fumbled with cigarettes. 'Go.'

'Aya!'

The mask-like face was suddenly, gratifyingly, all emotion. 'You don't talk to me. Why do you think I am here in the first place?' She turned her face from him. 'You failed me,' she said. 'You left me. Now look what I've become. It's too late, Craig Kirkpatrick.'

After the guests had retired and the torches had been doused, the woman and the man continued walking and talking. They paced the boardwalk and wore a rut on the beach. At one point, the woman stood on the sand with her fist in the air, shaking it with fury, tears running down her marble face. Perhaps the setting was too wild. Perhaps their separation was still too new. For at the night's long end, only one thing was definite. Aya had no intention of cutting short her self-exile.

'This is me,' she said passionately, gesturing at the deadened, desolate island. 'And you . . .' – her face was furious – '. . . all because of you!'

El Niño looked deserted as Craig's outrigger pulled away just after dawn. The guests were still asleep. The cottages were closed and lifeless. Craig thought to himself: *To the end of the earth I've gone. And now I return.*

THE PILLOW BOOK OF ALICE GILES, FOREIGN
CORRESPONDENT (CONTINUED)

A Letter

I was slamming all the drawers of my file cabinets when I found Craig staring at me quizzically.

'What are you doing, Alice?'

I slammed another file drawer, but the crash wasn't to my liking. I opened it wide and slammed it again. The windows shook gratifyingly.

'Therapy,' I said breathlessly. I kicked my steel garbage can across the office. It hit the door and bounced into the newsroom.

'My doctor thinks I hold in my frustrations. He says they should be vented.' I gave another slam of a file drawer, but it was an apathetic effort. I was tiring. Venting frustrations was heavier work than I had anticipated.

'I thought he was blaming the nerves in your left earlobe.'

'That was the other doctor,' I said, 'and it wasn't the earlobe. It was the sole of my foot.'

'You said it was working.'

'I had to. Those treatments cost seventy-five dollars each. A hundred dollars for both feet.'

'Couldn't you close the door,' Craig asked, 'so they don't have to hear it in the newsroom?'

I gaped at him. 'The whole *point* is for them to hear in the newsroom. What frustrations could I vent in here by myself?'

'Bridgette seems so upset.'

'Bridgette!' I cried. 'She was quaking the day I foolishly hired her twelve years ago and if she hasn't calmed down yet, it's not my fucking problem.'

'Speaking of,' Craig said. He handed me a vellum sheet with an impressive seal at the top. 'Let me know what you think.'

He left abruptly.

The first words I spotted were '. . . since you were a small boy . . .' *Poor Craig*. I quietly closed the file drawer, shut the door to my office and sat down at my desk.

Dear Craig, (read the sloppily-typed letter)

> There is no solution to the ages old debate: are journalists *made* or *born*? But after 35 years in the business, *I* have no doubt in my grizzled old head that journalists are too often *unmade*, sometimes by circumstances but usually by their own undoing. Drink. Laziness. A bad wife. A *tragically* wrong approach to their jobs. And *that's* why I'm writing you today.

Good lord, I thought. Do all photographers underline so much?

> Since you were a small boy, Craig, you *knew* you would be a writer. I distinctly remember telling your mother – you must have been no more than five – 'My God, I'll have to get him a typewriter soon!' Now you have your chance. In this generation, the name "Kirkpatrick" could very well refer to "Craig Kirkpatrick," not a couple of old, battling picture makers from a distant era. The *world*, Craig, is watching and waiting.
>
> But when I want to read the latest on the Karachi hijacking, or Lee Kuan Yew's rumble with Devan Nair – an old friend, by the way, give him our regards – or corruption in the Aquino government, where do I find the best stuff? In the *New York Tribune. Time* Magazine. The *Post* (if McEnroe is on the story – a fine Columbia grad *really* making good.) Sometimes, even, the networks. (I'm forced to watch these days. The world is changing so fast, even good old Columbia!)
>
> Son, I know you're proud of your writing style. I know you can do those feature stories, like that cave story from India, *which I read*, better than the average reporter. But Craig, no one ever became a star in journalism on fancy writing! You're not at the *Asahi Evening News* anymore, *thank the Lord!* You're pulling a hefty salary, you're working for one of the big publications. Now you've got to take a leap into journalism's mainstream. I'll tell you my basic theory of

journalism (I know you've heard it before). You got readers. Readers got expectations. Always work *with* or *against* those expectations. When you're in India, do a story about dirt or poverty – or do a story about an Indian town that's surprisingly clean and rich. Never go off the map – 'cause the readers just won't follow. Remember: the easiest thing for a reader to do is to *stop* reading a weird story. Like a story on Indian caves. Philippine lepers. Or Taiwanese umbrella makers. For God's sake, Craig. The Philippines is Marcos (or Aquino). Taiwan is China and unification. When I was at *Life*, we had a term for a reporter like you: he's writing like a local, we'd say. When the *World Business Journal* is paying you 75k a year to write like a pro. (I hope you're getting that much, by the way. You should see the results of our latest survey.)

Craig, get on the breaking story. You could run rings around the other guys if you tried. Leave this soft stuff to the girls. Do your best to avoid the economics crap because it belongs in the inside (no matter where the august *World Business Journal* prefers to run it). In fact, this whole issue has given me an idea for a new course: 'Real Journalists Don't Do Profiles.'

Let me repeat, my son, the *world* is watching. The industry is watching. Your mother and I are watching. We've been there.

Winn

(There was a pencilled P.S. in the journalist's characteristically ugly scrawl:)

A final cautionary note. I bumped into Peter at a dinner the other night. As you know, we used to play tennis in Japan and he was very fond of your mother. We made small talk and I waited for him to mention you. Craig – he *didn't*. Finally I said something and he, under compulsion, praised your McDonalds story. Your McDonalds story! From Chicago! He couldn't recall one of your stories from Asia – which, I might point out, is Peter's part of the world just as much as your mother's and mine!

With my green Pentel and in my girlish script, I wrote a note at the bottom of the letter: 'I've never known a father who wasn't full of shit. He mentions all your best stories!' I put the letter in an envelope, sealed it with tape – we have ferocious snoops at our humble edition and they open other people's mail for breakfast – and left it in Craig's mailbox. What more could I do? Friends are friends, after all. Fathers, unfortunately, are fathers.

Surely, I Am Not the Only Person

Surely, I am not the only person who wonders about the appearance of her colleagues' sexual organs. This is a natural response to working closely with people over long periods of time. I am rarely curious about the organs of people I meet on business trips or the journalists clustered around me on a breaking story. Never have I speculated about the organs of an interview subject. Or almost never.

But the people who work with me day after day, month after month, night after night: inevitably, there comes a moment when one has to wonder: Is it large or is it stubby? Are they smooth and pink or dark and rubbery? Commodious? Low and swinging? Bushy? Babyish? Terrifying?

With men, one can guess with some confidence, although verification is infrequent. Sometimes an erection shows through a pair of cotton trousers, or a detail is dropped unexpectedly in conversation. Both of these are possible when someone brings a pornographic magazine into the office and everyone gathers around to take a peek.

But with women, one has to examine peripherals and then extrapolate. And even then, it's nothing but a guessing game. The cleft between breasts is occasionally visible – but that tells you next to nothing of a colleague's nipples. The quality of a woman's skin can always be judged by her arms or shoulders. But how it looks naked is, I think, quite different.

I'm not just talking about Bridgette. After twelve years, I think I'm the only person in the office, male or female, who doesn't know what her organs look like. I remember a girl at the office named Harriet. The office was small – just a few of us, really –

and we endured a succession of Harriets, good and bad, all of them traipsing through Hong Kong for the worst possible reasons. One day, I found myself wondering how Harriet looked when she was naked. And this surprised me, for I disliked the woman and had, in fact, been conducting a low-key hate campaign against her by long distance to New York. I expected her to get the sack momentarily.

Harriet was long and wiry and pale, with hair to match. I took to wondering about her in bed. I concluded she must be the sexually-hungry type. I imagined her walking naked through her Hong Kong apartment, with the curtains ever open, her hair falling freely down her back.

Once, someone joked about a new brand of underwear being sold on the streets of Hong Kong. It was called 'Superman' underwear. Harriet said, 'I should get some for Billy.'

The remark could have been interpreted two ways. I chose to think that Billy disappointed Harriet in bed.

One day, Harriet returned from lunch and told us of a strange encounter. She had been washing her hands in the ladies' room of a Hong Kong shopping arcade. It was a small ladies' room. There were only two stalls and a sink.

From the occupied stall, she heard a strange female moaning. Harriet knocked gently on the aluminium door and inquired, 'Are you all right?' But the moaning persisted.

So she entered the cubicle she had recently vacated, stood on the toilet seat and peered over the divider. According to Harriet, she saw a young Chinese woman sitting on the toilet masturbating with her two middle fingers.

No one believed Harriet's story. It seemed too incredible. One of the other reporters said, 'She won't even tell that story to Billy. I think it was dreamt up for us.'

This amazed me. I felt that Harriet's fantasy had, in an oblique way, collided with my own. In the workplace.

My hatred campaign was a total failure. Harriet continued working at the office for many more months, until Billy was transferred to, of all places, Mogadishu. He was a schoolteacher: another reason to suspect his sexual capabilities.

My curiosity about Harriet's naked body faded after her tale of masturbation in the shopping centre. For the rest of her time at the paper, she was a model of propriety. (Her efficiency was another matter.) There were no more implausible tales; no further allusions to husband Billy. I wondered whether I had imagined that sexual current that seemed so palpable at one time. Or did it simply burn out?

Another Letter

I found the second letter in my mailbox, sealed in an eloquently blank envelope. Craig left no note, nor any penned comment. He left me the original of the letter. When I finished reading, I brushed aside a tear and wondered what to do with it.

> Dear Craig,
> I knew a man once at the magazine, an Irishman, who could write better than all of us put together. How we all admired his skill! He could take any sentence, turn it back to front and improve it. He could spot, as if by second sight, unnecessary words, phrases, sections of text. He could describe natural disasters 8,000 miles away with a feeling that gripped even the hardened reader. He could write anything, as we told him, but he knew it. To write, to him, was to *live*. He was always working on his novel. Then he was always working on his other novel. And then he was always working on his popular novel or his play or his screenplay. It was his example that taught me to tune out any human being who utters the fallacious phrase: 'If only I could get six months away in the mountains (or on the beach or at the lake house). Then I'd be able to write.' To *write*. To WRITE!
>
> He went to Hollywood once, my Irish friend. Is it necessary for me to fill in the rest of the story? I saw his obituary a few months back in the Post. His brief obituary.
>
> Writing is a real talent, Craig. There's no reason for you to ever forget that. So is photography, I might add. It's not just levers and chemicals and light meters. It's vision and eye. But neither are careers. Neither are lives, at least not for

working slobs like you and me. No one gets by on vision or eye or vocabulary. Let me be fatherly and give you counsel: journalism is your career and your life. You were born to it, my son. Journalism *is* Craig Kirkpatrick. Journalism is real. And then, let me sound forth like an editor once again, after all these years. If you don't become a real journalist soon, and do a real job for your cushy, overaccepting newspaper, you'll end up like my talented Irish friend. With a bloated liver, two paras in the New York Post and a closetful of half-typed fantasies. Neither I nor your mother intended that for you, our *bright* and *beautiful* boy.

Grow up, Craig. Join us in the real world. We're all waiting for you – you and, yes, your tremendous talent too.

Cheers,

Winn

(There was a P.S. written in purple ink by Ai. It read:)

Call Marina and Chris O'Connell when in KL. You remember them from Nashta in Key Biscayne? He's ambassador now, or DCM, and very buddy with the PM!

It Was A Restless Season

It was a restless season. I wonder what causes such a thing? We all felt it simultaneously, as if there was something in the air or the water, or their convergence. After all my years of scorn, do I have to admit there is something to the mysterious Chinese science of *feng shui*: the study of air, wind, water and fire, and their effect on human beings? I had thought expatriates were immune. But when we leave behind the plagues of our own society – the late-night sofa-bed advertisements, the extra-virgin olive oil, the Jon Voight movies – do we lose our defences and become susceptible to the elements of the Orient? Is this the expatriate's curse? And on a lonely pinnacle like Hong Kong, are there special times when the air rushes up, the waves rise beneath us and fire licks at our backside, prompting us to move on? To leave? To abandon, recklessly, the towers we once considered home?

That's the question. The answer was in the frantically smoky atmosphere of the FCC that season. It bounced atop the glinting waters of Hong Kong harbour, along with cigar smoke and the clinks of Bloody Marys, as journalists gossiped with ferocity at their Sunday launch parties. How many stringer jobs traded hands that season? How many bureaus relocated to Manila and Peking? Even La Rolla, the famous fabricator of stories, made a lucrative move from the *Chicago Times* to *Time* Magazine, sending the message to his less promoted colleagues that crime not only pays in journalism. It even pays a housing allowance.

Normally, I enjoy such things as a restless season. I love to see my colleagues on the go. It brings out the foolishness in them. But soon, that restlessness seeped into my own life. I discovered that the roots I had tried to bury in Hong Kong's rocky soil eighteen and a half years before had never penetrated its concrete skin. I felt an earthquake and tried to hide my fears. But my façade crumbled when Yrlinda also felt the rumbles.

She said one morning, 'I very scared.'

Her round face looked quite frantic. 'I had dream about Norma. I want to go.' (I hadn't thought Yrlinda dreamed about Norma, her illegitimate daughter in Kabankalan, or at all. Perhaps she didn't normally – and how frightening must be the dream that penetrates that bronze consciousness!)

'Don't go,' I said.

She looked at me queerly. 'You sick?'

I told her my paper was moving. It was abandoning its funky headquarters in Quarry Bay, astride a rat-ridden wharf, for tonier space in a newly-constructed skyscraper. At the top of the skyscraper. Not just any skyscraper. *That* skyscraper.

'The one you hate,' she gasped. 'Goodwill!'

'Evil will!'

But that wasn't the worst news, which I held back. I didn't think Yrlinda could understand. And I was afraid to stand ashamed and afraid before her. Life with servants is not all ironing and cooking. It's dignity. Shame. Dependence.

Before the official announcement was released, Bob Kingsley had called me into his office, shut the door, and spilled it. He was leaving for a post in New York. Joanne had already arranged a job on Wall Street. His replacement was Roger Mutterperl.

'And I promise you, Alice, he will do the right thing by you. With your health and your service to the paper. I'm writing him a memo now. He'll be a good editor, Alice. Young. Amibitious. Hands-on.'

He banged his pipe on an ashtray.

'I can't promise you your office, of course. I was just looking at the blueprints. Space is tight and the staff has grown. Look at Sue Philipps, stuck out there on the copy desk, while her counterpart in Brussels has – '

'Fuck Sue Philipps!'

Bob looked at me disappointedly.

'Fuck her! Fuck her, fuck you and fuck Roger Mutterperl!' I tried to put some robustness in my whispery voice. 'Where were you when there were no housing allowances? Where were you when there were riots in Hong Kong and it looked like the Chinese would invade?'

'I was here for those riots,' Bob said. 'I was staying at the Hilton. And I remember from the grill room – '

'I can't retire, Bob,' I pleaded. 'This paper is my life. I've given it everything. I have no other life. And if I can't write . . .'

'I know, Alice,' he said. 'We all know.'

'Even if I'm sick . . .'

'Alice, we know. We *appreciate*. We're a loyal paper.'

'How the fuck old is Roger Mutterperl, anyway? Where was he when the foreign staff was me' – I thumped my chest – 'and Saul Pearlstine and his girlfriend researcher in London? In those days, Tokyo was a backwater. In those days, we still believed in scoops! And who *got* the scoops?'

Bob gave me tissues and, as we left the office, he laid his hand on my bowed back.

'Alice, you were the best.' Bob enjoyed consoling people. He thought it proved his humanity. 'Don't ever forget that. I remember hearing about you when I joined the paper. "There's no story Alice Giles can't get," they said. And they were right.'

When I returned home that evening, the Tang jars with their orange lids were lined along the kitchen counter. My prescient Yrlinda. Oh, that tragically restless season! I can't say what element pushed my colleagues all around the map of Asia. I don't know if it was wind or water that uprooted my newspaper from its dock and plunked it atop the most hateful edifice in the colony. But I knew very well what element reached up to me in my green mansion, in ever-lengthening flames, aching to char the very soul of Alice Giles. It was nothing less than fire.

That night I drank the marrow soup. Yrlinda asked me if I wanted some music. I said no. 'No "Love Potion No. 9" tonight, my Yrlinda. No "Hello Young Lovers." No music at all.'

I went back to my Japanese books, looking for that unique sense of female abandonment they contained. I had found it time and time before. I found it again. In the tenth century, the rejected wife known only as 'Mother of Michitsuna' wrote:

> One day, as I sat looking out at the rain, knowing that today there was less chance than usual of seeing him, my thoughts turned to the past. The fault was not mine, there was something wanting in him. It had seemed once that wind and rain could not keep him away.

Yet thinking back, I saw that I had never been really calm and sure of myself. Perhaps, then, the fault was in fact mine: I had expected too much. Ah, how unwise it had been to hope for what was not in the nature of things.

I also found two poems that seemed to sum up my life in journalism and in Hong Kong. Oh the Japanese: those scurrying black beetles. In the tenth century, they had all the wisdom of the world. And they put it down on paper, expressly for the women of the world like me.

> *How sad to hear it is broken.*
> *Though not a spider's,*
> *It is a thread into which long years have gone.*

That is one poem I read that night. The other was an anonymously-composed poem. It spoke directly to me that restless season:

> *With the spring come the calls of countless birds.*
> *Everything is new, and I grow old.*

Book Two

THE TYPHOON

We are high above the South China Sea and it is, for the local correspondents, a time of high winds and rough surf. A 'restless season,' in the words of one eloquent veteran. We descend from the clouds over her colony, and the tumult is visible from a very great distance. The scurrying is unrelieved in Central, along Queen's Road, up those minor arteries that lead to Ice House Street, home of the Hong Kong Foreign Correspondents Club. On weekends, the bustling continues, with just a slight shift in pattern. Over Hong Kong's humps they go, flinging themselves lemming-like off the docks of Aberdeen into sampans and teak junks, slowed only by coolers full of Carlsberg and copies of the *Sunday South China Morning Post.* In formation, the boats veer out of Aberdeen harbour, headed through the same scummy seas to the same island coves, where the gossip and backbiting and job-jockeying of the night before will continue, interrupted by mere hours of sleep, a headachy cab ride, the passage out of the harbour (the engine noise forestalls conversation) and one or two Bloody Marys. The acutely hung-over start right in on the Carlsbergs. None of it stops until Aberdeen is back in view, with the sun darkening over the green and brown mountains that tower behind it. Followed by the return trip to Ice House Street, and a few more rounds.

A gust, and we are back in the clouds, flung eastward to the island nation of Taiwan. It too is a busy place, but we have no concern with the scurrying Taiwanese, and no need to descend to their level. Our view is into the penthouse of a glass-fronted building, the office of the chairman of a vast, yet grubby, industrial empire. In a heavy teak chair, an enormous man is sipping tea from a ceramic mug. He has a cloud of white, synthetic-looking hair and a pus-coloured smile. He wears a new-looking military uniform. With him is not a boy, but a mannish woman with dark skin, false charm and a large, dangerous smile. Her garb is an identical uniform, smaller and without ribbons. They are entertained by an oily Chinese man, the chairman. Everyone sips tea and smiles. The smiles subside; money changes hands; and the smiles resume. The Chinese businessman presses an electric button and leads his visitors to our wide window. They stand with their backs to us, their hands before them like schoolchildren, and a photographer snaps their picture. Vavasour nudges the mannish woman. She ignores it to smile at the Chinaman. Later, when he exits the room with the cash, she scowls at the fat man. He shoves her away, and with a doughy, prissy hand, fluffs his cottony white curls.

The wind gusts and once again we are airborne, moving south. A coach moves steadily down a Taiwanese highway. We descend to ground level and, racing through the landscape, peer inside the bus. There is a young man, possibly Chinese, possibly not, paging through an art book. The photographs show rough stone sculptures: large, black monsters, weird goddesses, fish with protruding tongues. But we lose our perilous position and, in a moment, we are back in the clouds, far from Taiwan. A southbound plane passes us and we duck. Through a tiny diminishing window we see a man with perfect, blow-dried, honey-coloured hair. He peers into the inky clouds with a worried expression.

The wind is getting fiercer and more frantic – it's a kind of typhoon – and in its tumult we lose a day. We descend over Taiwan, Taipei, over a hotel with its gargantuan outline celebrated by green and yellow electric lights on a string. It has an atrium interior, a popular recent design in hotels. Antlike hotel guests stroll nervously at its bottom, ignoring the mammoth space above their unprotected heads. Some actually manage to eat in the exposed restaurant, sipping nervously and blinking when their peripheral vision signals something swooping down from above. Of course, their eyes are playing tricks. It's just a light blinking – a guest shutting his door on a high floor – a maid watering the plants. But what if the clumsy maid dropped that watering-can? What if the guest catapulted over the railing? What if a child, left unattended, slipped between the railing and its glass panes . . .

A young man with dark eyes – possibly Chinese, possibly not – pages through an art book at one of the tables. Another man approaches him. From above, something seems wrong with his head. He stumbles, improving our angle. It's not a head, but a brown hat.

'Mr Kirkpatrick!'

'Adam?'

'What you working on, feller? A scoop? Or some economics story?'

Uninvited, Adam joined Craig. His fedora was fuzzy with Taipei's light rain.

'A Taiwanese sculptor,' said Craig. 'In the South. He does these.'

Adam gaped at the book. Violently, he whipped off his hat. 'Man, are you a foreign correspondent or what? You're supposed to write about life and death – not art!' He made a choking sound in his throat.

'This is one of his fishes.'

Adam nodded and motioned to the waitress.

'A fish with a tongue,' Craig said. 'See?'

Adam nodded again.

'Have you ever seen a fish with a tongue?'

'Craig, I don't know what we're going to do with you.' Adam sighed and ordered a Salisbury Steak. 'Fish with tongues!'

Adam explained, with obvious pride, his trip to Taipei. Hong Kong was making him restless – 'Rock fever,' he said – and the *New York Tribune* had suggested he write a few trial stories from Taiwan. It seemed the paper was looking for a stringer who, Adam said heavily, 'knew his way around.' They paid his air-fare plus the price of a moderate hotel.

'No barber shops.' Adam winked. Craig's look was blank.

'You don't know what they do in the barber shops here?' Adam glanced around the atrium and made a clumsy wanking motion in the region of his crutch.

'The barbers?'

'Girls!'

'Just wait,' Craig warned. 'You'll get enough of that when you join the *Tribune*.'

'You know who recommended me for the tryout?' Adam was smiling demurely at his placemat. He seemed to have fallen in love with a breadstick. 'Ted Augenstein himself. He sent a telex from New York.'

'You know Ted?'

Adam's attitude said, Oh yes. From way back. The ramparts of Troy. Those thrilling nights with the press pool on the wine-dark seas. 'He remembered me from the chilli contest.'

'Who makes the decision?'

'Huh?'

'On the stringer's job. Who chooses?'

'Chris Smart.' Adam was suddenly wary.

'I thought Chris Smart despised Ted Augenstein.'

Adam, a breadstick protruding from his pursed lips, looked stricken.

Craig explained he was booked on a flight to Japan the following day and on to Korea the day after – news Adam accepted with signs of relief.

'I'm looking for a high-profile story from Taiwan. Something that will really grab them in New York. Something exclusive.'

'What about the reserves?'

'No economics.' Adam wrinkled his nose. 'I want something interesting. Like an arms scandal.'

'In Taiwan?'

'Or industrial pollution. Children crippled for life. Mothers holding them, pathetically twisted, in the bathtub.'

Craig stared at him.

'"People Power"?' Adam said, with a discernible flagging of spirit. 'Who are the leaders of the opposition?'

'You could always write about the Taiwanese version of *Cats*.'

'Okay,' Adam capitulated. 'How large are the reserves? What the hell do you do with reserves?'

The lights have been turned down in the atrium. The guests have crept their way to their rooms, carefully, avoiding the railings and refusing to look down or up. Soon everyone is asleep, except the terminally hopeful and horny – who take long attentive walks around the darkened block – and the sleepy staff. Two black cars pull up to the deserted hotel. Three men in crew-cuts rush into the lobby. They disappear through a door marked 'Private.' In Craig Kirkpatrick's room, the phone rings.

'This is the Taiwan Information Service.' The voice was oddly mechanical. 'You are invited to a special press conference for foreign correspondents – '

'It's late . . .' Craig fumbled with the bedside lamp.

'– report to our officer in the lobby in ten minutes. Transportation to the conference has been arranged. I repeat, this is the Taiwan Information Service. You are invited . . .'

Five minutes later, an exciting banging rained upon Craig's door.

'Right place at the right time!' exulted Adam Fendler, already fedoraed and with gaping fly in his baggy pants. 'I hope it's something real hot. Wouldn't the *Tribune* be flabbergasted? They'd probably fire Christopher Smart. "Who needs you," they'd say, "when we have a Fendler, who's always at the right place at the right time!" To tell you the truth, I've always considered him a snot. Him and his shirts.'

'Adam, it's probably about the reserves.'

'The reserves,' scoffed Adam. 'You and your reserves. I knew that story was a dud. Ha! A midnight press conference on the reserves! It's probably war. They're taking over the mainland! Anything's possible these days. Maybe *that's* what the reserves were being saved for!'

'That is one theory.'

'Really?'

'A joke, Adam.'

But Adam was irrepressible. In the elevator, he said, 'You were alone? How surprising!'

'I don't care for Chinese girls.'

'You too? I'm incredibly happy to hear that. All the other guys – all they can talk about is Thai girls, Filipino girls, Cathay stewardesses. I can't see anything in them whatsoever. I mean, they don't share any of our jokes, our culture, our television shows. Try explaining a *Saturday Night Live* routine to an Asian girl. "Quien Es Mas Macho?" Remember that one? I wish there were more American girls in Hong Kong. There was this girl at school, her name was Lydia – '

'Adam,' Craig interrupted. 'I didn't say I disliked Asian girls. I simply don't like Chinese girls. If you need to know, I prefer Japanese girls.'

'I guess that's understandable,' Adam said in a betrayed tone. 'You being . . .'

'Adam . . .'

In the lobby, a Taiwanese official barked at the two men. '*New York Tribune! World Business Journal!* Your car outside. We go. No more in this hotel.'

'How did you get my name?' Craig asked.

The officer motioned towards the front desk. 'They tell us the journalists.'

'And the accountants? I'm an accountant for the *World Business Journal*. I'm here on holiday. You want the accountants too?'

The officer consulted his list.

'Craig,' Adam hissed. 'You'll miss the – '

'You from the *World Business Journal?*' the officer interrupted. 'From newspaper?' Craig nodded.

'Car outside. Let's go. Our schedule.'

As they walked to the car, Adam said, 'Don't fuck with the Taiwanese, Craig. I've lived here. They'll eat you for – '

'I know, Adam.'

'With chopsticks.' Adam chuckled. 'An accountant! An accountant on his way to the biggest scoop of this year! Okay Mr Accountant. Get out your bean counter. 'Cause we're gonna hit a million tonight!'

The streets of maze-like Taipei are dark and, amazingly, empty. The black car zooms to the outskirts of the city and towards the hills to the north. Another black car is snaking around a more northerly hill, but too far ahead for Craig or Adam to see. Two more cars follow in their wake.

'Driver,' Craig barked, '*where* are we going?'

The driver pointed and said in a harsh, Chinese growl, 'Peitou.'

'Peitou!' Adam repeated wonderingly. 'That's far!'

'I know Peitou,' said Craig. 'Or I've heard of it from my father. The old resort areas. The red-light town. Where the Literary Club was. Dad took his famous photo of the GIs in the massage room. What is it now?'

Adam shrugged. 'I didn't think anyone went to Peitou anymore. Maybe Japanese sex tourists.'

'So why would the government hold a midnight press conference there?'

'Must be something *really* big!' Adam exulted.

The roads continue to wind and climb, until the car pulls up to an old-fashioned resort and disgorges its occupants. They scurry through the hotel's front door. We descend to look through the windows of a large room, a banquet hall. But we see nothing. The windows are blocked by something opaque, yet something lovely and shining. Something new and something odd.

Craig said, 'This must be a press conference Taiwan style.'

'Ever read *1984*?' asked Adam. 'These people *live* it.'

Uniformed guards were posted at all four corners of the banquet hall. The doors were also guarded. A folding table with a single chair had been placed at the front of the room. Waitresses were passing around Chinese tea. For some paranoid reason, the windows had been covered with aluminium foil.

'Do you have beer?' Craig asked.

'Don't get drunk,' Adam said. 'Or I'll end up writing your file.'

The waitress returned with a glass of warm local beer. Craig decided to break the news to Adam. 'It's Friday night, Adam.' He looked at the back of his blank wrist. 'I mean Saturday morning. What time is it? I don't have a paper for seventy hours. I don't have a deadline for forty-eight. I'm not planning to file on anything that goes on tonight, unless, as you predict, it is war.'

Adam looked at Craig aghast.

'War,' Craig concluded, 'declared from a hotel dining-hall in Peitou.'

'And you call yourself a newsman!' Adam looked at his watch. 'The *Morning Post* is gone to bed. But I still have hours until my *Tribune* deadline. Scoop city! What time do you think the telex operators start work at the hotel?'

The journalists began their ritual chatting. It was a thin crowd. All present, both the foreigners and the local Chinese, represented foreign newspapers and magazines. None could recall such a strange location for a press conference. The timing, however, was unsurprising: the Taiwanese government was renowned for its hysterical spasms of PR.

The main door burst open and a rush of people entered the room. Someone breathed instructions into a microphone and the journalists obediently took their seats. Bulky men placed two heavy parcels on the table at the front of the room. Government officials took their place along the sides of the banquet hall. There was a woman in uniform: a peculiar, mannish woman who barely looked Chinese.

'Welcome, members of the foreign press,' said a sing-song voice over the microphone. 'This is a special briefing for the foreign press. You have often complained about access to news and we have registered your complaints. In reaction, the Ministry has decided to give a special briefing to the foreign press on an important news development. I must stress: you foreign correspondents are getting this story before the local press. The government of Taiwan is grateful to your coverage in the past and this is the way we have decided to express that gratitude. The local press will be given a similar briefing at noon tomorrow at the Ministry of Information. I believe for many of you that time gap will be a considerable help in getting your story in your newspapers.'

'Fan-fucking-tastic,' whispered Adam. 'I file at 11:00. The *Post* isn't here, or the *LA Times*.' He looked at Craig. 'Only the *World Business Journal*.'

'Don't forget McLeans – that little Chinese girl. And the slobby guy from Knight-Ridder.'

'Knight-Ridder!' Adam muttered. 'Don't make me laugh!'

The doors opened once more, and a modest-looking man in a Mao suit walked into the room. He didn't look at the members of the press or the officials lining the wall. He seemed most impressed by the windows covered in aluminium foil. The mannish woman in the green uniform strode towards him and gave him a push towards the table in the front.

'Please refrain from photo-taking for the time being,' said the disembodied, amplified voice.

The man in the Mao suit seated himself at the table. He sat alone. After a few moments he gazed at his audience. His plain stare caused a collective wave of uncomfortable shifting. Then, with no warning, he placed his hands on one of the rectangular parcels before him, pulled a string and removed a cardboard cover. Underneath was a brilliant square bar of gold. The journalists' discomfort was replaced by a murmur of surprise. A greedy murmur: they wanted more. The man in the Mao suit unwrapped the second parcel and beneath it was a larger bar of gold, newer-looking and more rectangular than the first. The journalists were thrilled. Adam could barely stay seated. The mannish woman by the wall smiled a dangerous-looking smile.

The man in the Mao suit spoke into a venerable microphone. 'Good evening, ladies and gentlemen,' he said in highly-enunciated, accented English. 'Or should I say good night.' He looked towards the foil-covered windows.

'Try good morning,' wisecracked the slob from Knight-Ridder.

'Thank you for coming at such a late hour. I am from the People's

Republic of China. I am a defector.' He looked nervously to the officials at the back of the room. 'I am, I should say, a fighter for freedom, who has escaped the oppression of China for the freer atmosphere of the Republic of China.' He paused, to add thoughtfully: 'What we Chinese erroneously call the province of Taiwan.'

'Hot shit!' said Adam, slapping his open notebook.

'Where's the plane?' asked Knight-Ridder. 'We've got to see the plane!'

Adam nodded fulsomely. 'Yeah, the plane!'

Craig whispered, 'Wait a minute. Where are the wires? I've never seen a press conference without the wires.'

'Here are the details of my defection,' said the man at the microphone. 'I defected to the Republic of China on August eighteen, which was three days ago. I came across the Formosa Strait by hired junk. How I travelled to Fuchou from Peking, where I formerly lived, I will presently describe. I got out just in time. It has been, I think, almost three months since the events of June fourth and fifth. The massacre in Tienanmen Square.'

The journalists began to buzz.

'Is he one of the students?' Adam asked.

Knight-Ridder laughed sardonically. 'Ever seen a student fly a jet fighter?'

'Before me,' the man continued smoothly, 'as you can see, is a block of gold that I have been given by the government of the Republic of China as a reward for my defection.' He gestured to the newer, rectangular block of gold.

'This bar' – he held aloft the smaller, square block – 'is also mine. It is what made me defect in the first place, in a fashion. This block of gold was in my fireplace in Peking. It was disguised as a brick in the fireplace. The government of Taiwan is also allowing me to keep this block of gold.'

In his fireplace! Craig thought, pulling himself up from an apathetic slump.

'You can see,' the man said, 'the imperial crest. Right here.' His finger made a circle around a shallow depression on the top of the block. 'And you can see some scratches. These are the scratches my father made with a shovel when he showed me the gold. The gold brick in our fireplace. I wonder if my mother ever knew of it. Events moved too quickly afterwards. I never was able to ask.'

'What's going on here?' growled Knight-Ridder.

Adam looked at him, then at the defector, then at Craig. His mouth was ajar in awe and confusion.

Craig noticed something odd about the defector's hand. Several inches below his new, blue cuff, a third thumb extended from the ball joint of his right hand. In repose, the defector covered the thumb with his left hand. But when he gestured, it became noticeable. It had no joint and its tip was a stretched, pale colour.

'It's kind of interesting,' suggested Adam. Knight-Ridder blew air out of his cheeks.

'I am – I *was*,' said the man, 'Assistant Chief Librarian in the All-China Technical Library in Peking, English language sub-branch. I have a friend – I *had* a friend – an old schoolmate, who works in the English Periodicals section of the main Peking library. I have – *had* – another friend who, in turn, knows someone working as a tour guide for visiting foreign dignitaries. I would say I would not be here today without these friends.' The voice paused. 'Without my father. Without the movement of Tienanmen. Without the massacre of innocent people. Without the prospect of change in China. And without this.'

His deformed hand caressed the square gold block.

'My father brought me into the room one day in July. I thought he wanted to clean the hearth. He took a metal shovel and scraped at a few bricks. I looked down into the hearth and, in the very centre, I saw a small streak of yellow. What, I wondered, would glitter so prettily in our old fireplace? My father scraped again with the shovel. And there, with magical ease, was a second glint. Gold. The centre brick, the filthiest brick, was made of gold. The soot was so thick, believe me, it took us a while to remove the brick. And even longer to clean it.'

The journalists continued to shift uneasily.

'I don't really get it,' said Adam.

'The problem, of course, is that a brick of gold is of no use to a citizen of the People's Republic of China. The second problem was that a citizen of the People's Republic of China doesn't know – and can barely find out – the worth of such a brick anywhere else in the world. Take my word for it. We Chinese live differently than you Taiwanese.' The voice paused for a moment. 'And, of course, you people from the West.'

The man described the difficult quest for knowledge. What was the current price of gold on world markets? How did Western weights convert into Chinese? How heavy was the gold? His trickiest question: what would the gold buy in a foreign country?

'It was with these questions that I turned to my friends who had access to books and to foreigners. I found out about salaries and house prices. As it happens, a visiting party of American Negroes related very valuable information on how much money was needed to set up a restaurant business. I realized finally what I had presumed all along: that in America, and in most countries in the world, my gold would make me a rich man. In retrospect, I realize that my decision had been made the moment my father made the second scratch with his shovel that warm morning in Peking. I was being sent from China. I would leave my whole life behind: everything I had ever known and everything I had ever cared for.'

He told of the dramatic flight from Peking to Taiwan. The near captures. The difficulty of concealing the heavy gold bar. The nights it was nearly stolen as he slept.

'And that brings me here, to Taiwan, an escaped Chinaman with not one bar of gold but two. Lives are changed, I have learned. By gold, by a massacre, by political turmoil, by arrests. But consider how frightening it all is. A few days back I was Assistant Chief Librarian at a technical library. And now, a couple of gold scratches later, I am something else altogether. I, a plain Chinese librarian, who had always thought life to be a slow trudge uphill, finds his life transformed into a reckless downhill race with no brakes. I remain a bit scared, I admit.' He looked to the grim-faced officials. 'Call me the frightened fighter for freedom.'

Knight-Ridder sighed and clucked.

'This sucks,' said Adam. 'If there's a plane, I'll eat my hat.'

Craig straightened in his chair and shouted, 'Who is your father?'

The disembodied voice said, 'No questions, please.'

The mannish woman on the sidelines looked at her watch and then at the foil-covered windows. She made an affirmative motion to the rear of the room. The amplified voice amended its command.

'Questions will now be taken. Please approach the microphone. Please identify yourself and your news organization.'

Knight-Ridder leapt to the microphone and repeated Craig's question.

'My father is Chia Yu Bang,' the defector said. 'My name is Pao Yu.'

The hands of the Taiwanese journalists made hurried scratchings in notebooks. The officials on each side whispered to each other and smiled at the engrossed journalists.

'Who the fuck is Chia What's-his-name?' asked Adam.

'The nuclear physicist,' hissed Knight-Ridder.

'Who was purged last month,' said the Taiwanese girl from McLeans.

'Purged by Deng after Tienanmen,' Craig whispered. 'Zhao Ziyang's crony.'

Adam's eyes were wide. He fumbled frantically with his hat and his notebook. 'How do you spell it? Where are you staying, by the way? Is that near my hotel?'

Craig caught the eye of the dark-skinned woman in uniform on the sidelines. She smiled and raised her eyebrows, as if to say: 'Good story, huh?' Craig watched the journalists' frantic pencils and pens, their folded, grimy notebooks. He stared at the tin-foiled windows. *What time is it?*

The defector coughed nervously. He reached into an inner pocket of his Mao suit and withdrew a soiled notebook. 'This is something else you should know about. My father gave me this. It's something important. To me, to them, to China, to Taiwan.' He laid the notebook gingerly beside the gold bar. 'My father knew my life, our family's existence, was over in China, and he wanted to make sure I could establish myself in the West. No matter what happened. Even if I lost the gold.' He touched the gold bar, and then the notebook.

'These are details of the Chinese nuclear programme. My father said that if I lost his gold, I could sell these. The government of Taiwan, these gentlemen here' – he motioned around the room – 'has expressed great interest in this information.'

A murmur went up from the journalists. Adam Fendler gasped.

Craig shouted, 'Where did your father get the gold?'

The defector stared at him. His six-fingered hand was poised intimately on the gold block. It took him several moments to reply.

'I have no idea,' he said.

And then the journalists were standing, the strobes were flashing and the woman in uniform was looking anxiously at her watch. The blue-suited defector was pushed through a door by security men and officials, with nothing but the frantic flash of strobes to bid him farewell. He raised a hand in farewell and the strobes illuminated it. Did the cameras catch the sixth finger? Would it grace the front pages of various US newspapers? Or would that vestigial organ be air-brushed out by a meticulous photo researcher in New York or Brussels, who'd think it a transmission error? The journalists filed out of the hall and the hotel, where they were surprised to see a strong midmorning sun.

'Time is of the essence,' said Adam, snapping his fingers triumphantly. 'Let's get a fucking move on.'

A group of journalists piled into a black government car. There was no room for Craig. Adam stuck his head out of the window and called, 'Sorry man! Deadline cometh!'

Craig was approached by the dark woman with the dangerous smile. She strode up manfully. Craig saw she was chewing gum.

'Hi!' she had a strong American accent.

He nodded and smiled insincerely.

'You didn't identify yourself.'

'Nope.'

'Where are you from?'

'*World Business Journal.*'

She flipped through papers in a folder.

'You're not on the list.'

Craig didn't reply.

'You were picked up . . .'

'. . . the Lai Lai.'

'Did you just arrive today – I mean Friday – in Taipei?'

He nodded. 'Overland,' he added.

'Ah!' She closed her folder.

'From Puli.'

The remark made no impression on the woman.

'The geographic centre of Taiwan,' he explained.

Her blank look refused to thaw. Craig realized the woman wasn't Taiwanese.

'You better come inside,' she said, grasping his arm.

Craig heard a happy shout from Adam Fendler. 'Man, squeeze in!' He nestled between two photographers and waved to the woman as the car crunched its way down the gravel path. *What*, Craig wondered, *is a non-Taiwanese doing at a government press conference? In uniform, no less.*

The car snakes its way down the driveway and around a hairpin turn, gaining the road to Taipei. We are airborne again, and our last sight is an angry, mannish woman, crunching her way across a gravel driveway and darting into the shabby, rustic hotel. The sun is climbing in the sky, and so are we: Peitou becomes a forest of tall green treetops, with a colourless plain to its south, followed by a belt of smog and grey concrete. We zoom over the city, the cars approaching it, pass it entirely, over the geographical centre of Taiwan, the entire island, and through to the steely waters of the South China Sea, which rapidly turn cobalt, and then aquamarine, and then as clear and green as a pool in Eden. The Java Sea. The clouds of North Asia, its winds and rain, are far gone. We are in the tropics. We are in the land of sarongs, cloves and mysterious shadow-plays. Jakarta looms, and another hotel, another atrium, another perilous balcony, another hotel-room door, another pair of flimsy curtains pulled against the sun for the benefit of a supposedly jet-lagged guest, another disturbing phone call, but a special one. An anticipated one. A crucial one.

'Ted,' said the long-distance voice. 'I'm sorry to bother you.'

'It's all right. I was just about to wake up anyway.' Ted Augenstein was, in fact, sitting by the window before several pots of depleted tea. 'I have to get ready for our interview.' He mimicked a yawn.

The voice described a crisis. Deadline indeed cameth. 'And Ted, we just got the loopiest story from your stringer, Fendler, in Taiwan.'

'Adam.'

'Yeah,' said the voice. 'Anyway, the story is about some kind of defector but it's hard to say . . . it's a pretty fucked-up piece of work.'

'What are the wires reporting?'

'That's the odd thing. There's nothing on the wires at all.'

'What does Fendler say? Did you call Taipei?'

'He says they weren't at the press conference. He says we've got to run the story or we'll lose a big scoop.'

'Kill it,' Ted said. He drained his last half-inch of tea.

There was a silence, broken only by the celestial sounds of long-distance phone lines. 'Kill it? I don't think that's – '

'Kill the story,' Ted repeated. 'We can't rely on that guy.'

'But Ted, he has a point. I mean, it *was* a government press conference.'

'Kill the story, Peter.'

'Jesus, Ted, the only story I've got is Fullman's 1992 piece, and it's not big enough for the hole. And it's lousy.'

Ted put down his teacup with painstaking gentleness. His were the slow motions of a man with an idea. 'How much of a gap do you have?'

He heard the sound of counting over the line.

'About five paras.'

'Run Fendler in five paras.'

'But that's nothing! This is a big kind of story, I mean, if it's true.'

'It's okay. We'll be covered if it turns into something. Just run him short.'

'. . . okay, but I'll have to disembowel . . .'

'Disembowel. And run a byline.'

'A byline on five paras? Ted, you've got to be kidding! And deadline – '

Ted replaced the phone in its cradle and went to pour himself another cup of tea. But all the pots were long empty. He spoke aloud to his empty hotel room:

'Five paras. With byline.' He stood and prepared to dress. He had showered hours before, but he felt soaked under his arms. He decided to shower again.

The hotel room is far below us. Just another hotel room, another coffee shop with rubbery cutlets, another bar, another pompous structure in cement and marble, another strange city, another assignment. How sad that he remains stuck down there on the ground, mired in the everyday of traffic jams and interviews. How much better to leave the mundane behind, to abandon facts and figures and spellings and quotes from 'well-informed' diplomats, to climb skyward. This is, in fact, something he knows: How much more buoyant life is among the clouds!

WELCOME BACK TO THE RAT'S NEST

I

'Inspiration strikes!' cried Anton Vavasour. 'Mamasan – bring me some paper!'

'*Hai! Wakarimashita!*' yelled the mamasan. The call was repeated by her winsome helper, Kikusan, who dived beneath the bar in search of paper.

'I have high hopes for my play,' Vavasour continued. 'And you'll appreciate the setting. It's Ermita. Your Ermita. That quaint little slum you call home.'

Vavasour's companion, a dark-skinned young man of unusual handsomeness, thoughtfully smoked a cigarette.

Kikusan found some paper, which she passed to Mamasan. Mamasan presented it to Vavasour. He nodded thankfully and said loudly, 'Pen!'

'*Hai! Boru-pen chotto matte!*' called Mama, with a meaningful look in Kikusan's direction. Once again, Kiku dived beneath the counter.

'Ermita!' continued Vavasour in an elegiac tone. 'I should say our Ermita. It was love at first sight, wasn't it?'

The boy exhaled, and in a soft, deep voice, said, 'Everyone's horny.'

'*Boru-pen dozo,*' declared Mama, handing it over with ritual politeness.

'Wonderful woman!' reciprocated Vavasour, with a wink at his companion. He struggled to balance his bulk on one of Mamasan's absurdly tiny stools.

'One thousand thanks, Mama. And two beers. *Kudasai*.' He said the Japanese word with outrageous self-satisfaction and gave Mama his pusiest smile.

'*Hai!*' she hollered, in a subdued tone.

'Perhaps I'll dedicate the play to you,' Vavasour continued in an oily voice. '"To Rudy. With Love and Tetracycline."' His wide, pasty face pursed itself into an ostentatious kiss.

'I told you,' said the young man, 'I want to be called "Rod."'

'You Filipinos,' Vavasour sighed. 'Always fiddling with your identities. But listen up. I've modelled the play's setting on your bar. I can't decide whether to leave it gay or transform it into a straight bar. It depends more than anything else on the marketability. Maybe a "mixed" bar – could there be such a thing? Perhaps I can leave it to the director. He can add pregnancies, abortions, irresponsible husbands who pick up diseases – the *family* things. I only insist the violence remains, gay or straight.'

The Filipino shrugged.

'So far I'm short on dialogue but I have a wonderful title. Are you ready to hear it? I'm calling the play: *Welcome Back to the Spider's Web!* You like it?'

'The Spider's Web?'

'Dear boy,' said the fat man, 'no one would believe in a brothel actually called "The Rat's Nest." They'd think me heavy-handed. Alternatively, I could call it *It's Great to be Back at the Spider's Web*. That has a cheery American sound. Or just: *The Spider's Web*, but that sounds so dire, so thematic. And I'm planning a comedy.'

The boy toyed with his cigarette.

'I have plans for a wonderful opening monologue by my foreigner character, my narrator,' said Vavasour. 'Imagine the set: the Rat's Nest in all its tawdriness, circa eleven a.m. Imagine the boys in corners – arms, tails, snouts intertwined. They are asleep. Trade hasn't begun. One boy is brushing his teeth in a sink at the back, spitting and making that loud hokking sound so beloved in your country. The Song of Manila!' Vavasour paused. 'I think there was a sink at the back of the Rat's Nest.'

'People pissed in it,' Rudy said.

'I'll remember that.'

'. . . the boys *and* the customers . . .'

Vavasour, the creator, nodded uneasily.

'. . . and it was never cleaned . . .'

'Okay, okay, enough,' he grimaced. 'Anyway, my narrator, dressed in a white linen suit and a Madras plaid shirt, strides downstage. He's a big man; not a stylishly thin type. I find them so *unsimpatico*. I picture him looking a bit like our friend E. G. Augenstein. He says, with no introduction whatsoever: *"There is rot at the heart of this city. A rot that makes one contract like no tropical sun . . ."*'

'Get them laughing early,' said the Filipino.

'That's what I adore about you, Rudy,' Vavasour oozed, leaning over and slapping the man's face tartly. 'You were the only Rat's Nest boy with even the hint of a sense of humour. That's why you're here with me today.'

'I was the best-looking,' said Rudy. 'And remember: "Rod."'

'You've interrupted the monologue.' Vavasour pulled himself erect, fluttered his eyes, and began anew. '"*. . . that makes you contract like no tropical sun. One feels it on the bayside boulevard with its beggars and baying dogs; in the obscene restaurants with their fat chairs and starving troubadours in Spanish costumes; in the concrete caverns of the business district, where secretaries earn their living by selling smuggled American peanut butter from under their desk. One feels it all day long, every day. Until night comes. And then, as the famous Manila Bay sunset turns labial red, one senses a strange relief. Rotten Manila is made bearable by night. The darkness covers the stench. And to obscure the darkness, there is . . . dare I say the delightful word? . . . there is light!"* The narrator lifts his arms of linen and the bar, which has gone completely dark during his monologue, blazes into life. The boys are awake and stroking customers' hands. Two are wearing G-strings and dancing in cages behind the bar. Another is totally nude, doing his "macho dance" with a large hard-on. (The scene will be short, for you, my boy, know how difficult it is to sustain an erection while disco dancing.)

'The narrator intones: "*Ladies and Gentlemen: Welcome Back to the Spider's Nest!*"'

'*Hai! Hai!*' Mama was refilling the beer glasses.

'*Hai domo!*' replied Vavasour magnificently, excited by his recitation.

Rudy yawned.

'And how about this scene, dull boy? It takes place upstairs in one of the cubicles. The cubicles, by the way, will hover above the main set. *Comprendes?* They'll hover right above the bar. Action will take place on two levels simultaneously.'

'Just like the real Rat's Nest.'

'Life imitates art,' Vavasour said astringently. 'Anyway, it's another monologue. The window of one cubicle is thrown open to the street. A boy stands in the window. At the proscenium I'll have beggars and flower girls, representing the life going by on M. H. Del Pilar. The boy is naked. No hiding of the bush. I despise that convention on stage. It lacks artistic integrity. His name is, let's say, "Rudy." No – *"Rod."* Standing there, utterly exposed, "Rod" tells the tale of his life. Starting with his seduction at the age of eleven. In a small room at the top of his house with a window overlooking the path leading to the front door. The only entrance to the house. His seduction by his own grandfather.'

Vavasour looked to his emotionless companion. 'Sounds familiar?'

Rudy smoked and nodded.

'Want to send tickets to Grandpa in President Roxas City?'

Rudy shrugged. 'Everyone's horny.'

'A philosopher!' Vavasour proclaimed. 'Mamasan!'

'Hai!' she shrieked.

'I want you to meet one of the great philosophers of his time and, in particular, his place. The Philippine Sartre. The Little Brown Nietzsche.'

'Hai! Hai!'

'One more beer, Mama, *kudasai* . . .'

'Hai! Hai! Hai! . . .'

'. . . and turn on that monitor. Let's look at the airport board.' Vavasour passed his hand over his shiny head. 'When I get to Hong Kong, I'm going to do something about my hair.'

'Your hair?'

'My *head*, okay? Look, there – both planes landed more than an hour ago!'

As if on cue, the door to the bar rattled angrily and slid open. Mamasan and Kiku sent up wails of greeting. The mannish woman with the dangerous smile ducked her head in.

'I'm here!' she bellowed. 'Has he come yet?'

'No,' called Vavasour.

'Hello Mama! Hello Kiku! Where's Fumi-chan?'

'Jean,' Vavasour said in a disgusted tone, 'wherever did you find this dump?'

'Food, Mama. Flying always makes me hungry.' She relieved

herself of several carry-on bags. 'Hey – did you see that moon outside? It looks like noontime. What's the matter, Anton? Don't you like Mamasan's place?'

Vavasour sighed heavily. 'Jean, Mamasan, despite her undeniable charm and tireless vocabulary' – he bowed in her direction and smiled – 'must run the most boring place in Japan.'

'Not usually,' said the woman. 'Normally this place is packed on Saturdays. Often there's a little cabaret.'

'Jean, you know how carefully I choose the sites of my rendezvous with Mr Augenstein. The Calcutta YMCA – you should have seen his expression! This time I proposed a most squalid little steamroom in Seoul. Near the station. Anything goes, and I mean *anything*. But he'd go no further than Japan. And this' – he gestured contemptuously around him – 'is the best you could come up with?'

'Anton, Sodom and Gomorrah don't have a franchise in Narita City yet.' She smiled and indicated Vavasour's sullen companion. 'And they're certainly not ready for hiring.'

She addressed Rudy. *'Filipino ka ba?'*

Rudy nodded.

'Ilongo?'

He raised his eyebrows. The Philippine affirmative.

'What's your family name?'

He stared at her for a moment. 'Fuck off,' he said.

'Charmer,' murmured Jean. 'Another one of your butterflies?'

'Business associate,' Vavasour answered.

'Looks like a professional.'

'And he works damn cheap!' yelled Vavasour, jumping up from his stool and throwing up his arms. Jean joined him and the two embraced and did a gay dance in the middle of the bar.

'That's what we could use, Mama, some music! Let's celebrate! Let's celebrate a job well done!'

'Hai! Hai!'

Saccharine Japanese bar music filled the small room.

'It *did* go well?' Vavasour held Jean at arms' distance.

'I told you on the phone.'

'The Claw didn't blow it?'

'I told you, Anton, he would do well. He looked the part. He read his lines perfectly. He is Chinese, after all.'

'Born in downtown Manila!'

'A chink's a chink.'

'Amazing,' replied Vavasour abstractedly. 'Maybe there's something in it: "Hire the handicapped."' The two danced a few steps, but the dull Japanese music defeated them. They returned to their stools.

'You're sure the journalists were satisfied?'

'The hotel telex operators were working full out by ten a.m. When I left at noon they were still sending.'

'Our friend in the hat?'

'First back to town. I saw to it. His telex was sent out. I xeroxed it.' She patted her handbag. 'Everything went like clockwork.' She lifted a frosted beerglass to her lips and drank greedily. 'He does not, however, seem to know the proper usages of "which" and "that."'

'No one seemed at all suspicious? We *must* have missed something: used some improper term, got our Chinese cities mixed up . . .'

Jean shook her head. "You don't know journalists,' she said dismissively. "And I do. They're like dogs with bones when they smell a story. And it takes them ages to realize that what they have in their mouth is not a bone but a boner.'

'Jean!' said Vavasour.

'The story, *our* story, is right now being set in print in the US. Trust me. I can almost see the headlines.'

'How incredibly easy!'

'I beg your pardon!'

'I take it back,' said Vavasour, his large head erect. 'What a triumph! What a feat of human ingenuity! If only the whole story could someday be told!'

'Which it will . . .'

'. . . when the price is right!'

'May I go back to the hotel?' interrupted Rudy.

'Go!' commanded Vavasour. 'Shoo! Leave the elders to their drinks!' He pushed money across the bar. 'I'll call.' Rudy stood to leave and Jean's eyes followed him. She was still watching him as he disappeared through the door.

'Wow!' she said. 'He looked puny sitting down. But he's an Adonis!'

'When God made the Filipinos,' Vavasour said, 'he did some of his best work . . .'

'Flatterer!'

'Present company excluded.'

The two traded documents and letters. Vavasour made the motions of tearing up a particular envelope.

'Tut tut,' she warned.

'I know,' he said. 'I just can't abide that dull little Mr Lee. "US dollah. US dollah."'

'What do you care? They aren't your dollars.'

Vavasour laughed theatrically. 'Of course they're not. Until I fail to distribute them. *Then* they are.'

'Here's the uniform,' she said, proferring a small parcel. 'I don't know if it was a good idea. I stood out. Oh, an unexpected journalist showed up. From the *World Business Journal*. I don't know how he got there. Tagged along with someone, I guess.'

'The *World Business Journal*. That's a stock market paper. What does it care about China?'

'They're in China,' Jean shrugged. 'We even have one in Manila.' She looked at her watch. 'Anton, I have to get going. I have other commitments.'

'Tonight?'

'Departing twenty-three hundred.'

'Speeding down to our gun-toting guerrillas in Mindanao?' Vavasour asked mockingly. 'I saw the *Newsweek* cover story.'

'*Newsweek* treats us well. So we give them the greatest access. They can't get enough of our guerrillas.'

'They looked so handsome and serious, plodding through the canefields, oppression pouring from every ripped seam,' Vavasour said. 'Or are you off to the generals this time? How I've always admired your commitment to principles.'

'I do have principles, Anton,' she said with a harsh smile. 'But I also have a living to make.' The smile failed to fade from her mannish face. 'Bills. Commitments . . .'

'It's coming,' Vavasour said dismissively. 'Any minute, in fact. You'll be paid as usual . . .'

'. . . two months late . . .'

'. . . and in pesos!' roared Vavasour, enormously pleased with his old joke. 'Mama! Cut this Japanese crap. Let's have some Western music.'

'*Hai!*'

The first notes froze Anton Vavasour in a posture of mock surprise. 'Sweet Jesus!' he cried. 'When you ask Mama for Western, you get Western!' He jumped up from his stool and started to sing, his hands on his huge hips. His massive bulk, dressed in an enormous, seersucker pants-suit outfit, nearly filled the entire bar. His globelike head bobbed with the music. *'I'm An Old Cowhand . . .'* he sang voluptuously, *'. . . from the Rio Grande . . .'*

'I just love the Japanese,' he said, wiping his greasy brow as he returned to his seat. 'And their choice plunderings of international culture!'

Vavasour panted and, with a tenting motion, pulled the damp seersucker away from his chest several times. A pensive look crossed his face. 'Jean . . .'

'I can't sing, Anton. My voice is like a rusted machine. Mama's always game . . .'

'No,' he said, 'I was just thinking about that *Newsweek* story. You've intrigued me. What if that journalist *hadn't* written the story the way he was supposed to? The way you wanted it written. What if he had written a negative story after you had given him access? How would you have reacted?'

'It depends on so many . . .'

'What I mean is: would you have had him killed?'

The door rattled and slid open. The first thing to appear through the door was a large, square parcel, wrapped in brown paper. Following it came Ted Augenstein, bowing to clear the low doorway.

Greetings were called from the Japanese ladies. Vavasour rose.

'Welcome,' he told Ted in a formal tone. 'To the Spider's Web.'

'Thank you,' Ted replied. 'Is that the name of this place? How uninviting.' He placed the parcel carefully on the counter and accepted Vavasour's offer of a drink. 'Scotch, please. Water. *O-mizu.* I didn't know Narita had bars.' Ted removed his raincoat and brushed from it a soft mist. He smoothed his hair. 'But it must. The locals . . .'

'This is an international hub,' proclaimed Vavasour. 'I am fresh in from Hong Kong. She's just arrived from Taipei. And you, Mr Augenstein?'

'Straight from Jakarta. We interviewed the president this afternoon.'

'I hope you gave him my regards,' Vavasour said. 'The corrupt bastard.'

'I fly back in the morning. The timing couldn't have been better.' He looked at Vavasour. 'That's why I had to say no to Seoul. It's an official trip this time. Totally accountable.'

Vavasour smiled.

'Did you see that giant moon outside?' Ted asked. 'You've been waiting long . . . ?'

'We've been watching your progress, haven't we?' Vavasour pointed to the monitor showing the airport's arrival board.

'Northwest eighteen arrived at nine thirty-five, twenty minutes behind schedule. I gave you forty minutes to do the needful at the airport, and ten minutes to make it here.'

'Do the needful?' asked Jean.

'Mr Augenstein, my colleague, Jean Yulo. Jean – meet the *New York Tribune*.'

Ted bowed gravely. 'Of *the* Yulo family?' he asked.

'No.'

'Jean directed the press conference,' Vavasour explained. 'And you did a fine job, Jean dear.'

'It went well?'

Jean nodded and handed Ted a long, taped-together Xerox. He murmured appreciatively, started to read and then stopped. He placed the back of his hand to his forehead. 'I think I'm getting a cold. It's just come on.'

'Flying,' commented Jean. 'The defences are weakened. And you get so ravenous!'

'I have a fever.'

'Fever?' cried Vavasour ebulliently. 'Fever! That's what we could use: some fever. Mama! "Fever" *kudasai!*'

'*Hai! Wakarimashita!*'

'Ask the Japanese for the simplest things,' Vavasour said, 'and they wail like they've been punched in the stomach.'

From the stereo roared a saucy, female voice: '*You Give Me Fever!*'

'The magnificent Peggy Lee!' exulted Vavasour. He jumped up and started to twitch his enormous striped hips.

Jean pulled him back to his stool. 'Anton,' she scolded, 'sometimes you go too far.' She threw her chin in the direction of Ted, who was nodding at the Xeroxed telex.

Vavasour said, 'You were damned lucky with that purge last month. A nuclear physicist's son – much more credible than your first suggestion. So much harder to check on short notice.'

Ted grunted and continued to read the lengthy telex.

'I think, Mr Augenstein, your fish is hooked.'

'You should teach your reporters the distinction between "which" and "that,"' said Jean.

'Newspaperwoman by training, Miss Yulo?'

'I write a little,' she said. 'But my occupation is PR. I work freelance.'

'Call it hit and run public relations,' said Vavasour. 'Slash and burn PR. Guerrilla PR, by guerrillas and for guerrillas – '

'Shut up, Anton,' she said. 'My main work, Mr Augenstein, is bribery. I don't think that will shock you.'

'And bribe reduction,' added Vavasour. 'Don't forget that, Jean. Very important.'

'It's a major part of doing business in Southeast Asia. I think you know that quite well. The little project we've just completed: what was it but a round of bribery?' She gathered together her carry-on bags. 'I'd love to see this treasure' – she patted the box on the counter – 'that I've heard so much about but I'm sure it's all wrapped up, and opening it . . .'

'Yes,' Ted said.

'I have a plane waiting. I'm sure Anton can be relied on to do . . .'

'. . . the needful,' Vavasour suggested.

'Au revoir, Anton. Send me my cheque this week.' The sliding door rattled and she was gone.

'She ran the conference?'

'I thought it wiser for me to be absent. She's extremely efficient. Ruthlessly so. She takes no shit whatsoever, especially from bureaucrats. I, by contrast, am hopeless in the face of authority. Fall entirely to pieces. I always feel like reaching for my gun.' He patted his clutchbag.

As is often the case with important meetings long anticipated, the dealings between Ted and Vavasour took a surprisingly short time to accomplish. A few customers entered the bar and the scene they saw was an unusual one: two bulky foreigners exchanging slips of paper and talking in low, confidential tones. Vavasour was surprised at the sombre fervour which Ted applied to what was, in essence, a frivolous project. *He has done as much as an individual can to bring credit to his newspaper and himself,* Vavasour thought. *Now he's applying the same dedication to the opposite goal.* He wanted to laugh aloud.

'Is it possible to get a more detailed accounting of these expenses?' Ted asked.

'I'll forgo the customary comment about honour among conspirators, Mr Augenstein.' Ted smiled an obligatory smile.

'Mr Augenstein, why do you think I request payment in these' – he patted the box on the bar – 'in lieu of cash?' Ted shook his head.

'You see, Mr Augenstein, you have antiques. You have an antiques appraiser. And you think you know the value of these pieces. You think you know how much you are spending on this little project of yours. And you are willing to spend that much. Now you ask me to show you receipts. The receipts, of course, will add up to the amount your appraiser scribbled on a piece of paper one rainy afternoon in midtown Manhattan.'

'He's downtown.'

'But you are being a remarkable ass for someone who has spent much time in this part of the world. The value of your porcelains shifts depending on where they are sold. On who purchases them. A wise man or a fool. An honest man or a crook. A man with clean money or dirty. There are many more factors than you and your appraiser appreciate. The simple fact, Mr Augenstein, is that you don't know how much I will get for this vase. You have no right to know. It's my risk, my profit. It makes no sense for you to request receipts. We've made a deal. Let's stick with it.'

Ted placed his hand against his forehead. 'I'm feeling awful . . .'

'Which hotel . . . ?'

'The Nikko.'

'Mamasan,' Vavasour bellowed, 'another round and – '

'No,' said Ted. 'I'm feeling . . .'

Ted used his fever as an excuse. He referred to a few outstanding details. He promised Vavasour a letter from New York. He gathered his belongings, except for the square box he had arrived with, and exited.

As Mamasan's door shut with a startling bang, Vavasour rubbed his hands together diabolically. 'Act Two,' he said to himself. 'Which I have entitled: "The Mask Slips."'

Mama dialled and passed the receiver to Vavasour. As he waited, he thought of the steamroom in Seoul and the dramatics that had been sacrificed. He imagined Ted Augenstein, with his perfect, honey-coloured hair, neck-deep in the communal bath as an unexpected scrotum descended slowly, seductively, on his outstretched foot.

'He's at the Nikko,' Vavasour instructed Rudy. 'He's wearing a blue silk blazer and khaki pants. No tie. He has a pocketwatch on a gold chain. You can't miss him. Check all the hotel's restaurants. You have money. Go *now!*'

Vavasour ordered more beer. 'Did you like my friend, Mama?'

'*Hai!*'

'Truly? Did you find Mr Augenstein a handsome man? Or merely *simpatico?*'

He lifted the square box a few times, as if its weight alone could disclose the beauty or value of the vase within. All the while he talked to himself.

'Perhaps my play needs an innocent. A *simpatico* innocent, stumbling unawares into the Spider's Web. How do I get him inside?' He rubbed his hands. 'He'll have to come in on his own. Yes, he will. But I have great ideas for him once he's inside.' He pulled the paper and pen towards him and began to scribble.

2

Fever, jet lag and sixteen hours of intermittent scotches combined to disorient Ted Augenstein. He had unusual difficulty deciding what to eat for dinner, and there was some confusion with the waitress over which courses he could order with his airline coupon. Annoyed and harassed, he settled on 'Spaghetti Vongole,' and when the pale, watery pasta was placed before him, he ordered it away and demanded a steak. This caused more confusion but it cleared his mind and revived his spirits. He mulled over the interview with Vavasour and the report of the successful press conference in Peitou. He mused nostalgically on his precious, surrendered vase. And with buoyancy, he daydreamed about life after the *New York Tribune*. He imagined an existence far removed from the hideous parody of life that transpired in lower Manhattan. He luxuriated in the idea of escape from sisters, aerobics, humorous messages on telephone answering machines, 'addictive personalities,' vulgar talk-show hosts and hostesses, Bruce Willis, 'blackened' food, Manhattan's ostentatious tolerance of blacks, burglaries and AIDS patients, tuition chatter, doltish cab drivers, Vuarnet sunglasses, tasteless Thai food, skirts and running shoes, *Vanity Fair* sensibilities and the dutifully insipid opinions of Michiko Kakutani. He foresaw renewal abroad in a life centred about an exquisite apartment in Harajuku, or behind walls off a busy Bangkok street. Or at the bottom of a brilliantly moonlit rain forest.

Halfway through his toughened 'sizzling' steak, Ted found a young man gazing at him from an adjacent table. He was an unusually handsome man with a large, sculpted face and soft, olive-coloured skin. He was clean-shaven and his T-shirt read: *If Found, Return Immediately To The Rat's Nest*. His mossy brown eyes were the magnetic kind, and they were directed at Ted. He toyed with a cup of coffee.

Ted unfolded his *International Herald Tribune*. After a few moments, he found the man gazing at him again. Ted played the game one plays in foreign countries: staring at a stranger for intervals that would be unacceptable in one's own land. He wondered if the man would ask him for a hand-out, perhaps for the airport taxi.

'I like your nose,' the man said to Ted.

'Thank you,' said Ted, amused by the comment. He tried briefly, but failed, to picture his own nose.

'It's a perfect nose,' the young man said. 'Beautiful.'

'I try to keep it in shape,' Ted joked, unconsciously smoothing his hair.

'Asian noses are flat,' the man said. He ran a finger around his own nose. 'American?'

'Yes.'

'America is Number One.'

Ted considered replying, 'It's our noses,' but decided to cut short the absurd encounter. He nodded amiably and returned to his newspaper.

'You have a family?'

Ted shook his head.

'Not married?'

'No.'

'How old are you?'

Ted replied.

'Not *so* old,' said the stranger. 'Where do you stay in America?'

Ted knew Asians were disappointed with Americans who didn't come from New York. He replied, 'The Big Apple.'

The man's next remark, Ted predicted, would concern his relatives in New Jersey or Long Island. All Asians had them, Filipinos in particular. And this young man was unmistakably Filipino, with that extraordinary forwardness, the unabashed passion for America, those magnetic eyes.

'I love New York,' the man continued. 'I have – '

' – relatives . . .'

'No,' said the man strongly. 'I have *friends* in New York. No relatives. All my relatives are in the Philippines. In the province.' His tone was unfond.

'Filipino friends?'

The man scowled harshly. 'I hate Filipinos. They'll always lie and cheat. Americans are the best friends. I have twelve friends in New York.'

'Twelve?'

'Yes,' he said. 'One is a priest. Father Mallory. In Stoneybrook. You know him?'

Ted shook his head.

'I have a picture,' the man said. He rooted in his wallet and produced a creased snapshot of an overweight American man in a bathing suit by a swimming pool.

'He's a priest?'

'I have seven friends in California. One in Chicago.' (He pronounced it with a hard 'ch.') 'I also have friends in Germany and England and New Zealand. But Americans are Number One.'

Ted lowered his paper and looked at his watch. 'I have a call to make. A call to New York.' Ted smiled. 'You'll have to excuse me, it was nice, good luck . . .'

'Let's go,' said the man. 'Waitress. *Waitress!*'

'She's coming,' Ted said. 'Be patient . . .'

'*Waitress!*' called the man. '*Waitress!*'

Alarmed by the sudden shouting, the Japanese waitress hurried over.

'Check,' said the Filipino imperiously. The waitress pointed to the bill, nestled in its plastic container on the table, Japanese-style.

The man removed his own bill and then reached over and took Ted's.

'No!' cried Ted.

'C'mon,' said the man, pulling notes from his jeans pocket.

'No!' Ted continued. 'Please. There's no – '

'You're my friend,' said the Filipino. 'I pay.'

'Please,' said Ted. 'My company – '

'*I* will pay.'

'This is absurd,' said Ted.

'Then will you join me in a beer?'

'Yes,' said Ted. 'Fine. That's fine.' The Filipino relinquished the tab and, in a loud voice, called the waitress anew.

'Two beers,' he said.

'But I have this call – '

'Okay,' said the man. He looked at the waitress. 'No beers. Forget it.' And he stood up.

Ted also stood up, took both his bill and the young man's, and proceeded to the cashier. The boy didn't object. Nor did he thank Ted as they walked from the restaurant to the elevators.

Ted asked him, 'Are you in transit?'

The man nodded.

'Where are you going?'

The boy shrugged.

'You don't know where you're going?'

'Hong Kong.'

'Are you working there . . .'

The man nodded ambiguously.

'. . . or in the Philippines?'

The boy looked at Ted and sighed.

'Well?' Ted asked.

'I'll be a houseboy in Hong Kong.'

As the elevator doors opened, Ted wondered to himself: *What's a houseboy doing in Narita?*

Ted pressed the button marked '5' and asked the man:

'Which floor?'

The man said, 'I'm not staying in this hotel.'

He stood across the elevator from Ted, his arms folded on his broad chest. Ted noticed for the first time his magnificent physique.

'Where *are* you staying?'

He gestured with his chin. 'The Holiday Inn.'

The two men stared at each other across the elevator.

'What are you doing?' Ted asked.

The man smiled.

From outside the elevator came the muted sound of a bell. The lights above the doors showed the elevator was stopping at the fourth floor.

The Filipino looked quickly at the doors. The elevator slowed. He stared hard at Ted.

'I want to embrace you.' His voice was soft and deep. He unfolded his arms and made a praying gesture with his brown hands.

The doors slid open soundlessly. A hotel employee entered the elevator, bowed politely to Ted and the boy, pressed a button and bowed once more.

Ted averted his gaze from the Filipino. As the elevator neared his floor, sounding another muted tone, he wondered whether the boy would dare follow him into the corridor. But his worry was unfounded. Ted escaped the elevator and glanced back to see the boy staring sadly. The hotel employee bowed and muttered Japanese pleasantries. The boy pointed downwards and formed a word with his mouth: *Lobby*. He made the imploring gesture with his folded hands. The doors slid shut. Ted's heart raced and his pulses pounded. He had trouble concentrating as he traversed the dim hotel corridor and he mistakenly passed his room.

The phone was ringing when Ted entered. He recognized the piquant New York accent of Florence, amplified by a satellite echo. Florence assured him that all was well in New York, apart from a minor crisis with the computer system, which had affected deadlines. Ted inquired about some European stories and certain reporters in the Middle East. Finally he asked: 'How about Taiwan? Anything more about that defector?'

'Nothing,' Florence said. And with a pleasant series of high-pitched beeps the connection was severed.

Ted couldn't decide whether the hotel room was too warm or his fever was rising. He waited with impatience for Florence to call him back. When the call didn't come, he wondered if she realized, or cared, that the connection had been cut. Then, to calm himself, he turned to the television, but it took several minutes of unwilling concentration to read its instructions, find a channel with an English soundtrack, and discern the knob that transformed the guttural Japanese to English. The movie was *Bye Bye Birdie*.

Ted fell asleep swiftly, but he suffered a thin sleep disturbed by a succession of unpleasant and feverish dreams. At first, he dreamed he was in a Japanese jail. Then his traditional erotic fantasies, which he summoned to stimulate himself, were replayed in his mind with alterations. In most of the dreams, the object of desire was transformed into a well-built Filipino boy with wet eyes and a distinct signature line: 'I want to embrace you.' One dream featured Vavasour's Malaysian boyfriend Ramse removing his satin gym shorts. An erection further troubled Ted's sleep. He dreamt of weird scenes at the paper: of Abe ripping up telexes in the newsroom and Florence standing on a desk shouting obscenities. He dreamt of a loud banging sound and that voice, once again, pleading in its musical Philippine accent: 'Open the door, Ted Augenstein. Let me in. Please.' But the door was locked in a strange way and wouldn't open. At one point he awoke to find his pillow drenched in fever's sweat. He dreamed of his mother, which always upset him, and he had the recurring dream in which his teeth exploded like overcooked sausages. The voice returned to him, like moonlight shining in through a window, coming again through the door. 'Ted! It's me! Open the door! Do I have to get a key from the roomboy?'

Ted awoke so many times during the night that he was able to recall, the following morning, many of the dreams in disturbing detail.

3

Craig Kirkpatrick descended from the rooftop Japanese restaurant. He too had thrown away his coupon to purchase, on company money, a superior and absurdly expensive dinner. His *Herald Tribune* had disappointed him: it had no news on the Chinese defector. But Craig's thoughts quickly shifted. The unique sensation of being back in Japan – discernible at a mere airport hotel – had brought his thoughts back to Aya. Even the sight of the red, yellow and blue public telephones brought him pain. He knew he could not stride to one, as he once could, deposit some coins and talk to her.

On his way to his room, Craig saw a well-built young man banging gently on a door, making ardent entreaties to someone inside. 'Ted, it's me,' called the man in accented English, 'open the door!' Craig tried to avert his eyes. He mused on the commonly-accepted notion that handsome men always turned out to be gay, and wondered if this was a mystical vindication of the gay life or an ironic curse inflicted on the overly-handsome. He reflected on the old concept of gay names, like Bruce, and how quickly it had gone out of fashion. Certainly Ted was as heterosexual a name as one could choose for a boychild. In his room, he debated writing yet another letter to Aya, which would either be sent back or go unanswered. Instead, he flicked on the television set and giggled through a broadcast of *Bye Bye Birdie* dubbed into Japanese.

4

Anton Vavasour was drunk, singing and dancing with abandon. His seersucker shirt showed dark triangles of sweat in the front and the rear. His shoes had been discarded to reveal milky, leavened feet. Mamasan's customers watched him with pleasure, and even Mamasan, with a closing-time cigarette in hand, laughed at his histrionic rendition of 'My Way.' When his Philippine companion returned, the bar was closing and Mama politely offered to call a taxi. The two men decided to walk. Rudy guided Vavasour down the dark, tree-lined road, which was free of cars. In three directions illuminated hotels rose like mountains. Vavasour carried his shoes, occasionally dropping them. Rudy carried the vase.

'He didn't bite!' cried Vavasour. 'He didn't bite! Don't take it personally, my own little morsel. You did your best, I'm sure. I have utmost faith in you. You're a professional, and please take that comment in the best possible way.'

Rudy guided the enormous, weaving man back to the side of the road as a taxi slowly cruised by.

'But we haven't finished with the serene foreign editor with that oh-so-perfect hair, my boy. That hair!' He rubbed his shiny head.

'I know a mask when I see one!' He pushed the Filipino away from him and swivelled to confront him. 'And I intend to rip this one off even if half the face comes away with it.'

The fat man stood in the middle of the road, his legs spread wide, his hand in the air with a sausage finger pointing at the moonlit sky. With his ancient-looking shirt and his bare feet, he could have crawled from a grave.

'Because, my boy,' he exulted, 'while you were on your abortive mission, I formulated a plan! I have it here' – he patted a pocket at his rotund rear – 'and this barbed hook will bring Mr E. G. Augenstein face to face with all his own, personal demons.'

'Anton,' said the Filipino. 'Everyone's horny.'

'Shush, my boy,' said Vavasour, throwing his arm around his companion. 'Everyone's horny, yes. You Filipinos are so accepting. What I have in mind is a kind of game. Yes, a mere game. A highly expensive and dangerous game, which no one in his right mind would like to play. But life is that kind of game, isn't it? Isn't it, Rudy? You and I know it. Now it's time for Mr E. G. Augenstein to discover that fact of life.'

The two men stumbled down the shiny, empty road, with the illuminated hotels hovering in the distances and that small, brilliant moon above, throwing its moonbeams in all directions with equal celestial mischievousness.

THE PLEDGE

Both the Knight-Ridder chain and the *Christian Science Monitor* gave good runs to the Chinese defector in their Sunday editions. They printed grainy photos of the modest man in the Mao suit waving a blurred hand above a bar of gleaming metal. The *Monitor* story was particularly effective, filled with finely-wrought, poignant, somewhat-stretched details. The *New York Tribune*, with a prescient sense of paranoia, assigned the story a mere six paragraphs filled with 'allegedlys' and 'purportedlys' and even: 'The Chinese Home Ministry was unavailable for comment.' The byline – 'By Adam F. X. Fendler' – stood out atop such a miniature dispatch.

Within hours, the Chinese denied the story, saying the purged Chinese nuclear physicist had no family. The defector, they pointed out, claimed a job in a non-existent library. The Chinese statement was followed by one from the Taiwanese, who stated they had authorized no recent press conference. The kicker came in an article by a Yale China scholar, appearing on the op-ed page of the *New York Tribune* itself, which pointed out that the defector had the same name as the protagonist of *The Dream of the Red Chamber*. By Monday, the State Department had confirmed the hoax and condemned 'a shadowy attempt to embarrass both the People's Republic of China and the Republic of China.'

The American press took the expected line, condemning both the mysterious perpetrators and the careless victim newspapers. As usual, the *World Business Journal* spearheaded the editorial assault, vituperatively connecting the scandal with high tax rates and excessive regulation of forest lands. It was days before the stunned *Christian Science Monitor* and Knight-Ridder chain issued contrite retractions. The *Tribune*, thanks to previous experience perhaps, had an announcement in its late Monday edition and an editorial the following day promising quick action from its weary ombudsman and, yet again, 'rigorous checks on editorial controls.' The paper also warned its readers, in a worldly, accept-the-inevitable tone, that 'in the hustle bustle of newsgathering, mistakes are made – not due to carelessness or haste, but as a necessary accompaniment to the rigorous job of distinguishing truth from fiction.'

The foreign correspondents of Hong Kong took the hoax with a scared shiver, for there were few among them who wouldn't have been equally fooled (despite blustering claims to the contrary). An FCC committee was convened to investigate the hoax and it released a pompous statement to the *South China Morning Post* on the danger of a press under attack 'from mischiefmakers, with possible government backing.' It was a wild charge, for the correspondents had no first-hand information whatsoever about the hoax. They couldn't get hold of the *Monitor* and Knight-Ridder correspondents in Taipei; Craig had disappeared, as usual, into Korea this time. And Adam Fendler had yet to return to Hong Kong. After all, Adam F. X. Fendler had a stringer's job to clinch. Days went by. By the end of the week, it is no exaggeration to say that the entire FCC held its collective breath in anticipation of the return from Taiwan of Adam Fendler, as astonishing as that statement sounds. Someone even suggested that an official party meet him at the airport. It was Milo Schindo who shot the idea down.

'If I know Adam Fendler, he will personally fly from Kowloon to get back to the FCC as fast as possible,' he said, flapping his long Italian arms. 'A greeting party would only slow him down.'

The day he was due to arrive, the correspondents huddled impatiently around the bar staring at Adam's premier story in the *International Herald Tribune*. The story was about the Taiwanese version of *Cats*.

'And this is the guy who *didn't* get fooled?' asked Matt Mell, throwing down his baseball cap. Christopher Smart merely shook his head.

'Six paras,' Milo reminded with a Mediterranean wag of his forefinger.

'With byline,' added Christopher Smart grumpily.

'That's fooled!' insisted Milo.

They all looked down at the byline.

'What do you think "F. X." stands for?' asked Matt.

'"Francis Xavier,"' said Carl Rolla, reaching for a cigarette, in a pocket of his fishing vest. 'What else?'

'But surely Adam Fendler is Jewish,' said Matt.

'Or *half* Jewish,' suggested Milo plausibly.

'He made the initials up,' stated La Rolla. His definite tone convinced everyone at the bar that Adam Fendler had made up his middle initials. It went on to suggest that such fictionalization was not only possible, defendable and desirable, but a commonly-exercised journalistic prerogative. The next day, Matt Mell and Christopher Smart held newspapers at arm's distance to critically contemplate their own, initial-less bylines.

Adam Fendler, at 30,000 feet, stared at a plastic cup containing an inch of brown liquid and muttered to himself, 'I shouldn't do this!' A plump Chinese matron across the aisle watched him with unabashed curiosity. Adam drained the brandy and suppressed a hiccup, a signal of alarm from his virgin stomach. 'Maybe I should have had a lite beer,' he thought, burping. The immigration and custom formalities at Kai Tak passed dreamily. As Adam's taxi flew by the windows of Kowloon's terrible tenements, he wondered at the placid pace of life inside. Could life be so still for some while the world around one person revolved so sickeningly? Christopher Smart's telex had disclosed the extraordinary news: that the FCC was awaiting his return. Adam's first dilemma was how he'd walk through the door. He wondered what he'd say and what facial expression he should adopt. He hugged his fedora to his chest, which produced yet another dilemma: to enter hatted? Or to wave the fedora triumphantly, a jubilant remark on his lips.

'Here I am!'

No, no, no, no.

'Gather round! Gather round! Hear all about it!'

Oh my God! What am I going to say? What am I going to do?

'It was a trap, fellow newsmen! A commie trap!'

Adam felt like throwing the fedora out the window of the cab. He imagined his name and even his picture as they would appear in the following day's *South China Morning Post*. And in a sickening rush, Adam realized the momentousness of the evening ahead of him. The inevitable had sunk in: He, Adam F. X. Fendler, was the story of the night. In the days to come, newspaper readers around the world would see him as the symbol of the Fourth Estate pinned in an ugly corner. They would judge him either an honest newsman led into a blind trap or an unprofessional nincompoop. His chance of joining the *New York Tribune* or any other mainstream paper depended on his artful description of the hoax press conference and his own professional conduct. (Adam's stomach heaved. He frantically wondered how many people had seen his original file. *Did Christopher?*) Everything hinged on how his colleagues played their stories: his career, his name, his reputation. He began to resent his colleagues in advance. *They'll take my comments out of context*, he inwardly moaned. *Just one ironic, facetious or nonsensical statement could ruin my life.* Adam wondered whether he should quickly prepare a formal statement. Or maybe he could go off the record! But neither tack would do for a newsman with nothing to hide. *Hide! Perhaps I'll check into a hotel and hide out for a few days! 'Sorry guys, a small bout of cholera!'*

Adam profoundly regretted his whimsical adoption of those middle initials. How foolish he had been to credit Carl Rolla's opinions on 'good' bylines and 'forgettable' bylines! *The initials did improve the byline. And who would have known – that six paragraphs, with that damned byline, would go into the annals of journalism?* What would he reply if someone actually asked what the 'F.X.' stood for? The only words Adam could think of were 'Feroz' and 'Xanadu,' and they seemed unlikely middle names. *Unless one's father was a professor of literature, perhaps. At an extremely obscure university . . .*

The FCC door opened and Adam climbed a small flight of steps to confront every face he recognized in Hong Kong. There they were: the old and venerable, the diminished but experienced, the young and ambitious, the liars, the bores, the alcoholics, the *Morning Post* sub-editors, the Australians, the Indians, plus a few public relations men. He had envied them all for months – except for the public relations men and the Indians, of course. There were photographers with flashing strobes and there were even diplomats. One murmured into a walkie-talkie. *Diplomats! Oh Lydia! If you could see me now!* Each face was directed at him in varying attitudes of eagerness, curiosity, joy, suspicion, disdain and, from the *Far Eastern Economic Review* table, practised petulance. A ragged cheer went up from the AP people, who anticipated several stories from Adam's revelations, and there was a rush from the bar by the hearty regulars: Matt, La Rolla, Milo, Christopher Smart and Georgie Tam. They led Adam back to the bar and demanded that he steel himself for the evening with a beer. Adam was forced to oblige. When Adam's first beer was gone, consumed instantly by his ferocious nervousness, he found his fist grasping a second. The crowd milled around him and Adam wondered at their terrible enthusiasm. Much of the crowd had waited a bit too long for Adam's arrival. To put it plainly, they were drunk.

Milo shouted at him, 'Adam! What a fuck-up! What happened? *Really?*'

I don't know . . .

Georgie Tam, standing nearby, asked with blinking, sober curiosity, 'Do you think the Taiwanese were actually involved, Adam, and if so, at what purpose were they striking?'

I simply don't know. I have no idea.

Christopher Smart approached Adam with an urgent wave and this provoked Matt Mell, who despised Christopher. He yelled to the assembled crowd, 'Please hold the questions, people, hold the questions! Let's do this according to plan.' (For Matt was chairman of the Hoax Committee.)

And only La Rolla, pressing a warm hand into Adam's back, had the words that Adam so desperately needed. 'Oh Adam, good job! *Good* job,' he whispered in Adam's ear. 'We can't wait to hear all about it.'

Adam had never liked Carl before, with his fishing vests and his Zippo lighter. The image of the foreign correspondent as adventurer was one that Adam could never aspire to. But in an intense instant, he felt a flush of unrestrained loyalty. *Maybe he's not so self-centred after all.*

As a third beer was pushed into his hand, Adam felt a tug on his sleeve. He swivelled and saw a ghost-like woman with red-rimmed eyes and lank, greasy, white bangs.

'Adam,' whispered Alice Giles with a kind of urgent sweetness. 'Welcome home . . .'

What could this horse-faced bitch want?

Like everyone at the FCC, Adam had heard dim tales of Alice Giles' journalistic triumphs, set in an era so distant they failed to mean anything anymore. As far as anyone at the FCC knew, she hadn't written a story in years. In Adam's eyes, she had ceased being a real journalist. She was the underside of the profession: the old journalist who neither writes nor dies nor vacates her office. That office had been coveted by many an aspiring financial journalist, according to La Rolla, and several had waited anxiously for Alice to do the decent thing and retire. They had all been outwaited.

An aura of grave-dust issued from the old woman. Instinctively, Adam stopped breathing through his nose.

She's nothing but a Nosey Parker.

'Adam. Was the fat man there? At the press conference? Did you see an enormously fat man? An Englishman?'

'No,' Adam said with some puzzlement. The crowd parted to reveal a path leading to the club table. At the head of the path stood Matt Mell, in his red sweater, beckoning impatiently. As Adam pushed away from the bar, he watched the crowd jostle the horse-faced old woman. Disappointment crossed her haggard face, along with a spasm of hatred or pain.

Soon, Adam was seated behind a bank of microphones with Matt Mell at his right and a confident Carl Rolla at his left. Adam came through his interrogation with surprising ease. His awkward moments were few and, if anything, Adam's hackneyed eccentricity helped sway the crowd to his side. He employed nearly all of his funny faces, his slogans, and he made numerous asinine comments. But the crowd was happy and it desired to laugh. By midnight, it became clear that the only real victim of the night was going to be the fedora. For Adam had made the tough decision to enter the FCC without it. He had sacrificed it to the thundering fates. Adam left the hat jammed beneath the taxi-driver's seat, a pefectly good $65 fedora from Brooks Brothers. As the taxi had pulled up to the FCC, a stroller along Lower Albert Rd. could have peered into its interior and seen a beady-eyed man kissing his fedora farewell. The sacrifice was a wise one. Adam's photos in the next day's paper looked more innocent and earnest for his lumpy bald head.

The reporters asked Adam the exact location of the press conference. They wanted a precise description of the invitation as it was stated over the hotel telephone. They demanded the actual words used by the purported officials when the bogus defector was introduced. Hardly any reporter strayed from this line of questioning. Their collective attitude was apparent: let's pin this event on some government and then the story will die a natural death. Which was for the common good. Because each reporter in the room knew he could have been fooled along with Adam Fendler – a truth the Fourth Estate deemed best left unstated. One reporter even asked, to Adam's delighted surprise. 'Do you think the conference was held late at night to disorient the journalists' natural scepticism?'

'Fellers!' Adam replied with a smile. 'A headshrinker I'm not . . .'

Adam's relief was so profound that he accepted too many beers. He became drunk for the second time in his life. When the one tough questioner rose, from *The Economist*, Adam was in a dulled and careless mood. No one had seen *The Economist* reporter before. No one caught his name.

'Firstly, Mr Fendler,' he said, 'can you tell us your full name. Do you go by "Adam Fendler" or by your byline, "Adam F. X. Fendler"?'

La Rolla lowered his foot atop Adam's and flashed his Hollywood smile for the benefit of the crowd.

'We all know Adam,' Carl breathed into the microphone with a comradely pat on Adam's back. 'And Adam, as long as we've known him, has just been plain old Adam. Plain old *weird* Adam!'

The crowd loved it. They cheered, drowning out the sputtering follow-up from *The Economist*.

But he was a persistent newsman. 'Mr Fendler,' he continued. 'What was your procedure for checking this story before you filed it? Or the procedures of the *New York Tribune?*'

La Rolla nudged Adam's knee encouragingly.

Checking? Who thought of checking? I spent half an hour deciding whether to change my byline.

'In New York,' he muttered, swallowing some more beer, 'the *Tribune* made its routine check with its other bureaus.' He felt a congratulatory nudge from Carl.

'Which bureaus were those?'

'Which bureaus were whose?'

'Which bureaus were alerted to the story for the purpose of checking?' *The Economist* was holding a very large legal pad.

I don't know. Probably none.

'Peking,' Adam ventured with a gulp. 'But the Home Ministry, I understand, unfortunately, because of the time difference, wasn't . . .'

'In Taipei,' continued the interrogator relentlessly, 'did you call anyone after the press conference to get some confirmation? Anyone at all?'

La Rolla's nudges had ceased.

'No,' Adam said. 'You see, the conference was a very late press conference. And my deadline . . .'

'Was at eleven a.m.,' said *The Economist*. 'Mr Fendler, were you accredited to report in Taiwan?'

Adam gaped.

'On what kind of visa did you travel to Taiwan?'

'On a tourist visa. This was just a tryout. I was bucking for a job.' His voice took on a new confidence. 'I don't see the point of these questions. I really don't.' The crowd made agitated and approving sounds. An aggressive rustle swept the room.

They're on my side!

'You know, it wasn't me, Adam Fendler, who tried to fool the readers of the *New York Tribune* or the *Christian Science Monitor* or the Knight-Rider chain . . .'

'Knight-Ridder,' corrected Matt Mell.

'I was as much a victim as anyone. More so, I'd say.'

On Adam's other side, La Rolla was staring with admiration. *I'm free*, Adam thought. *And I'm accepted.*

'And I would just like to say at this juncture,' Adam continued, 'that I have thought long and hard about what this scandal says about our industry. What it says about the world in which we work, the world for which we make our endeavours. I have wondered to myself: what does this whole thing say about Truth and about, and about . . .'

'Unattributed quotes!' called Truman Toto.

The crowd laughed, and some blushed.

'Fictionalizations,' corrected Milo Schindo, known as one of the club's strictest sticklers with his facts.

'No,' shouted La Rolla. 'Not fictionalizations. Lies. Deliberate, malicious untruths. There's a difference!'

'*Vive la différence*,' shouted someone from Agence France-Presse.

'Yeah!' said Adam vaguely. 'Truth and untruth. Or, as my mama would say, the difference between the truth and a lie is getting caught!'

The crowd roared its approval and some called for Adam's mother. The next morning, Adam recalled a volley of confused responses, all shouted in what sounded like Australian accents. The uproar drowned out the final, impotent question of the correspondent from *The Economist*, who was calling to a host of sweaty, male backs, 'Mr Fendler, as our only witness to this hoax can you say who you think organized and executed it?'

Before he knew what had happened, Adam found himself standing once again on the bar of the FCC, reaching vainly for his fedora, his arm in the air and a merry crowd at his feet. Evangelically, Adam vowed to uncover the perpetrators of the hoax. 'I'll travel to the ends of the earth, even to Kowloon,' he said, 'if it takes my last Hong Kong dollar. In fact, I'm booked on a flight to Taiwan next week' – the crowd roared its approval – 'to start my investigation! And I'm not coming back until those scourges of the Fourth Estate are exposed!'

The rest of the night would forever be an embarrassing blur to Adam Fendler, the virgin drunkard. The next day he struggled to remember his exit from the FCC and his arrival at his apartment. He counted the money in his wallet over and over again, for Adam didn't know that bacchanals are costly in a mysterious way. The last thing he recalled was sharing a taxi home with Carl Rolla, which in itself was peculiar. Carl lived in the opposite direction.

In the taxi, Carl declared his intention to join Adam in his quest. 'It's a great story, man,' he said. 'I'm with you all the way!' The two made made various vows: to pursue the story relentlessly, no matter how much it cost or what editors said. To share bylines. (This was Carl's suggestion.) To share awards when they came streaming in. (This was Adam's.)

'You've never done investigative reporting,' Carl lectured. 'That's where I come in. And Adam, I hope you'll take this constructively, but your writing could use some work.'

'I am the moral centre,' Adam proclaimed woozily. 'I am the aggrieved party. I represent the Fourth Estate's honour. The industry must be vindicated!' *And I won't have to travel alone.*

'What a name we'll make for ourselves,' La Rolla enthused. 'We'll decide who gets the first byline later.'

'Exactly,' said Adam. 'It's nothing less than ritual purification for the industry.' And then Adam described to Carl his concept of the press as a priesthood that worshipped Truth as its God. It was a theme he had devised for one of his *Morning Post* columns. He had hoped the column would be reprinted in the *Columbia Journalism Review* and, perhaps, be the premier chapter in a published collection of his columns. Unfortunately, the theme had dried up after three uninspiring paragraphs.

Carl, lighting a cigarette with his Zippo lighter, chuckled at Adam's pronouncement. 'Yeah,' he said, exhaling fulsomely. 'A priesthood. With vows and rites and all that. Yeah, that's us. The fraternal organization: that we have. The best part of this profession, in my view. The wine: we have that too. The bells on the altar, the acolytes. You, Adam, make a fine acolyte.'

Adam didn't like the way his idea was evolving.

'The terrible God,' he mused. 'Yes, we have a terrible God. If you let him get on your nerves.' He smoked and talked on as the taxi wound around the illuminated concrete ramparts of the Midlevels. Adam noticed that Carl's voice had taken on a natural ease it normally lacked. Usually La Rolla spoke like a summer stock actor.

'Hacks as priests,' La Rolla said dreamily and contentedly. 'I like it Adam. I *like* it. And like priests, we all sin from time to time. Who can blame us?'

THE PILLOW BOOK OF ALICE GILES, FOREIGN
CORRESPONDENT (CONTINUED)

I Love My Friends

I love my friends, all of them, in New York, Hong Kong, even those half-forgotten faces scattered to Atlanta and Toronto and Jakarta. I always have. I adore Lennie, Nikki, Norm, Felicity and the rest of the old bunch. But I hardly trust them. Who truly trusts their friends?

This is the life of the professional tale-teller. In a business that requires one to sing above the chorus, one tends to keep one's mouth open and to search for new notes wherever they can be found. To a journalist, a friend provides background harmony, counterpoint, the temporarily-forgotten melody – and when he walks away from the bar, he becomes the next song. We all do it. And as we learn to live for the songs we sing, we learn to live with the songs sung about us. Would Nikki be surprised to hear her sexual woes being discussed animatedly at the FCC? Hardly. She'd be surprised if they weren't.

To the outsider, it sounds inhuman and rather exhausting. But it becomes a way of life. And if the journalist grows slightly deaf to the delights of a quiet duet, she becomes an expert in subtly directing the tune from the back benches when the song title bears her own name.

There are some melodies one keeps from the crowd. People have secrets. And a secret, when it is revealed, requires more than a friend.

Of course, everyone around the globe knows the teary tale of my romantic tragedy. It's an old standard by now. Left at the altar in her youth by a man of low degree, Alice Giles inevitably lost her health but not her reporter's spirit. She retreated from her beloved New York and went into self-exile in the mysterious East, where she became a legend in journalism circles and a doyen of Hong-Kong-based foreign correspondents. (The Curse of Alice Giles: May You Someday Be Called a 'Doyen'!) And then she dried up like a stick. I think that's how the tale ends now. If only it could somehow be decently told: what passion raged in Alice Giles for so many years! How well she knew the pangs of recurring infatuation and love! How unwithered, if enfeebled, she remains today! But that's not how the song goes, alas. And it's too late to rework the melody now.

Over dinner one evening, I sang for Craig my sad song. My tones were breezy and mock-tragic but I ended with genuine tears in my eyes. (After more than twenty years, this presents no challenge.) I could see him inwardly comparing my aria to the pop version he had heard – where? New York? Hong Kong? Brussels? Those recessed, half-Japanese eyes of Craig's: they didn't let on which version he believed or preferred.

But I trilled no secret.

Until months later. I had just returned from another stay in Canossa Hospital. Professionally, my neck was in the guillotine. And the blade was rocking. I suggested to Craig a moonlit drive to Repulse Bay.

'Craig,' I warned. 'Paul is flooding the phone lines with vitriol about you. What did you do to him? Steal his wife?'

'I didn't go to Pakistan,' Craig said. 'You know, last night I forgot to take the phone off the hook. When it rang, I thought it was you. It was Paul. Alice, I can't seem to get it up anymore. None of these stories seem real. Pakistan! My word processor can write that story. Push a button and you get: '. . . Ms Bhutto's audacious gamble . . .' Push another button: '. . . to avoid a firestorm in the US Congress.'

' "Window of opportunity," ' I said. 'That's my least favourite. Along with "drift." '

Craig and I glided over Hong Kong's hump in my ageing, still-stunning aquamarine automobile.

'This is what I'd miss most of Hong Kong,' I remarked, 'were they ever able to drag me away. This view of Repulse Bay.' At its rear, Hong Kong no longer towered. Light showed in mere pinpricks on rounded, fuzzy hills; dark surf pounded and inky islands, barely visible, jutted from the waters. The road at Hong

Kong's back had mysterious curves. How many times had I driven it? How many surprises it continued to hold for me!

'Craig, I've been thinking. I want to confide in you.'

He looked at me uncertainly.

'You see, it's a certain secret of mine. A secret I've never told anyone. Something I considered, let's say, *sacred*. But now, so much has happened . . .' My girlish voice caught in my throat. 'Craig, if anyone . . .'

We flew by the site of the old Repulse Bay Hotel, demolished now, a wasted plot of sandy soil awaiting an upturn in the fortunes of the greedy real-estate barons.

And I told Craig about my green car.

'It's a classic now, of course. No one would dream of scolding me anymore, or calling it a rustbucket. Because it's worth money. That's it, you know. Money. They hectored me for years!'

'You're so lucky it kept going. How much is it worth? These are original seats?'

'Craig, this car was old when I moved it to Hong Kong. It was old when I had it driven by a reckless teenager from New York to California. All my friends told me: "Alice, cut your losses and get something new in Los Angeles." My ghastly brother Frank suggested a Dodge Dart. A Dodge Dart! Only Frank could have thought of that!

'But Craig, I couldn't abandon my Thunderbird. It's such a nice car. So substantial. So safe. So sleek. It's the only car I've ever learned to drive. And the colour: it's such a pretty colour. Don't you agree?'

He nodded.

'He bought it especially because of the colour.' I spoke in a special tone. 'It was my colour. Even then.'

Craig looked alarmed.

I said the next words slowly. 'Craig, this car was bought for me by my fiancé a week before our wedding. I was to be driven to the church in it. We were to drive away in it, together, down the happy highway of life. Our life: the life we all expect. The life that only some of us get. The rest, like me, get consolation prizes. Like this. Like my green car.'

I couldn't restrain my tears. 'If they knew, Craig! No one can ever know!'

In the West, we have such a narrow literary frame of reference.

Every adulteress is a Hester Prynne. Every bemused traveller is an Alice. Every widow is a Wife of Bath and every dead beauty is a Catherine Linton. And Alice Giles: unless she was careful, she would be consigned to the uncrowded banquet table of the yellowed Miss Havisham. Miss Havisham, with her constant, low sob. Miss Havisham – *If you knew all my story, you would have some compassion for me!* Miss Havisham – bursting into flame at the hearth, going out with a shriek and a flame 'soaring at least as many feet above her head as she was high,' in the words of dear Pip.

Miss Havisham. Was there ever a more pathetic, false, hateful fictional character? Dickens is my kind of author. But I will never forgive him Miss Havisham!

No, not me – Alice Giles is no Miss Havisham, pacing the courtyard and sobbing. I have strode across the world. Why does everyone forget that? My girlish voice has made governments tremble and tycoons reach for their digitalis. And yet I, Alice Giles, am considered nothing but an old woman once abandoned. An old woman? Abandoned? I have been a foreign correspondent. I have searched, found, and sung the truth! I have lived, and loved, and even judged a world that, in turn, sees nothing in me but my age, my looks, and my tragic personal failure.

'Craig, when you were in Japan, did you ever read the *Kagero Nikki?*'

'Heian era?'

I nodded.

'I remember Aya recommending it. She loved those sad tenth-century women.'

'The *Kagero Nikki* was written by an abandoned second wife,' I said. 'It's quite a dreary tale, really. I read it often. There are parts I know by heart.'

And as we glided back to Central in my antique aquamarine chariot, sweeping past the quiet waves and the invisible, jutting islands, I recited for Craig my favourite poems of the abandoned wife. Never can I recall my whispery voice, rasped from illness, sounding so wonderfully appropriate.

> *One would not mind waiting*
> *If the night wind were not so cold.*

'Yes,' Craig said from the darkened passenger seat. 'That one

I've heard. Aya must have told me. There's another famous quote. What does Genji call those women?'

'"Rotting stumps."'

'What?'

'"Driftwood,"' I said. 'You must be thinking of driftwood.'

'Yes,' Craig said. 'Driftwood.'

'Craig,' I said, 'I'm so frightened. Everything is changing and changing so fast. Once Roger Mutterperl arrives . . .'

'Alice,' he said, 'how – '

'Just listen to me,' I said fervently. 'I know. I can feel it in my old lady's bones. He's going to chop off my head, Craig, and all for the sake of some space – so someone can get an office. My life, my career, for a few square feet. He is, Craig! He is!' My driving became erratic. 'He'll probably give the office to Matt Mell!'

'Alice. We'll stand by you.'

I blew my nose. I didn't have to look: I could visualize its redness, my blotchy skin, my eyes made even more haggard.

'Maybe I should strike a deal with him right off, the day he arrives. My office for a chair. A coffee cup. Postal meter privileges. A mailbox.' I blew my nose again. 'You work all your life and what does it come down to? Begging for a mailbox!'

I let Craig think he was consoling me. But I knew in my heart I was right. I was old and sick and, in the eyes of the world, a rotting stump. And to all in life come Roger Mutterperls. Personally, I prefer the notion of the Grim Reaper: one particular agent, of a certain, dependable look, who deals the final blow to everyone. How horrible is the reality – *customized* reapers – and who wouldn't resent meeting his or her fate from a Roger Mutterperl? Roger Mutterperl with his rubbery neck!

As we flew over the hill and Central appeared before us in all its shining glory, I thought again of *The Tale of Genji*. That strange book, so foreign, which seemed, as the years progressed, to come closer and closer to describing my life.

Who in the city, now bathed in the light of the moon,
Will know that I yet drift on through the gloomy world?

A Telex

This was the telex sent to Craig and discovered by one of the office's many computer snoops:

83828 WBJ HX
CRAIG KIRKPATRICK
WORLD BUSINESS JOURNAL
HONG KONG
CRAIG,
I AM CONVENING A FAMILY POW WOW AUG. 28. I AM WILLING TO PAY THE AIRFARE. LET ME KNOW IF YOU'RE NOT FREE. AI WILL BE HERE. PLAN ON BRINGING ALL OF YOUR CLIPS FROM THE PAST 18 MONTHS.
CHEERS,
WINN

The Paper Moved

The paper moved premises in a whirl of confusion, excitement and ceremony. A dragon dance was held outside the Goodwill Centre. There were photos in the next day's *South China Morning Post* of the dragon being confronted by the edition's fresh editor and publisher, Roger Mutterperl. Roger beamed rather ferociously. The dragon looked alarmed.

The vernacular press gave the story especially large treatments. Each paper ran several photos of the cylindrical Goodwill Centre, known to the polite Cantonese as 'the stone cigar,' and by cruder epithets to the less genteel. It was a building that had entered the folk history of Hong Kong. Erected at the nadir of the real-estate cycle, it had stood empty for years. The Cantonese, in their characteristic way, transmuted its financial failure into rumours of its imminent physical collapse. Our paper's move to the building – to its two top floors – was considered proof that both collapses had been averted. Several photos showed the cylindrical building and the grassy knoll directly behind it, with the graceful little house I called my own. Two Japanese banks had quickly followed our lead and signed leases on less exalted storeys. I noticed a sign outside the building for a planned health club, a Japanese restaurant and a Maxim's fast-food joint. I felt sorry for the Cantonese: being robbed of a potent paradigm of overarching, doomed greed and receiving, in its place, yet another shopping mall.

My forced retirement from the paper was announced before the move. I was a dirty chore that needed tidying up before new premises could be occupied. Roger Mutterperl, in a straightforward and unembarrassed encounter, informed me of the details. He admitted that Bob Kingsley had asked New York for a different arrangement.

'But we all know, Alice,' he said, 'and this is just between you and me for now, what an ineffective editor and manager Bob was. That's why New York has sent me. There's no room for sentimentalism in today's business climate.' Roger had a peculiar way of dropping his head sharply to the side when he wanted assent from his subordinates; and who could disagree with a man whose neck seems to be breaking before one's eyes?

'Bob also wanted to stay around for the move,' he further confided. 'The dragon dance, the reception, all of that. I nixed that plan.' Again, the head dropped violently toward his shoulder.

There are certain occasions one rehearses for. You rehearse in the shower, over the dishes, driving to work in the morning and home at night. But the rehearsals never really help when that moment finally comes. And life, for evermore, becomes a rerun of that scene whenever the shower starts to spray, the dishes cry out for washing, the car starts moving forward – not to work anymore but to a market, a friend's house, to a Repulse Bay joyride, if such a term can be used in such grim circumstances. A cry ride. A ride to rail at the fates! I'm no different from anyone else. I blew the big scene of my life and went out with a whimper. How easy I made life for the man who ruined my own! And no, I'll never send the letter I've composed hundreds of times. The gossip I spread will never, truly, hurt the impervious Roger Mutterperl. And he will surely never call to ask how I'm doing, and to give me the long-fantasized second chance at the opportunity I blew.

I cleared out my office on a Sunday morning, when I thought I would be alone. It went well until, carrying my last box, I reached the door of the *South China Morning Post* building. That's when the guard demanded my keys. My keys! I realized all I was leaving behind: not just an office and a job, but a postal meter, a stationery closet, long-distance phone lines. My very lifelines were being severed.

The last word comes from the tenth century:

> *Look down upon me from your cloudy summit,*
> *Upon the dying autumn which is my world.*

THE BIG STORY

I

It's a hotel lobby, any hotel lobby. The smell of polish is in the air, the gleam of brass, the lustre of marble and the bright smiles of crimson-liveried bellboys with dark Asian faces. It is any time of day or night, for time never matters on deadline, only time differences. This is a story, a *big* story, but at the same time, any story. An assassination, a *coup d'état*, a controversial election, a hijack – what's the difference? At the front desk, *Newsweek* is shouting at the staff over a delayed telex. *Time*, in the person of Carl Rolla, has just burst through the bevelled glass doors, his shirt grimy with sweat, his fishing vest swinging heavily with vital equipment and his face bathed in a self-satisfied glow that says, 'I've *got* something. And you guys don't.' Carl is lying (as always) in his first suggestion. But his second assertion is, as usual, absolutely correct. Nobody knows anything but deadlines are near, stories are precipitating from the energized vapours, and one can only hope the spellings, if nothing else, get transmitted correctly.

It's one of those stories.

The English reporters are here and there, clasping notebooks to their chests, wearing those dun-coloured trousers that never quite fit around the crutch and spouting arcane bits of history. The Americans – who better rise to journalism's sartorial demand for the unconventional but picturesque, shirts and vests suitable in the jungle or at the presidential palace and pants that fit snugly about the crutch – are airing their instant, insistent theories and pecking at the very latest lap-top computers. The women reporters are there too, of course, tired and greasy-haired. The Japanese confer volubly, but no one listens, for in the race called journalism, they are the perennial nonstarters. And there is the requisite pair of female reporters from the Mediterranean, journalism's lost tribe, who travel the world on unimaginable means, working for unpronounceable and possibly unreal publications, living at press conferences and airport lounges, and continually demonstrating their sole and ever-astonishing professional ability to ask questions (in stilted English) that manage to be both obvious and outrageous at the same time.

Lastly, leastly, there are the television crews, attached to each other by cables, lugging equipment from the front door to the elevator, from the elevator to the coffee shop, from the coffee shop to the front door, and never deviating from these three paths. They are journalism's beasts of burden and they keep their eyes on the floor to avoid getting caught up in any excitement or discussion. According to rumour, they are so uninvolved they don't even go out to fuck.

To an outsider, the reporter's huddles would appear curiously passionless. Opinions are clashing but there's no real dissonance. There are no raised voices. There's only one emotion in this lobby: a hyped-up examination tenseness, as the men and women labour to *absorb*. To accumulate opinion. To capture just a few vital words to put before that desperate fallback phrase, '. . . observers say.' For no one knows anything tonight. The endless siege is in its ninth day, with no killings since the sixth; the opposition is still hopelessly divided; the military, despite all printed predictions, hasn't seized power; the release of the official report, which no one intends to believe anyway, has been delayed. It has been hinted at before: journalists live their lives on the razor edge that separates truth and fiction. They dance upon that edge, sometimes playfully, often frantically, and this is what gives them their particular verve and despair.

It is the journalist, and only the journalist, who knows the beauty and the gain in a small lie. Careers thrive or die on nights like this one. And in the rooms upstairs, where the lie is devised, decided upon or succumbed to; from ambition or carelessness or the inaccessibility of truth. When one contemplates the journalist, think of him in that anonymous room: the curtains pulled against the reality of the coming dawn, his fingers poised above the keys and the lie lying in wait. The lie that will prevent the story from being stillborn. The lie that will make all the other assertions make sense. The lie that could propel the story onto the front page. Or the lie that presents itself by default because the truth is playing hooky and no one in the government is answering his telephone. The fingers are poised. A crack of dawn appears in the chink between the curtains. What if the Japanese are hogging the telex machines again? The lie is typed: 'Analysts say it is unlikely . . .' or '. . . no sooner than next week, according to well-informed ministry sources.' It is dispatched and disseminated. Or is it suppressed? Does he yank the curtains shut, start all over again, go back to last week's notes and pray that the Japanese are asleep and the telex is free? After which he can retire to the coffee shop for a Pakistani omelette, or Islam's beef bacon, or bready English sausages, to recover from his searing test of energy and integrity and hope that Carl Rolla won't burst through the coffee-shop doors with the words: 'I *love* this story, and let me tell you, I am *burning!*'

But Carl Rolla can't burst through these coffee-shop doors. The big story of the month was Pakistan, and all the region's top journalists were there. Except for Carl Rolla.

According to the *Time* guy from Cairo, who was flown in instead, Carl was hunting down a different kind of story. Where? He wouldn't say. What kind of story could keep Carl away from the breaking news? 'Sorry, guys. Even I don't know.'

'It's really nothing less than an "investigative" piece,' Carl said to himself as he sipped the thick, bitter coffee of the Lai Lai, a stack of rumpled newspapers on the bench beside him. 'Sometimes you've got to take a break from the breaking story. Go a bit deeper. Broaden your skills.' He tried to savour the word 'investigative.' But he recalled all the bad things he had said in the past about 'investigative' colleagues. 'Lazy assholes,' he called them. 'All journalism is investigative!' he'd proclaim convincingly. '*They* just can't meet a deadline!' Carl devoured another newspaper, hungry for more news from the big story a quarter of a world away. *If I was there*, he thought, *the story would be solved by now*. Oh, the joy of tumultuous breaking news, when there is never a shortage of leads to be tracked down or doors to be knocked on or tips floating around the hotel lobby or topics to be argued with your colleagues. When there are hundreds of speculations that, with a choice phrase or two, can easily become fact. (Or what passes for fact in breaking news journalism.) When there is always something to file and New York, that voracious bitch, can always be placated by telex after telex, the longer the better.

When you never wake up in the morning wondering: *What next?*

Adam Fendler ambled into the coffee shop, waved goofily to Carl, bumped into a waitress and received half a glass of orange juice down the front of his white shirt.

'Well, Adam,' Carl said sternly. 'What do we do next?'

'I had a great idea,' said Adam excitedly. 'I can't believe I didn't think of it before.'

'What?'

'I'm going to change hotels. Someone told me last night that the Brother Hotel is *half* the price of the Lai Lai. And perfectly comfortable. It's kind of a Japanese hotel.'

'Adam,' growled Carl, 'don't worry about the goddamned hotel when we have a dying story on our hands. A dying story! Do you know what a dying story is?'

'I think you need a little patience, Carl. Some stories need a little age. Think of Watergate. And remember, not everyone is on *Time* Magazine's ticket.'

'And this story is so hot,' Carl groaned, pointing at the rumpled front page.

Adam looked at the paper and its fuzzy front-page photo of army tanks on a runway. 'Where is that?'

'Pakistan,' answered La Rolla incredulously. 'Haven't you been following it?'

Adam wrinkled his nose. 'Who gives a shit about Pakistan? May I have one?' He lifted one of Carl's croissants and started eating hungrily. 'You don't think they'll charge me for the buffet?'

In three days, the two journalists had met numerous officials and local journalists, grilled hotel employees and drunk countless cups of tasteless Chinese tea. But the few facts they had gathered added up to nothing. The government information officer insisted that he and his office knew nothing of the hoax press conference. At the same time, he acknowledged that the hoax had neither annoyed nor embarrassed the government. 'Look at this from our point of view,' he said. 'Nearly all publicity of this sort is good publicity for the Republic of China.' He smiled a mysterious smile. 'Someone, somewhere, read that story and believed it.'

'Yeah,' said Adam as they exited the office. 'My editors. That fucker was in on it.'

The manager of the hotel in Peitou portrayed the press conference as nothing more than a routine banquet booking. When Carl asked how many midnight functions the hotel holds, he smiled suggestively.

'More than you would think,' he said. Carl and Adam became excited when he offered to show them the documentation for the booking. It was written entirely in Chinese.

The theory of the local journalists was that the government, for obscure reasons, was somehow involved. They said the owner of the hotel, a leading industrialist, was influential in the ruling party. But they could come up with few coherent theories and absolutely no proof.

'It's funny,' mused Carl as the two men returned to the hotel after their third day of work. 'When people are interested in a story, like a breaking story, you never need any proof for theories. You just print them. But on a story like this, if you don't have any proof, you don't have any story. It's excruciating.'

'If we could just get three good sources to spill the beans, even off the record,' said Adam.

Carl looked at him. 'Three?'

'Didn't you read *All The President's Men?*'

Silence descended on the taxi. 'Well didn't you?'

'For God's sake, Adam,' shouted La Rolla. 'This is reality!'

Carl's temper was better the next morning but he was convinced he was trapped on a sinking story.

'Maybe we could go back to Peitou,' suggested Adam wiping the crumbs of a third croissant from greasy lips, 'with a Chinese-language speaker. And look at the documentation again. It might give us something.'

La Rolla sighed heavily and gulped the last sip of his coffee. He passed Adam a copy of a telex. It read:

'LEAVING TAIPEI FOR BANGKOK TODAY, FRIDAY. STRINGER SAYS COUP RUMBLINGS ARE GETTING SERIOUS. TAIPEI STORY NEEDS FURTHER COOKING. NO CHANCES FOR EARLY BIRTH, ROLLA, TAIPEI.'

'Have you sent this?'

La Rolla nodded gravely.

'You're coming back?' Adam begged. 'If I change hotels, you can find me at the Brother . . .'

La Rolla shook his head. 'That's just a lie so *Time* can't accuse me of wasting money on a dud story.'

'A dud story?' Adam cried. 'You're giving up?'

'I'm cutting my losses,' said La Rolla. 'The good journalist knows when he's spinning his wheels, Adam. If I were you . . .'

Tears filled Adam's eyes.

'. . . I'd go back to the FCC and admit defeat. Call it a day. There's always another newspaper coming out tomorrow, Adam. Remember that first axiom of journalism. Tomorrow is another paper.'

'This isn't just a story to me,' Adam said. 'It's life. It's reputation. It's career.'

'Bullshit, Adam.' La Rolla rose and unfastened the third button on his shirt. 'Journalism is a business with a short, short memory.' He winked and gave Adam a broad, handsome smile. 'Thank heavens,' he added in a lower tone. 'It was fun, buddy. My plane's at noon. Let's hope for some boom-boom action! See you back at the farm.' And in a heady rustle of khaki and newsprint, La Rolla was gone.

Twenty-four hours later, Adam stared queasily at a raw egg, a greasy piece of fried salmon, rice and two slices of pickled yellow radish: the complimentary Japanese breakfast served to all guests at the Brother Hotel. He picked up his newspaper, with its front-page photo of uniformed men standing before a bank of microphones. The dateline was Bangkok. The coup had broken just after La Rolla's arrival, and just in time for *Time*'s deadline. Bangkok had a shortage of foreign correspondents thanks to the Pakistan siege. Adam rifled through his paper to find the Pakistan story; it had been exiled to the back page. La Rolla, 'The Best Journalist In The World,' had been visited once again by his famed good luck. Adam threw down his paper in disgust.

With his mouth full of rice and salted fish, Adam took the newspaper up again. Something about the photo from Bangkok caught his attention. He stared, stared again and then stared so hard his eyes could have burst. He leapt to his feet, still chewing, and ran to the hotel kiosk. He grabbed three other morning dailies. Each paper carried the same wire-service photo. In each photo Adam spotted the figure in the back row: a mannish, dark-skinned woman, dressed in khaki, her mouth flashing a wolfish smile at the military man to her left.

Adam spent $22 on a telex to Bangkok.

'CARL ROLLA TIME MAGAZINE GUEST ORIENTAL HOTEL
URGENT URGENT URGENT
CARL
   HOT LEAD ON HOAX STORY. BELIEVE IT OR NOT, THERE'S A BANGKOK CONNECTION. DEFINITELY DON'T LEAVE BANGKOK AND MEET ME TONIGHT AT BANGKOK TROCADERO HOTEL
  I PROMISE YOU MAN SCOOP CITY
  ADAM F. X. FENDLER, TAIPEI'

He used his last $140 to buy a plane ticket to Bangkok.

2

This was a story Carl Rolla could sink his teeth into and his energy and enthusiasm nearly swept Adam Fendler off his brown Oxfords. Adam was astonished at how a simple photograph could provide so many leads to an enterprising reporter like La Rolla.

'I'm learning loads from you,' Adam told Carl.

'This is what we needed in Taipei,' Carl scolded as their taxi bumped its way through Bangkok's impenetrably clogged streets. 'You find the photographer. You identify the other people in the picture. You hunt until you drop!' When Carl first used this expression, Adam had presumed it hyperbolic. Until he completed his first day's hunting with La Rolla and actually dropped into his bed at the tacky Trocadero Hotel, remaining unconscious until the heavy black phone at his bedside jangled. His wake-up call from Carl.

'Haven't we been to this office before?' Adam asked Carl.

'At *Time* you learn the value of persistence.'

'I worked for *Time* once, you know,' Adam said. 'Fact-checking.'

'*Fact*-checking?'

'First job,' Adam muttered humbly.

'Adam,' Carl said, deliberately changing the subject, 'I'm glad you're with me on this story. Yes I am. I don't like doing these stories alone. It's better reporting as a buddy team.'

Adam thought this a queer remark since Carl rarely allowed

him to talk during interviews. He had perfected a modest, sober nod from the sidelines.

'I even think *Time* can cough up some stringer pay for this week.'

'And credit?'

'Let's work on the pay.' Carl patted Adam's rounded shoulder. He produced, for the millionth time, the creased photo of the coup leaders. Each face was circled, with arrows pointing to marginal notes and scrawled addresses. La Rolla's settled into a determined squint.

'This is the guy, Adam,' he said, pointing to a military man with half-closed eyes in a square face. 'He's the key to our quest. I've had my eye on him for a year. I knew he'd rise in the next coup. And I'm sure he can tell us what the rest of those hairballs have been covering up.'

'But what about the Filipina?' Adam asked despondently. (For this was their only breakthrough: the woman's nationality.) 'We've made no headway . . .'

'It's the same damn thing,' Carl said. 'You find one, you find the other. But for God's sake, Adam, we must be crafty. No Mike Wallace stuff. And if I've told you once, please stop talking about democracy at these little chats. No one gives a shit about democracy in Thailand. This week especially.'

Adam blushed guiltily. 'I thought you always talked about democracy as a journalist.'

'Who gives a shit about democracy?' Carl asked. 'Nobody wins prizes for writing about democracy. Leave it to the columnists. And don't even think about it when you're with generals. They prefer to talk about US military aid and how stingy it is. And here's another tip: sometimes say you're Canadian.'

Silence reigned as Adam wondered how it would feel to impersonate a Canadian.

'But never, ever say your paper is Canadian,' Carl continued. 'That would be deadly. And when they ask you where you're from in the States, always say New York. Cut out this Massachusetts bullshit.'

This statement amazed Adam. 'You're not really from New York, Carl?'

Carl shook his head roughly. 'I'm from Toledo,' he said. 'The suburbs.'

Adam marvelled to himself: *From the suburbs of Toledo!*

The taxi rides continued, the skipped lunches, the abuse given to obtuse cab drivers and taken from them in return, instant coffees in offices and bottles of warm Coke at roadside stands. At the end of the fifth day, the two men had no new information but Carl was glowing and content. They had done the required rounds. They had met new people and 'schmoozed' with them (as Carl liked to say). Carl had distributed his business card to half the population of Bangkok, offering 'big money, my friend, *Time* Magazine money' to anyone with a lead on the Filipina. 'Just call the Oriental and the money's yours.' Adam had obeyed Carl's command to talk little, and he never, ever mentioned that he was staying at the Trocadero.

'They won't take us seriously if they hear you're staying at that fleabag. Isn't that where Indians stay?'

'There do seem to be a fair number.'

'And I'm glad,' Carl added, 'you stopped wearing that hat.'

Adam nodded self-consciously.

'What happened to it?'

'I always retire it during the summer months,' Adam lied.

One night, after a dinner at the Patpong Pizza Hut, Carl disclosed that he wasn't feeling at all tired. He was, in fact, ready for some 'fun.' Adam responded amiably. He enjoyed girlie bars. He had yet to experience the raunchy sex shows of Bangkok, but the idea didn't trouble him, especially with La Rolla providing amoral support. For Adam Fendler believed in the value of 'experience,' as long as he didn't get robbed, hurt or embarrassed in front of too many acquaintances. He had three condoms in his hotel room, which gave him triple insurance against most of Bangkok's diseases.

'Where shall we go?' asked Adam gamely as they strolled through Patpong's lanes. His question seemed almost pointless. Around them swarmed everything anyone could desire: food carts, sugar-cane peddlers, hawkers of illicit drugs, videotape vendors, standing diners, hustlers, prostitutes and legions of touts. To the merely curious, there was no need to even move; one could merely stare. To the sexually eager, there was no point in proceeding. One need only reach. To the disgusted or the uninterested, walking required the dull gaze of an unworldly ascetic. But few unworldly ascetics could be seen strolling through Patpong after 9 p.m.

'It's not a question of *where* we go,' replied Carl. 'It's what you want.' A tout approached proferring photos of black-haired females in arousing postures.

'Why don't we go to a bar?'

'C'mon Adam. You can loosen up with me. I know this city. Just tell me what you like and I'll lead you to it. I'm easy. I'll do anything you do. Or I can just watch.'

'I thought we'd go to a bar.'

La Rolla slung his arm around Adam's shoulders, pulling him confidentially to his side. It was a firm grip.

'Adam, we'll go to a bar. The question is what do you want to do *afterwards*. What do you like?'

'Or a sex show . . .'

'No sex shows, Adam. We ain't a couple of hair-bag tourists. Tonight is our night for action. We've earned it. And it's up to you what kind of action we're going to get.' Carl's claw gripped Adam's shoulder. 'What do you like, Adam? Tell papa. Girls? boys? A *couple* of dirty girls for you alone, you and your little weenie? A couple of dirty boys?'

He pulled him closer. 'I won't be shocked, Adam. Really, I won't be. After all, boys make a nice change . . .'

'Girls!' Adam yelped.

That's how Adam Fendler, with a crimson face and overly courteous nods to the hotel staff, escorted two young Thai prostitutes back to his room at the Trocadero Hotel. He was mortified to be stopped at the elevator and directed back to the lobby guard, who asked him to register his guests in a large, worn ledger. Adam waited behind a strapping Indian man in a crimson turban, accompanied by a pockmarked Thai woman in a revealing blouse.

'Fuck, they do this even at the Trocadero?' asked Carl, who had his arm around the prettier of the two girls.

Adam could barely respond. His throat was tight and he felt like weeping. He needed to pee.

'I can assure you,' continued Carl, 'they give us a harder time at the Oriental. Sometimes they make you pay extra after you've had a guest. Isn't that fucked in Bangkok? It's much better here, buddy.' With his free hand he patted Adam. 'Even here. And I'll be glad to give you some pointers, you horny bastard.' The Indian had embarked on an obscure argument with the lobby guard. Another Indian, with yet another Thai whore, joined the queue behind Adam and Carl.

'Gridlock at the Trocadero elevator!' announced Carl in a booming voice, and he laughed a long, theatrical laugh. The two prostitutes giggled behind their hands. The bellboys across the tacky lobby laughed and rudely pointed.

Adam served drinks from the room's outsized refrigerator. He gave the girls Cokes and reserved the beers for Carl. There was a jolly hunt as all four looked for a bottle-opener. One of the girls turned on the television. She wanted to watch a local television show, but Carl refused. He turned to an in-house movie about surfers in Australia.

While he was in the toilet, peeing nervously and checking his condom supply, Adam heard whispers and giggles. Instinctively he felt for his wallet. When he came out, the two girls were standing between the beds stark naked.

'Say surprise, girls,' commanded Carl. He had removed his shirt to reveal a tanned upper torso. 'C'mon. Say "Surprise" for Uncle Adam.'

The girls giggled and tried to hide behind one another. They were thin but wonderfully winsome. The large nose on Adam's girl no longer seemed to matter. Her nipples were dark and hard like pencil erasers. Her thighs were like a teenager's. She covered her bush hurriedly, but not before Adam had stared at it. He felt a throbbing in his baggy trousers. He noticed Carl's hand familiarly caressing the ass of the girl with the big nose. *How easy it is for him,* Adam thought. *How does he remain so relaxed?* He wondered if Carl was aroused. But he spotted no telltale bulge in his faded jeans.

Soon, Adam lost control of the night. He relinquished it to Carl. On his instructions, the girl with the big nose brought Adam into the bathroom, where she disrobed and bathed him. He was erect in the shower, but she didn't seem to notice. She scrubbed with practised thoroughness. Adam made a few attempts to soap the woman's belly, her breasts, a quick pass at her groin. But she took the soap from him and did it herself.

When they came out from the bathroom, Carl and his girl were lying on a bed watching television. It was their turn to wash. Carl removed his jeans and pulled Adam's girl aside for a brief chat. She nodded knowingly. He poked her chest demandingly with his finger. Then the door to the bathroom closed and Adam was alone with the woman. His first woman. In his entire life.

By the time Carl and his woman returned to the room, Adam

and his companion were engrossed in their act. The woman with the broad nose performed every sex act Adam had dreamt of, and though there weren't many of those, she did each with consummate skill and a thrilling absence of fuss. Adam had never imagined a woman without embarrassment, a woman who didn't moan, a woman who performed sex with admirable simplicity. He allowed her to take control when it seemed easiest and he took over when his urge demanded. In a distant part of his consciousness, Adam knew that Carl was watching. He heard: 'There's that weenie, and not a bad one after all!' and later: 'Ride 'em cowboy!' But he couldn't concentrate on anything but his woman and, to his own surprise, he didn't mind being observed. Only once did Adam take a look at the couple on the other bed. Carl was sitting and the Thai woman was kneeling between his knees. He was moving his long, tan cock in and out of her mouth. She accepted it mechanically. Carl chanted steadily: 'More, take it, more, more, take it . . .' Adam could see the woman gag as Carl pushed too hard. 'C'mon,' he insisted. 'Take it, girl . . .'

The heavy black phone exploded. Both women jumped and grabbed nervously for sheets. Adam plucked up the receiver and gasped, 'Yes!'

He stared at Carl, who was standing nude between the beds with a scowl of surprise on his face.

'Just a minute!' Adam put the phone down. 'Where are my shorts? I can't talk on the phone without my undershorts.'

'Who is it?' Carl barked.

'I don't know,' said Adam, struggling with his jockey shorts. The startled girls had fled to the far bed.

'He asked if I was the journalist from Hong Kong.'

'Who?'

'Him,' Adam said, struggling back to the phone with twisted underpants.

'Give me that!' Carl barked into the phone. 'Who is this?'

Adam was deflated within his undershorts. But Carl, bronzed and lean, was fully erect as he bellowed at the telephone. His long phallus seemed to gain strength from its master's shouts. The girls touched each other's hair and giggled.

'This is Carl Rolla,' he shouted into the phone. '*Time* Magazine. I think I'm the party you are calling. Who is this, please. Hello? Who is this, please? Hello?'

But the phone was dead. The operator, when finally reached, couldn't help. It was an outside call. No name had been left.

'He didn't ask for you,' Adam said after La Rolla had slammed the phone down. Adam sat on the bed with his arm around his girl – his first girlfriend. 'He asked for me. He asked for me, quite precisely, by name.'

3

Adam's dreams were happy, erotic celebrations of a homely Thai girl with an endearingly clinical attitude towards the male sex organs and a particular way with the testicles. They were dispelled by another volley of angry rings from the phone. As he answered, Adam marvelled at the emptiness of the hotel room compared to the previous evening. Weak light showed through the room's filmy curtains.

The male voice from the previous evening commanded him to descend to the coffee shop.

'We'll give you four minutes,' it said.

I'll call Carl later, Adam thought.

Two Thai men were standing in the coffee shop awaiting Adam's arrival. They escorted him through plateglass doors to a car outside.

Adam squinted against the bright sunlight. 'Where are we going?'

'Not far,' replied the men.

It was a silly answer, for every car drive in Bangkok is endless. But Adam was getting to know the layout of the city. He recognized Sukhumvuit Ave. By the time the car veered into one of Bangkok's walled residential bylanes, he knew he wasn't very far from the city centre.

The car honked at a pair of high steel gates, which rapidly swung open. Inside was a shambling wooden structure with deadened neon signs suspended from the roof. It was a cabaret of some sort, closed for its deserved morning rest. Adam was led to a narrow doorway and up a flight of steep wooden stairs. He was ushered into a room containing a large, soiled double bed and three wooden chairs. A bare bulb was suspended from the ceiling. As the door shut, he heard it being locked from the outside.

What if there's a fire?

After a few moments, he heard his cell being unlocked. A shrunken old man brought in a tray with two cups of instant coffee, already whitened and sweetened. He placed the tray on the floor and gestured towards it. The door was locked again when he left.

Adam sipped his coffee and stared, unavoidably, at the bed and its historic-looking stains. His erotic fantasies began anew. He inwardly marvelled at his previous lack of interest in Asian women.

The door was unlocked and it swung open with urgency. In the doorway stood the Filipina from the press conference. She smiled at Adam and said, 'I hope you're an early riser. Like me.'

She was a commanding presence, with a dangerous kind of interpersonal warmth. She sat on the bed facing Adam, accepted the coffee that Adam passed her, gulped it, and stared ferociously into Adam's eyes.

'Yeah,' she said. 'That's what I needed.' She gulped again. 'Hey – why do you stay at the Trocadero? It took me a coupla days to find you.'

The curse of people who learn English as a second language is that along with grammar and vocabulary, they adopt accents and timely slang that remain embedded in their speech like linguistic time-capsules. The Filipina had learned English in America during the late 1960s or early 1970s. She had the gratingly flat accent of middle America and a tendency towards gum-snapping 'yeahs.' Her voice held the memory of pot parties, long drum solos and 'pig' jokes.

'Yeah,' she repeated, talking to her coffee. 'Now. What can I do for you? I hear you've been asking for me all over town.'

'Do you remember me?'

'Yeah.'

Adam gave her his goony stare.

'Yeah, I remember you,' she said impatiently. 'From the press conference in Taipei. In Peitou. You were the eager one.'

Adam continued staring.

'What about it?' she asked.

'That press conference was a fake.'

The Filipina nodded. 'And you,' she said as she bent to place the drained mug at her feet, 'got fooled.' She gave Adam a bold, satisfied look.

'All I want to know,' Adam blurted desperately, 'is who did it. And why.'

The woman barked an insincere laugh. She raised her arms above her head and performed a long, languorous stretch. 'Oh!' she said, recovering from her exercise. 'It *is* early for this kind of talk, isn't it? Are you always so blunt, Fendler?'

'Yes,' Adam replied. The way she used his last name made him feel like a schoolboy.

'So you want to know who planned the hoax. Who paid for it. And why anyone would waste his or her time and money on such a stupid trick. Do I get you right? Is that what you want?'

Adam nodded.

'What if I say *I* did it all?'

'Then I'd ask you your name.'

'My name is Jean. Jean Yulo.' She extended her hand and Adam had no choice but to shake it. 'There,' she said. 'We're friends.'

The two stared at each other for a few moments. 'Look, uh, Jean . . .'

The woman cut him short. 'I'll give it to you straight, Fendler. You weren't the only person fooled over that press conference. I worked hard on that little charade. It all came off beautifully, thanks to me. And I haven't been paid. No honour among thieves, you might say, but it makes me damn mad. So here's my proposition. You help me make up my loss, and I'll give you the information you desire. I have some photos you can use. I have names and addresses. I promise you the information is good.' She paused. 'And very, very newsworthy. But I must be paid. I'm not in this business for charity or to kill time.'

'In journalism,' said Adam, struggling to gain control of the situation, 'we don't buy information.'

'Bullshit,' said Jean. 'Everything has its price. And someone will pay if you don't. If you turn me down, I'll sell it elsewhere. I'll call up, I don't know, *Time* Magazine. I know the guy in Tokyo.'

It dawned on Adam: the woman knew nothing about La Rolla. She was offering the story to him, Adam Fendler, alone. Adam was being offered a world-class scoop – for a price.

'I have to talk to my editors.'

The woman stood mannishly. 'Go ahead.' She walked to the

door and knocked. Adam could hear the sound of a padlock being removed from the other side.

'We'll be in touch.'

'Wait!' Adam called. 'I'm planning to change hotels!'

She swivelled militarily. 'Yeah? Where?'

'I don't know!'

'Fendler,' she said. 'What's your problem? We will call you at the New Fuji Hotel. Move there today. And just wait. It's near the Trocadero. And it doesn't get all the Indians.' She turned and walked away. The door shut casually. There was no sound of the padlock being replaced.

As Adam packed his bag, he watched the telephone fearfully. As he checked out, he kept one eye on the door, waiting for the arrival of Carl Rolla, refreshed after an evening's fuck and ready for another day on the streets. But Adam was in luck. La Rolla had decided to dedicate his morning to communications with New York. Adam crept out of the door of the Trocadero and lugged his suitcase to the New Fuji, which was less than two blocks away. To Adam Fendler, the trip seemed a journey into a new, eventful, potentially glorious future.

4

Adam waited for the Filipina's call for three days – the three longest days of his life. He was afraid to leave the New Fuji. He was afraid to reclaim his wondrous bedmate with the large nose from her Patong bar. He imagined Carl sitting in wait. So he dreamt of her and masturbated with the image of her lips and tongue lapping delicately at his testicles. He ate nine meals alone in his room. He watched local television, because the New Fuji didn't have in-house movies. His only stealthy outing was to a local department store to buy a fedora. For Adam felt lost and insecure and he knew the comfort of a familiar prop. On the way back in the taxi, he felt happy with the fedora fitted snugly on his globe-like head. *Everyone should wear one,* he thought. As he drove through Bangkok's streets, he kept a concerned eye on the heads bobbing along the pavements. Every time he saw a foreign head, he caught his breath. *Is it Carl?* And he'd snatch the fedora from his head.

Adam made three phone calls during those three days, and received one. The first call was to Christopher Smart, who said with a frantic tone in his voice: 'We got burned on this story once and I don't think we should get burned again. The *New York Tribune* does not pay for information and Adam, let me make this perfectly clear, you were given no authority to negotiate on behalf of the *New York Tribune*. I don't know why you're in Bangkok. I don't know why you went to Taipei. This whole story, and your involvement in it, gives me the willies.'

And he calls himself a newsman?

The second call was to Ted Augenstein in New York.

'Yes, I remember you Adam, quite well. I was quite concerned about that hoax story in Taipei. But from all I know about it, you seemed to have done the best you could.'

That's better.

Adam explained the situation and his chance to get information about the perpetrators of the hoax. Ted's reaction was hesitant.

'As a very firm rule, Adam, we do not purchase information at the *New York Tribune*. If your source was to *give* you the information, and give it to the *New York Tribune* exclusively . . .'

Adam explained the impossibility of that option.

'I am planning a trip to Hong Kong and China this week, Adam. Perhaps we could talk about it then.'

Too late, old man. It's gotta be now.

Again, Ted became thoughtful. At one point, Adam wondered whether the line had been cut.

'In that case, Adam, I must instruct you not to offer any money for this information. That is a clear directive. Information that is sold is often poor information. If those are the terms of the deal, I think you ought to withdraw from the story and return to Hong Kong. I don't care if another news organization gets the information as a result. I'd be glad to see you for a meal sometime this week. I arrive Monday.'

Withdraw from the story? No one gets it! I can't just drop this one and go onto something else. This isn't just a story. This is my life. This is my vindication. This is my shot at a job with the New York Tribune *– not breakfast with its foreign editor.*

Jean Yulo's call came through on Sunday morning. She sounded very far away. The operator spoke Chinese.

'Where have you been?' Adam wailed. 'I've been waiting for three days. Where are you now?'

'Do you have some money for me?'

'Listen, Jean . . .'

'Do you have money?'

'You know, there are rules at my paper. I talked to New York . . .'

'All of you guys are such amateurs. Forget it, sonny boy.'

'Don't hang up!' Adam begged.

'Why?'

'I need that information. I really do.'

'I need that money.'

'No you don't,' Adam said boldly. 'I need that information to redeem myself. I made a fool of myself at that press conference. You made a fool of me. Give me a chance to get some back.'

There was a hesitation on the other side of the line.

'And I've waited for you,' Adam continued, sensing success. 'I've been waiting by this god-damned telephone for three whole days. What took you so long?'

'I was travelling.'

'So give me a break. C'mon. Give a person a break.'

'But we had a deal . . .'

'Okay,' Adam said, rushing to compromise. 'You don't have to tell me everything. I'm a reporter. I can dig up facts. But give me a hint. Give me a good hint so I can get these guys on my own. The ones who didn't pay you.'

There was a chuckle from the other end.

'A *good* hint,' Adam repeated. 'Otherwise . . .'

'Here's your hint,' said the harsh voice. 'Go to San Fernando in the Philippines. And look for the fat man.' She chuckled again. 'Good luck.' The line was cut.

Adam stared at the receiver. He replaced it gently in its carriage. He looked around the room and could hardly bear what he saw. For three days he had tolerated the New Fuji. Now, the look of every piece of furniture enraged Adam Fendler.

His last call was to the Oriental Hotel.

'No,' he told the desk, 'don't put me through to Mr Rolla's room. Just take a message. I said just take a message. Tell Mr Rolla . . . No, I don't care if Mr Rolla is coming through the lobby now. Do not connect me. Do *not* connect me. Do you understand? Just take this message. Tell Mr Rolla I'll return his computer in Hong Kong. Yes, *computer*. Tell him this is Mr Fendler calling. *Adam*. Tell him Adam called.' And Adam tossed the receiver back to its cradle.

This dump is history, he thought, his heart racing with fear and ambition. *I'm off to the Philippines.*

THE PILLOW BOOK OF ALICE GILES, FOREIGN
CORRESPONDENT (CONTINUED)

Craig Had A Share

Craig had a share in a junk, or, to be precise, a share of a share. Every second Sunday, he and a diplomat took possession of a battered teak boat with an unreliable engine and a sleepy 50-year-old 'boat boy.' They invited friends, purchased food, laid in bottles of vodka and cans of 'Mrs T's' and Carlsbergs and spent long Sundays drifting in a Hong Kong cove. When they got bored, they waved and shouted to everyone they knew in Hong Kong, who were jammed onto their own junks in the same idyllic bay. (So close were the boats that the *South China Morning Post* suggested 'No Smoking Coves' and a total ban on cigars.) All were determined to enjoy their shares of shares, even if it took more Bloody Marys than were prudent while trapped on a boat with pompous bankers, scrounging journalists from magazines like the *Far Eastern Economic Review* and *Insight* and, even, accountants. Thanks to these junk parties, Monday mornings had a particular ache in Hong Kong. An implausible number of people phoned in sick with food poisoning. The telephone lines were jammed with calls of awkward apology.

How emblematic these parties are of the expatriate life. Somehow, a cove draws us to its waters. And there we float, utterly unanchored and blind to the dangers of our wanderings. There we chat: with people we like and people we disdain, never making much distinction and drifting further and further from the family and friends that moor most lives. There we sail, oblivious to changing weather, for who can worry when everyone around, in identically worn and leaky vessels on the same scummy seas, is smoking and drinking and emitting peals of Sunday laughter that reach all the way to the shore? Oh, how we laugh! We can laugh and chat until the moon comes out – until a thousand moons rise and fall! Until the weather finally changes and that endless summer idyll turns into shipwreck. It happens! I know! But no one believes. In Hong Kong, there are too few half-submerged hulls: when people crash they are instantly whisked home. Hong Kong is for those still sailing. It is an endless Sunday with all of the traits of Sunday: the sun in the sky, the drinks in the hold, the patient conversation with the dull Japanese wife, the careless insults traded between journalists, the little boasts that annoy the next day, the trilling laugh of the fat Indian matron gobbling up the kebabs, the insincere compliments to the odd-looking children of mixed races, the latest outrageousness from the *South China Morning Post* – read aloud, of course, in a mock English accent – the sun still high, the beers still cool, a certain tremor beneath the feet, but not to worry: it's nothing but the tremor of a boat engine that will never give out or, even, ever, ever run out of gas. Life is a lark for expatriates. And how desolate it becomes when the lark finally flies away.

I had found, with a hideous crash, my submerged rock and his name was Roger Mutterperl. Craig was being buffeted in a crosswind between parents and bosses. It's no wonder that we came together to break the story of the year, one of journalism's most significant and telling sagas. For we had a special edge on everyone else. We were trying to outrace the wind. We had the energy of those who have to bail furiously or drown.

The diplomat was out of town, so Craig boarded early Sunday morning, climbed to the boat's top deck and, with his shirt collar raised against the morning chill, watched the towers of Hong Kong recede into a thin mist. He banished from his mind the distracting, ugly crowd that had made life so painful for him: his parents, his colleagues, the disembodied voice over the phone line that symbolized New York. Craig wanted to think clearly about the career that was pulling him over the precipice. There was only one figure he couldn't vanquish: that Japanese woman with the sculpted face, the full hair and the warm, husky singing voice that penetrated his very essence. With pain, he recalled her sing in El Niño:

> *You can't know how happy I am that we met.*
> *I'm strangely attracted to you.*
> *There's someone I'm trying so hard to forget.*
> *Don't you want to forget someone too?*

Craig despised the journalism his father revered: Hot Shot journalism, filled with fake authority and fantasy analysis, created in an endless daisy-chain of hasty journalists talking to diplomats talking to other journalists talking to still shallower diplomats, with the truth receding irrevocably like the image in a pair of parallel mirrors. Craig had a fantasy: he would come home after a business trip to find Aya lying on the couch reading a novel. She would say, 'How was Pakistan?' and he'd reply, 'Okay.' He'd close the door and everything would be all right. But Aya wasn't on his couch reading a novel. Craig thought of the life expected of him: spending his days chasing phantasmic stories that climaxed, '. . . according to well-informed sources,' spending his nights blowing foam off beer glasses.

Before he knew it, his boat was anchored in a cove and surrounded by three other junks. One of the neighbouring junks was filled with rich Chinese continuously visited by friends in loud, gaily-coloured speedboats. The other boat seemed to be all men: large European men with smaller Chinese men. *A gay boat,* Craig thought. *The first I've ever seen.* The third boat was the usual collection of bankers in loud pants and wives with fussy haircuts. Craig read his *Morning Post* and spied on his neighbours. On one side, he watched a harassed-looking amah taking care of an ill-behaved toddler. Its rich, well-groomed Chinese parents sunbathed on the top deck. On the all-male boat, the drinks were flowing along with significant, sexually-tinged laughter. Craig was surprised to spot a woman on board. He watched as she moved confidently among the men, slapping asses. She put her arm around an Asian man and the two huddled in a serious talk. Then she came out from the shaded area to take a reading of the day. She looked as if she could change the weather if she wished. She had dark skin, short hair and a mannish way of walking. She leaned on the rail and scanned the cove.

It's her.

He called excitedly to the napping boat boy and, after much grumbling, the anchor was hoisted and the boat pointed towards Aberdeen Harbour. Craig's heart pounded and his mind raced along with the engine. But he could summon few coherent thoughts. He felt alone and inadequate to the coming challenge. *They don't train us for this,* he thought. When he docked at Aberdeen, he ran to the boat club's pay phone and dialled my number.

'Craig! I'm so glad!'

'You sound happy, Alice,' Craig said. 'I was concerned. I haven't seen you . . .'

'Happy? I'm distraught! The worst thing in the world has happened!'

'You don't sound ill.'

'My spirits are fine, no thanks to Roger Mutterperl, that life-wrecker. But Craig, everything else has turned to crapola. The landlord had my house fumed yesterday. Every corner, Craig, has been sprayed with some vile concoction. It's never happened before in almost twenty years. I don't know if I can stand it. I had to open all the windows and still I couldn't sleep. Not one wink. Yrlinda is airing everything. Craig, I think I'm being chased out of my home. My wonderful home! I have these allergies, you know.'

'Alice – '

'It's more than terrible, Craig. This house is all I have left.'

'Alice, listen – '

'They want to send me home, Craig. To some fucking nursing home, I think. Everyone is on it – '

Craig interrupted to tell me of his discovery.

'I have to follow her, Alice. I know you have your troubles. But I need a car. And I need help.'

'I'm so excited!' I affected girlish glee. 'I'll worry about the bugspray later. I wish I had a pistol. And what to wear? Do you have food?'

'No.'

I shouted a command to Yrlinda. 'Don't worry, Craig. We'll be there in a jiffy.'

When we pulled up in the Thunderbird, Craig was waiting with a tense look on that odd, mixed face. When Yrlinda unloaded the hamper, she dropped one of the Tang jars. Greasy brown fluid leaked onto the road.

'We have plenty!' she cried. 'No mind!'

'Soup,' I explained. 'It's a taste of the bronze age, Craig, a recipe from the amino-acid pool. Life was created from that soup.'

Yrlinda nodded happily. 'You crack the bones,' she said, pantomiming some extraordinary physical effort, 'and then you pull the white out. Sometimes you have to . . .' She made an ugly sucking noise.

Craig looked disgusted. 'You eat that, Alice?'

An hour later, the junk again approached the Lamma Island cove. The gay junk was moored in its original spot. The boring bankers were still docked alongside – collapsed in chairs and on foam mats – but the chi-chi Chinese had moved on to more fashionable waters.

I peered through the junk's dirty window with my mother-of-pearl opera glasses. 'I don't see her.'

'Maybe she's down below. Or up above. Check the deck.'

'Everyone on the deck is topless. One man has a shaved head. He looks like Daddy Warbucks with an earring. But where is our little Orphan Annie? She seems . . . Wait! I see her. The female has been spotted. What nationality is she? She doesn't look Taiwanese in the least. The aboriginals don't look like that, you know, although they have dark skin. She looks like a Filipina to me.'

'Everyone looks like a Filipina to you, Alice.' Craig snatched the opera glasses.

Yrlinda, standing on the deck in full view of the neighbouring boat, hands on hips, called into the boat, 'She's Filipina. She *has* to be Filipina. Her companion too. Two *Pinoys*.' Yrlinda was excited. She was wearing her green man's pants.

I ordered Yrlinda inside. Craig looked through the opera glasses and saw the woman standing at the rail with a young Asian man. The man had a T-shirt that read: *If Found Return Immediately to the Rat's Nest*.

'I've seen her friend too, Alice. I know his face. *Where* was that?'

'He looks like a hustler. Good-looking hustler.'

'It was Japan. In a hotel. At Narita.'

I strained to make the connection.

'I saw him around the time of the hoax, Alice. In fact, it was the next night. I was on my way to Korea. But he wasn't in Taiwan – he was in Japan. It doesn't fit. Nothing fits.'

'Sure it fits,' I said. 'There they are. They're our only two pieces in this puzzle and they fit right together. Let me remind you, Craig. Coincidence is something we journalists don't believe in.'

If only Craig and I could have heard that conversation: what pain we would have been spared in the next 48 hours! Later we knew it all: that he, the hustler, was the messenger between her and Vavasour. That she had spoken to Adam Fendler in

Bangkok that morning. That she was *en route* to Manila, to make final preparations. That everything was going well and that the conspirators' target date, three days hence, was still operative. We saw her gesture at the raucous white men, and give the boy an unmistakable lecture on the evils of the gay life. The boy spat some insult and walked away.

Craig said, 'I think we have to follow both of them.'

'If they split up . . .'

'You take . . .'

'. . . the boy.'

'Perfect,' said Craig. 'I don't think they'll dock at the club.'

'Nah. They're public pier.'

At the dock, the woman and boy separated. She tried to kiss his cheek but the boy pushed her away, raising a laugh from the rest of the group. They hailed separate taxis, and as Yrlinda and I clambered into the aquamarine Thunderbird, I shouted across the road, 'Craig! What about later? I can't go back to my house: I'll choke!'

He gestured in the direction of his apartment and stepped into a cab. I saw his dark head disappear up the road. On the dock, the Filipino kissed a white man goodbye, gave his balls a mock-squeeze, and jumped into another taxi.

Yrlinda commented, 'He not good boy. Not a good *Pinoy*.'

Craig related later: when his taxi had followed the Filipina's through three tunnels, he realized she was headed to Kai Tak Airport. He wondered if she was meeting someone or getting on a plane. His answer came when the cabs pulled up the departure ramp. Craig stood at a careful distance and watched the woman check into a flight to Manila. Behind his grimy airport pillar, as he wondered whether to approach her, the woman turned his way. Their eyes met and Craig stepped backwards guiltily. She smiled, turned, and walked rapidly to the entrance of the immigration section. Craig couldn't follow without a boarding pass. He raced to a counter and inquired about a ticket, but the flight was full. Craig had lost her. He had failed in the most rudimentary tail job. He told me later, 'I was so embarrassed.'

'Craig, journalists are really much better on the telephone.'

The Philippine man-boy's taxi skirted the tunnel leading from Aberdeen to Causeway Bay and, instead, started climbing the back of Victoria Peak.

There's only one reason a guy like this would be visiting the peak, I thought.

The taxi pulled up to an apartment building on one of the choicest pieces of real estate in Hong Kong. Directly beneath it glowed the brilliant stalagmites of Central.

Government flats. He's visiting a civil servant.

The boy paid the taxi, slammed the door, and walked with a confident gait up the path. Yrlinda peered out the window and repeated her earlier judgement. 'Not good boy,' she said.

'Shush, Yrlinda.' I opened my door and struggled to extricate myself from the overly-youthful bucket seat. 'Watch the car.'

'I can't drive!' Yrlinda wailed.

'I didn't say drive it. *Watch* it. I'll be back in two seconds.' I hurried, with my head down, following in the boy's footsteps. By the time he reached the front door, I was directly behind him.

I stopped at the mailbox and fiddled with some keys as the boy began to climb the wide, concrete steps. He seemed uncertain. He was looking for numbers on the doors but there were none.

I followed slowly. *I hope he finds it soon,* I thought, *or I'll have to pass him and come down again.* But just as I pulled alongside, the boy rang the bell of a second-floor door. I heard a voice from inside. I continued walking up the stairs. A greeting echoed through the stairwell, followed by a door slam. When I descended, the hallway was empty. I walked out of the building, down the path and out to the car.

'Where you go?'

'Never mind, Yrlinda. Do as I say. Go over to that railing and look up at this building and see if the lights are on in the second-floor apartment facing Western.'

'Western?' Yrlinda excitedly arranged her shirt and pants for her vital mission.

'Western,' I scolded. 'That way.'

'Second floor,' Yrlinda repeated. 'One up from ground? Right?'

'Yes. And hurry.'

Yrlinda waddled to the observation point. She leaned over it. I worried she'd tumble down the hillside. Then she jogged back, her bulk jostling her brightly-coloured blouse.

'The lights are on!'

'The other apartments?'

'Some on. Some off.'

'But the second-floor apartment light is *on*?'

Yrlinda nodded eagerly.

'Did you see anyone?'

She shook her head excitedly.

'Okay. Now – Step Two. Walk down to the Peak Tram station. You know the station? Get us some hamburgers and French fries and I would like a strawberry milkshake. Strawberry, okay? Here's the money.'

We ate our dinners sitting side by side in the car's bucket seats.

'What flavour did you get?'

'Vanilla.'

'Vanilla? I didn't think you liked vanilla.'

'I have to lose my weight,' Yrlinda giggled. She slurped the remains of her milkshake.

'Yrlinda, that's my kind of diet.'

It was after eleven when the boy exited the building. As he waited for a passing taxi, I ducked in my seat. Yrlinda was asleep in the back. When he had entered a cab, I started the ignition. 'Yrlinda. We're going!' Yrlinda sat up like a sleepy child. With a hefty groan, she tumbled heavily from the back into the passenger seat.

'Home?'

The taxi took the winding roads to the harbour and headed for the Kowloon Tunnel.

'Kowloon!' There was awe in Yrlinda's voice.

The cab exited the tunnel in an area of plush apartment buildings and in the shade of a gleaming white train station. We continued onto Nathan Road, the centre of the tourist district, with its tailor shops, its camera shops, its hotels.

He's going to a hotel, I thought. *To meet someone else.*

But the cars proceeded several more miles, until the stereo shops had given way to open-air food stalls, and then several miles more, until the bright lights of the food stalls had dimmed. We drove slowly through a neighbourhood of blackened, ancient-looking industrial buildings. It was a part of Kowloon that I had never seen before.

'Kowloon?' Yrlinda asked. 'Still?'

The boy's cab stopped at a forbidding building with a number of signs arranged on its front. In a flash, he was out of the cab and inside. The cab slowly pulled away. From across the street,

Yrlinda and I peered into an inky rectangle: the loading dock of an industrial building. It was the only opening in the blackened concrete façade.

'We'll wait,' I said nervously. 'Surely he can't remain long in *there*.' I turned on the radio and sought the cheeriest music on the air.

After thirty minutes, I said, 'We'll give him five more minutes.'

Yrlinda looked at me fearfully.

After ten minutes, I said, 'What's in this building?' I stepped gingerly out of the car, darted a glance at the loading dock to see if I was being observed – I wasn't – and gave a reassuring nod to Yrlinda. I strolled to a light post and peered up at the building's façade. Most of the signs advertised knitting and weaving companies. One sign stood out. It advertised a health club on the third floor.

A health club? In this wreck of a building?

'I'm going inside,' I told Yrlinda through a crack in the passenger window. 'The third floor. There's a health club there.'

Yrlinda gazed at me sadly, as if in farewell.

'It will be all right,' I said firmly. I walked bravely across the darkened street. *Lord, give me courage. I'm too old for this.*

I entered through the loading dock. There was a dim light burning. I spied elevators. Tiny red lights, in arrow shapes, showed they were operating.

The elevator's jaws opened to reveal an empty interior. I stepped in gingerly: every surface of the elevator had grease stains. I pressed a button, which threw the machine into noisy life. It was consolingly slow. Finally, the doors swung open

Before me was a wall; behind were the elevators. To the left and right there were identical folding iron gates. Closed iron gates. Above one gate was a sign for a garment factory. Above the other gate was a miniature version of the health club sign.

I took a tentative step towards the health club and a pile of rags and trash started to move. From the pile arose a toothless Cantonese male. From his face came an ugly scream in the uncharming vernacular of Hong Kong.

I put my hands to my throat.

'Health club,' I begged.

A rag-clad arm waved threateningly. I realized he was a watchman. He was informing me the club was closed.

'But what time . . .'

I received another rude growl. I stepped to the elevator and pushed the button hastily. A dim red arrow lit up.

'Excuse me,' I said in my kindest, most helpless voice. 'Is there a back exit to this building?'

The watchman didn't respond. He slowly resumed his previous position, becoming once again an unnoticeable pile of trash.

Protective camouflage, I thought. *Had I an M-16, he never would have stirred.*

I could see Yrlinda agitating in the bucket seat. She was happy to see me alive.

'He's gone,' I said. 'I don't know how we missed him.'

'Not good boy,' repeated Yrlinda.

'You can say that again. And a tricky one.'

'Very tricky,' Yrlinda agreed with a disapproving cluck. 'Tricky boy.'

As I drove to Craig's apartment, I lectured Yrlinda on the strengths and weaknesses of journalists on the trail of a story. 'They do this better in films,' I said wistfully. 'They do it in every scene. But can those cinematic journalists spell, Yrlinda? Can they read a balance sheet? Can they even meet a deadline? There's not a journalist movie made that has a reporter worrying about a deadline! See them. You'll see I'm right.'

'Not your fault,' Yrlinda said. 'Not your fault, no. He tricky boy.'

The remark softened me. 'No,' said I, 'you're right. It's not my fault. None of this is my fault.' I drove through the empty Kowloon tunnel and its dim, aquarium lighting turned my skin and hair a putrid shade of green.

'But it doesn't matter whose fault it is in the end,' I said in a weakened whisper. 'When it all ends in failure.'

I Couldn't Sleep

I couldn't sleep, and then found myself on Craig's balcony chaise, wrapped in a bedspread, blinking and yawning at an orange harbour. A morning mist snaked amidst the skyscrapers. Such an unsettling dream! I shivered and went back to the guest room, stepping carefully over a snoring Yrlinda. I wrote, for the first time in my adult life, a poem.

> *From beneath the moon, through night-time clouds*
> *Towards jagged, upturned daggers.*
> *Heaven's outcast or gravity's slave?*
>
> *The column's smooth skin rushes by.*
> *The pavement can't be far.*
> *To welcome me? Or swallow me up?*
>
> *I refuse to look, and then damn the dark.*
> *Too curious not to see*
> *Home. Did I jump or was I pushed?*

Before Craig left his apartment for work, I called an old gay friend. He explained, somewhat shyly, my dilemma of the previous evening. The establishment with the charming night watchman operated as a legitimate health club during the day. Its official closing time was midnight. After midnight, it turned into a gay club. There was a trick: at midnight the club actually closed. Its doors were locked and anyone remaining inside could not exit until it opened its doors the next morning.

'Obviously,' said my friend, 'that's when the "fun" begins.' It was all a ruse to fool the local police, who undoubtedly were completely unfooled and were paid handsomely to go along.

'It's a dirty place, Alice,' said my friend. 'To tell you the truth, I'm surprised to hear it's still operating.'

'When you've got a great concept . . .' commented Craig. 'How gross!'

I gave a stage sigh. 'Had I only got there a half hour earlier! Yrlinda and I could have entered as a couple!'

I had nothing to do all morning, so I left Craig's apartment forty-five minutes early for our lunch date. I sat and gazed down upon my Hong Kong. The venue was my choice: the tacky tourist restaurant on the Peak. It felt like my birthday. Hong Kong was spread below me like a gorgeous buffet, so white and clean in the noon sunlight. To the right was the Goodwill Centre and, slightly further, my own abandoned house. *Will I ever return?* I wondered. *Or have the wanderings of old age begun?* The sight of the two buildings juxtaposed gave me my first bright idea in two days. But at that moment, Craig arrived.

'I'm really sorry you couldn't sleep,' he said. 'I was worried about you all morning.'

'I think all Hong Kong must use the same insecticide. Probably from China. We're being poisoned by the Reds.'

'What will you do?'

'I've asked Bridgette to put me up,' I said, avoiding Craig's gaze. 'She owes me.' *Who cares if she is personally contaminated. It's an uncontaminated bed I need. Is it possible Bridgette does it in every bed in turn?*

'Maybe you should go back to Anderson & Partners.'

'I'll be fine at Bridgette's,' I said bravely.

'You need a doctor, Alice.'

How horrible I felt. How horrible I must have looked. Even Yrlinda had been embarrassed when I prepared to leave Craig's flat that morning.

'Don't tell *me* about doctors,' I cried. Tears poured down my face. Craig clasped my hand across the table.

'I think all of this has been too much.'

'It has,' I said, searching for tissues. 'But let's get back to business. Let's talk about our story – anything other than allergies and Anderson & Partners.'

'You mean our deceased story?' Craig was angry at himself for letting the woman slip at the airport. He was equally angry at me for losing the Filipino, although he didn't say it.

'I don't know,' I said coyly, wiping tears. 'I did some thinking last night, Craig. I've got an idea!'

I proposed to get the name of the Filipino from the civil servant who lived on the Peak. We could lean on him, I suggested. The man obviously liked the company of Filipinos more than the law allowed.

'You mean blackmail, Alice?'

'Extortion,' I corrected.

'That's a terrible idea.'

'It's illegal in Hong Kong, Craig.'

'But . . .'

'And they do arrest people. They arrest civil servants for it! I could show you files.'

'I won't do it.'

'Of course you won't do it,' I said sweetly. 'This is *my* job.'

'That's not . . .'

'I know what you're about to say, Craig, and I couldn't agree with you more. It's reprehensible to frighten a poor, timorous civil servant, who has done nothing more than take the wrong sex organ into his mouth in his own, modestly-appointed apartment . . .'

'Alice!'

'. . . or into another body cavity, but I should remind you, Craig, that we have no other course. We are at a brick wall. And our brick wall is the one that holds up that civil servant's bedroom!'

As everyone knows, it's easier to speak of deep matters when you're in a car. It's a function of staring out the window and not having to meet another person's gaze. This is particularly true at night, when the darkness adds its own layer of intimacy. But it's true in the middle of the afternoon too.

'As I lay in your guest bed last night,' I said, 'tormented by communist insecticide, I thought of nothing but this story. I dreamt they'd have to take me back once we cracked it. It's a fantasy, I know. But surely they'd have to do something! Imagine: an employee on permanent disability winning the Pulitzer Prize!'

'I was thinking about this story too.' Craig stared out of the windshield at the scurrying crowds. 'And all I could think of was what it said about journalism. Journalism is a lot more fucked than anyone ever admits, Alice.'

'Craig! How could you?'

'Don't tell me it's one of democracy's pillars, Alice, or you'll sound like my father. And don't say it's "fun," like all the other journos. I detest that line!'

'It's a calling, Craig. Nothing less. It's a commitment to the truth.'

'That's it, Alice,' Craig said. 'It *is* a commitment to the truth. But so many journalists fail in their commitment. They can't live up to it. That's what I was thinking last night. That's what this hoax was all about. Someone, somewhere, has the same ideas about journalism that I do. And he was demonstrating them with that hoax.'

'Someone, somewhere,' I mused. 'That's not much use.' But Craig wasn't listening. He was staring out of the window, oblivious of the crowds without and my comments within.

'If I wasn't born to write this story,' he murmured, 'I've sure as fuck earned the right over the past eighteen months.'

Before I proceeded to the Peak that evening, we had a preparatory drink at the FCC and a small debate.

'It depends, I guess, on how many times you can do it in one night.' I adopted a clinical tone.

'Not how many times you *can* do it,' Craig countered, 'but how many times you want to do it. And Alice, there are limits.'

Craig's point was sensible: would the Filipino have proceeded to an all-night sex club if he had just had sex with the civil servant? Or wasn't it more likely that he and the civil servant had merely had dinner? A mixed grill, perhaps.

'I saw the way he walked up that walk. And it wasn't a going-to-dinner walk.'

'But in all likelihood – '

'He's a horny bastard, Craig.'

'He'd better be,' Craig said, 'because if he isn't you've got nothing on this civil servant. You can't blackmail. You can't exort. You will sit in his living-room, make a false charge – and then what will you do? Ask to be excused?'

'I'll threaten to expose him on a *false* charge,' I said. 'What does it matter? I'm trying to intimidate the man. It doesn't matter if

I've got something on him or not. I can picture this man: he's a poor, scared civil servant who wears a kimono around the house. Even if he didn't do it last night, he wanted to! And that's enough. Fear is the key, Craig. And tonight, my role is the monster mother who catches her son with his cock in his hand! Or someone else's. I intend to scare this guy so fully, he'll tell me anything I ask!'

Craig didn't say it, but his look was eloquent. He took in my face, my hair, my dishevelled clothes. He was thinking that no one in Hong Kong, or anywhere else in the world, perhaps, could better portray the Monster Mother than Alice Giles.

Craig saw me off from outside the FCC. 'Give him hell,' he said. 'No mother jokes.'

I hesitated for a second. 'We're in this together, Craig? Aren't we?'

He clasped my arm. 'You bet,' he said. 'One hundred percent. This is our story, Alice, and we're going to rock the world with it.' He squeezed the arm again.

'Where are you going?'

He motioned to the office.

'Why?'

'I have to send a message to Paul. He thinks I'm on a plane to Pakistan!'

He looked at me and grinned. Those dark eyes were as expressive as I've ever seen them.

I Traversed That Same Path

I traversed that same path, climbed those same steps, and rang the bell of the second-storey flat. After a few moments, I heard a muffled shout. It sounded like, 'Wait Wait Wait.' The doorlatch clicked, a pale hand made a gesture through the crack of the door. I heard vague welcoming noises. I pushed the door open tentatively.

'I'll be with you in a second, sweetheart. Something's cooking. John's Famous Pork Roast.'

I saw the retreating back of a large man dressed in gym shorts and a stained grey T-shirt. In a moment, I heard facetious singing, clearly performed for my benefit.

'Someone's in the kitchen with Dinah . . .' It was a hearty voice. 'Feel at home, sweetheart. You must be thirsty. It's damned *hot!*' He called the last word in a dramatic sing-song. 'A drink?'

I closed the door gently and walked to a chair in the living-room. I chose not to call out a drink order. Friendliness seemed a poor tactic.

'Hard or soft?' came the voice again. 'What's the difference between cumin and coriander? One of the great world questions! I'll tell you the answer: there is no difference. Go on, sweetheart. Have a stiff one!'

What a cheery soul. How does he know I'm not a murderer? A bill-collector? Or, for that matter, a blackmailer?

The living-room was decorated in a remarkable, unbachelor-like style. The furniture, standard civil-service issue, was covered with huge black sheets. All the fittings had been painted black; the carpet was white. The walls were covered with reproductions of Egon Schiele prints, displayed in black frames. I felt uncomfortable being watched by all those twisted Schiele men and women, bent in positions of passion. They made me dizzy.

'Don't be shy, sweetheart.' The man re-entered the room. He handed me a glass of club soda and bowed with exaggerated formality. 'Pleased to meet you. Whoever you are. You didn't specify hard, so you got soft.' He grabbed a cane chair from his dining-room set, pulled it around backwards, and sat facing me with his long arms around the chair's back.

'I'm John,' he said. 'The smell is my pork roast, for which I will someday be famous. Remember that smell. Remember that name.'

'My name is Alice Giles.' I soberly sipped the soda water.

'Never heard of you.'

You'll wish you never did. 'I won't take much of your time.'

John was the kind of large, unihibited man who dresses with intentional sloppiness. His face was oval, clean-shaven, with lank, traditionally cut black hair. He had cocker-spaniel eyes that fixed on a face with aggressive calm. He was a huge man and powerfully built. He was starting to settle around the hips and waist but there was nothing feminine about him. He had tremendous, excess bodily energy; already he had abandoned his chair and was circling around me. His accent, surprisingly, was American and faintly New England.

'You won't take much of my time?' His voice shifted to a mocking tone: '"I won't take much of your time." How sorry I am to hear that, sweetheart. For I have plenty of time, plenty of stew and no one around to share them with.' He shifted into an Elvis Presley imitation:

'*Are you looo-onely tonight?*'

'I've eaten.' I realized that John wasn't the timid civil servant I had described to Craig. 'I've come on an awkward matter.'

'Blurt it out sweetheart. I won't tell a soul.' John was back on his chair, but his feet were tapping the floor.

'It's not about me, I'm afraid. And please stop calling me sweetheart. It's about you. You and your Philippine boys.'

John shot out of his chair with a look of shock on his face. The shock was feigned. He then exploded in a gust of astonished laughter.

'Did I hear you right, sweetheart?' He was bent over with

artificial laughter. 'Me and my "Philippine boys?"' He mimicked my feathery voice.

'I simply need some information,' I rushed on. 'You entertained a Philippine boy last night in this flat. What you did was illegal under the laws of Hong Kong. As a civil servant you can be fired summarily for the offence of indecent assault or gross indecency. *If* someone exposes you. If *we* expose you.'

John was pacing the room in great, wide, happy circles. 'Yes!' he proclaimed, gazing thoughtfully at the ceiling. 'I'll never forget his look when he said to me, "John, I want to indecently assault you!" There was fire in his eyes. John had assumed a horrible, mincing voice.

'. . . just a little information.'

'And I said to him, "I haven't had a good gross indecency in a dog's age." That's what I said. I couldn't help myself. And how it turned him on! We had the grossest gross indecency of our lives!'

I wondered at my misjudgement.

'And was it ever gross!' John fixed me with a look from across the room. 'Who are you, sweetheart?'

'If you tell me some simple facts . . .'

The big man approached me. He extended his index finger. He brought the finger to the end of my chin. With his fingertip, he raised my face until I looked into his glittering eyes.

'Who the fuck is "we"?'

I looked at him with shame and terror.

'How old are you, ma'am?'

I tried to pull my face downwards. He raised it again with his brusque finger. I felt enormous power emanating from him and could imagine being struck.

'How old?' he repeated. 'Tell me. Don't be modest, sweetheart. I won't tell a soul.'

'Forty-six.' I had a catch in my voice.

'Forty-six?' said John. 'You don't look a day under seventy.'

'My health. Everyone thinks . . . It's my tragedy!'

'So why's a forty-six-year-old woman, who looks seventy and can barely catch her breath after two fucking flights of stairs, blackmailing a Hong Kong policeman?'

John's voice was enraged. His finger actually hurt my chin. 'A policeman?'

John nodded. He whipped his finger away from my face. I stared at him with open mouth.

'Yes, sweetheart. I'm an CID inspector. Been one for eight years.'

'Oh, no. A professional interrogator . . .'

'At work *and* in my spare time.' He was circling the room once more, making ever wider circles and working off his vast amounts of energy. 'When the opportunity walks in my front door.'

'An expert in criminal evidence . . .'

'And I know quite a bit, believe me, about buggery in the civil service. Now, Ms Alice Giles, what is your profession?'

He grabbed my chin once more. He raised my head. 'Tell me, sweetheart! I want to hear this loud and clear!'

'I'm a foreign correspondent.'

'A *what?*'

'A foreign correspondent.' I spoke loudly. I was regaining some spirit, and a glimmer of defiance.

John leapt from his chair and threw his arms out to the far walls. '*That's* it! A journalist! One of my favourite professions! The seekers of truth! The know-it-alls who never err! I should have guessed. What wonderful publication do you do your blackmailing on behalf of, sweetheart?'

I had begun to loathe this man. 'I work for the *World Business Journal*.'

John roared laughing. He flopped on the couch and waved his legs in the air. He gaspingly made his way to the kitchen and after several moments returned with a bottle of Macao wine and two glasses.

He poured two glasses.

'I apologize,' I said, 'I do. And I think at this point . . .'

'No,' John said. 'Don't go. Finish your wine. You've had a tough evening.'

'I wasn't planning to go. You misunderstood me. I haven't completed my job.' I drained the glass of wine, my first alcohol in years. I sat erect in my chair and spoke simply and unemotionally. 'I came here for some simple information. I tried to bully you but it was foolish. I should have just asked. Now I will. Can you, or will you, tell me the name of the Filipino who spent the evening here last night? It's very important.'

John took a gulp of his wine. 'Why do you want to know?'

'It's too complicated to explain. Who is he?'

'Is it murder? Robbery?'

'It's for a story, John. You know that. One of our stories. That you consider so ridiculous. Please tell me!'

'A story!' John rose and towered over me. 'A bedtime story? Or some other kind? I must say, it's been a long time since I busted my butt for a "story." You know that some of us work for good and evil? For life and death?'

'Some of us work for truth,' I said. 'I don't expect you to understand. But I can assure you it has nothing to do with sex or the law or the civil service. It's all about newspapering. It's all about . . . may I have another glass of wine?'

I was forced to explain, in a truncated way, the significance of the Philippine boy.

'You're working on a pretty slim case, sweetheart.'

'I know. He's all we have. Please!'

'His name is "Rod,"' John said. 'Your problem is that he has no address or phone. He's one of those boys. I've only met him a couple of times.'

'He's *what* kind of boy?'

'Casual,' John said. 'Real casual.'

'Where will he be tonight? I followed him last night to the Nathan Road baths. Would he go there again tonight?'

John shook his head. 'Not on Monday. It's closed. There's no place people go on Mondays.'

'No gay bar?'

'Not on Mondays.'

'But I need him tonight!'

'If you can wait until the weekend, try the Dateline in Central. He's been there every weekend for the past few weeks. He's new in town. Otherwise, you'll have to troll for him on the streets. On any of the million streets in Hong Kong.'

'Isn't there some park? Some public toilet? I know that sounds disgusting but I've always read . . .'

John leapt to his feet, tossed off his third glass of wine and started his enormous rings around the living-room. 'Alice Giles cruising the gay toilets of Hong Kong? My God, who could credit it? Where would you lie in wait? What would you say? What if you got caught?' He started to laugh. 'We'll read in tomorrow's

Morning Post that you were being held for indecent assault inside the Hilton toilet?'

He walked to me and said, 'I knew who you were, you know.'

I gaped at him.

'I was a journalist myself, sweetheart. At *Newsday*. Long ago. Before law school and the SEC. I've seen you at the FCC but we've never met. Old Alice Giles. The journalistic tiger.'

'Why didn't you . . .'

John shrugged. 'I wanted to see your technique. It started off piss poor, old dear. But you're recovering nicely.'

'You fuckhead.'

'And,' John continued in a more serious tone, 'I wanted to see how far you'd go, and for what cause, as a journalist. I have a lot of opinions, you know, on these two institutions: the press and the police. Sometimes I think the police are the most fucked-up people in the world. And sometimes I think journalists are.'

'And tonight?'

'No contest.'

I bowed my head.

'I'm sorry,' John said. 'You won't stay? For my speciality. Really, it's not half bad.'

'No. I have work to do.'

'You won't find him tonight . . .'

'I understand.'

'Do you need help?'

I made my way out of the apartment, down the steps, and out of the building with its hallways covered with thousands of coats of paint – one for every occupant in its history. I strolled to the railing at the edge of the hill and wondered why the thought depressed me. Isn't it our fate to be less than we hoped? To be a mere coat of paint, covered by someone else's coat? I leaned over the railing and looked up at the apartment. The lights were on.

I looked out at Hong Kong's jagged towers and thought of John and his interrogation.

They have a method, I thought. *Why did he ask my age?* John had penetrated my most sacred secret, the truth that I couldn't reveal to new friends because of the unbearable pity it would elicit. *They go for the weakest point. The bastards.*

'I'm forty-six,' I said to the gleaming spikes ranged below me. 'Forty-six and ready to die.'

Unnerving Things

1. A phone off the hook.

2. Skewed scissors on the floor.

3. An whole egg on a kitchen counter.

4. Not the wandering eye, but the other one that looks directly – and fiercely – at you. How happy, in those moments, seems the wanderer.

5. Swivel-hipped walkers with painfully thin legs. In Hong Kong.

6. That skin disease that makes brown skin peel away to reveal sickly white skin beneath. This is common in India.

7. Albinos. In China.

8. Japanese people with steel teeth.

9. Laughing, friendly people who, surprisingly, have no molars. This reminds me of the Philippines.

10. Big gums.

11. The landing by plane in Hong Kong, when you can peer in the windows of the Kowloon tenements as if you were on a slow, inner-city elevated line. Can those people see you, with tense face and rigid smile?

Things That Horrify (and Make the Heart Catch)

1. The phone call at 3 a.m.

2. Hare lips.

3. A beggar girl walking down the street with a salvaged Q-tip sticking proudly out of her ear.

4. A note that reads: 'See me.'

5. Hairy spiders.

6. Goitres.

7. A four-year-old child running gaily towards the top of a staircase.

8. A cockroach tickling your ear as you sleep.

I Can Only Relate These Events

I can only relate these events in the dreamlike way I picture them: through a cloud of disbelief and incomprehension. Craig is a genius in some ways. And a fool in others.

As I was suffering through my disastrous attempt at intimidation, interrogation and extortion on the Peak, Craig waited for me at the FCC. He proceeded straight to the bar and informed the bartender of my impending call. Christopher Smart approached a few moments later.

'When you have time, Craig,' he said, 'I'd like to introduce you to Ted Augenstein.'

Craig saw Ted, in a jacket of yellow linen, entertaining an assemblage of journalists.

'He's back?' Craig asked. 'Again?'

Christopher nodded.

'You have enough ass-kissers over there?'

'We do, actually.'

'Where's Adam Fendler? He's conspicuously absent.'

'Don't ask,' said Christopher, shaking his head and making a kind of shudder. 'Believe me, don't ask. Ted's on his way to China.'

'China needs more visiting foreign editors,' said Craig. 'And US senators. Bosses are the pits.'

'He's technically my boss,' Christopher said, 'but in day-to-day matters . . .'

Craig cut Christopher off with a false promise to join the group later. He could imagine his introduction to Ted Augenstein. 'Yes, I know your mother and father quite well . . . Winn mentioned you when I last saw him at the Yale Club . . . He thought your performance in Asia lacked a certain . . . and I would have to agree in many . . .'

What happened then to Craig Kirkpatrick? Did he sink into a hateful reverie against Paul, Winn, Ai and the whole world of journalism? Did he succumb to another kind of reverie, a sticky dream of Japanese girlfriends walking on his back and manipulating other, more sensitive organs? Or did he simply fall asleep? How did he miss, at the other end of the bar, one of the most significant visitations in the history of the FCC? How did he miss the man who had the answer to all the questions? The man dressed, unbelievably, in a huge, brand-new, snow-white sailor suit? The man with the music-hall voice, sitting alone with a large pink drink? The fat man with the billowy clouds of puffy grey fake hair: which sausage fingers continually pulled and primped and poked?

To continue: How could Craig miss the moment when the fat man sent a bottle of champagne to the stocky, visiting foreign editor? How did he not hear the hearty cheers of welcome as the bottle was delivered and opened? Who could have mistaken the foreign editor's 100-Watt blush as he read the scribbled note with the bottle? His awkwardness in acknowledging the gift? The painful, long-distance toast from bar to table? The whispered questions at the club table: *Who is he?* And Ted's bullshit reply: *An old acquaintance from Singapore.* The follow-up question from the implacable journalist (was it really one of Les Misérables?): 'But, Mr Augenstein. What does his message mean? *"Congratulations from me and my companion for the story of your career"?* And Ted's *sotto voce* reply, 'An allusion, I guess, to an old story of mine . . .' The utterly logical riposte, 'But he doesn't have a companion!' Not yet, oh Misérable, you who are so sensitive to who is with companion and who is not. But you were on the right track! If only the same could have been said for Craig Kirkpatrick!

Or is the blame on me? I had known from the very beginning that Anton Vavasour was the touchstone to the mystery. I had recounted my theory numerous times to Craig. But did I forget that vital point? Did I not tell Craig that Anton Vavasour was a fat man? Was I protecting my own, little scoop, the scoop I had earned by ambushing Ted Augenstein at a chilli contest? All journalists guard their scoops, of course. Sometimes, we even hate to reveal them in print.

So there sat Anton Vavasour, blissfully alone, twirling the umbrella from his fruit drink and darting glances and grins that Ted Augenstein desperately tried to avoid. There was Craig, muttering blasphemies into his beer against a different foreign editor. And there I was, 2,000 feet up, battling wits with a trained interrogator for the Hong Kong police! Life can be so foolish! Ah, the wonder of it all. Ah, the pity!

Craig was retrieved from his reverie by the sight of a newcomer approaching the bar. He was a slim, good-looking man who decided to share his looks with every other man at the bar. After he had traversed its length, he took a seat next to the enormous Englishman in the sailor suit. The young man tried on his elder's sailor hat, eliciting a great gust of guffaw from his companion, and teasingly pulled at the fuzzy wig. He ordered a beer, returned a wink to Craig's astonished stare and embarked on a whispered set of confidences with the fat man.

It's him, Craig marvelled. *He's strolled right into the FCC. It's what my dad always said: a good journalist can't count on luck, but he sure gets a lot of it.*

Craig knew to hold onto his luck. He ordered another beer and repositioned his chair to keep his eye on the Philippine boy/man.

The fat man struggled out of his chair and placed his sailor hat crookedly on his grey curls. He embraced the Filipino in a bear hug, held him by the two shoulders and said in a loud, ostentatious voice, 'Wish me luck, Rudy. I'm off to sea! Don't mourn me! War is hell!'

His name is Rudy.

The fat man proceeded to Ted Augenstein's table, made pleasantries, elicited a giggle or two from the crowd and shook Ted's hand twice. Ted seemed annoyed.

Then he departed, waving his sailor hat to the entire bar.

Nigel Harris, also known as 'Jabbah the Hut,' said to Craig, 'What in God's name was that?'

'Haven't you met the new *Time* Magazine correspondent, Nigel?'

'What happened to Carl Rolla?' Nigel was in a state of shock.

'Didn't fit the corporate culture.'

The Filipino drank his beer and, with some loose bills left on the counter by the fat man, ordered another. Other drinkers came and went. There was a stir when Ted Augenstein finally broke up his happy party and the ass-kissers regaled him with best wishes. His exit was less dramatic than that of the fat man. It concluded with a lame joke about China Airlines.

And finally the boy jumped up from his chair, gave a final searching look around the bar – with a meaningful look at Craig – and jauntily exited.

Craig followed him down the curving lane towards Queen's Road. The boy turned into a dark connecting street. He stopped to light a cigarette. Craig strolled up beside him. 'Rudy.'

'Have we met?'

Craig shrugged noncommittally.

'You were staring at me,' said the boy.

'You were staring at me,' Craig replied.

'I was admiring your nose.'

It took Craig a moment to reply. He had never been complimented on his nose. 'There were lots of other noses at the bar.'

The boy laughed. 'It's "Rod,"' he said. 'You have a place?'

'How about a cup of coffee?'

'I don't like coffee.'

'Neither do I. I have a better idea.'

Craig and the boy strolled to D'Aguilar Street, a good twenty minutes away, and spent another twenty minutes choosing a bar, ordering drinks, making preparatory chit-chat. By my reckoning, Anton Vavasour was boarding his plane to the Philippines by the time Craig finally called the FCC. I was waiting there. He told me, 'Hold on, Alice. I've got him.'

'Who was your friend?' Craig asked when he returned from the phone booth. The boy looked around.

'At the FCC, I mean. The fat guy.'

'An old friend. An Englishman. A lot of fun. Where are you from?'

'New York.'

'I have twelve friends in America. Real friends. I don't sleep with that guy, Anton, anymore. We meet to talk. He makes me laugh and brings me places. Sometimes I bring other boys to his room. He likes Japanese boys. Thais.' He wrinkled his nose in disgust. 'You're not an all-American boy, are you?'

'I'm half Japanese.'

'Oh.' After an awkward pause, he asked, 'You're cut?'

'What?'

'You know. Circumcised.'

Craig didn't answer.

The boy's eyes narrowed. 'Hey, you're not wasting my time, are you? I hope you've got a place.'

'I have a place, yes. And I can give you some money. Afterwards. Don't worry.' The boy nodded.

'But,' Craig continued, 'for the time being I just want to talk.'

The boy laughed good naturedly, showing large, beautiful teeth. 'Look,' he said. 'I know there are lots of bullshit guys. I'm not one. If we're going to screw, let's screw. You don't have to worry. You can fuck me. I have a condom.' He patted his jeans pocket.

Craig turned serious. 'Rudy, you were on a boat yesterday with a Filipina. She arranged a fake press conference in Taipei last month. At the same time, you were in Japan. I saw you there. You need to give me some information. Who arranged the press conference? Why did he, or they, do it?'

The boy looked at Craig incredulously.

'I was at that press conference,' Craig said in a low, sincere tone. 'Now I need some answers.' Craig withdrew five red $100 bills from his pants pocket. He placed them on the bar. '*If you give me information.*'

The boy laughed his handsome laugh. He put his hand on Craig's shoulder. He took one of the red bills from the counter and pushed the others towards Craig.

'I told you I'm not a bullshit guy,' he said. 'Keep the rest. I'm not worth it. I was in Japan with my friend. With Anton. The fat guy at the FCC. He's the one who organized your press conference. He was sitting there, right next to me, and you followed me instead. You blew it, *pogi*. You wanted Anton Vavasour.'

'That was Anton Vavasour? In the wig? The sailor suit?'

The boy stood up and readied himself to leave. 'Thanks for the drink.' He drained it. 'And the cash.' He patted his pocket. 'Sorry we couldn't do something more exciting.'

'Wait!' said Craig. 'Where's Vavasour?'

The boy made a flying motion with his hand.

'Where?'

The boy shrugged and moved away.

'Rudy!' called Craig. 'Where?' He put his hands up in a praying gesture.

Rudy returned to Craig's side. He looked around the bar to see if they were unobserved. He put his hand on Craig's crutch and whispered closely in his ear.

'I shouldn't tell you. But I like you.' He squeezed. 'Go to the San Fernando in La Union. Anton will be there during the race. And so will some of your other newspaper friends. They're having a kind of reunion. You'll get your story, or your revenge, or whatever.'

'When?' asked Craig desperately.

'Now.'

When I saw Craig rush into the FCC, I knew something serious had happened. I spoke first. 'I blew it!'

'It doesn't matter,' Craig said. He quickly told to me the confusing story.

'Anton Vavasour!' I cried. 'At our bar? The insolent pig!'

Christopher Smart strolled through and Craig and I repressed our emotions. 'You didn't come to meet Ted,' Chris said. 'He said he knew your dad.'

'Ted who?' I asked.

'Ted Augenstein,' Chris replied. 'He was here earlier.'

I kicked Craig under the table but comprehension was already dawning on his face.

'What's he doing here?' I asked innocently.

'China trip.'

'He's been here quite often in the past few months,' I said. I felt Craig kick me under the table.

'Yeah, I guess,' said Chris.

'How long in China?'

'He's back Wednesday night.'

'And he leaves . . .'

'Tomorrow.'

'On Cathay or . . .'

'The CAAC morning flight.'

'He's scooping you again?' It was simple to divert the attention of Christopher Smart. All you had to do was mention him.

'Well you know, Alice, technically he's my boss. But in day-to-day decisions, I call my own shots now. It's been that way for six months.'

When he finally left, I said to Craig: 'It's Ted! He's in with Vavasour. He has to be.'

'But he wasn't with Vavasour . . .'

'It doesn't matter, Craig. The point is that he didn't expose him! Tonight, at the bar! They're conspirators!'

'And he's going to China – '

'Bullshit,' I cried. 'He's not going to China. Don't you see? Don't you *see?*'

Tuesday morning, Craig was once more loitering behind a pillar in Kai Tak's departure area. He watched a group of CAAC passengers as they stood in roped-off seclusion. The flight would leave in forty minutes. Ted Augenstein was not in the group.

A uniformed woman demanded the attention of the passengers. She began reading off a list of names. When each passenger responded, she ticked a name off her list.

'Augenstein!' she called. She said it again, changing the 'steen' to 'stine.'

A hand raised above the crowd. The uniformed woman nodded and called the next name.

Craig changed pillars to get a better look at the man who raised his hand. A Chinese man had taken Ted's place. An ordinary-looking Chinese man, with nothing peculiar about him unless you looked at his right hand. The hand he chose not to raise in the air. The hand with the six fingers.

For one magic moment, the man's awed attention locked onto Craig. But Craig couldn't dawdle. His plane to Manila was starting to board.

A Brief Word About The Philippines

The Philippines: that unique land that is drawing to it, as a candle beckons to the darkened corners of the moth-filled room, nearly all of my acquaintances in this tale. The Philippines is a land unto its own, a land whose faults are obvious to all but whose cheap perfume continues to beguile. It's a land of twisted violence, heartless poverty and a kind of political and social chaos that the locals seem to enjoy. At the same time, it's a land of family, of humility, of sparkling seas, of ardent passion. It's a place where killings are done for a quarter and kindness is even cheaper. It's a land where foreign journalists thunder down dusty roads to find the spot where an Italian priest was murdered; to discover where his balding pate was crushed with a stone; to interview the bystanders who saw the assailants lean down and eat the priest's brains with rusted spoons. After filing their stories, the same journalists lie down with ageless Filipinas, stroke their silken skin or take them roughly and murmur, 'No, I will never leave the Philippines! No, never!'

I've already told you my theory about Pandora and her box. The entire world was rocked by the furies she let loose, but no place more than the land where the box was pried open. This must be the permanently-wretched Philippines. According to legend, Pandora was left with only one consolation – Hope – but the Philippine Pandora found something different at the bottom of her box. Sex. For Filipinos and Filipinas have a special attitude towards sex. They aren't much interested in opium or hard work or mumbled mantras, like the poor of other countries. The Filipinos prefer to screw their troubles away: to screw everyone and anyone, at all times of the day, for a fistful of pesos or for free. As one Filipino would say, 'Everyone's horny.' And he's perfectly correct – about his jazzed up, ever-confused native land.

Such a strange convergence! Later, Craig and I would piece together, minute by minute, the odd minuet in Manila of Anton Vavasour, Ted Augenstein, Adam Fendler, Jean Yulo and, of course, Craig himself. On Tuesday afternoon, Craig was striding through Benigno Aquino International Airport, past a mariachi band that sang, whistled, jigged and waved at arriving passengers. It performed near the very spot that poor Mr Aquino took three bullets in the head from the gun of a soldier. (The Philippines does it best to overwhelm even first-time visitors with its unique mix of the happy-go-lucky and the macabre.) He waited on the immigration line that Ted Augenstein had gone through only hours before, Anton Vavasour half a day before that, Adam Fendler two hours before Vavasour, and Jean Yulo the previous night. On the way to his hotel, the cab driver asked if Craig was a newcomer to the Philippines and Craig said yes. He desired to bask in tawdriness. He spent the rest of the drive turning down the driver's offers of an astonishing catalogue of sexual encounters with girls and boys, all of them college graduates, even the virgins. The taxi rumbled by canals with decrepit slums hanging tenuously above them; past tiny discos with red lights and decoration done in bamboo and thatch; it barely missed pedestrians dashing across the darkened boulevard like terrified animals. Craig could see the prayer on their lips.

Craig stayed at the Manila Hotel. He ate in the grill room, with its dusty seashell decorations, and the maître d' greeted him by name.

'How is your father, sir? We haven't seen him in several years. And your mother? Tell them we are holding the "Kirkpatrick Suite" just for them.'

Anton Vavasour, we later realized, was not far away. He was in a Spanish restaurant on M.H. del Pilar, Manila's tenderloin 'strip,' eating a vast platter of smoked hams and *chorizos*. The maitre d' had also greeted Vavasour by name and the boys behind the bar had whispered and giggled.

'I'm always hungry before a big job,' Vavasour told a very hungry new friend, who wore a new pair of jeans, a new shirt and his first pair of real shoes in half a year, all bought that afternoon at the nearest Shoemart. 'And I have to get up very early,' Vavasour continued between bites. '*Very* early. So no carousing tonight. It will have to wait until tomorrow, when this whole job is finished at last. If you can wait, my little morsel. Just one more day. Tomorrow.'

The boy looked up and nodded, his jaw slack and shiny with sausage grease.

Ted Augenstein was staying at a downtown hotel never patronized by journalists. He ate dinner in his room. How he longed to go to the bars on M.H del Pilar! To immerse himself in the world of night, drink, talk and expatriatism, the jokey, jazzed-up, hyper-autonomous existence for which he was sacrificing a career and a respectable public image. But Ted realized the foolishness of impatience. He too had only a day or two to wait. He stared out of his hotel window at the glow that came over the rooftops. He could almost see the neon, hear the music from the jukeboxes, see the journalists with their feet hooked onto bar rails and their hands wrapped around brown beer botles, talking as if the night would never end. They'd be talking truth and lies all mixed up together as they always did at this time of night. They'd talk so much it would seem they'd never go home.

Adam Fendler was dining on the outdoor patio of a modest seaside resort in San Fernando, three hours drive north of Manila. He had spent the whole day patrolling the town's resorts, sweating beneath his fedora. No one seemed to know anything about 'the fat man.'

The fat man, Adam grumbled to himself. *Am I being jerked around or what?*

Adam was tired, discouraged and very hungry. Until his meal was placed before him. 'Is this Chicken Kiev?'

The waiter nodded.

'It doesn't look like Chicken Kiev.'

'I told you to have the fish,' the waiter said.

'I don't like the taste of fish.'

'Or the mixed grill.'

'I had that last night. It was horrible.'

'Tomorrow,' shrugged the waiter, 'try the fish.'

In Hong Kong, at that exact moment, I was enjoying slurps of Yrlinda's sustaining beef-marrow soup between snatches of conversation with Florence in New York. Why hadn't I called Florence before? Weakness! Sloth! Lack of vision! She gave me information that would have tipped us off several days back. For one thing, Ted had practically jumped on a plane, according to Florence.

'No one can explain his sudden interest in China,' she said. 'Lila's doing a bad job in Peking but she's always done a bad job.'

When Ted Augenstein jumped on his plane, Florence related, he forgot that Arthur Ecclestein was coming to stay with him. Arthur showed up at the newsroom. Florence was forced to take pity on him.

'He *was* a staffer,' she said. 'Once. Although I think he still owes the *Tribune* money. And you know how much he gets at the *Monitor*.'

She gave him, against all regulations, the office's spare key to Ted's apartment. And the next day, Arthur returned to the newsroom with news of his own. He reported that Ted's apartment was stripped of its porcelains. Each shelf was bare, except for a few blue and whites in the guest bedroom. There were no signs of burglary or forced entry. The priceless vases and bowls had been spirited away! Sold! For what possible purpose?

'Keep going,' I told Florence.

That night, as Arthur sat in front of Ted's television, he heard a bizarre but familiar noise emanating from the master bedroom. He went to the room and opened the closet. Inside he found a telex machine. A telex installed in Ted Augenstein's closet! And on the telex roll, there were more than 50 cryptic messages from Hong Kong, the Philippines, India, Thailand and Taiwan.

'I went through Ted's expense reports just now,' Florence said. 'No telex bills. Anthony Pasquale is saying that Ted is a spy. I say that's nonsense. "We don't have spies at the *Tribune*," I said.'

'Only assholes.'

'That's right,' replied an unfazed Florence. 'All recruited from the *Journal*.'

I was so elated with Florence's intelligence that I called Craig at the Manila Hotel.

'I'll leave for La Union tomorrow morning,' he said. 'If we only knew, and knew for certain, that Ted's here.'

'He's there, Craig! He's there!'

'You're calling from Bridgette's?'

I told him no.

'You've gone back to your house?'

'No,' I said. 'I can't face it. I'm sure it's contaminated for three hundred years. I'll explain when you get back, Craig.'

'Where did you stay last night?'

I didn't know what to say.

'Alice, where are you? Where can I get hold of you when I return?'

'It's all taken care of, Craig,' I said. 'I will know when you return with our story. Don't worry. And then, when we have the time, I'll explain everything. Don't worry about me. I'm doing fine.'

Later that evening, I stared down at the tiny lights of Hong Kong. The moon was full and only partly obscured by clouds. Yrlinda was preparing some more soup. We even had music: she had retrieved my portable cassette recorder. Somehow, despite the scrabbly circumstances, I was feeling remarkably content. My strength was returning. I felt restored to my old life. I had wrenched back my phone and computer lines and reconnected myself to the world. I had everything back that I had lost, just one floor up. In addition, our story was breaking. The right reporters were at the right place at the right time, riding the story's crest. It's the same feeling a general must have when a battle is going so smoothly that he can take a few hours' nap. As I looked down at my colony below, I listened once again to that anthem of the old and semi-forgotten, 'Hello Young Lovers (Wherever You Are.)' In the past, I've loved the song for its sadness. This evening I began to appreciate its difficult optimism.

> *All of my memories are happy tonight.*
> *For I've had a love of my own.*
> *I've had a love of my own, like yours.*
> *I've had a love of my own.*

I've had a *life* of my own. And somehow, that Tuesday night, touching the clouds 55 storeys above Hong Kong, that seemed almost enough.

CONSOLACION

There isn't an island in the Philippines that lacks a sign promising, in peeling blue and yellow letters, 'A Taste of Paradise: Cabins Available' or 'Sunset Villas' or 'Costa del Sol Holidays' down an uninviting dirt track. Most newcomers are intrigued by the signs. Which of these lush 7,000 islands, they wonder, couldn't support a small, unpretentious beach resort? A resort with warm hosts and cool beer, delicious seafood, gentle sands and becalming surf. But down that dirt track is nothing more than the miserable, abandoned dream of some Swiss or Australian man who once had $10,000, an exotic fuckmate and unoriginal ideas of an easy life. These days, Hans or Fritz or Al is only a face in a dimpled snapshot. The resort is run by Hans' abandoned Philippine wife Baby and her truculent brother Julius, who dreams of going to Manila. The work is too much and the guests too few; enormous spiders now dangle above each hard bed. The beach is a ghastly stretch of black, volcanic cinders – an oversight by Hans – 'but there's a white beach just ninety minutes away by jeepney and pump boat,' according to Baby. Dinner is spaghetti with meat sauce or canned corned beef, because they closed the fish market. 'Or would you prefer Spam?' Dreams die fast in the Philippines, as fast as thatch rots. Only slightly more durable is wood and yellow and blue paint. And the cast-iron determination of Julius to get to Manila. All he needs is the money the average visitor will leave in his cabin the day he visits the white beach. (Which isn't very white, in truth, and takes 2 1/2 hours to reach, not 90 minutes, and only if the pumpboat works.) Julius will also take the gold watch, the portable radio and the packet of 20 Japanese condoms. All will come in handy in the big city. Until they're stolen, hocked and used up.

San Fernando, in the province of La Union, is the apotheosis of faded Philippine dreams: a full-fledged resort town, with once-good roads, once-high hopes and a bundle of uncollected promises from the local boy who was Minister of Tourism. *Before* the revolution. Now, a stroll along the two kilometres of pebbly, unlovely beach is a harrowing tour of dreams dead and dying. The closed resorts have been looted and shaken to their foundations, as if singled out by earthquakes of unusual precision. Next door, the speakers are still blaring 'Sex Over the Phone' and the beer is still cold, but the game room is permanently closed and the gift shop has long run out of T-shirts and toothpaste. The porch is rotting and ants draw maps on the vinyl tablecloths. The Chicken Kiev smells funny. The mixed grill is very, very mixed.

The only successful resorts of San Fernando are filled with East Europeans, who spend their days gobbling mangoes and beers and growling to the female mango vendors, 'Fuckey fuckey fuckey?' The most energetic entrepreneur is the seashell vendor who makes eyes at both the European ladies and the European men, knowing that sex appeal increases his shell sales. (He brags, quite plausibly, that he's been in every hotel room in San Fernando.) The hoteliers spend their days hoping for an invasion of Australian or English perverts, who have done such wonders for other Philippine resort towns.

When Ted Augenstein drove through San Fernando in a sealed car with black-tinted windows, the town was preparing for the imminent arrival of the Ninth Annual South China Sea Regatta. It was a rare boom week for modest San Fernando. Already the main street bustled with foreigners and not just the dun-coloured East Europeans with the ever-full mouths. These foreigners wore bright yachting duds and white belts and shoes. They bought shells and souvenirs. They smiled charmingly and their sunglasses were held around their heads by fashionable straps. Need I say more? They were Americans. Many of them wanted the same 'Fuckey fuckey fuckey' as the East Europeans, but they had a much nicer way of asking. They actually looked good when they took off their clothes and they paid more. These were San Fernando's favourite foreigners and the fact that they came just once a year added an evanescent beauty to their visits. Their subsequent letters, first bearing 'Love' and greenbacks, later 'All the Best!', were eagerly awaited. The snapshots they sent from Hong Kong and Tokyo were displayed with particular prominence in the high-ceilinged, sparsely-decorated living-rooms. For Filipinos love good-looking Americans; they adore good-looking Americans with money; and they become ecstatic over good-looking Americans with money who return over and over to the Philippines. What more could a Filipino desire: good looks, sex, money and an assurance that he and his country are truly, if temporarily, loved? For America and Americans could fuck the Philippines and the Filipinos for the next 50 years and the Filipinos wouldn't mind. As long as they got paid and the fucking was regular.

Vavasour had chosen San Fernando for the camouflage it provided. As Ted sped from the town and into the hills beyond, he admired the unexpected subtlety of the fat man. If anything went wrong, both Vavasour and Ted could move to the city and be lost, instantaneously, in a gay holiday crowd. How different it would have been in any other small town in the Philippines, where the only foreigners are Peace Corps, pederasts, and missionaries. Vavasour was, Ted realized, a man used to covering his exits.

Not that anything vital could go wrong, despite the guns and Vavasour's small army. *It's little more than a joke,* Ted thought. *An elaborate prank. For everyone but me.*

The barrio of Consolacion was tucked behind the scorched hills that overlook San Fernando and its grey-green sea. A road condescended to touch Consolacion and twice a day, on paper at least, a bus route. Consolacion had nipa huts along the road, and one of them sold candies, hard-boiled eggs and, for the village toughs, warm, brown bottles of beer. The land sloped down from Consolacion's road and then up again and then down, like the landscape in a strange storybook. The houses were either perched on top of hills, fragile little castles of thatch and frame, or they shivered at the bottom.

Consolacion was a barrio that accepted its place in the violent scheme of Philippine life. Its people, like the people in all the lawless hamlets of the Philippines, knew when forces larger than them were on the prowl. They knew when a military ambush or a meeting of the communists – or both – required their tolerance and discretion, for which they would receive some food, some gratitude, gassy promises of protection or 'liberation.' The people of Consolacion knew, instinctively, when to call their children inside and when to gather the pigs and chickens from the road. They knew when they weren't allowed to look out of the window, or, at the very least, when they must forget what they saw out of those blank holes in the bamboo walls. And like all Philippine villagers, they had seen too much and lost too many friends and relatives in hellish incidents they couldn't report or even remember, except on those rare nights when the various bands of interlopers were tormenting other barrios and Consolacion's mothers and wives and sisters could mourn their dead with as much noise and anguish as they could bear.

All this had to be learned, of course. And there was at least one villager in Consolacion who was simply too young. Too young by a year, perhaps, by a day, or maybe by just a few hours. His name was Arturo Mission, but everyone called him 'Boy Boy.' Though only 10 years old, Boy Boy was already used to sweeping the house, running errands and taking care of his two-year-old sister Pinky for whole mornings at a time. Boy Boy could dress Pinky and feed her. He had been holding her in his arms and chasing her around the base of the hut since he himself was an infant.

Boy Boy's mother had a morning job in town. His father lived with a second family a few villages away. So Boy Boy's mornings were dedicated to fantastic adventures denied boys with stricter supervision. He climbed thousand-foot palm trees and hurled the coconuts down to his sister – or so he dreamed. He went to war in the mountains of the Cordilleras and the plantations of Mindanao. He celebrated long, solemn masses. He did all this in the darkness of his house, behind queerly vibrating eyes. Neighbours saw him gaping out of the window. When they waved, his eyes would make their strange shifting motion. He would smile shyly. And the gallant soldier or fearless tree-scaler would duck his head into the darkened room and peer out again through a smaller crack in the thatch.

Boy Boy first noticed strange goings on when a crowded jeepney roared past his window after dawn. He yelled excitedly to his mother. She responded warily. After she had left for town, two more jeepneys roared up the road, followed by a fancy sedan. The cars and strange men were exciting, but Boy Boy was most thrilled by the guns – what his mother called Armalites. Boy Boy couldn't get enough of Armalites. He listened for them in adults' conversations. He dreamed of them. Somehow he had concluded that Armalites were only carried at night, by shadowy men who disappeared with the sun. Yet here they were, the guns of his dreams, scuffed and green and perfectly visible at nine o'clock in the morning! Boy Boy looked to the cot where Pinky, luckily, was taking her morning nap. He jumped down the house's steps and ran as fast as he could, in his drooping shorts of no recallable colour, to the sari sari store that doubled as the bus stop. He stood at the corner of the store and watched the uniformed men get in and out of jeeps. He watched them shift and even trade their guns. Boy Boy stared with his vibrating eyes. He was close enough to see the guns' 'banana clips,' which his father had once drawn in the dirt outside the house. In the midst of the soldiers he saw a large bald man with pinkish skin, dressed in a huge olive-drab uniform, barking angry orders and mopping his brow with a handkerchief. An American general! Overwhelmed by the overlapping novelties – soldiers, banana clips, an American – Boy Boy ran to the house, checked Pinky, and without pause raced back to the bus stop. But the American had disappeared along with the bulk of the soldiers. Only a few remained behind to watch the cars. Boy Boy heard the grumblings of the adults within the sari sari store, angry because they were forced to close for the day, but he didn't share their disgruntlement. His only potential unhappiness was that the adventure might peter out without any gunfire – that thrilling sound he had never heard. Boy Boy had not been regaled by the song of the Philippine hills!

Less than an hour later, another imported sedan sped up the hill. Boy Boy watched from the top step of his house. Pinky toddled up to join him and he held her hand protectively. *Another American general?* Boy Boy kept his ears open and, when Pinky allowed him, sat by the window, his large eyes fixed on the downhill portion of the road where new troops would come from. Occasionally, he'd shift his gaze uphill, to the scrubby mound that the soldiers had passed beyond. *Maybe they'll come back.* Then he'd panic and return his gaze downhill, prepared for whole caravans of troops to move up the road for the Battle of Consolacion. The road remained disappointingly empty in both directions.

It was the closed-down Consolacion that Ted Augenstein entered in his air-conditioned auto. The town's sari sari store was boarded up. The pigs and chickens had been collected from the road. Laundry was being pulled inside a house by a pair of worried brown arms. Ted's driver parked the car behind another sedan and three dusty jeepneys. One jeepney was occupied by four slovenly men in unmarked military uniforms. Each had an M-16 rifle. Each gun, had it been fired at the instant, would have sent a bullet through the head of one of the other men in the group.

Vavasour's men, Ted thought, staring at the guns. *God help us.*

After the long drive, Ted stood on the road's shoulder and stretched his cramped muscles. The sky was a deep, tropical blue and the heat had already risen. He leaned into the car, retrieved a large parcel and indicated to the driver he was ready. The driver stepped down a steep path. It was another ten minutes of trekking around small fields and between knobby hills before they encountered a larger group of armed men. They stood defending a small hill with a single nipa hut at its peak.

A group of losers, Ted thought. *Where did Vavasour get them? Prison?*

'Good morning, men!' Ted called briskly. He knew the power of a foreigner in the Philippines.

The men reluctantly stood at attention and paid their grudging respects. Only one continued to lounge against a tree, picking his teeth. He had a melon belly and an insolent look. Two belts of ammunition were crossed on his chest like a Mexican bandit. He gave Ted a closed-mouth smile.

The leader, Ted thought. He nodded his recognition to the melon-bellied man – it was returned – and he inwardly recited one of the mantras of the foreign correspondent.

Never argue with a guy with a gun.

Ted's guide pointed to the straw house at the top of the hill. Ted could perceive people and movement inside. He set his mouth, changed the parcel to his other arm, scaled the side of the hill and entered the tiny hut.

Vavasour, in a commodious military outfit, was seated on the floor like an Oriental despot. Jean was dressed in surprisingly stylish matching pants and blouse. She paced the room above him.

'Now we are complete!' Vavasour proclaimed, smiling a wide pus-coloured smile. 'The conspirators, that is. All we need is our guest of honour.'

Jean, with a smile of relief, took the parcel from Ted. She squatted on the floor, placed it between herself and Vavasour and started unwrapping.

'Where is he?' Ted asked.

'He slept late, Mr Augenstein,' Vavasour replied. 'I had once thought you journalists got up with the dawn. But after seeing the Foreign Correspondents Club of Hong Kong. I fully understood your sleeping habits. Who wouldn't need a good snooze after a night at that place!'

Jean stood, went to the window and made an urgent hand motion.

'They were assembling the crowd,' she explained to Ted. She returned to the unwrapping of the package. 'But now they're on the way. It should take another twenty minutes.'

Ted gave her a questioning look. She said, 'We have walkie-talkies.'

'That was a stupid trick at the FCC, Vavasour,' Ted said.

'I had to see it after all these years. And I had this new sailor suit. Plus you know what.' He swirled his hand around his shiny, bald head. 'It's much too humid to wear it here, in the province. Although I look so much older . . .' He sighed. 'Anyway, there I was, all dressed up and nowhere to go! You ought to make that a motto of your club in Hong Kong, Mr Augenstein. My friend Rudy was curious too, because I gather he has a journalist friend. Several journalist friends!' Vavasour gave Ted a wink. 'He was hurt you didn't "greet" him, as he put it. God knows what constitutes a greeting for that boy. Something illegal. We didn't actually *know* you'd be there, of course.'

'The Foreign Correspondents Club isn't exotic?' Jean asked. 'Glamorous?'

'Mock-exotic, I'd say. Heavy on the ceiling fans. The problem is the people.' Vavasour rolled his eyes voluptuously. 'Deadly!'

'You could have ruined the plan,' Ted stated.

'Nonsense. I would have regretted that as much as you. Perhaps even more. You shouldn't be such a Nervous Nellie, Mr Augenstein. Please sit.'

Jean was withdrawing from the box a perfectly round pink and green Chinese vase. 'It's lovely!' she cried. 'Oh, it's perfect!'

'I saved it for this day,' Ted said. 'It's less valuable than the other pieces. But it has such a shine. It looks so precious.'

'Oh, it does!' said Jean, giving Vavasour a meaningful look. 'I'm keeping my hands on it.'

'That's not in the script, dear.'

'Let's improvise!'

Vavasour leaned over and took the vase from her with a saccharine smile. 'You'll get paid. After seeing your boys outside, I'd be a ninny to do anything else.'

Her boys, Ted realized.

'That's wise, Anton. And the moment of reckoning is coming soon.' She looked at her watch.

'Mr Augenstein, I was just telling Jean an amazing story about Philippine-French friendship, which I heard only last night.'

'Oh Anton,' said the woman. 'Please no!'

'It seems there was this difficult Frenchwoman living in the Philippines. Her husband was posted in Davao for a year, or it might have been Cagayan de Oro . . .'

'I can't bear this story,' Jean said with a shiver. 'Excuse me.' She trotted out of the hut and ran manfully down to the base of the hill.

'One of those rough spots,' Vavasour continued.

'Shouldn't we prepare?'

Vavasour showed his palms to the ceiling. 'We're prepared!' he proclaimed. He pantomimed the handing of the vase to Ted, and then the receiving of the vase. 'That's the whole performance.' He placed the vase gently on the floor between them.

'Anyway, this Frenchwoman didn't get along with her servants . . .'

Ted glanced around with impatience.

Vavasour barked, 'We have time, Mr Augenstein. Please relax. You'll put Jean's boys at edge. That we shouldn't risk.'

Vavasour continued his story. 'Anyway, the woman slapped one of the maids, or so the story goes. She made them eat rotten food. She put the maids on the birth-control pill . . .'

'Oh come on.'

'. . . and she scolded the driver in front of the maids next door. The incidents themselves seem small. But in the mind of the staff they added up to a very large and very violently-coloured mosaic of abuse. I can understand this, you know. Foreigners so often refuse to tune into the natives' wavelength. I've seen this thousands of times. They uphold some abstract values: "Cleanliness," "Responsibility." And they never get in touch with the very people they live with. Somewhat primitive people. People who can creep into their bedroom any night. The people who are expected to put away their birth-control devices each morning, and wipe the lubricant off the bedside table. Having servants is a responsibility as well as a privilege . . .'

'Yes,' said Ted.

'. . . and it's particularly dangerous to have sex with them. That is a fact.'

Vavasour stared at Ted. 'Did you have servants in your foreign postings, Mr Augenstein? In Saigon? In Hong Kong? House-boys, by chance?'

'Get on with the story.'

Vavasour shrugged. 'Anyway, no one knows what incident broke the camel's back. Perhaps it's impossible to pinpoint when a human being runs out of dignity. Maybe a scolding did it. Perhaps the maid was forced to pay for something she broke – something costly. Or maybe the driver was fired and couldn't bear to be separated from the cook he had grown to love. For drivers and cooks do love. Yes they do. Sometimes it's hard to believe when you stare at the man's pathetic, oily hair every day from the back seat, or eat the woman's wretched cooking. But they love. And they hate. They can hate the person whose eyes burn into the back of their heads each day. The person who sighs each evening when the meal is put before him.

'One Sunday night the Frenchwoman and her husband went for dinner at the barbecue buffet at the local hotel. Sunday, as you know, is the servants' day off. When the couple returned, they were surprised to see the front door open and all the lights in the house blazing. The Frenchwoman was immediately angry and started to complain. The house, she discovered, had been abandoned by the servants. Later, some valuables were declared missing.

'And on the floor of the living-room, surrounded by certain intimate possessions the couple stored in a remote drawer of their bedroom wardrobe, the Frenchwoman found the severed head of her eight-year-old son.'

'Oh my God,' gasped Ted.

'All of the servants disappeared, of course – back to their home villages I would guess. One interesting question is whether they were all involved. Did one of them try to stop the crime? Or regret it afterwards?'

'That is terrible.'

'The French couple separated and divorced, as you'd expect, and both went back to France with distinctly poor memories of their time in the Southern Philippines.'

Ted's face was wrinkled in revulsion.

'But in a way, I like that story,' said Vavasour reflectively. 'I find it a valuable cautionary tale.'

'Against what?'

Vavasour looked at Ted slyly. He raised his arms, his palms upward, gesturing to the tiny bamboo room and the rolling hills outside.

'Against this kind of project, Mr Augenstein. Against trusting people you don't care for.' The fat man paused heavily. 'Against dabbling too deeply in lands you don't understand.'

'I know this country better than you.'

The fat man emitted a stage laugh. 'Do you, Mr Augenstein?' he asked. 'Because you've been here often? Because of your Pulitzer? Yes: I know of your Pulitzer. I have done my research. I'm sure it was an incisive look at the country's politics and the challenges martial law presented. I believe that's the proper locution. "Challenges."'

Vavasour smiled oilily. '"Tightrope." "Bold gambits." "Failed agenda." These are all terms I read in newspapers time and again. I can't say I ever understand them. But they must mean something to someone. Perhaps even to the journalists who write them.

'But don't you think knowing a country, or a continent, is something different, Mr Augenstein? To *know* a land, mustn't you have something in common with it? Look down there.' Vavasour gestured out of the window into the hot, mid-morning air. His tone had turned harsh. 'Jean's boys. Do you *know* them? Would you know when to push them, or to praise them, or to just leave them alone? Would you know when to run from them, as fast as your legs could carry you? Do you know the range of an M-16?'

'This is ridiculous talk,' Ted said.

'Do you really think you know the Philippines, Mr Augenstein? Asia? Any country outside your own?'

'Vavasour, I'm sick of you. Let's start our business.'

'Oh! Your mention of business reminds me. Do you know what the Frenchwoman said to the police later?'

Ted shook his head wearily. 'She said: "And I paid them so well! They just got a raise!"' Vavasour laughed and clapped his hands. He scooped up the lovely vase and crooked it in his arms. He petted it, laughing long and hard, and gave Ted a queer look.

Ted thought: *It's him. He's back.* It was the Vavasour that had surfaced only once before, but whose image had haunted Ted for months: the young, handsome Vavasour. *Is it the eyes? It had seemed so in Thailand, but now . . . I can't tell . . .* For Ted was confused. The other Vavasour, released once again from his cave, his cracked bubble in the rock, did seem younger, eager, more pointed. But now, the new Vavasour terrified Ted. *What happened to the handsomeness?* Had Ted misinterpreted, in Thailand, those dim sparks that had seemed to reflect a hidden, shrunken, but fundamentally good quality within the fat man? In Consolacion, they seemed different sparks altogether.

What happened to the man with the childhood? The man who could be loved?

'Oh, servants!' called Vavasour. He giggled ridiculously and fixed Ted with a glittering stare. 'Can't live *with* them – can't live *without* them!'

Adam Fendler had been sick through the night and was surprised to hear banging on the door of his hotel room in the morning. It was a roomboy. 'Sir, someone downstairs.'

Adam went down in his baggy pants, fumbling with his belt and fly. A greasy-looking man in a faded T-shirt said to him, 'I hear you're looking for the fat man.'

Oh boy, thought Adam. *I knew this would work.*

'Indeed I am,' said Adam. 'Shall we talk this over at the coffee shop?'

'How *much* money are you offering?' asked the greaseball.

The question threw Adam. He had found it easy to imitate Carl Rolla by offering 'big money' all over San Fernando. But he had never seen La Rolla actually cough up any of *Time* Magazine's cash. And Adam had no cash but his own.

'Enough,' Adam said firmly.

'Enough for what?'

'Enough already. Just a minute. Let me get dressed.'

'Pack your bag.'

'Pardon me?'

'Check out. Bring your bag.' The greaseball shuffled his feet nervously.

'Are you kidding?'

The man shook his head.

When Adam returned with his suitcase he was met by three new men. The greaseball had mysteriously disappeared. A young man in a crisp yellow shirt offered to take Adam's bag.

'Who are you?' Adam asked. 'Where's . . .'

'We'll bring you to the fat man,' the young man said. 'Check out first. I'll hold your bag.'

'*I'll* hold my bag.'

When he had checked out, he encountered a varicoloured jeepney filled with an assortment of men and women. 'What's this?'

'This jeep is going to Consolacion. That's where you'll see the fat man. We'll bring you.' The man in the yellow shirt gestured at the dozen people in the jeepney. 'Don't worry. Trust us.'

Adam saw twelve Filipinos staring and smiling at him.

'Trust them!' he muttered. He bumped his head as he clambered onto the back of the vehicle. His fedora fell into the dust.

The young man brushed off the hat and handed it to Adam.

'Thank you.' Adam straightened the hat on his head. An old crone on the opposite bench treated him to a wide, toothless grin. 'Americano?' she shrieked.

Adam wondered if other journalists found themselves in similar situations. He looked to his right and his left. Everyone on the jeep was staring at him and smiling. He looked back at the old lady, whose smile had grown even broader. Her head nodded vigorously up and down.

'Yes,' Adam admitted. 'Americano.'

'Yay!' cried the lady, clapping her hands. She offered him a half-gnawed mango. He looked down the length of the jeepney. Everybody was nodding their heads, insisting he take the mango. *I hate mangoes. Do I have to eat it?* And he began to laugh. The old lady was the first to notice, but soon the whole jeep began to laugh, just as it bolted away from the hotel with a violent start. Adam nearly fell into his neighbour's lap and, as he straightened up, everyone laughed even harder. The teen sitting beside him plucked off the fedora and the hat was passed up one side of the jeepney and down the other. Everyone tried it on for size. The old lady was the last to get the hat. It suited her best of all. Adam contemplated giving it to her.

'Mango!' shrieked the old lady, the fedora falling onto her leathery face. '*Gustoko* Americano!'

The jeepney laboured up the hills to Consolacion. Adam day-dreamed of banner headlines, offices with windows and indoor plants, acceptance speeches and a broad-nosed Thai bride with dark, rubbery nipples. When the jeep arrived, the town seemed dead in the mid-morning heat.

The young man in yellow jumped down and headed for a steep path leading from the road. 'Follow me.'

Adam disembarked and straightened himself bravely. He felt prepared for the biggest adventure of his life. He had courage. He had a guide. And he had a computer – Carl's computer, which was, he had to admit, heavier than any journalist's computer should be. It pulled him down on his left side, giving him a strange and inelegant gait.

He nodded farewell to his new friends on the jeepney but the vehicle didn't roar off in a cloud of dust. Adam heard its ignition kick off. A few people clambered down and started stretching and squatting on the ground.

It must a scheduled stop, Adam thought.

When the two men got to a small cornfield, the young man halted. He pointed through some trees and said to Adam, 'Over there. That house. On top of the hill.'

Adam looked through the crops.

'I see people.'

The young man nodded.

'Are you coming with me?' Adam tried to mask the nervousness in his voice.

The young man shook his head. He placed an encouraging hand on Adam's back. He smiled grimly.

Adam returned an identical smile. He inhaled deeply and thought to himself: *Okay. Let's go.*

He felt foolish strolling through the cornfields laden down with an overnight bag and a bulky computer. He felt even more self-conscious when he arrived at a group of slovenly soldiers wearing uniforms with no markings. *Insurgents*, he thought. *Armed insurgents. Something like that.*

He was about to awkwardly introduce himself when he recognized a figure at the far end of the group. It was a woman in pants and blouse.

'Hey! Jean!'

It took the woman several moments to recognize Adam. Her first reaction was to glance nervously at the house at the top of the hill. Then she strode purposefully towards him.

'What are you doing here?' she whispered. 'You must leave. Now!'

'What's going on?'

'You can't stay. If they found out . . .'

Adam's nervousness, and even his fear of the armed men, melted away as he became cognizant of his position and of hers. The tables had been turned. He was on top now and she was at his mercy. Adam's face broke into a small, confident smile.

'Hey,' he said. 'Wait one minute. You tipped me off, remember. What's going on here? Where's the "fat man"? *Your* "fat man."'

Again, the mannish woman looked up at the hut above her. 'Everything's changed,' she blurted. 'You're not allowed here now. Come with me. I'll bring you back to town.'

'Yeah,' Adam said happily. 'I know everything's changed. You've been paid.'

Tough shit, lady, he thought. *Now it's my turn.*

'I'm press,' he said proudly. 'Foreign press. And I've got a job to do. Excuse me.'

He dropped the canvas overnight. *Who needs it? It's only clothes.* With the computer in hand, Adam Fendler ran with all his might up the ridiculous, lumpy hill. He took the four steps of the hut in two bounds. Inside the hut, his eyes had to adjust to the dim light. When they did, Adam Fendler saw a strange and unexpected scene.

The fat man, a hideous, sweating creature in a kind of fake uniform, was seated in the middle of the floor glaring at the doorway with the anger of interruption. He held in his puffy hands a delicate Chinese vase of diaphanous colours. Standing next to him, with a blank look that could have spoken of shame, fear or boredom, was Ted Augenstein, foreign editor of the *New York Tribune*. Ted held a wooden carton dripping with packing materials. He didn't react to Adam at all. He didn't signal recognition. He didn't blink. It seemed he didn't breathe.

'Who is this!' demanded the fat man. His voice was smooth and fruity. He looked angrily to Ted Augenstein.

'You?' Adam said.

Ted made an almost imperceptible nod of his head. He said to the fat man, 'I know him. He's a journalist.'

'You arranged it,' Adam blurted. 'You arranged the press conference. You sent me there. *You* did the hoax! You fooled your own paper!'

Jean entered the room with an alarmed look on her face.

'Get him out of here!' commanded the wrathful fat man. 'Tell your boys to dump him in the river! There's too much to lose!'

'Wait!' commanded Adam. 'I want some answers. On behalf of the press.'

The fat man smiled horribly. 'Dump him in the river "on behalf of the press," Jean dear.'

'No,' said Ted Augenstein. 'Let him go. Nothing can be done to him. He's press. We don't want to make things worse.'

'But our agreement!' wailed the fat man.

Jean made a signal to someone outside the door.

'Bring him to town,' Ted said. 'That will give us time.'

'Hey,' said Adam. 'You've got this all wrong. Where do you think you can run? All of this is going straight to the paper tonight. Your paper. Your editors . . .'

Two rough men in uniforms attempted to pull Adam out of the nipa hut.

Adam yanked himself free. 'Don't you see, Ted?' he cried. 'The game's up. It's all over. Tell your friends they can go, I don't care, but *you've* got to stay. You're news now. You will soon be history. You've *got* talk to me. You owe an accounting before the world.'

'Jean,' scolded the fat man, as he struggled to his feet. 'Please. Let's get on with it.'

Adam was pulled struggling from the room. He hit out at the uniformed men with the portable computer. But they restrained him with little difficulty. They pulled him down the hill and tossed him through the air until he crashed at the base of a stately mango tree. Adam got to his feet as fast as he could. It was his duty, he thought, not to lie on the ground: the journalist's refusal to surrender his dignity. He grasped the computer with one hand and readjusted the fedora with the other. As he regained his breath, he saw Jean racing down the hill. She was followed by the fat man, descending clumsily. Ted Augenstein remained on the crest of the hill, a dark and solid presence in the morning glare. His hand betrayed his nervousness by carefully smoothing his honey-coloured hair.

Adam was stunned at the unexpected vision that met him at the base of the hill. His friends from the jeepney, all twelve of them, were assembled in a concentrated-looking group. Somehow, for some inexplicable reason, they had followed him. They faced off against the armed men. Standing to the side were Jean and the sweating fat man, his hands on his huge hips. He barked orders at the armed men.

Adam saw his only chance. 'I am the foreign press,' he called to the impromptu jury. 'These people' – he gestured to the soldiers and their keepers – 'have tried to meddle in the press freedom of the world.' Adam's mind was racing desperately. 'And the press freedom of the Philippines!

'They want to kidnap me,' he continued. 'And I appeal to you for help. Don't let them take me. Who knows what will happen? *You* take me with you. You – the guardians of freedom in the Philippines!'

It was a split-second judgement on Adam's part, but he knew he had chosen wisely. As a kicker, he added: 'People Power! People Power!'

The crowd took up the familiar chant. The young man in the yellow shirt led them.

'People Power!' they cried. Adam could hear the harsh shriek of the old woman. *I give her my fedora,* he thought, *and fifty bucks if we make it out of here.*

'Freedom!' Adam cried. 'Down with the US–Marcos dictatorship!' But he was aware that a line of soldiers still separated him from his supporters.

'Help me!' he called to the peasants. 'Help me *now!*' The crowd responded ebulliently. All twelve began pushing against the uniformed men.

'Stop!' cried Jean.

Adam could no longer hear any words, but he watched as the fat man barked another command. His hands were still on his hips but his face was contorted with rage. Jean looked briefly at him. He repeated the order sternly. And finally she called something to her men.

The next few moments were a break in time and cognizance. Adam knew, though he could hardly recognize, the sound of gunfire. In one way it seemed too popcornish; but any doubt was dispelled by the accompanying visual image. His twelve supporters writhed and arched and ran and fell. The old lady slumped to the ground, instantly dead. Soldiers ran too, and chaos reigned in the cornfield. Adam looked up to see the looming silhouette of Ted Augenstein. When next he looked around, everything was stained the colour of blood. The old lady was face-down in the grass with a blood-splashed back. The man in the yellow shirt was almost out of sight, running as fast as he could. The soldiers frantically scurried, waving their rifles. Jean was out of sight. Vavasour stared at Adam with a ghastly smile. His hands were on his hips: his right arm swivelled out and a puffy hand pointed at Adam, mimicking a gun. Vavasour's fleshy mouth formed the soundless words: . . . *bang bang* . . .

Ted Augenstein remained atop the hill, a dark, passionless observer of the entire scene.

Adam ran easily and swiftly, despite the computer. Soon the carnage and gunfire were far behind him. His story was forming in his mind. Hoax! Massacre! His was a mega-scoop! Adam ran for the road, his hand steadying the fedora as he scrambled up a crumbling hill, in a flight that could only be described as jubilant..

Ted returned to the cool shade of the hut. He sat on the floor. Soon Jean joined him and, several struggling minutes later, Vavasour, wiping his brow.

'Mr Augenstein, please,' Vavasour said. 'You are needed outside.'

Ted hoisted himself to his feet and, guarding his eyes, re-entered the fierce, noon sun.

'Our performers!'

Ted squinted down at the stilled, bloodied pile of bodies. There were ten of them. On Vavasour's announcement, the bodies began to stir. The corpses stood and stretched. They laughed and slapped each other on the backs. The sound of chatting and laughing rose to greet Ted. The younger men had fun with the fake blood, painting patterns on each other's faces. The old lady rubbed her face of dirt and kept craning her head to see the bloodstains on the back of her shirt. She looked up at the men on the hill, raised her hands in the air, and waved at them triumphantly.

'Make some acknowledgement,' hissed Vavasour.

Ted hoisted his arm in the air.

'Papa!' shouted Jean, motioning to Ted, and the bloodied Filipinos clapped their hands appreciatively.

Vavasour raised his own arms theatrically, waited for a lull in the crowd noise and exulted immodestly: 'Maestro!'

The soldiers joined the townspeople in the applause.

'How do you like that,' Vavasour asked. ' "Papa"!'

'Give them their 100 pesos,' Ted said. He returned to the shade of the hut.

Just as some householders refrain from buying cars or appliances until they have saved the last penny, Ted Augenstein had tried to discipline his fantasies over the previous months. Now he could surrender to them completely. He imagined the front page of his own newspaper, with the grisly, over-large headline. Shame would compel the *Tribune* to overplay the story. He could see the sombre passport photo of himself that would run not only in the *Tribune* but in papers and magazines around the world. It was an extremely unlovely shot, in which his hair was too short and his face too plump. It would be the perfect accompaniment to a story about a lying, mass-murdering foreign editor. He could picture the byline – 'By Adam F. X. Fendler' – and he wondered how long he could prolong the cat-and-mouse game of the next few days. *Until Sunday,* he thought. *So the newsweeklies will also be fooled.* And then what? A news conference? A quiet interview with the wires? Or a succession of gradually revealing interviews, one per day, each held in a different Asian city, all with rivals to the *Tribune*. Sunday it could be the *Post*; Monday the *LA Tribune*; Tuesday a Japanese daily. How Abe would hate that: a Japanese paper! He imagined the photos that would accompany those stories: the psychopath replaced by a handsome gentleman in linen or silk who, far from harming anyone, had merely tried to illustrate a point that every newspaper reader in the world suspected deep in his heart: that newspapers and newspapermen lie, sometimes for the sheer fun of it.

'If you'll excuse me,' Vavasour said with a courtly nod. He struggled to his feet. 'The maestro is needed.' He giggled and left the room.

Perhaps he could become a Daniel Ellsberg-style folk hero, Ted fantasized. An ungreedy Clifford Irving. The man who is always called when a harsh opinion is needed on the subject of the press. Called long-distance in his glamorous exile in Phuket or Penang or Mindanao. He was reminded of Vavasour's tale of the Frenchwoman and the beheaded child. *Maybe a nice apartment in Hong Kong . . .*

Adam scrambled up the crumbling hill to find an utterly deserted road. The nipa huts along its side were either boarded up or abandoned. He began to run back towards town, but he soon realized that the goons with the machine guns could easily track him. His alternatives were poor: one side of the road was rocky cliff; the other was a series of sloping hills. As Adam wondered which route to take, he noticed a small boy staring at him from the window of one of the houses. It was the first human he had spotted since he reached the road.

'Let me in!'

The boy merely stared.

Adam pushed his way through the curtained doorway and into a darkened trio of rooms. One was a living and eating room. The other two held the kitchen and a primitive commode.

Adam said to the boy, 'Do you speak English?'

The boy didn't reply. He just stared at Adam.

Adam sat down with his back against the front wall. He told the boy, 'Get away from the window.'

The boy continued staring.

Adam leaned over and pulled the boy by the back of his sagging shorts.

'I'm your friend,' Adam said, although he could barely hear his own words with the heavy pounding of his heart. 'And you're gonna sit right here by me. Just like a friend.'

The boy made no effort to resist. Adam removed his fedora and plunked it on the boy's head. The boy played with the hat.

Adam sat in the dim bamboo room and realized he was less fearful than he was excited. Adam pulled the computer to him, opened its lid and typed for a few seconds on the bamboo slat floor. He knew the uniformed men would be searching for him. But he put it out of his mind. Logic told him that his personal danger must decrease with every minute that went by. The soldiers had shot in panic. They hadn't meant harm. The people killed were civilians while Adam was press, accredited and formally identified as such, which was a big distinction. It was highly dangerous to kill members of the press, he thought, Amnesty International and all. In any case, Ted Augenstein was undoubtedly calming his men right now. Perhaps Ted would stroll down the road any minute, calling Adam's name. He'd sit down and reveal the entire, tawdry tale as Adam typed notes into the computer. This gave Adam an idea, and he typed a bit more. If Ted and the soldiers didn't discover him, Adam planted to hitch a ride into San Fernando. He could file his story from a hotel. Ted's personal confession could come later, a second-day story.

'Is there a bus?' Adam asked the boy. The boy looked up at him. Adam noticed his queer eyes. They vibrated rapidly from side to side, even when the boy's attention was fixed.

'There must be a bus,' Adam muttered. He looked down at the computer screen. He scowled at what he saw and started all over again.

Low guttural voices could be heard outside, along with the sound of boots on dust. Adam peeked through a crack in the thatch. The soldiers were walking by each house, peering into the windows from the roadside. Ted wasn't with them.

The little boy tried to rise. Adam pulled him down. 'Stay here, little feller. Let them pass.'

The boy bent down and peered through the thatch. He watched the soldiers approach his house.

There was a crying from across the room. A shapeless pile of blankets stirred and gave birth to a small, dirty-faced girl with wide, panic-stricken eyes. She stared at Adam and bellowed. She extended her arms to her brother. Adam restrained the boy, but finally said, 'Okay. Go to her. Get her to shut up.' He released his grip from the back of the boy's shorts.

The boy jumped up and ran out of the front door, down the steps, and to the soldiers passing in the street. The girl continued to wail.

'Oh shit,' Adam said. He closed the computer with a plastic crash.

A large shadow was thrown across the floor of the room and the little girl's eyes grew even wider with terror. She started wailing furiously.

Adam wondered: *My press card?*

Only three soldiers remained outside Boy Boy's house. They all had guns, which frightened Pinky, but not Boy Boy. They looked like guns that didn't get used. Boy Boy watched through the window and wondered if some soldiers got to shoot their guns while others had to stay behind to do the less exciting things. He held Pinky's hand and, with nothing else to look at, directed his wobbly gaze at the three bored soldiers on the road.

And then it happened: the sound Boy Boy had waited for! The popping sound of bullets echoed through the neighbourhood. Boy

Boy's dream was realized. Gunfire! But it was so short! And the sound came from behind the house. He had wanted to see the shooting as well as hear it. Did fire really shoot out from those green tubes, as his father said? Was it true that a shot man never heard the explosion – some kind of mercy given by the great God above? A few minutes later, the shadow once again grew across the living-room floor. Pinky's face darkened, but Boy Boy squeezed her hand. The soldier wiped his feet, entered the room gingerly and placed on Boy Boy's head a memento that only a ten-year-old of Consolacion, La Union, the Philippines, could appreciate. The hat of a dead man, still warm with its owner's last sweat. The soldier departed, respectfully fixing the curtain in the doorway as he left.

Vavasour was standing in the doorway of the thatched room, blocking the sun. 'Mr Augenstein, I have something to show you.'

'When do we go back?' Ted said as he struggled to his feet. 'Is there another route? I don't want to meet Fendler on the road. There's only one road to Manila.'

'Don't concern yourself.' Vavasour made way for Ted. 'You first,' he said. 'At the bottom of the hill, please. Under the mango tree.'

Ted ran down the hill. He moved towards a clump of soldiers. He called to Jean, 'How do we know we won't pass Fendler on the road to Manila?'

He didn't understand the awkward look on her face until the soldiers parted. It was the last theatrical gesture of the day: Vavasour's final screen. And now the final mask was removed.

Behind the soldiers lay a crumpled pile of black and brown. Adam seemed to be attempting a difficult swimming stroke. Adam's beady eyes were open. Their expression was no different than when Adam, the live Adam, asked for a ride home from the *Post* or ordered a Coca Cola at the FCC bar. It was his goony face. The fearful mask of death had not made its visitation on the face of Adam Fendler. Perhaps he had been too busy thinking of his story when he expired. Perhaps he never believed it possible he could be killed, even at the last.

'Why?' Ted asked wearily. 'What did *he* do?'

The question was directed at Jean. She directed Ted's

attention to the house on the hill. Standing next to it was Vavasour. He stood, hands on hips, waiting for Ted's return to the hut.

Ted looked at Adam's pitiful, hatless head.

Ted lunged in an attempt to grab Jean and beat her with all the violence he could summon. But she moved too swiftly, retreating behind her men. The slovenly soldiers forced their gun barrels at Ted with surprising speed.

The fruity laugh of Vavasour floated down from the hilltop. 'Now Mr Augenstein, sink to your knees in grief. Put your head in your hands. And call out with anguish: "It wasn't supposed to be like this!"' The laugh pealed down from the hillside. 'I believe that's how the script goes.'

Ted turned abruptly and started walking to the road. He ignored the calls from behind. He kept his eyes on the path before him and began to trot. His mind raced with panic and he found tears in his eyes.

He heard the sound of running behind him. Hands grabbed him and threw him to the dirt. He struggled but he was no match for Jean's squad. Jean approached in a strong trot. Vavasour followed, wheezing.

'I'm going to the police,' Ted protested. 'Let me up.'

'You're going nowhere.' Vavasour laboured to catch his breath. It was exactly noon and rivers of sweat poured down his face. 'Until we put you in a car to Manila. To the airport. To Hong Kong. This was all arranged.'

'This was all arranged? What the fuck do you mean?'

'Calm down, Mr Augenstein, or you won't understand my orders to you and the whole point of my little variation on your plan will be lost. And that would be a shame. It's so elegant.'

'Your *orders*?'

'I wish we could have done this inside.' Vavasour wiped his head with his sleeve. 'Jean, do you have a handkerchief?'

'Let me up,' Ted said.

Vavasour gestured. The man with the melon belly kicked savagely and Ted fell back into the dust.

'Stay down, Mr Augenstein, and listen. I have added my own dénouement to your original plan.

'You desired to change your life in the most dramatic way, with headlines and scandal and revenge and some kind of exile. I think

I sum up your wishes properly. And with no blood shed – except pig's blood, of course. That's a sweet touch. Very American.'

Ted glared at the fat man.

'I decided to improve on your little game. I have added a little blood at the end, because I don't share your squeamishness. Please note – and this is important – that I *devised* the new ending but you *paid* for it. You financed this killing with your exquisite porcelains. That's how these gentlemen, and this lady, have been paid. And me.'

Vavasour gave a little bow. 'And paid well, we admit.'

He gave a repulsive smile. 'So I don't think it's a good idea for you to go to the police in San Fernando or in Manila. Anyway, you'd have trouble finding many police in San Fernando this morning. We have most of them with us here.

'Mr Augenstein, this is a lesson in power. I will soon send you back to your hated job at the *New York Tribune*. You must go back to establish your alibi. You were never here, remember? That's part of your original plan. Right now you are in China, on a tour. You are expected back at the Mandarin Hotel this evening, straight from China. I will deliver you back there in time. I wouldn't want to welch on my part of the deal. You know nothing about the Philippines or the strange disappearance of Adam Fendler, who was, after all, not really an employee of the *Tribune*. You will placidly return to your high-paying job, and enjoy the life of an ageing, once-famous journalist. If you do anything else, the local police will be given evidence of your part in this murder. The evidence will always be there, along with the body, buried right beneath that mango tree. There's only one thing that can make that murder disappear this afternoon – and that is your return to your former life. There's only one person who has the power to make that murder reappear sometime in the future.' Vavasour bowed formally. 'And that is me.'

He hissed: 'You thought I was some kind of a joke, Mr Augenstein. The joke's on you. It's one of my magic tricks. You didn't believe that I am a magician, did you? But I have just pulled the tablecloth out from under your plan. You don't know your Greek, Mr Augenstein, being American. But I say now: "Flow backward to your sources, sacred rivers. And let the world's great order be . . ." – Vavasour's arm poised in mid-air – ". . . restored!"'

Vavasour circled around Ted with delicate steps.

'You gave me money, Mr Augenstein. And that's all it takes in this part of the world to be good or to be bad, to be benign or treacherous. A little money. You didn't know that. I guess you don't win Pulitzer Prizes when you write about money and blood. Only "tightropes" and "bold gambits" and "incomplete agendas." And the other terminologies of your tongue-twisted, lying trade.'

Vavasour was soaked with sweat. He turned to go back to the hut.

'You might as well go, Mr Augenstein. Your plane is at four. I tried to warn you earlier today about playing games that you can't control. But you wouldn't listen.' He looked down at the man sprawled beneath him in the dust. 'You lose. You're a fool, Mr Augenstein, if you don't mind my saying so. I'd spit on you but it's too hot.'

The fat man toddled off with a half-weary, half-jubilant step. Jean talked rapidly to the soldiers and then chased after him. Ted was prodded to his feet by a soldier and led back to the road. At first the soldiers were silent and sombre. But it wasn't long before they were back to their joking and laughing. It wasn't clear to Ted how many of the jokes were on him.

In the back seat of his car, Ted found Adam's computer. *How honest they can be,* he thought, *in the smallest things.* His car sped between rice and tobacco fields towards Manila. He opened the lid of the machine. It was still on. He found three files slugged 'EG1,' 'EG2' and 'EG3.'

He opened 'EG1.'

SAN FERNANDO, the Philippines – A massacre in the northern Philippines, leaving at least 12 dead, was engineered by E. G. Augenstein, Pulitzer prize winning foreign editor of this newspaper, and struck yet another blow to press

Horrible, thought Ted. *And inaccurate.* He thought briefly of his sister, Angie, whom he had yet to consider. *What would she have thought of such a story?*

'EG2' read:

SAN FERNANDO, the Philippines – The puzzling hoax that mystified the world of journalism last month was solved here Tuesday. Its perpetrator was no other than

Ted mused on the struggles of a reporter with a complicated

story. It hadn't occurred to him what a difficult assignment he had pitched to poor, unprepared Adam Fendler. He couldn't imagine how the desk could rewrite either of Adam's first two leads.

'EG3':

SAN FERNANDO, *the Philippines – All was peaceful in barrio Concepcion here in this bucolic part of the Philippines. Farmers planted their crops and little children took care of their smaller brothers and sisters as their mothers attended to domestic chores. It was a normal, summer day.*

Until shots rang out, leaving at least 12 villagers dead and bringing to a close one of the strangest chapters in recent journalistic history. At the end of the day, 12 were dead. A puzzling, journalistic hoax had been solved. And an admired journalist, a Pulitzer prize winner, had been indicted in both.

Inaccurate and clumsy, Ted thought. *But on the right track.* For the very last time, he imagined the reaction in the newsroom as they read the story that would never be filed. He tried to picture the faces of Florence, Anthony Pasquale, Abe and even Alex Postlewaite III. It was the reverie that had sustained him over several months. Then he dismissed it. Ted ordered the driver to stop. He opened his door and hurled the computer as far as he could. It made a dry splash in the middle of a tobacco field.

'Hoy!' proclaimed the driver.

'Drive!' Ted was surprised at the authority remaining in his voice. He looked out of the windows at the yellowed crops that rushed past the car window.

Goodbye, Adam Fendler, he thought. *God help you. You and me both.*

2

Craig anticipated an easy quest. In the Philippines, everyone wants to talk. Everyone watches everyone else. No foreigner goes unseen or unremembered. It took Craig only one hour to find a lead.

'I don't know the fat man,' the roomboy explained. 'But someone else was looking for him too.'

Craig asked for a description.

'He said he was a journalist,' said the roomboy. 'Although he didn't look like a journalist.'

As they were flipping through the register, the roomboy added, 'He wore a strange kind of hat.'

And so it was unnecessary for the last page of the ledger to be flipped, although it was and it contained the entry, 'Adam F.X. Fendler/*New York Tribune*' underlined in Adam's bold, silly hand.

Craig's next chore was to drive to town and to wait forty minutes for a certain Emilio in a flyblown café. He drank two warm Cokes against the heat. Finally, Emilio was brought into the café by an impromptu crowd, struggling and denying any knowledge of 'the fat man.' Craig knew the whispers and nudges of the average Philippine crowd. In the Philippines, there is always a crowd; they always know the truth; and a lady in the crowd always nods her head when the truth is spoken.

'What do you do?' Craig asked.

The man shrugged.

The crowd agitated. Someone poked the roomboy.

'Policeman,' whispered the roomboy.

'Bring me to the fat man,' Craig commanded.

'I don't know any fat man,' said Emilio.

The crowd swelled and agitated. Craig made a quick mental calculation. Fifty pesos in normal times. One hundred and fifty when the situation was tricky. Two hundred and fifty for a blood secret.

'Tell me where he is and I'll give you three hundred pesos.' Craig withdrew the worn bills from his wallet and laid them on the plank table. There was a gasp from the crowd. Emilio was in deep trouble. The crowd would demand he tell the truth when so much good money was offered. It would resent him keeping the entire three hundred pesos. And some compromise of food and drinks for all would have to be arrived at. Of course, there would be no nastiness. It would all be gay and enjoyable – the Philippine way. Craig saw an old woman in the front of the crowd nodding her head at him, approvingly and confidently. He would get what he wanted, she suggested. And he had gone about it in the right way.

By the time Craig arrived in Consolacion, it was a reborn town. Soldiers and interlopers were gone. The villagers wandered in small clumps, trading excited reminiscences of the violent day. They went through the story over and over again, arguing over inconsistencies. The sari sari store did booming business that afternoon and its owner nearly forgave his lost morning. When Craig arrived, the townspeople rejoiced to have an audience for their tale. They insisted Craig write down all the details, including their full names, addresses and ages. They brought him to the mango tree and showed him the freshly dug earth. They described each of the soldiers. They heaped scorn upon the Philippine female who led them. They described the death scene of Adam – for some peeked – and the hurried abandonment of the village by the soldiers and their keepers. To atone for their cowardly behaviour of the morning, which doomed Adam Fendler to a bloody death in the midday sun, the people of Consolacion treated his colleague to an avalanche of information.

Craig understood most of what the villagers had to offer. Except for one detail. It was Vavasour who gave the people of Consolacion their biggest narrative trouble. In some accounts, he was a foreigner, in others a Philippine *mestizo*. Some said he arrived all alone, while others claimed he roared up with the soldiers. One woman swore she saw him fly away from Consolacion, making hideous shrieks from the clouds.

Craig also had trouble with their description of the fake massacre. 'Joke,' said one man. 'Joke only.' Craig soon realized that the victims of the fake massacre were all townspeople of Consolacion. They had been hired to meet Adam Fendler at his hotel and go through with Vavasour's charade. They were paid one hundred pesos each. A few men displayed the wan-looking bills and offered, with sad faces, to relinquish them. Craig politely declined their offers. They insisted to Craig that they had no idea of what would follow their performance. A man imitated the sound of M-16 automatic fire. A woman wiped away tears. 'Joke,' said the man. 'Joke only.'

Craig kicked at the freshly dug earth. He wondered how long an exhumation would take.

'Are you sure,' Craig asked, 'that it was the third white man who was shot and buried? The smaller man?'

Half the people nodded eagerly. But the other half disagreed and a debate began.

'I have to know,' Craig emphasized. 'I must know if it was him or the other man. The larger white man. Not the really fat one: the one with the hair.'

The debate continued noisily and one villager started shouting at his wife. An older matron in a faded house dress tried to calm the crowd. She looked imploringly at Craig. She extended her hands gently to the fighting pair. And then she put her hands to her mouth and started a strange call. 'Boy Boy!' she called. 'Boy Boy!'

Craig wondered what was happening. 'I have to know,' he repeated. But no one was listening.

The whole crowd took up the chant. 'Boy Boy!' they cried. 'Boy Boy!'

Craig couldn't tell what had come over the village.

The chant continued. 'Boy Boy! Boy Boy!' In the musical lilt of the Philippine tongue, it sounded like a call to prayer. 'Boy Boy! Boy Boy! Boy Boy!'

On the path leading from the road, a Philippine woman appeared. She stood at the top, near the road, blocking the sun behind her. She peered at the chanting crowd. Abruptly, she turned and made a welcoming gesture. She squatted. Again she beckoned. A tiny girl in a droopy dress ran into her arms. The woman picked her up, hugged her to her face and placed her back on the ground. The mother stood, holding the small hand of her daughter. With the afternoon sun behind them, they made a handsome tableau of mother and child. And then they were joined by a third figure. A larger child, whose naked upper torso glowed slightly in the bright sunlight. The chanting ended and Craig realized that this was Boy Boy. In silhouette, something looked wrong with Boy Boy. His head was misshapen.

Then Craig recognized his error. A hat obscured the shape of Boy Boy's head. A fedora.

Craig climbed to the road and squatted beside Boy Boy. He shook his bony brown hand.

'You're Boy Boy?'

The boy's face didn't move except for a queer vibration of his eyes.

'Boy Boy. May I have the hat?'

He held out his hands and asked again: 'Please, Boy Boy?'

The boy removed the hat and placed it gently in Craig's hands. He looked up at him with fear and excitement. He ran back to his mother, who enfolded him in her faded skirt.

Craig held the fedora as one would a small child. His mind raced with the confused combination of details. But he looked at the fedora and realized, as the professional journalist learns to: 'It isn't clear yet. But it will be.'

THE PILLOW BOOK OF ALICE GILES, FOREIGN
CORRESPONDENT (CONCLUDED)

Fifty-five Storeys Over Hong Kong

At Kai Tak airport, Craig raced through immigration and customs and was the first passenger to enter the arrival hall. The first things he saw were two brown arms hanging wearily on an orange-painted railing. Yrlinda's arms. The two noticed each other at the same moment and Yrlinda jumped up and down and waved.

'Sir!' she called. 'Here!' She held a sign – lipsticked letters on a piece of discarded paper – that read, simply: 'CRAIG!!!' He recognized Alice's script.

They met in the middle of the crowd. Without thinking, Craig bent down and kissed the round, brown woman. 'How long have you been here, Yrlinda?'

Yrlinda was energized, which did bad things to her blend of English words and Philippine sentence structure. 'There six planes from Manila,' she said, pronouncing the last word as *Ma-nee-la*. 'This last plane. First one at 6:40. Ayem.'

'You've been here all day?'

Yrlinda nodded. 'Only six planes.'

'Did you eat?'

She nodded enthusiastically and gestured at the snack bar in the arrival hall.

'Oh my God!'

'Phone!' Yrlinda announced, pulling at Craig's shirt. 'You phone!'

'Good idea,' Craig said. At the public telephone, before Yrlinda could intervene, he dialled the number of the Mandarin Hotel. He covered the mouthpiece and said, 'Wait, Yrlinda. Just wait. This will only take a minute.'

He asked the hotel operator for Mr Augenstein and nodded at the reply. 'Please give me the front desk.'

He asked the receptionist, 'Do you know when he will be back? No, of course you don't. He has returned from his China trip? Ah. Yes. Thank you.'

He's here.

Yrlinda had engaged the adjacent telephone. She was reading from a scrap of paper and dialling intently. She listened with wide eyes and handed the receiver to Craig.

'Ma'am!'

'Alice! I'm going straight to the FCC. Go there right now. If Ted Augenstein is there, and he *must* be, stick with him. Don't let him leave the club. Sit on him if you have to. It's more than a hoax now, Alice. Believe me. And you and I are going to get this guy.'

Craig hung up. He watched Yrlinda carefully fold the paper with the phone number on it. 'Let me see that.' He lifted the paper from her hand. The number was unfamiliar to him.

'Where is ma'am?'

Yrlinda gazed at him guiltily. Her body danced with nervousness.

'Never mind, Yrlinda,' he said wearily. 'Let's go.'

The long, lonely drives in the Philippines had worn Craig's nerves, and he was glad to have company. Yrlinda spoke little and kept her ever-fascinated eyes on the crowds of Kowloon and Causeway Bay and Wanchai. Say what you will about Hong Kong's coldness, its hardness, the roughness of its people, its crowds alone impart a feeling of humanity absent in those dark odysseys in the Philippines, through black fields where insurgents patrol, past sunny mountains where gunshots ring out like churchbells.

Outside the FCC, in the light of a large, silver moon, Yrlinda said, 'I'll wait here.'

'Nonsense, Yrlinda. You're allowed in.'

She plucked the bag from his hand. 'I'll carry this!' Yrlinda: never a guest, always a maid.

'Wait one second. Put the bag down here.' Craig squatted on the sidewalk and rummaged urgently through it.

I was sitting at the bar finishing a banana split when Craig climbed the two small steps and halted in the doorway. Yrlinda hovered anxiously behind him.

The hour was late and the bar itself, except for me and Anthony Lawson, was deserted. A waiter desultorily wiped glasses. I had made him angry with my ice-cream order. Neat shots of liquor, I concluded, were far simpler to prepare. By that standard, Anthony Lawson must have been the staff's favourite member.

But Craig hadn't looked to the bar. He hadn't acknowledged my presence. His eyes were focused on the only occupied table. It was always hard to read those difficult eyes, but that night I knew their secret message: *Exactly. Exactly the scene I expected.*

It was a lively group at the club table and all its activity centered about a well-dressed, freshly groomed man telling a fun-filled story about Papua New Guinea. The observant would be forced to comment that Mr E.G. Augenstein's group was not the best and brightest of the FCC. But there's nothing wrong with Indians, after all, and Nigel Harris ('Jabbah the Hut') can be a pleasant companion, or he could be back in the late 1960s before his teeth rotted and his mind quickly followed. Kelly Plant, though a PR man now, was once a foreign correspondent before the expense-account scandal. And wife Sonia, though hardly a journalist, had a reliable stage laugh that Ted's woeful little group was grateful for. Les Misérables, of course, filled the remaining chairs, as was their fate in life.

I tumbled out of my bar chair and rushed to the door. 'Craig! What happened? Tell me *everything*!'

'Get him!'

I gaped but Craig offered no explanation. He gazed at the table beyond. I gave Yrlinda a questioning look, but all she could offer was a seismic shrug.

But knowledge isn't everything, after all. Confidence is. I smoothed my orange tunic and approached Ted's table with my head held high. I didn't know what I was doing but Craig had convinced me of my errand's justice. I went straight to the man with the perfect hair and for the first time in my eighteen and a half years ignored the glare of searching eyes. I wondered whether Craig had cured me of my hunchback.

'Alice,' Ted said. 'I saw you but you looked engrossed . . .'

'Ted,' I said in a horrible, frightened whisper. It was all wrong. I decided to start all over again.

'Why don't you join us,' Ted said magnanimously. 'A veteran, after all . . .'

'Ted,' I repeated in a firmer tone. 'Would you come with me, please?'

The tone might have puzzled an innocent man, but not Ted Augenstein. He ran his hand over his hair, coughed slightly and rose to join me. The rest of the table stared with surprise.

'Take your magazine,' I said.

I don't think I'll ever forget the queer expression on his face. It wasn't that he avoided the gaze of the rest of the journalists. Rather, his attention seemed to have been retracted, like a coil, the moment I commanded him. I realized later what a superhuman effort Ted made to act normally that night. And how quickly his façade crumbled.

I brought him to the doorway and said, 'Ted, this is Craig Kirkpatrick.'

'Winn and Ai's son.' But Ted's eyes never reached Craig's face. They remained fixed at the level of his hands. They stared at a dusty brown fedora that Craig held forth like an offering.

'I didn't kill him,' Ted said in a flat tone.

'Oh no!' My hands flew to my wretched face. None of it made sense but the expression on the two men's faces affirmed the ugly truth.

Ted continued to gaze at the fedora. Craig held it forward, as if he was waiting for Ted to claim it.

'Where can we go, Alice?' Craig commanded. 'We need a private place. Near the office would be best.'

'I have the place!' I said. 'Oh God, do I have the place!'

As I drove, an icy silence reigned within my car. Craig's eyes were shut as if in meditation. I peeked at Ted Augenstein in my rear-view mirror. He stared blankly out of the window as if he had never seen the colours and the Cantonese before. Yrlinda shifted continually and darted glances at the sad man beside her. *She wants to console him*, I thought. *His gloom is too much for sunny Yrlinda.*

When the car halted, Craig opened his eyes. 'We're at the office. I don't want to go to the office. Keep going, Alice.'

'Shush, Craig,' I said, patting his hand. 'Trust me.'

'Alice, the desk people are there. They will see us . . .'

Ted was already on the sidewalk outside the Goodwill Centre. Yrlinda tried to engage him in conversation. He stooped to comprehend her question.

'Trust me,' I repeated emphatically.

In the elevator, I pressed the button marked 55.

'You've made a mistake, Alice,' Craig said. 'That's an empty floor.'

I caught his hand as it reached for the button marked: 'The World Business Journal. Penthouse/57.'

Yrlinda laughed with gleeful pride. 'You see,' she babbled. 'Everything so nice. Just like home. We do it and everything so nice. Even burner!' Yrlinda was proud of herself. Inadvertently, I had discovered an untapped talent of our Philippine maids. They have learned, through generations of fires, earthquakes, raids and ravaging typhoons, how to pick up the pieces when their houses come tumbling around their ankles. It's second nature to them. Again I stake my claim for my Yrlinda: she is the most accomplished expatriate in the world.

As our elevator zoomed up the core of the concrete column, I shut my eyes and imagined myself flying up the outside of the building, unaided by elevators or other machinery. This was a habit I had adopted in the previous few days. Something about the building, its shape and its emptiness, aided the fantasy. Along with the kaleidoscope Hong Kong night. The dark sky, with the lights straining up from below. My incredibly rapid progress, straight up the tubular glass skin, aiming for that shining crown. Two rings of diamonds at the top, with sheer, shiny darkness below them. The elevator started to slow, a bell rang, and I opened my eyes.

'Watch your step,' I said as we stepped out of the elevator. Construction rubble covered the hard concrete floor. There were nails scattered around, jagged sheets of aluminium and the strange kind of dirt only encountered in a high-rise construction project.

'If I had known,' I said, 'Yrlinda would have swept.'

Both Craig and Ted walked gingerly through the rubble to the full length windows. For all of its exterior hideousness, the Goodwill Centre does have marvellous views. Through an uninterrupted semicircle of glass skin, all of Hong Kong was ranged before us. We could see the harbour on our right, the icicles of Central in the middle, and the hills and apartment blocks of the mid-levels to the left. My house was visible, but only if you scooted over towards the loos. The moon was in place over Tsim Sha Tsui, hovering beneficently and matching, but not surpassing, the artificial brilliance of its obeisant colony.

Yrlinda had taken my words as a command and she rushed to

find a broom. Craig turned from the view and watched her scurry across the concrete. 'You're *not* living here, Alice.'

He saw the neatly arranged bed, with my special pillow and the table lamp at its head. He saw the gas burner and the Tang jars arranged around it. He saw the cassette recorder, the suitcases, the small refrigerator swiped from the computer room one floor up.

'I had nowhere else,' I cried. 'This is the only place in Hong Kong where I can sleep! I've tried everywhere, Craig. The whole colony is contaminated. Either that or my allergies have gone beyond the point of tolerance.'

'But *here*?'

'It's perfect!' I exulted. 'There's a fire door that leads up to the computer room on the fifty-sixth floor. They have telephones, a postage meter, a few terminals. I snuck down and propped open the door.'

'How did you get the keys? Roger Mutterperl took yours.'

'From Bridgette,' I said. 'I wept until she gave me her set.'

'You wept?'

'The tears were real, Craig! I needed those keys! I gave my life to this paper and it threw me out like garbage. This paper was my life and it still is. It has to be – I have no other. I'd rather live here, on the floor, sneaking up at night than to give it all up, Craig. How could I give it up? To retire to my house waiting for people like you and Bridgette to call once a month and ask me to dim sum? Then once a month becomes once a quarter? "How is Alice? I haven't seen her in such a long time. I really should call." Do you think I can live that way? At least, now I have the computer and the phones, even if I have to sneak around like a ghost. I am a ghost, Craig. That's what I've become. But it's better than being dead! At least ghosts get to see what's going on back at their old haunts.'

Yrlinda was dispatched to the streets of Wanchai for a bottle of scotch. The request of the condemned man. Craig snuck up to the 56th floor for a couple of folding chairs and to alert New York to the coming story. As we stood staring out of the gigantic window, I made small talk with Ted.

'Do you remember this autumn moon?'

For the first time since he left the FCC, Ted emerged from his fog. He looked at me. His expression was pained, but my question seemed to bring him some relief.

'Yes, Alice. I do remember it. I remember my first autumn in Hong Kong.' He looked out of the window again and touched the pane gently with his hand. 'So long ago. I remember my last – I left a few months later. You know, there wasn't a week that went by in New York that I didn't look out of my window and conjure up that moon.' We both stared at it over Kowloon. 'Is it true, what I've read, that only moonlight makes the lotus bloom? Not sunlight?'

Ted drank a large neat scotch and began to tell his tale. He spoke in a plain, unembarrassed tone. He sat in a folding chair facing Craig and me, his back to the lights of Hong Kong. He didn't have another drink until he finished talking two hours later. Craig listened with his eyes closed, opening them only to ask questions. I sat erect with paper and pen taking rapid notes.

What did Ted Augenstein tell us that night 55 storeys above the shining streets of Hong Kong? He told us of a peculiar but happy life that had warped out of shape. He told of his alienation in his own country. He told of his mistaken notions of power: how he had tried to bully some changes in his life and got bullied instead. None of these were his words, of course. I have his exact words in my notebook. The task facing Craig and I was to get behind those words. To understand the truth behind them and to put that truth into words of our own. Words that sang. Words that wept.

As a newsman, Ted knew how an interview was conducted and he was precise in his details and orderly in their presentation. He carefully stated when he was unsure of a fact or was uninformed. He plunged into awkward and embarrassing details with valour. Craig and I were able to gather the necessary facts and details with little cross-examination. We were free to delve into deeper matters. Craig's strange eyes would suddenly open and he would say, 'Why didn't you just quit and move back to Asia? Why didn't you hunt around for a new job?'

And: 'Would you really have gone back to the *Tribune*? How could you have done that? What would you have done about Fendler's disappearance?'

My questions were more motherly. I asked Ted to articulate his disorientation in Manhattan. I was the one who asked how he felt about Vavasour. It was Alice who had the last question: 'Ted, what will you do now?'

He leaned down and reopened the bottle of scotch. As he poured, he said, 'In some ways, I will lead the life I had planned. I will be outcast from journalism, which doesn't trouble me. I'll have made an enormous splash in the press and my name will forever be known in the business. I will have disgraced the *Tribune* even more than I had planned. I will live abroad, which was, at heart, the main idea.'

He drank the scotch thoughtfully.

'He was a fool, we all know that. But his death makes such a difference. I wasn't planning murder. The joke was not supposed to be on me. I was the fooler. Not the fooled.'

Ted told his story with such dignity and sadness that I fell under its spell. Perhaps it was the setting – the bowed man alone in the darkness with the wall of blinking night behind him – but he reminded me of a fish that strayed too far from its school. A fish who descended to those strange depths where there is no light and fearful pressure. The fish adapts to his environment: heavier scales grow and a phosphorescent appendage sprouts, shining its own light before his tiny eyes. He comes to love the dark depths. And then, in a swirl of sand and seaweed, he is restored to the bright, shallow waters of the reef. Can that fish go back to the school, moving in perfect synchrony? Can it disregard the pale phosphorescent light that had become its private beacon? Or wouldn't that fish swim as hard as it could to reclaim its black depths?

And I sympathized with Ted's original notion, which was now doomed to obscurity thanks to Adam's pathetic demise. To lash back at the industry he had grown to hate by revealing journalism's dirty little secret. That the truth-tellers lie. The priests sin. The devoted lovers cheat. Truth may be their child, but truth has a brother – a twin brother. And more often than any journalist cares to admit, the twins get confused.

Actually, I hadn't asked the last question. There was one set more. In one way they were the least difficult: Ted's age, the date of his Pulitzer, the number of years he had worked at the *Tribune*. But in reality, they were the toughest questions. They did violence to the confiding spirit of the night. They introduced the ugly reality that Craig and I were minutes away from writing the story that would destroy the life of Ted Augenstein.

Ted looked at us with pained eyes. I don't know what made him say it: a last appeal for sympathy, perhaps.

'Do you know, you two, how feelings can stay buried for so,

so long? And how unpredictable everything becomes when those feelings rise to the surface?'

Craig opened his eyes with an abrupt shock. He said deeply, 'Yes, Ted. I know.'

I nodded my head, perhaps too eagerly. Craig and I might have been too sympathetic a duo of inquisitors.

After Ted returned to his hotel, Craig lay down on my bed.

'Craig, New York will be anxious.'

Without opening his eyes, he replied, 'They said we could start filing as late as five.'

'Craig, it's four-thirty and we haven't even begun to write. How can we start to file in half an hour?'

Craig raised a hand. 'Please Alice.'

Twenty minutes later he rose and beckoned me up the stairs to the computer rooms. He sat before a telex machine and said, 'I'm going to write it straight. We don't have time for a first draft.'

'Impossible! This is for Page One. You can't just start typing.'

He smiled for the first time that night and tapped his head with his finger.

'I have it all here, Alice. That's what counts. And what I don't have, you will get. I want you to read over my shoulder. Then you open up that line' – he pointed to the adjacent telex machine – 'and send corrections. We'll be done in one hour, two at tops.'

And so the great story was written in a matter of minutes by a young man with mysterious, dark eyes locked in a furious embrace with a telex machine.

'I need a beer,' Craig said.

'Let's get take one done first,' I said as gently as possible.

I watched over his shoulder as the first words were typed.

SPELLMAN, DAVIS, WITBOLD, NEW YORK
ATTN. FOREIGN DESK
ATTN. ART
ATTN. LEGAL – ALL DETAILS CLEARED BY AUGENSTEIN HIMSELF IN INTERVIEW. NO INPUT FROM VAVASOUR. FENDLER DEAD AND BURIED.
   HERE IS PG. ONE SCOOP BY KIRKPATRICK AND GILES. MUST RUN TONIGHT. EXPECT MAJOR REACTION. ART SHOULD GET DRAWING OF EG AUGENSTEIN, FOR. ED. OF NYTRIBUNE, AND IF TIME ALLOWS ADAM FENDLER STAFF MEMBER SOUTH CHINA MORNING POST HONG KONG AP CAN TRANSMIT.

WHAT HAPPENS WHEN A NEWSMAN, THE SEEKER OF TRUTH, TURNS AGAINST HIS TRADE?

THIS IS THE TALE OF A JOURNALIST GONE BAD. IT'S A STORY THAT BEGAN IN A NEW YORK NEWSROOM AND WHICH ENDED IN A SMALL PHILIPPINE VILLAGE, AT THE BASE OF A MANGO TREE. WHERE ANOTHER REPORTER LIES DEAD AND BURIED IN A SHALLOW GRAVE. ALL FOR THE SAKE OF A LIE.

Craig had succumbed once again to his trance. I took my seat at the second telex machine, turned it on and punched the buttons to connect with New York. It was a marvellous feeling: it had been so long.

SPELLMAN, DAVIS, WITBOLD, NEW YORK
ATTN. FOREIGN DESK
FROM ALICE GILES, RPT. ALICE GILES HONG KONG.
HERE ARE FIXES FOR KIRKPATRICK/GILES STORY FOR PG. ONE THURS PAPER. IT'S GREAT TO BE BACK ON THE JOB. LOVE, ALICE
1. KILL FIRST PARA. START STORY XXX THIS IS THE TALE XXX
2. HERE IS NEW SECOND PARA:
THIS TALE OF HOAXES AND MURDER SHOWS HOW ONE NEWSMAN, E.G. AUGENSTEIN, TRIED TO THROW AWAY HIS OWN LIFE AND, INSTEAD, CUT SHORT THE LIFE OF ONE OF HIS COLLEAGUES. AND IT SHOWS HOW MR AUGENSTEIN, IN HIS LIFELONG SEARCH FOR THE TRUTH, BECAME OBSESSED WITH THE DARKER SIDE OF THE PROFESSION: THE TELLING OF DELIBERATE LIES.

We continued to work this way, Craig grinding out the original, me fixing and polishing on the other machine. When I tried to explain to Craig my changes, he waved me silent. 'I trust you, Alice. Do whatever needs to be done. Pay attention to my spelling.'

Later, Craig shouted, 'We missed a point, Alice. I'll TK it. You call Ted at the Mandarin.'

My voice was whispery over the phone. 'Ted, it's me. I hope I didn't wake you.'

He said I hadn't. What was he doing as we toiled over his undoing? Lying in a darkened room? Standing at the window gazing at that moon?

'Ted, how many porcelains did you sell? And how much were they worth?'

He told me and I thanked him.

'Call if you have any more questions.' Good old Ted. A professional to the very end. I decided that if another question came up, Craig could make the call. I couldn't bear to speak to him again. The poor man, gazing at the moon over Hong Kong. I knew which moon Ted Augenstein had been beguiled by. I had read about it long ago:

> *A ray is caught in a bowl*
> *And the cat licks it, thinking that it's milk;*
> *Another threads its way through tree-branches,*
> *And the elephant thinks he has found a lotus-stalk.*
> *Half asleep, a girl reaches out*
> *And tries to rearrange the moonbeams on the bed*
> *To share the warmth.*
>> *It is the moon that is drunk with its own light,*
>> *But the world that is confused.*

'Seventy thousand bucks,' I told Craig. 'An expensive farewell to journalism.'

A reflective look appeared on Craig's face. He stopped typing.

'The sad thing,' he said, 'is that Adam's killing probably didn't cost more than seventy dollars. All the rest went to hotels and to Vavasour. It makes you wonder. Seventy bucks.'

'I used to despise him,' I said softly. 'It sounds terrible, but it's the truth. He seemed to me the kind of man journalism least needs. The man who would do anything, and now he's lost his very life, for a byline. But maybe I was too harsh. Is it such a bad motivation? Why not dedicate your life to a byline? What motives do the rest of us have?'

I read over Craig's shoulder as he typed the following:

'THE JOKE WAS NOT SUPPOSED TO BE ON ME,' SAID MR AUGENSTEIN, WHO WON THE PULITZER PRIZE IN 1973 FOR DISTINGUISHED INTERNATIONAL REPORTING. 'I WAS THE FOOLER. NOT THE FOOL.'

'That's not the exact quote, Craig! He said "fooled," not "fool."'
'It's better my way, Alice.'
'It's better the way he said it, Craig.'
'Alice,' Craig said wearily, 'I've never known a story that couldn't be improved with a little less truth.'

I wished we were back on the 55th floor, where the darkness and the moon and the glittering lights would have bolstered my argument. In the telex room, with its synthetic floors and its artificial light, Craig had the upper hand.

'Tonight of all nights, Craig Kirkpatrick! This story of all stories! We must be true! What does it all lead to but this moment? Truth at five in the morning. Truth when you're tired. Truth when, as you would say, a lie would actually read better.'

'That's all very noble, Alice, but I can't believe in it any more. I've lost faith in this truth business.' Craig leaned over and pushed a tan button, severing his connection with New York. 'This business altogether.

'None of the things I thought about journalism have turned out to be true, Alice. Where are the unexplored turfs? Every story I've ever written has been crawled over by droves of reporters. Where are the scoops? They're nothing but daily titillation and half of them turn out to be false two days later. Journalism is different from my parents' day, Alice. We do nothing but follow each other around and pretend that television hasn't scooped us all. We're not chasing truth. We're chasing each other. The only thing that is real is what comes from here.' He tapped his head. 'Creation! Invention!'

'Oh, Craig! What you say is true! Very true! Very often! But look at us tonight. *Look* at us. We've got a real story. We've got the scoop of the decade. Let's not blow it with fabrications.'

'No one would know, Alice, and no one would care.'

'It's faith, Craig. They *would* know. I believe in our bond with the readers. They know when a mere name is mis-spelled. They tolerate it, but they can feel the untruth creeping in. You must keep the faith, Craig, or all else falls away.'

My voice fell to a hush. 'I must believe that, Craig. I have nothing else.'

'Okay,' Craig said gently. 'We'll make it true, Alice. For you. Go ahead and fix the quote.' He returned to his machine, but before he could transmit to New York, an incoming message clattered across his machine.

KIRKPATRICK/GILES. HONG KONG NEWSROOM NOT RESPONDING OVER COMPUTER. CHEUNG SAYS YOU CAN'T BE REACHED. WHAT'S GOING ON? PAUL, FOREIGN.

Craig replied:

WE ARE BOTH IN TELEX RM ONE FLOOR DOWN. PLS COMMUNICATE DIRECTLY TO HK TELEX RM.

Paul responded:

OKAY. STORY IS INCREDIBLE. THE BRASS IS AT PG ONE WAITING FOR REMAINDER. HOW MANY MORE TAKES? WHAT IS DATELINE?

Craig typed:

THREE MORE. FOR CHRIST'S SAKE PAUL GET OUTTA MY WAY.

He continued typing and I hovered over his shoulder like a guardian angel. Outside the computer room, day was breaking.

Later we ascended to the deserted newsroom to wait for follow-up calls from New York. We were grimy and happy and Craig put his feet on the copy desk. I slurped bone-marrow soup. Yrlinda was sent out for beer.

'Could he possibly be arrested?' I asked. 'Or detained? Would the CID even get involved?'

Craig shrugged. 'I don't think he ever feared arrest. He didn't kill Adam Fendler. That's a fact. He feared this.' Craig patted our telexes.

'Those who live by the sword . . .'

'It is the natural fear of all newsmen,' Craig said. 'To be written up as a fool. We know how it's done. We know how the mirrors are used, the strings that are supposed to be invisible.'

'That's a nice way of putting it.'

We both laughed.

'You know, he might have become an actual hero.'

'Oh Craig. Come on!'

'Alice, people hate the press more than we admit. And look at those bank clerks who walk off Friday evening with the money from the vault. Don't people love them? Aren't they heroes? And wasn't Ted's plan the journalistic equivalent?'

'When your money's stolen, you don't consider the bank teller a hero,' I said. 'And Ted was planning to fool the very people he was trying to impress. People don't like being fooled.'

We could see the start of a traffic jam on Des Voeux Road.

'It's much nicer than the old newsroom,' I said. 'I bet they don't even get any rats on the fifty-seventh floor. Except Roger Mutterperl.'

'He'll be here in a few moments. I guess it's time for your big scene. I'll let you break the news to him.'

'I'm not prepared,' I protested. 'I'm not showered.' (I couldn't imagine what my hair looked like.) 'I don't even know what I'd say!'

'You don't know what you'd say?' Craig laughed. 'I thought you'd have practised for weeks.'

I laughed and pushed away the last of my bone-marrow soup. The taste had begun to seem insipid.

'I have, now that you mention it.' I took Craig's beer-can and took a large swallow. 'My only worry is which version to give him. What time does Roger get in?'

Our Story Ran In Column One

Our story ran in column one, accompanied by a drawing of a plump Ted Augenstein with very short hair. Roger Mutterperl was extremely annoyed that the Asian edition missed the story. His readers would have to wait until the next day, when both the *Post* and the *Standard* would be filled with wire-service follow-ups.

'God damn it, Alice, you should have told us and we could have held our print run. For a story like this, we don't mind if the papers miss the planes to Singapore. This is some kind of award-winner.' Roger's head dropped onto his shoulder.

'I would have come up and told the desk, Roger,' I said sweetly. 'But I didn't have any keys.'

'Don't give me that,' he said. Large blue veins bulged in his neck. 'You could have called.'

'I forgot the new phone numbers.' I batted my eyelashes.

'Let me get this right,' he said, scraping his ear on his shoulder. 'Are you angry at me? Do I get the feeling you're bitter about that disability thing? Or are you trying to rehash that business about Felicia's baby and the funeral? Someone said you were badmouthing me about that. I don't have time to go to funerals, Alice. I've got a paper to put out here.'

It is important, I feel, that when one has something vital to say in life, one be well rehearsed. That morning I was well rehearsed on the topic of me, the paper, and corporate cruelty. I had to wing it on behalf of Felicia and her poor baby. In the mirror that evening, I did the customary replay. And, if I do say so myself, I think I did justice to mothers, children and the disabled.

The media went wild over the story, of course, and I was chosen as the paper's spokesperson. My name was on the story, after all, even if it came second. Craig was unavailable for comment. Officially, he was taking a 'well-deserved vacation.' In reality, he was on a plane to Manila. After that, he would fly by charter to Palawan province. To an island known as El Niño.

Before he left, he kissed me and held me in a sweet, giant hug.

'I don't know if I'll be back, Alice.'

'Come on, Craig,' I said, tears coming to my eyes. 'Your career is just begining. We're famous as of this morning.'

'I've been famous all my life,' he said. 'You enjoy it. I'll go and see if I can do something worthwhile with my life.'

'I'm sure you can,' I declared. 'What was that song?' (For I realized Craig wouldn't come back if he had to come back alone.)

He laughed and burst into a bombastic version of 'Fly Me to the Moon.' Excuse me, 'Fry to the Moon.'

Long pieces about Ted Augenstein, Adam Fendler and the dangers of a hijackable press clogged the newspapers for days. No paper managed to communicate both the facts and the theme of the story as our original story did. There was talk of it being a 'classic' – whatever that is – plus the inevitable rumblings about Pulitzer prizes. One rumour said we'd be awarded a 'special' Pulitzer because our story was about journalism itself. In a newsroom performance that reeked of false modesty, I disputed this notion. Our story was like any other story, I said. We simply got the facts and put them in a readable order. If a prize was to be awarded for showing up the flaws of journalism, it belonged to Ted Augenstein. Or Anton Vavasour. Or, perhaps as a consolation prize, to poor Adam Fendler.

The only organization that produced something new was *Time*, thanks to the ever-resourceful Carl Rolla. *Time*'s photo was an exclusive: a crystal-clear, heartbreaking shot of Adam Fendler's exhumed corpse. Adam looked like a little boy, with that bald head and a puzzled expression on his dirty, dead face.

Finding the grave wasn't easy, Carl Rolla explained in one of his endless brag sessions at the FCC bar. And he was right. With all of the cross-telexes, a single error crept into Craig's and my story. The dateline was printed 'CONCEPCION' instead of 'CONSOLACION.' The journalists who poured into the Philippines couldn't find the scene of the crime.

Except for Carl.

'One of my good sources,' Carl told his bar buddies. 'A Philippine guy who really knows his way around. In fact, when the call from New York came through, the guy was bunking at my place.' (Sure enough, in the background of the *Time* picture one could see the figures of Carl Rolla, a sceptical look on his face, plus a Philippine man, inappropriately smirking and wearing a T-shirt that read: 'If Found Return Immediately to the Rat's Nest.' I had always presumed that Carl Rolla did vile things to his sources. Now I have the satisfaction of knowing they do it back to him.)

There was much talk about the arrest and deportation of E. G. Augenstein. But when he finally surfaced, in Sri Lanka of all places, he claimed he was as much a victim as anyone else (except for Adam). After an initial blaze of publicity, we never heard of him again. Ted Augenstein rumours became an FCC staple: that he was living in Penang or that he had moved to Borneo. Once I heard he was running a bar in South Korea, not far from the DMZ. Over and over again, I have tried to picture Ted's life, but my imagination always fails me. All I can see is that beefy hand pressed against the glass skin of the Goodwill Centre and that hopeful face staring out at Hong Kong's harvest moon. The lotus waiting to bloom.

I see Rudy occasionally, hanging around Sutherland House or cruising the beach at Repulse Bay. For fun I once spread the rumour that Anton Vavasour had walked into the FCC bar. All the correspondents rushed away from the dining-room and flew downstairs. How shocked they were to find Jabbah the Hut, silently sipping a stiff one. Nigel looked pleased by the unexpected attention. And then so devastated. I was actually ashamed of myself.

Before he left, Craig showed me his memo to Peter in New York, copied to Roger Mutterperl and, of all people, Winn Kirkpatrick. It stated the facts of my case and urged I be given office rights.

'I'm sure the *Columbia Journalism Review* would be interested in a piece,' Craig wrote, 'on how one newspaper treats the reporter who broke the year's biggest story. It might show the other side of our business: the side forgotten in all the talk about 100K salaries.' Within days, I was given a terminal, a telephone, a set of keys, a company coffee-mug and a cubicle located near the office kitchen. This began a new, comic office ritual. When he was thirsty or bored, Roger Mutterperl would round the corner from his office, jingling the change in his pocket. I could hear him coming. When he turned the corner and saw my hideous, inescapable grin, he would turn heel and flee back to his office. The newsroom joke is how thirsty Roger is getting! Sometimes I put coins in my tunic pockets and do a cruel Roger imitation, with my head dangling onto my neck. Even Matt Mell, Roger's pet, has to laugh.

I returned to my house on Bowen Path. I had to. Norma, Yrlinda's daughter, is coming to live with us. I couldn't sanction raising a 10-year-old on the 55th floor of the Goodwill Centre, however convenient and despite the wonderful view. Even a Philippine child who, God knows, is used to worse.

Yrlinda was jubilant the day I proposed it.

'Let's get Norma out of that place,' I said. I meant the Philippines, of course. Yrlinda thought I was referring to Norma's school.

'Yes,' she said eagerly. 'There no roof!'

'No roof? Was there a typhoon?'

'No,' she said. 'Typhoon last year. This year cholera.'

'Cholera?'

'Yes,' Yrlinda said with a less than appropriate giggle. 'All the parents dead.' She grasped her throat and made a ghastly death-rattle.

The fedora I have kept, as macabre as it sounds. Craig handed it to me with solemnity. 'You keep it, Alice. So I know it will always be safe.' I haven't shown it to anyone except for Yrlinda, who always wants to clean it, which I won't allow. I consider it a genuine souvenir of journalism. It is artificial in its intended iconography. (To Adam's credit, he never put a card reading PRESS in its band.) But it is poignantly true in its crumpled, dusty mis-shape: the hat of death. I consider it a typically journalistic combination: lots of bullshit plus lots of truth. Perhaps Adam Fendler's fedora says it all about my peculiar trade. Perhaps it sums up the good in us along with the bad. Image is important. So too is truth. And maybe that hat brings it down to an even simpler statement. Maybe we journalists simply try too hard. Possibly, it's no more complex than that. Off we go, with our fishing vests and our press-conference voices, our grabby leads and our bent quotes, taking on the very earth – its generals, its diseases, its crooks, its morals, its shifting core and its heady ozone layer – and all the time we're just trying a bit too hard.

'When Are You Coming Home?'

'When are you coming home?' people ask me quite frequently, even people I barely know from places I'd never want to call home. What they mean is 'Why do you live abroad?' The question is inherently cheeky. Would I ask them, 'Why do you live in Canada?'

In eighteen and a half years, my replies have varied widely. When I was younger, it was simple to say 'It's fun!' and people would accept, if not entirely believe, the reply. Older women, I have learned, are not supposed to plead the cause of fun, so I have different excuses now. 'I've lost touch with the States,' I say at times, although this is received sourly: Americans deny the possibility. 'I wouldn't know which US city to settle in,' is an alternative and people accept that more graciously, although some have the temerity to suggest a city or two. 'What about Phoenix?' they say. (Never do they suggest their own cities, but instead, some godforsaken retirement spot where an old aunt or incontinent uncle has been exiled. Perhaps they're afraid I'll visit.)

Other, more flippant lines have come to mind in idle moments, when I'm impatiently shaking water on the plants or waiting for a call from New York. 'The statute of limitations is twenty years,' or 'I can forgive, but never can I forget.' Occasionally I say my job and my life is in Asia, but this rings too pompous, especially in my whispery voice.

How can I tell the truth? In America, I feel like someone just off a bus. It's age, I know – the sagging, the whitening and the horrifying settling of the face into an eternal mask of discontent – but who wants to look like a perpetual rider on a bus that continually circles without ever spotting a skyline or even a bucolic field or two?

I was born of the suburbs, overly modest ones, and I can't imagine a return.

> *There's no way out* (wrote Louis Simpson in 'In The Suburbs')
> *You were born to waste your life*
> *You were born to this middleclass life.*
> *As others before you*
> *Were born to walk in procession*
> *To the temple, singing.*

My escape from the suburbs eighteen and a half years ago was accidental – let us all toast ill health! – but I knew instinctively the liberation I had achieved. I have chosen my own temple now, atop a hill in Hong Kong. It's an old girls' school on Bowen Path, separated from the world by 218 stone stairs. I have the top floor and my rent is fixed. The ground-floor flat has seen a succession of families headed by highly-paid bankers and executives. I know the subtle sounds of marriages subsuming. The families are ever wonderful when they move in! The kids bound up the 218th step, the wide-eyed mother is close behind and the father, hassled and angry, takes up the rear with helpers. When they depart, it's the mother first, defiance wrinkling her brow, the children dawdling, the father remaining behind to listen to the stereo and someday to pack. He takes a different plane, often in a different direction.

You can see me in most nighttime photos of the skyline, when the accursed Goodwill Centre doesn't intervene. I'm a small twinkle against a dark hillside. (Rarely is the downstairs apartment visible.) Darkness extends all around the house, before it gives way to enormous housing blocks and zig-zags of illuminated highways. Those roads are molten in the time-exposure photos: red for the lane proceeding away from the camera, a pure white for its companion.

My twinkle is always there. That's how I see myself, the former suburbanite, as I drift into old age in the Far East. I stand alone. I have found a place that sets me apart. I shine my own light: not a white one, actually, like that of my lovely old dormitory windows. But green. For green is my special colour.

In The Spring

In the spring, it rains so pitifully. The tram tracks fill with water and the cars splash the pedestrians with no mercy. I do this myself and want to cry at the misery left in my wake. The party dresses ruined! The family outings! The first dates! Spring should be the opposite, I think. But the rains come regardless of our preferences. What choice have we but to splash through them?

In the winter, it is merely cold. There are occasional days of glory, but unless they coincide with Christmas or New Year's, no one notices. The Chinese don their padded, blue jackets – extra cushioning for their bruising strolling style. The nights are damp and surprisingly bitter.

The summer heat pushes one's eye to the pavement. Has it always been this way? Or does my life lack the joys that never wilt, even on a brutal summer day?

For me, there is only one season.

Autumn brings the Moon Festival, Hong Kong's most sublime celebration. Children carry paper lanterns into Victoria Park and onto Hong Kong's peaks. Each lantern glows with the light of a single candle. How I adore looking at the tiny lights. And the stately moon, handsome on its night of honour, making a wide arc across the autumn sky.

A Hindu aphorism says life is four nights of moonlight and then darkness. On the night of the Moon Festival, high on my grassy knoll, I am a light honouring the moon. I quaver slightly, and my light is tinged with unhealthy green. But shine I do! Alice Giles shines still from her squat tower above Wanchai.

Is it her fourth and final moonlit night?

No! I say. *No! Not yet!*

ACKNOWLEDGEMENTS

I am indebted to two esteemed translators of Heian Era literature.

The first is Edward G. Seidensticker, whose translation of the Kagero Nikki, *The Gossamer Years* (Charles E. Tuttle Co., Inc., 1964), inspired my first chapter ('These times have passed . . .'). The Heian Era passages and poems on pages 3, 153 ('How sad to hear . . .') and 187 are taken from that translation. His pellucid *The Tale of Genji* (Martin Secker & Warburg Ltd., 1976) has provided the allusions on page 187, the poems on pages 186 and 187, and the final poem on page 135. I am also indebted to his translation of the Sarashina Diary, *As I Crossed A Bridge of Dreams* (The Dial Press, 1971).

Ivan Morris's translation of *The Pillow Book of Sei Shonagon* (Columbia University Press, 1967) inspired my final chapter ('In the Spring') and many of Alice Giles' lists.

The poem on page 283 is translated by John Brough in *Poems From the Sanskrit*, page 74 (Penguin Books Ltd., 1968).

The passages on page 28 are from Frederic Prokosch's *The Asiatics* (Chatto and Windus Ltd., 1935).

The passage on page 30 is from *Memoirs of an Anti-Semite* by Gregor Von Rezzori (The Viking Press, 1981).

The passage quoted by Anton Vavasour on page 267 is from Rex Warner's translation of *The Medea* by Euripides (John Lane The Bodley Head Ltd, 1944).